AMERICAN ROYALTY

Also by Tracey Livesay

AMERICAN ROYALTY

A Novel

TRACEY LIVESAY

AVON

An Imprint of HarperCollinsPublishers

P.S.™ is a trademark of HarperCollins Publishers.

AMERICAN ROYALTY. Copyright © 2022 by Tracey Livesay. All rights reserved. Printed in the United States of America. No part of this book may be used or reproduced in any manner whatsoever without written permission except in the case of brief quotations embodied in critical articles and reviews. For information, address HarperCollins Publishers, 195 Broadway, New York, NY 10007.

FIRST EDITION

Designed by Diahann Sturge

Crown illustration © mashakotcur / Shutterstock

Library of Congress Cataloging-in-Publication Data has been applied for.

ISBN 978-0-06-308450-6

22 23 24 25 26 LSC 10 9 8 7 6 5 4 3 2 1

To Ruth Eva Watson, my late grandmother.
I miss you—your unconditional love, your wise sayings, and
your incomparable cooking—more than I can ever express.

AMERICAN ROYALTY

Chapter One

"Duchess is here! Bitches better bow down!
D to the A to the N I / You wanna know why / Dudes go
sky high / When I say jump? / I have no need to lie / Open
up your eyes / The lush between my thighs / Dudes wanna
pump . . ."

—Duchess, "Sky High"

Virginia Beach, Virginia

Sitting forward in the red leather club chair, Dani braced her elbows on her knees and bobbed her head, lip-syncing in time to the playback booming through the large airport hangar. The nasty drumbeat and thumping bass—courtesy of famed hip-hop producer SuzyQ—flowed through her, transforming her from Danielle Nelson, the tenacious young woman who'd survived being bounced from one relative's house to the next, unwanted and unappreciated, into Duchess, one of the fastest-rising female rappers in the game, who'd snatch your balls before she'd let you touch her heart.

That's all they see of me
My femininity
They think they have the key
Silly little guy

She stood and tossed her honey-blond curls, staring down the camera on the movable crane several feet away from her, swaying her hips, seducing the lens, looking beyond the equipment to all of the guys who'd soon be watching her.

Wanting her.

Eventually downloading the song because it was the closest they'd ever get to her.

She'd recorded her close-ups of this verse earlier today, full of sass and sex, giving them her signature head tilt and arched brow. But this part of the performance was about her movements and her body, clad to perfection in the stunning silver sequined Alberta Ferretti pantsuit the designer had lent her from the up-coming Limited Edition Fall Couture line. Dani channeled all of that charisma and raw sex appeal and felt her success in the sudden thickness of the atmosphere around her, the telltale prickle against her skin that told her she was the sole focus of everyone's attention.

You could never see
What I'm meant to be
I belong to me
D to the A to the N I

She knew what she was supposed to do as the bars to the verse ended, but she refused to execute that choreography. Instead, she freestyled some moves and struck a standing power pose.

"Cut! Going again," the assistant director called out.

The music stopped, and, as if roused from stasis, people in the darkened background continued on with their tasks. The dolly grip pulled the main camera operator off to the side while the cameramen bordering the set hefted the heavy equipment off their shoulders. Someone wearing a headset handed her a bottle of water as hair and makeup swarmed, patting her face with more setting powder and taming any loose curls that dared to fight the bobby pins and extra-hold hair spray.

"That was fire, Duchess," Amal said, clasping his hands together. The in-demand video director appeared from the surrounding shadows and stepped onto the set, which was decorated like a luxurious home office in a mansion.

"Thanks. It felt good," she said, handing the water back to a passing PA and waving off the beauty technicians.

"You looked strong, regal. Powerful. Buuuuut," he said, drawing the one syllable out like taffy, "what happened at the end?"

Here it comes . . .

She wasn't going to make it easy for him. She widened her eyes, feigning innocence. "What do you mean?"

He pointed to the pile of dollar bills heaped on the Aubusson rug. "You were supposed to tumble down to the ground and roll in the money, rub it all over your face and body. The point was to temper your strength with your femininity but make it gritty. Raw, y'know?"

It would have been one thing if she'd fucked up or he'd wanted additional coverage for the scene. But he'd loved what she'd done while on her feet; he was just pissed he hadn't forced her on her knees.

Dani closed her eyes and pictured herself in a Missy Elliott–type video where she grew several feet, her head swelled like a hot-air balloon, and she chomped down, biting the director's head clean off his body.

How's that for temper, bitch?

But when she lifted her dramatic false lashes, Amal was still standing there—head intact—smugly licking his lips, rubbing his hands together, and waiting for Dani to acquiesce to his demands.

The point was to temper your strength with your femininity but make it gritty. Raw, y'know?

Dani did know. She'd heard some version of that asinine reasoning numerous times over the past ten years. Each time she was asked to twerk while wearing a gold string bikini, pose suggestively and touch herself while half naked, or wrap her body around a pole like a member of an X-rated Cirque du Soleil troupe.

However, the real reason she didn't want to go down on all fours for this video was because she was tired of having her image dictated by men. She wasn't ashamed of her sexuality; it was a part of her, and she owned it. But she was also aware that she viewed it differently than the men who controlled her career and dominated the industry did.

Unwilling to simply comply, she wrapped her arms around her waist, cocked her head to the side, and allowed her curls to tumble over her shoulder and rest against the brown skin of her cleavage. Amal's dark eyes followed where she led, his Adam's apple bobbing.

God! Why were men allowed to rule the world? They *thought* they were powerful, but it didn't take much to redirect the blood flow from their brains to their dicks. Even now, without uttering a single word, she'd caused beads of sweat to form on Amal's upper lip as he stared at her. He'd do anything she asked him to do.

And wasn't that true power?

You keep telling yourself that.

Because they both knew Amal was going to get what he wanted.

There was a time and an occasion for confrontation and this wasn't it. As long as Dani's future—and success—was tied to the music industry, she had to play the game. And Amal was too famous for her to consider burning that bridge.

Dani thought back to the time just after her grandmother had died. For as long as she could remember, it had been her and Nana; Dani didn't know her father and barely remembered her mother. Nana had raised her with a loving, firm hand until a stroke had taken her life. Dani had been devastated and terrified. She'd felt like a small tree violently uprooted by tornado-force winds from the only forest she'd ever known. What would happen to her? Where would she go? Family had stepped in, vowing to keep her out of the system. But that claim, pledged out of love and generosity, quickly deteriorated into resentment and obligation.

It was while staying at her fourth home that year—with her mother's third cousin, Little Jessie, his wife, and their two kids—that she'd seen Eve on BET. The lyrical powerhouse had been imposing, dynamic, and everything fourteen-year-old Dani had yearned to be. She'd been certain that if she could command respect and attention like the rapper, she could finally live her life on her terms.

No more couch surfing with unenthusiastic relatives, having no say in where she landed next.

No more busting her ass doing their menial chores to "earn her keep."

No more fending off inappropriate quid pro quo sexual advances from distant male kin who should know—and do—better.

Though it hadn't seemed like it at the time, young Dani had had more autonomy over her situation than grown-ass Dani did now.

Wasn't *that* a bitch?

"So, we're going to do it again and this time you're going to stop, drop, and roll, right?" Amal crossed his arms over his fashionably ripped T-shirt.

Annoyance heated Dani's blood but she knew better than to let her irritation show on her face. "Yeah."

He tilted his chin up and stared at her down the line of his nose in that cocky, arrogant way she hated. "That's my girl."

The fuck she was.

Still, even as Dani mouthed the lyrics, rubbed the bills over her body, and made love to the camera, she forced herself to keep her inner eye on the real prize. It wouldn't be long before her fortunes would be defined by *her* decisions, and she wouldn't need to placate Amal; her manager, Cash; or any other men of their ilk. Three years ago, she'd debuted Mela-Skin, a skin-care line created for and geared specifically toward women of color. Everyone she'd initially approached to invest had rejected her, claiming she was developing an entire product line for a niche market. Roughly seventy million women were a "niche market"? The lack of respect and their inability to "see" her prompted her to do it on her own.

To everyone's surprise but hers, it was an immediate success. A year ago, a small cosmetics company had approached her about bringing the line into their portfolio. They'd wanted to buy her out completely, leaving her no say in the future of the brand, so she'd declined the offer. But it had gotten her to thinking. Running her business, not becoming a famous rapper, might be the real path to the power and autonomy she sought. And if one company had seen potential in what she'd built, wouldn't others? Upcoming meetings scheduled with the top four cosmetics and beauty companies in the world suggested the answer was yes.

The music playback ended and the assistant director yelled, "Cut!"

Amal approached her, pink tingeing his golden brown skin.

"Now that's what I'm talkin' 'bout! That was sexy as fuck! Go on. I'll see you back here in a bit."

He motioned to the AD, who added, "Moving on! Setting up the club scene."

Dani nodded her thanks, her pleasant expression collapsing as she turned away. Trying not to trip over the thick cables and lines running along the concrete floors, she headed to meet her assistant, who handed her a mason jar filled with her favorite iced vanilla coffee.

"Bless you," Dani said, taking a sip of the sweet nectar.

Tasha's lip quirked and she adjusted the black square frames on her face. "Figured you'd need it."

"You figured right. Now, as much as I love how these shoes look," she said, lifting one foot clad in a red four-inch Sergio Rossi Godiva Steel pump, "I need to get out of them."

"I got you. In four. Three. Two—" Tasha broke off as a white golf cart driven by a large black man came to a stop in front of them.

Dani grinned. She'd met her bodyguard, Antoine, when he'd been providing security for an event she attended. He'd impressed her with his top-notch skill and quiet confidence. Since celebrities were some of the most photographed people in the world, bodyguards were often caught in the frame and a lot of them started caring more about themselves and less about the people they were supposed to keep safe. But in the four years Antoine had worked for her, he hadn't shown any tendency toward that inclination. He protected her person and her privacy.

Dani settled next to Antoine. "Hey, big man. What's good?"

"You, lil' ma," he boomed in his deep voice. "You *wearing* that suit!"

Dani laughed and squeezed his shoulder as he maneuvered the small vehicle out of the hangar and along the parking lot, past tables filled with food, and the hair, makeup, production, and wardrobe trailers. With so many people milling around, it resembled a small town instead of a video shoot.

Dani braced an arm on the back of her seat and asked her assistant, "Did we hear from Estée Lauder?"

"Earlier today. They confirmed the meeting for next month. They just need to know if you'd prefer the New York or L.A. office," Tasha called over her shoulder from her rear-facing vantage point.

Dani nodded, excitement fluttering in her belly. Make that the top *five* companies.

"I just want the meeting. I don't care where we do it. As Janet said, 'Any time, any place,'" she sang.

"I'll check your schedule and see where you'll be then." Tasha shook her head. "You really should sing more on your albums. You have a great voice."

"Truth," Antoine said, pulling up in front of Dani's trailer.

If things went according to plan, there wouldn't be any more albums. But she was keeping that information to herself.

"You both have to say that. I pay you," Dani said, getting out of the cart.

She climbed the steps and entered her temporary home on set, the hardwood floors, dark cabinetry, and light granite surfaces screaming anonymous luxury. The bright smell of citrus essential oils was the only nod to personalization. She didn't even allow her eyes a moment to adjust to the cool, darkened interior before she slipped off the gorgeous but torturous pumps and sank down on the leather couch, moaning as she massaged the pad of her right foot.

"Up. Up. Up!" Zoe appeared from behind the door that led to the bedroom, her expression molten with horror. "You do not *lounge* in Alberta Ferretti!"

Dammit! Dani stood and quickly shed the suit, handing it to her stylist in exchange for a silk robe, which she wrapped around herself before sinking back onto the sofa. She patted her hair. "Can I take this wig off?"

"Sure. Miss K only spent an hour getting it to lay right and making your baby hairs look natural. I'm sure he won't mind doing it again."

So that was a no.

Dani frowned. "Your sarcasm isn't attractive."

"Says you."

She leaned her head gingerly on the cushion. "Do you know how much time I have before the last scene?"

"They called and told us they needed you back on set in two hours," Zoe said, zippering the pieces back into a garment bag and disappearing into the bedroom.

Which meant she had thirty minutes to relax. Maybe. She needed to contact Mela-Skin's marketing director to discuss arranging a photo shoot for their new revitalizing face mist. She also wanted to scope out the feeds of her favorite beauty influencers, see what kind of products and posts were getting the most engagement. Which reminded her . . . She hadn't checked her own social media accounts all day! She had sixty-four million Instagram followers who would be waiting to hear from her. She should go live and tease the upcoming video release, have Tasha post a few pics from the set.

The door opened and "speak of" bounded in.

"Do you have my phone?" Dani asked, not bothering to bleach the impatience from her tone.

Time was limited and her feet were still throbbing. The gladiator stilettos she was supposed to wear next wouldn't help their condition at all. But she wouldn't complain. She'd suck it up and perform her ass off.

Like she always did.

Instead of answering, Tasha responded, "It made the blogs."

Dani's head shot up so quickly she was relieved she didn't give herself a concussion. Had news of her meetings leaked?

While there was an obvious bidding war strategy to everyone being aware of all parties involved, she didn't want the companies to know she was playing them off one another this early in the game. Nothing could affect contract terms and concessions quicker than an executive's hurt feelings at learning they weren't "the only one."

She'd learned that lesson the hard way on her first album.

"Which one leaked? Coty? Genesis? L'Oréal?" She'd barely gotten the words out through gritted teeth.

"Samantha Banks."

"Samantha Banks? What does she know?"

"No. She gave TMZ a story about that incident at the club and it's trending on Twitter."

Relief slumped Dani's posture, causing her to sag back before aggravation restiffened her spine. "Can't that bitch find another coattail to ride?"

She immediately regretted her outburst. Not the sentiment— never that!—but the fact that she'd permitted Samantha Banks, of all people, to generate that amount of emotion in her.

The pop sensation with the neon-colored hair had burst onto the scene two years ago with a catchy dance tune that had become the song of the summer. Everyone, including Dani, had eagerly anticipated her follow-up . . . and they were still waiting. Banks had released several remixes of her hit, featuring famous DJs, but no new original music. That hadn't stopped her from trying to remain relevant, showing up anywhere someone even thought to erect a step and repeat.

At the VMAs last year, when Dani had accepted the award for Best Hip-Hop Video for "Who You Gon' Tell," the camera had cut to the audience for reaction shots and caught Banks rolling her eyes. The press had latched on to the incident, and for weeks, they'd speculated on the tenor of Dani and Banks's relationship. Since she'd received word from Banks's camp that the singer had been reacting to the person next to her, Dani hadn't taken offense. So, she'd been stunned when the other woman had gone to Twitter to discuss their "feud."

Whenever questions arose about the existence of new Samantha Banks music, she resuscitated her "feud" with Dani. In private, Dani had no problems making her feelings known—"If she spent as much time working on new music as she did stalking me, she'd have a fucking Grammy Award–winning album!"—but she refused to comment publicly on the situation. As Nana used to say, the dog may bark at the moon, but when the moon barks back, the dog becomes important.

Dani would've felt sorry for Banks. Fame was addictive— invitations to the best parties, loads of free goodies, people knowing your name and singing your songs. It was difficult to experience the consuming phenomenon and then slide back into anonymity. But Dani hadn't been resting on *her* laurels. In addition to Mela-Skin, she'd dropped a new album and her third song from it, "Sky High," had reached number one, hence the video.

Dani hadn't worked her ass off to make Samantha Banks famous.

"Let me see," Dani said now, holding out her hand for Tasha's phone.

The TMZ headline read, "Duchess's Rebuke of Samantha Banks Has the Pop Star's Fans Calling for Her Head!"

Wait, what?

Dani knew the incident they were probably referencing. She'd been hosting a party at a club in New York last weekend and Banks had made her way to Dani's VIP area. Antoine hadn't let her in, so she'd proceeded to insult Dani and make a scene.

"How desperate is she? No one picked up the story, so she sends a video to TMZ? Nothing about what happened will make her look good."

Dani clicked the video link embedded beneath the headline. The footage was grainy, the bouncing camera was nausea inducing, and the weird vantage point meant Dani spent the first twenty seconds looking at everyone's crotch.

Had she been recording this from her purse?

The music was loud but the singer's interaction with Antoine was clear.

"You can't be here," he said, calmly and professionally.

"It's a free country." The retort was peevish and juvenile.

"True. So, feel free to go stand someplace else."

Samantha's plaintive voice offscreen: *"Look, Duchess promised to appear on my track and now her people aren't returning my calls. My fans are waiting for my new music. I just want to know if she's still going to do it."*

A hard cut to Dani, leaning over the railing yelling, *"Are you serious? You gonna come up in here and say that shit to me? You're a fucking clown. Get the hell outta here."*

Antoine took Samantha's arm. *"It's time for you to go!"*

The video ended abruptly.

Dani turned wide eyes to Tasha. "What. The fuck. Was that?"

"Banks's new attempt to capitalize off your fame?"

"That's not what happened. When Antoine told her to leave, she basically assaulted him trying to get at me in the section. She started yelling that I was talentless and that the only reason I'd made it was because I'd spread my legs for all of the big producers in hip-hop. Security had to escort her out!"

Tasha bit her lip. "Unfortunately, she came out with the story first. And it's gaining traction."

"I wasn't aware that I was in a race to release trash takes on my career."

Tasha took the phone, swiped her thumb over the screen, and handed it back. "*Bossip* had a better take. They got your back."

Dani enjoyed *Bossip*'s clever headlines . . . when they weren't about her.

"Duchess, You in Danger, Girl! Is Rainbow Brite Pop Star Going Single White Female on Rap Royalty with Doctored Documentary?"

At least everyone wasn't drinking the Kool-Aid.

"You want to do a post addressing it on your Insta?"

Dani pursed her lips. "No. That would just be giving her the attention she wants."

"Are you sure?"

"Yeah. The only people who gain by me responding are Banks and the press. And since it won't put coins in my pocket, I'm not gonna participate."

Dani looked at the picture of Banks. "You tried it, little girl."

She wasn't about to let some wannabe dictate her actions. There was only one Dani "Duchess" Nelson.

And when she vacated her throne, it'd be on her terms.

Chapter Two

*"Growing up, it was very clear that I was a member of
a royal family with a potential function later on. The
question was: when and how and if?"*
— Pavlos, Crown Prince of Greece

Buckingham Palace
London, England

The moment His Royal Highness Prince Jameson Alastair Richard Lloyd, the Duke of Wessex, crossed the threshold into the intimate sitting chamber, he was inundated by an inexplicable feeling of sadness. His gaze flew around the area until it settled on a hanging oil portrait of a distant relative he recognized.

Oh, this room.

Though it looked luxe and ornate—with the walls and picture frame moldings painted a buttery yellow, silk draperies covering the floor-to-ceiling windows, and gleaming antique pieces dotted throughout the space—he'd secretly dubbed the room the Den of Despondency. He'd come here after the helicopter crash that killed his father, Prince Richard, when Jameson was seventeen. It was also where he'd learned his grandfather, Prince John, had passed away. For some reason, certain members of the royal family chose this room to deliver bad news. Maybe they believed the sunny color would counteract the melancholy.

It didn't.

Coming to the palace always did this. Reminded him of his loss. Of what his father's behavior had cost the monarchy. Of what Jameson was failing to do.

He ran a finger along the collar of his crisp white dress shirt, seeking some give in the fabric. The dark suit was tailored to perfection and came from one of the most established shops on Savile Row, but he disliked dressing so formally. He always had. It was one of the benefits of being a college professor of philosophy, with an emphasis on environmental theories. His usual uniform consisted of trousers, jumpers, and trainers.

But his grandmother, the queen, had summoned him to Buckingham Palace. Dressing casually wasn't an option.

As if on cue, the door opened and a footman announced, "Her Majesty the Queen."

Jameson flicked his gaze upward. Who else would it be? This was one of *her* private sitting rooms. But the cheeky thought didn't stop him from rising to his feet and standing tall with his chest out and shoulders back, just as his mother had taught him.

Muscle memory.

Queen Marina II strode into the chamber, her bearing as regal as you'd expect from her title. Only of average height, she always seemed taller, her trim figure striking in a mint green dress that fell just beneath her knees, her silver hair styled in puffy curls around her angular face.

"Lovely to see you, Jameson."

"Thank you, Your Majesty," he said, bending over her hand.

He never thought of her as his grandmother. Only as the queen. He'd always chafed at the formality present in their interactions.

Unlike the easy camaraderie he'd shared with his grandfather.

When he straightened, she eyed him from the top of his wavy dark hair to the tips of his John Lobb oxfords.

"You're much taller since I last saw you."

Unlikely. He'd stopped growing over ten years ago and he'd seen the queen as recently as last May at the christening of the newest member of the royal family.

But all he said was "Maybe it's the shoes."

"Maybe," she conceded. "I know the spring term begins next week, so I appreciate you coming into London on such short notice."

He cleared his throat. "Well, when the queen calls . . ."

She dipped her head, fully aware that he couldn't refuse her request to see him.

"I only have a few minutes. I'm meeting with several newly appointed ambassadors down in the Audience Room today," she said, perching on the edge of an ornate yellow armchair.

Once she was seated, Jameson settled in the matching chair opposite her. The fact that there was no tea service bolstered her assertion that this was meant to be a quick visit.

His hand tightened into a fist on his thigh. A two-hour drive to get here for a fifteen-minute conversation? Why not? At least he was missing only meetings instead of lectures. He hated missing lectures. Fortunately, he wasn't summoned often. He'd listen patiently to whatever the queen wanted to tell him and then head back to the safe anonymity of his ivory tower.

"As you, and most of the world, know," Marina began, "it's been a . . . difficult few years for the Company."

Despite the expressed sentiment, Jameson smiled at the name the royal family actually used when describing themselves. The public thought it was "the Firm," thanks to a joke ascribed to the queen's youngest daughter, his aunt Princess Bettina. Now, the press believed they had "insider" information and dropped the term into every story or documentary where the royals were mentioned.

"That would be an understatement," he agreed.

"Between Calliope's divorce, Alcott's crises, and the children not doing well . . . it's been challenging."

Princess Calliope, the queen's sister, had left her husband of thirty years after letters he'd written to his twenty-three-year-old lover had been printed in the *Daily Mail* online. According to Jameson's mother, and the royal ladies who tea, Calliope could've gotten over the affair. But having everyone read the elderly Lord Fulham rhapsodizing over the "supple smoothness" of the much younger woman's hair and skin had been too much for her to bear.

The queen's brother, Prince Alcott, while still married, was facing scandals of a financial nature. He was currently being investigated for fraud, and the Tea Trust seemed to believe Alcott irrationally blamed his situation on the fact that his sister, instead of him, had succeeded to the throne by virtue of King George V's letters patent establishing the rule of absolute primogeniture.

"They wouldn't dare do this if I was king," he'd been heard to say.

The term "the children" referred to the queen's grown offspring: Julian, Catherine, and Bettina. Between predilections for partying, constant whispers of infidelity, and severe lapses in judgment— big-game hunting endangered species, anyone?—it appeared the next generation wasn't doing any better handling royal life than their predecessors had.

Jameson knew most commoners weren't brimming with sympathy for these public faux pas. They assumed life as a royal was filled with incredible clothes, famous people, and glamorous events, a snap of the fingers bringing anything one's heart desired.

He didn't deny there were perks, but he knew most of his family would agree those benefits were a balm for a demanding way of life. Cameras always flashing, documenting everything, even when the attention was unwanted; people feeling free to comment on their choices, whether they were asked or not; and the inability to beg off attending an event, no matter what they'd been through or how they felt.

It might seem inconsequential, but day after day, year after year—with no end in sight—the negligible added up. A gilded cage was, after all, still a cage.

"Now I'm being informed there are renewed calls for the abolishment of the monarchy," Marina was saying.

He frowned. "That's not new."

"No. But this anti-monarch sentiment has been gaining traction since we asked for the money to renovate the palace several years ago."

The dissolution of the monarchy was Marina's biggest fear. From the moment she'd ascended to the throne, she'd taken her responsibilities seriously and truly considered herself the steward of a dynasty that had spanned a millennium. The idea of losing it on her watch was untenable.

"Other countries have gotten rid of their monarchies by public referendum, but I'm fairly certain ours isn't going anywhere anytime soon," he said.

The pale skin between the queen's brows furrowed. "Public opinion shows strong support for the monarchy as an institution but little for specific members. In fact, there have been suggestions that Julian and Bettina devalue the solemnity of the monarch."

Jameson squelched his instinctual amusement at her statement.

The queen was paying attention to and quoting polling? The situation must be more dire than he thought.

"There was a time when the royal family enjoyed considerable approval from the public. When John was alive, and the children were young . . ."

Though her posture remained stiff, she looked away, a shroud of grief seeming to seep over her at the mention of her late husband and Jameson's grandfather Prince John, who'd died from a heart attack ten years ago. Jameson averted his gaze, offering her the privacy she needed.

After several moments, the queen cleared her throat and continued.

"Sixteen years ago, when Julian married Fiona, over a billion people around the world watched the wedding live. The heir to the throne and his beautiful bride. The press abandoned their usual snide coverage for an overwhelmingly positive tone, and Julian and Fi's images were printed on everything from teacups to place mats."

Jameson was astonished at the wistfulness in her voice. "I thought you hated all of that."

"I do. We're not celebrities. As queen, I'm the head of state and the family is supposed to support me in carrying out my many duties. But it . . . matters when the people you represent think highly of you. In fact, I'd say it's essential. We have to be viewed as an ideal and beyond reproach. If not, we're no different from any other family of privilege. And the public will start to wonder why they're spending funds on us."

Is this why she summoned me? To discuss her thoughts on the public's current sentiments regarding the monarchy?

He'd thought she was far too busy for such musings. He was.

She set her jaw, her blue eyes resolute. "I think the country—no,

the world—needs to be reminded of our worth, our global contri-
butions."

He had no reason to disagree. It sounded like a creditable goal.
Did that explain her nostalgia about Julian and Fiona? A royal wedding would've been ideal. The pomp and circumstance involved
in those occasions never ceased to bring the nation together. Unfortunately, no one in the family was engaged. He wondered what
Marina had in mind.

And what any of this had to do with him.

His heart stuttered to a stop. She hadn't called him here to force
him to marry, had she?

It wasn't an unlikely possibility. The queen had forced his parents
to wed thirty-two years ago, when her youngest son, the eighteen-
year-old Prince Richard, had gotten the seventeen-year-old Lady
Calanthe pregnant.

And look at how *that* had turned out.

Acid churned in his stomach. Over a decade and a half later and
the world was still fascinated by the death of Prince Richard and
his reality TV star mistress, Gena Phillips, en route to a romantic
getaway in the Swiss Alps. The scandal had rocked the monarchy
for years. Not only because of the infidelity, but because of Richard's total abdication of his duties in the months since they'd begun cavorting in such a public and spectacular fashion.

After Richard's passing, Jameson should've taken his father's
place and begun carrying out engagements on behalf of the queen.
As her grandson, he was duty and destiny bound to live his life in
the public's eye. But his mother had intervened, requesting he be
allowed to hold off on his royal duties so he could devote himself
to his studies. Maybe it was the timing or the bad press, or the fact
that it was unlikely he'd ascend to the throne or become a working royal, but the queen had acquiesced. He'd always be grateful to

his mother for the unprecedented act. And to the queen, for recognizing he was better suited for life in a lecture hall and not St. George's Hall. That concession, and his mother's sensibility, meant he'd been able to have a normal life.

If constantly being hounded by the press and tabloid media documenting his every move counted as normal.

The queen answered his questions with her next words. "We're going to host a celebratory concert!"

"Pardon?" He swallowed incorrectly, the action bringing on a coughing fit. She couldn't have surprised him more if she'd stood and started dancing in front of him.

"We're going to host a celebratory concert," she repeated.

"A concert?" How did that help bolster the family's image? "That's the idea you came up with?"

"With help from Louisa."

"Louisa?"

Now he sounded like a bloody parrot.

"Yes. Louisa Collins, our events coordinator. You don't know her? Her husband is the stable master at Primrose Park."

Jameson couldn't recall the name of his stable master, let alone know the man's wife. Primrose Park, the country seat where Jameson resided, consisted of over seven hundred acres managed by a staff of close to one hundred. He left the handling of them to his trusted estate manager.

"We hired Louisa last year," Marina said, "to manage a broad range of official, ceremonial events."

She pressed a button on the table next to her. Seconds later, the door opened, and a footman strode in followed by a pretty young woman. Jameson stood, the movement automatic.

The woman executed a small curtsy. "Your Majesty."

Louisa Collins was tall with sleek auburn hair twisted into a knot at the nape of her neck. In a knee-length navy sheath dress and sensible but stylish matching heels, she was dressed as the queen preferred for all of the palace's senior aides: tailored, pared back, professional.

Marina smiled. "Louisa, my grandson Prince Jameson."

Louisa curtsied again, this time in his direction, the sunlight gleaming off her pearl earrings. "Your Royal Highness."

The formality threw Jameson, as it wasn't something he dealt with on a daily basis. Inside the bubble of academia, at the University of Birmingham, his most ceremonial title was "Professor."

In the beginning, the faculty and students had been fascinated by the idea of having a member of the royal family on campus. But it didn't take them long to realize he actually planned to lecture on *philosophy*, not sit around in a smoking jacket, *philosophizing*, drinking single-malt whisky, and spilling secrets about his relatives and the famous people he knew. Being on campus afforded him some sense of normalcy. That was why he hated leaving.

Marina toyed with her diamond wedding band before wringing her hands in her lap. "John would've been seventy-nine in June if he had lived."

Louisa nodded. "The queen and I were discussing ways to honor His Royal Highness."

Marina's lips curved softly. "He really believed in his environmental philanthropy."

Jameson knew that all too well, considering it was one of the interests he and his grandfather had bonded over. They'd always been close, but after Jameson's father had died, the prince had gone out of his way to connect with him. John had suggested weekly lunches, framing the get-togethers as being for the prince's benefit, as a way for him to remember his son and to stay abreast of the current generation's thinking. It wasn't until after John's death that

Jameson realized their time together had been more for him. John had sensed Jameson's loss, his directionless anger, and had stepped into the emotional chasm.

He'd learned so much from his grandfather. There were times when he'd seemed to have more in common with him than he'd ever had with his own father. In fact, it had been his conversations with John that had developed Jameson's interest in the ethics of environmentalism and the study of man's relationship with and responsibility to the environment.

"I mentioned the Americans and their tribute concerts," Louisa said. "They're always having them to bring attention to one cause or another."

Marina nodded. "A concert for John could bring attention to the issues he believed in."

"Prince John still polls extremely well, and we now accept as fact many of the tenets he endorsed when he was alive," Louisa said.

"The concert can tap in to those feelings," Marina stated. "Give us all something positive to rally around."

And if the press was busy remembering John and covering the concert, they'd have less time and "space" to expose any other royals acting badly.

"We can showcase Prince John's favorite musicians and bring in some current popular ones, to appeal to a younger crowd."

Jameson imagined John would've enjoyed that idea. He'd more than loved his grandfather. He'd respected him. John had been smart, funny, and exceedingly kind. He'd nurtured Jameson's love of philosophy and reading, and had encouraged him to be himself, even if that was slightly different from other royals his age.

And John had loved Queen Marina. With a loyalty, depth, and acceptance Jameson hadn't believed the royals were capable of. He hadn't seen it in his parents' marriage. Or any of his other relatives'.

John had been the emotional linchpin for the family and Jameson knew that his death, and lack of counsel, had led to many of the scandalous behaviors recently exhibited.

"A concert sounds wonderful," he finally said, endorsing the idea.

Although he was still confused by his need to be here. Maybe the queen thought he had an in with the "younger crowd" by virtue of his work at Birmingham. He supposed he could ask around. Or, once the date was set, he could get permission to advertise on campus.

"I'm glad you agree," Marina said. "Because you're going to be the royal family representative for this event."

Blood flooded his head and pounded in his ears and he was immediately bombarded with the terrifying recollection of the weight of pressing bodies, blinding camera flashes, reporters calling his and his mother's names, and streams of inappropriate questions. Of photogs recklessly crashing into the back of his car and of almost being run over by a reporter who lost control of his bike trying to get a picture of him and his mother after his father died.

The queen wanted to put him out there to subject himself to that? Willingly?

Perhaps he'd misheard her. "Sorry, what?"

"Once Louisa puts the event together, you will be the primary representative for the royal family."

The queen wanting to host a concert was one thing but wanting him to be involved?

He was gobsmacked.

Anxiety twisted his belly into knots. "But . . . I have a job. I'll be busy."

"Louisa said the summer term ends mid-June. The celebration wouldn't be before then."

Jameson shot a look in the event coordinator's direction before saying, "While I appreciate you thinking of me, ma'am, I did have plans for the break."

None of which included working on a high-profile event for the Crown.

"Louisa and her staff will take care of the logistics. At most, she may need your help with the talent," Marina said.

He shifted in the chair. "The talent?"

"The musical acts," Louisa clarified.

Since when was his musical opinion sought? His tastes were more Bach than Beyoncé, Chopin than Céline. In fact, he couldn't name the songs at the top of the popular music charts if his life depended on it.

Jameson didn't go out much, preferring solitude or the company of a few friends. He wasn't a partier. That was his uncle's and aunt's area of expertise.

And his father's.

"Wouldn't Julian and Bettina be better suited for this?" he asked, referring to said uncle and aunt, the latter who'd infamously followed a rock band on their world tour when she was nineteen.

Marina's lips tightened, practically screaming her displeasure. "The last thing they need is to be in the spotlight . . . or within close proximity of musicians."

Jameson would've laughed if he hadn't been preoccupied with the vise tightening in his chest. "I just think they may have a better idea—"

"Louisa, would you please excuse us?"

"Yes, ma'am," the younger woman said, dipping into a quick curtsy before disappearing behind the door the footman held open.

"This is more than a concert, Jameson," Marina said when they were alone . . . save for the ever-present household staff. "Though

I'm elated to be honoring John's legacy in this way, I need to change our reputation and the public's view of us. Quite literally, the monarchy could be at stake."

"Ma'am—"

"It's time for fresh faces," Marina interjected. "The public loves you."

And hates Julian.

She didn't have to speak the words. Everyone was aware of the public's feelings about the next in line. And Julian's complete indifference.

"The public barely knows me!"

Not for lack of trying.

"Before your father . . . passed away, he'd let the numerous important duties he performed for the Crown lapse. Responsibilities that came with the title. After his death, there was a lot of work to do. You should've taken his place. But your mother came to me and begged for more time. And John . . . John agreed with her." Her expression hardened. "But there was always the understanding that at some point you would take your father's place and assume his duties. That time is now."

Grinding his teeth, Jameson tried one more time. "I don't think I'm suited for what you—"

"I suppose I could tell you it doesn't matter. That earlier today I drafted an announcement officially naming you a Counsellor of State."

He sucked in a breath. Counsellors of State were senior members of the royal family who could carry out official duties on the queen's behalf. They were usually the sovereign's spouse and the first four in the line of succession who were over the age of twenty-one. Once an appointment was made, one was unable to refuse acceptance.

The queen's counsellors had been Julian, Catherine, Bettina, and the queen's brother, Alcott.

"You already have your counsellors."

"I never replaced John after he passed. Appointing you remedies that breach. I could tell you that I've made my decision and you *will* be the public face of the royal family for this event." She folded her hands in her lap. "But I don't want to do that. Not when this situation could benefit us both."

He didn't see how him voluntarily stepping into the public eye, when he'd spent his life trying to avoid its glare, could ever serve his interest.

Until Marina said, "For the past ten years, John's charitable patronages have sat untended, almost in shambles."

Jameson inhaled sharply. Each member of the royal family was linked to numerous public service organizations, to which they lent their names and, if they were so inclined, their efforts. The money was essential, but having the involvement of a royal patron made a world of difference. It took a charity from being just one in a crowd to one with top-notch exposure, drawing in other well-connected donors and driving thousands, even millions of pounds into the coffers each year. John had been passionate about his trust, having given his time and attention to a carefully curated list of worthwhile but lesser-known environmental charities.

"They've received the money he'd allotted, but the guidance, the counsel, the events that would continue garnering attention and donations . . ." Marina eyed him steadily. "If I don't find a new patron for it, I may have to dissolve his trust."

Jameson's stomach dropped at the thought of disbanding all the work his grandfather had done. During their lunches, John often talked with great excitement about the new charity he'd discovered doing good works in the areas of conservation or urban sustain-ability. He'd practically radiated enthusiasm.

She sighed. "I'd thought about giving it to Julian. He's been ask-ing for years."

Give John's esteemed and revered trust to his son? Whose idea of environmentalism was throwing his bloodied bow in the recycle bin after shooting an endangered rhino?

Bloody hell.

Despite his haze of anger, Jameson was aware that Marina was playing on his affinity for John. He was under no obligation to take over the trust. But how could he stand by and watch the life's work of the man who'd mentored and advised him—who'd influenced him more than his own father!—be placed into the hands of a self-indulgent reprobate?

Willingly participate in this concert and Marina would give him John's charitable trust. Fight her in any way, she'd force him to comply . . . and make him watch her dissolve the trust or, worse, give it to Julian.

Swallowing, he accepted his fate. "I'd be honored to represent you and the family in the celebration of Prince John and his life's work. But once it's over, I'm returning to Birmingham and my work there."

"I knew I could count on you, Jameson." With a tiny smile of satisfaction, the queen stood and smoothed her hands down the front of her dress. "The newly appointed ambassador from Den-mark is waiting for me, but you don't have to rush off. Stay as long as you'd like."

She swept from the room in a cloud of rare, elegant florals, tak-ing the aura of regality with her.

He wanted to throw something.

Kick something.

Yell.

He settled for loosening his tie, undoing the top button on his shirt, and raking a hand through his hair.

His grandmother had been correct. This *was* more than a concert. It was a gateway from the normal life he loved into the royal life he dreaded.

But at least one thing remained the same.

It was *still* the Den of Despondency.

Chapter Three

"I'm busy 'bout my coint with a t on the end..."
—Duchess, "A Hard Road"

Manhattan, New York

Dani stared straight ahead as the elevator car ascended the many
floors of the Upper West Side skyscraper at a dizzying speed.

Tasha reached over to squeeze her arm. "Don't be nervous."

Dani frowned. "I'm not nervous. What makes you think I'm
nervous?"

"Oh, I don't know. The fact that you're biting your lower lip the
way my Aunt Gladys tucks into short ribs?"

Tasha would be the only one who'd noticed the habit, since Dani
went out of her way to ensure she always projected a flawless image.
If she was anywhere in public, anyplace where there was a chance
a camera could focus on her, she made sure she was never caught
looking any way other than how she wanted to be seen. Especially
these days. She couldn't eat out, go shopping, or even travel without
a hoard of cameras attached to unrelenting paparazzi—hassling
her and shouting out for a quote.

When she'd left her favorite nail salon and tried to get in her car, they'd surrounded her, holding her door open to get as many shots as possible. She'd finally yanked it from them, yelling, "Let go of my fucking door!"

The photographer had smirked in triumph. "Why you so aggressive, Duchess? Is that how you treated Samantha?"

Goddammit!

Pushing the memory aside, she released her lip and grabbed the lipstick wand Tasha was holding out for her. Correcting the flaw, she inhaled.

"This is make or break, Tasha. We can't lose this."

"We won't."

Dani placed a hand on her churning belly. "You don't know that. The other four companies dropped out. Genesis is our only chance."

"You're worried they're going to do the same?" Tasha asked quietly.

"Of course I am! But they're a thirty-five-billion-dollar corporation. They should have more important things to do than read celebrity gossip blogs."

Unlike the other four companies.

Although, to be fair, the story had reached epic proportions, moving beyond gossip blogs to mainstream media. When the video had made Hot Topics on *The View*, her mentions had exploded. Out of context—and thanks to Banks's Spielberg edit—the video wasn't flattering for Dani. The takeaway was that Duchess was unwilling to help another up-and-coming female artist. Mainstream media was quick to side with the pop star over the rapper. Oversexualized, vulgar black woman versus innocent-looking young white woman?

No contest.

When the first beauty company had canceled their meeting, Dani had shrugged it off, buying their scheduling conflict excuse. When the second company called, she grew a little apprehensive but told herself the story would burn hot then flame out when the next A-list celebrity couple called it quits. By the time companies three and four had called, she'd accepted what she was up against.

Aided by Banks's craven need for attention, the entertainment industry had found its newest gladiators for the Colosseum. And in the eyes of the beauty trade, Dani wasn't the winning bet.

Fortunately, people in the music business and her fans knew the truth. As they liked to point out on Instagram and Twitter. Daily.

"It'll be fine. Everyone wants this deal to work," Tasha said.

Dani hoped so.

The elevator doors slid open and they stepped into a bright, sleek reception space. The slate gray tile floors and glossy white interior were warmed by bright orange lounge chairs and a colorful over-sized area rug.

A young woman stood waiting, cute and professional in a white shirt and basic black skirt, box braids piled into a bun on the top of her head.

"Welcome, Duchess."

Showtime.

Dani straightened and smiled. "Thank you."

"Can I get you anything? Water, coffee? Champagne?"

Her love for all things bubbly always preceded her.

"I'm good," she said.

"Then they're ready for you in the conference room. Would you please follow me?" The young woman started down the hall, then stopped and turned back to Dani. "We're not supposed to bother you, but I wanted to let you know that I'm a big fan."

Some of her fellow artists took these interactions for granted. Dani never did. Maybe because she still remembered being on the other side of the exchange when she'd first gotten into music. Her foray into the industry had begun with a part-time job at a recording studio in Norfolk. She'd never forget the day she saw one of her idols strolling the carpeted hallway. Dani had gone up to her, expressed her admiration and gratitude, and confessed that the woman's music had gotten Dani through some hard times. The woman had looked Dani up and down, sucked her teeth, and said, "Get me more ice in our studio lounge," before sashaying off, muttering about "young bitches trying to take her spot."

Dani had been shocked by the woman's attitude and had mentioned the incident to a fellow intern. "Oh, girl. Get used to it. Women don't take other women under their wing. And they definitely don't play nice with us. Do you know how many boyfriends and husbands have been lost to the woman you thought was your friend?"

That experience had made a lasting impression on Dani. The disappointment she'd felt, meeting an entertainer she'd looked up to, informed her own interactions with her fans. She always took time to speak with them, especially the young women. And if they ever expressed interest in the business, Dani encouraged them to go after their dreams. Fuck that "Highlander, there can be only one!" shit.

It was an additional reason why she was pissed with Banks for propagating the impression that she would intentionally hurt another female artist.

Dani fought her way back to the present. "Thank you. It's always nice meeting fans who support women in hip-hop."

The receptionist recoiled. "No, not of your music. Though it's good," she stammered when she realized what she'd said, color blooming on her cheeks. "I meant of your skin-care line. I love your exfoliating skin wash."

Assumptions, Dani!

But she recovered quickly. "Isn't it great? I use all of my own products, too. We actually have that wash coming out in a couple of different scent options. Give your information to Tasha and I'll make sure we send you some."

"Really?" The woman's eyes widened. "Can I post this on Insta?"

"Of course. Tag me, okay?"

"I will. Thank you, Duchess."

Dani smiled and Tasha handed the young woman a business card.

"That's happening more and more often," Tasha commented, as they headed down the long hallway to the conference room.

"Being approached by fans? It happens all of the time."

"Not just fans. Fans of Mela-Skin. It used to be a rare occurrence. Now it's happening with the same frequency as you being approached by fans of your music. And the skin-care fans are more women."

At the beginning of her career, most of the people who approached Dani and asked for pictures were men. Over the past few years, she'd begun noticing that she was approached by more women, but Tasha's statement was the first time she realized that most of the women also spoke to her about the skin-care line. This all seemed to confirm her decision to focus her energies on the venture that would help her achieve her long-term goal of true independence.

"Mela-Skin made you more approachable," Tasha said. "It softened your image, excuse the pun."

When they reached the glass door to the conference room, Andrea Thompson, Mela-Skin's CEO, was waiting for them. "Are you ready?"

"Aren't I always?" Dani asked.

"Put everything that's happened out of your mind. Remember, they want your company," Andrea said.

"I know. So, let's get in there and do what we have to do not to lose it."

Andrea opened the door and stood back to allow Dani to enter. By the time she'd crossed the threshold, Dani had buried the nervousness she felt layers deep beneath the cool image she wanted to project.

The room was large, and the floor-to-ceiling windows offered a breathtaking view of downtown Manhattan and One World Trade Center, the sun sparkling off the Hudson River. Three rectangular-shaped wooden tables were configured into a narrow U that dominated the space, and a large digital screen was built into the far wall. An assortment of men and women, mostly white, sat in various chairs around the tables.

Instinctively, Dani made eye contact with the only black woman on Genesis's team. Neither would ever betray it outwardly, but the slight head bob was all that was necessary for each to confirm they were allies, a quick moment that most people in the room hadn't noticed.

At the far end of the table, Henry Owens, the company's point person, stood to greet her, buttoning the jacket of his navy suit. "Duchess. Welcome. It's good to finally meet you."

The familiar sensation of eyes on her body tingled along her skin as she traversed the length of the room to reach Henry. She'd wanted to project business while also using all of her charms to her advantage. Hence, the black Tom Ford pin-striped suit that hugged her curves, the skirt ending just above her knees, white lace bustier, and four-inch black-and-white Jimmy Choo pumps.

She kept her eyes trained straight ahead, so she felt, more than saw, each chair swivel discreetly as she passed.

Just as she wanted them to.

Control the image. Control the narrative.

"Thank you, Henry. I hope you're well," she said, presenting her cheek for an air-kiss instead of a handshake.

Pulling back, she smiled, noticing the blush high on his cheekbones and the way his gaze lingered on her cleavage. She dropped gracefully into the chair he held for her and glanced at the stony faces. "We're finally doing this thing!"

"We've had our eye on you for a while," Henry said above the laughter, taking the seat to her left.

"You and everyone else," she said.

"Right you are. You and your company burst onto our scene and made quite the impression."

"Mela-Skin is the real deal," Andrea said, chiming in. "We're honored that a company of your stature has recognized what Duchess has created."

"We have. Which is why we were excited about bringing Mela-Skin into the Genesis family."

Dani's chest tightened, making it hard for her to breathe.

Were?

Andrea caught her eye and nodded imperceptibly. "It's a great match. And we're willing to do what's necessary to ensure the process goes smoothly and there are no surprises."

"Excellent," Henry said. "Then let's begin."

Almost as if it had been choreographed, they all swiveled to face the large screen on the wall. Henry pressed a button, the lights dimmed, and the Mela-Skin logo, a capital M topped by a crown, appeared.

"Mela-Skin has done what other companies haven't: you've specialized in one area and perfected it. Other companies we've acquired in the black beauty space try to be all things to all people. They'd be great with hair, but their skin products weren't as good. Or they had a great makeup line but tried to branch prematurely into skin care. Your company started with skin care and stayed in that lane. That takes a wisdom and patience we recognize and appreciate."

Some of Dani's anxiety eased with his words.

Dani had started Mela-Skin because one of her favorite brands had made that unsuccessful move Henry had mentioned. Dani had wanted skin care to be her sole focus. Whenever an investor or executive tried to convince her to branch out, she refused.

But she understood why some of those companies made the choices they did. Women of color had long been an underserved market. No one had been reaching out to them. Those companies saw an opportunity to serve a market in need and make money. She wasn't going to judge them for that.

"Financially, your company appears sound. Some look great from the outside but upon closer inspection they turn out to be a collection of dysfunction and chaos. Luckily, that hasn't been the case with Mela-Skin," Henry said, his smile testing the bounds of condescension.

Luckily?

It wasn't luck, it was hard work. Periodt. End of sentence.

Dani didn't consider herself a real businesswoman. Yet. But she was smart. When she'd started her company, she'd been honest in her assessment of what she could and couldn't do. Those things she didn't excel at? She hired people to do them for her. But that didn't mean she abdicated her responsibility. Mela-Skin was her company. She owned eighty-four percent of it. She made sure she always knew what was going on.

She held her tongue, nodded, and smiled, keeping her eyes on the future and not willing to risk offense before a deal had been signed.

"Once we'd conducted our initial due diligence, we wanted to get you in here. See if we could do business."

Dani crossed her legs. "Seems like you believe we can."

"Yes, well . . ." Henry's assured demeanor began to crumble. "That was before."

Dread wrapped its frosty fingers around her heart. "Before what?"

Andrea frowned and leaned forward. "What's going on?"

Henry cleared his throat and nodded across the table to the black woman Dani had noticed upon entering the room. "I'm going to let Barbara address this."

Barbara? Really?

Dani turned her chair and caught the resigned annoyance on Barbara's face before the executive covered it with a practiced mask of professionalism.

Been there, experienced that, sis.

Barbara folded her hands on the table. "We're concerned about your latest altercation with Samantha Banks."

Dani stiffened, the heat of frustration burning away her earlier apprehension. She'd worked hard, paid her dues, and established a good reputation in the business. Before two years ago she'd had no idea who Samantha Banks was. Now, it seemed they were joined at the tit.

She mentally reached out for patience. "I didn't have an altercation with Samantha Banks."

"The video all over the media says otherwise."

Dani rolled her eyes. "Has anyone bothered to really look at that video? Y'all can tell it's doctored, right?"

Barbara glanced quickly at Henry before responding. "Personally, I can understand why you were driven to say what you did. But your feud with her has gained traction."

Dani wanted to slide her freshly manicured nails into her silk press and pull the straightened strands out. "I'm *not* in a feud with her."

"The public believes you are."

"The public is wrong! Connecting my name with hers is insane. Before this incident, I'd never even met her. And my response had nothing to do with some bogus promise to appear on her track. She assaulted my bodyguard and pretty much called me a whore. I've never said anything negative about her online. I haven't even acknowledged her existence. And yet we're in a feud?"

"It's really semantics at this point," Henry said.

Heat swamped Dani's body. Sweat gathered beneath her arms and slid down the valley between her breasts. She wished she could shrug out of her jacket, but she focused on keeping calm. After all, the last time she'd lost her cool was the reason she was here now, having this conversation.

"I make my living with words," Dani said. "They matter. If you're going to accuse me of something, the words you use to do so matter."

Some of the executives around the table began shifting in their seats, as if uncomfortable with the discussion.

Join the fucking club.

"No one is accusing you—"

Barbara held up her hand to prevent Henry from continuing. "You're right. But the perception is out there and, as we all know, perception is reality."

Dani knew. Her own persona was built on that very idea.

"What are you saying?" Andrea asked.

"Everything Henry mentioned was correct. We love you. We love your company and your products. What you've done is show you're more than a pretty girl who spouts suggestive lyrics. We want to do business with you. Bring you into the Genesis fold. We want to take Mela-Skin to the next level."

Though the words sounded nice, Dani waited.

"But . . . we can't have our brand tarnished. Companies are getting canceled left and right these days. Samantha Banks has a large following of young girls and they've taken exception to your treatment of her. We can't afford to be on that growing list."

Had she heard right? The big corporation was going to use cancel culture as their excuse to side with a pop star over her?

Wasn't *that* some shit?

Henry jumped in. "It's not a good look online. Half of why we wanted to acquire Mela-Skin had to do with your products. The other half had to do with you. Take Rihanna and Fenty. Her image is tied to that brand. It's a more valuable commodity because of her. And Mela-Skin is more valuable because of who you are. Because of your image. Sexy. Fearless. Glamorous."

Good to know all the work she put into projecting that vision was paying off.

"We understand creative types are driven by emotions. This didn't have to be a big deal. But the mainstream media latched on to the story and young girls, our target demographic, are seeing you differently. And it's affected how we're seeing you. And your company."

She read the continent of space between the lines.

Their target demographic.

Young *white* girls.

The same demographic that was taking Samantha Banks's side on social media.

So, a group of women who had nothing to do with her business and who would never buy her products, because they weren't *her* target demographic, could play a role in whether this deal would even happen?

A knot formed in the back of her throat, making it difficult for words to emerge. She opened her mouth then closed it.

"What does this mean?" Andrea asked.

Dani sent her CEO a look of gratitude.

Henry tapped his index finger on the table. "You're going to need amazing press to turn this all around and get people on your side again. The only way we see that happening is if you apologize."

Dani was certain she hadn't heard him properly. "Excuse me?"

"This is outrageous!" Andrea said, confirming that Dani had indeed heard him properly.

"It doesn't have to be a big deal. Put something out on your social media saying you regret what happened. Try to squash the beef. That's what you call it, right?" Henry offered with a smile.

Dani didn't find the situation humorous.

"Why would I apologize? I haven't done anything wrong. None of this is my fault."

Henry leaned back in his chair. "It doesn't matter. You're the one who's seen as wrong. Your image has taken a beating. You need to apologize. Surely we aren't the only people to tell you this."

This was a nightmare!

"And if I don't?"

Henry's features hardened and he issued the final blow. "Then this meeting is over and you're going to have a problem. This is a small industry. We knew the other top companies were interested in Mela-Skin and we were aware when they dropped out of the running. Heed my words. Apologize. Now. Or there will be no deal. With anyone. And you'll become a cautionary tale smaller companies tell themselves about not missing their opportunity."

Despite her earlier apprehension, Dani hadn't allowed herself to believe this would actually happen. Fate wouldn't be so cruel as to once again render her a puppet in her own life, the success of her plans and attainment of her goals dictated by the whims of people who couldn't give a shit about her, would it?

At the moment it looked like fate would, indeed, be that bitch.

Chapter Four

"I cannot teach anybody anything. I can only make them think."

—Socrates

University of Birmingham
Birmingham, United Kingdom

J ameson stood in front of the large lecture hall as eighty pairs of eyes stared back at him from the seats that rose up and spread out in a fan pattern, almost like in a Colosseum. An apt analogy, as in the beginning, each class had seemed like a Roman public spectacle, with him lecturing and waiting for the thumbs-up or thumbs-down that would determine if he'd managed to entertain. Unfortunately for him, if it had been the Colosseum, he would've been sentenced to death.

At the beginning of each term, his Introduction to Philosophy course was always filled, as it had become a rite of passage for the students who came to Birmingham. They wanted to see the prince teach a class. It didn't take long for people to learn it was Professor

Lloyd, not Prince Jameson or the Duke of Wessex. He'd had loads of information he'd been eager to convey, and that, combined with his distinctly not royal style, had led to high dropout rates.

He'd quickly learned to adapt his teaching style. Modern students had a shorter attention span than their predecessors and they needed time to process the information. They tended to get more out of a lecture if they had the opportunity to engage with him versus sitting and listening to him spew material. That shift in technique had helped him improve each term, which had boosted his already high gratification in his job.

Some terms were better than others. This class, with its ninety percent capacity, counted as a personal victory. If they could do their part and show up, he could ensure the subject matter caught and retained their interest.

He glanced to his left at the three students sitting in chairs facing the far wall. "Masks on and covering your eyes. Ready?"

When they'd donned the black satin eye masks and given him the predetermined ready sign, Jameson turned back to face the rest of his class. "Book seven of the *Republic* gives us Plato's Allegory of the Cave, one of the most famous images in all of philosophy."

He pressed the button on the clicker in his hand and the lights dimmed. Nervous snickers filled the air and Jameson smiled.

Same reaction every time.

He grabbed the industrial-strength flashlight off the lecture stand and strode over until he was on the other side of the room, facing the backs of the students sitting in the chairs.

"Masks off," he told them, before beginning. "A group of prisoners have been confined in a cavern since birth, with no knowledge of the outside world. They are chained, facing a wall, bound by feet and necks, unable to turn their heads, while a fire behind them gives off a faint light."

He turned on the flashlight. The students' shadows were projected on the wall in front of them.

"Occasionally forms pass by the fire, carrying figures of animals and other objects that cast shadows on the wall. The prisoners name and classify these silhouettes, believing they are perceiving actual entities."

Jameson gestured to the two students sitting in the front row, who stood and walked in front of his flashlight, holding their bags and books aloft.

"Thank you," he said when they scurried back to their seats. He continued his tale. "Suddenly, one prisoner is freed and is dragged outside for the first time. And since we're not in the habit of inducing physical violence and if I send you outside you probably won't come back"—laughter followed this remark—"everyone except Isla, put your masks back on. Isla, keep yours off, but stand and face the class."

The girl sitting in the chair on the far end did as he directed. Jameson turned the overhead lights back on.

"The sunlight hurts her eyes, and she finds the new environment disorienting. When told the things around her are real, while the shadows were mere reflections, she cannot believe it. The shadows appeared much clearer to her. But gradually, her eyes adjust, until she can look at reflections in the water—for our purposes that will be your classmates—and then at actual objects directly. And finally"—he pointed overhead—"at the sun, whose light is the ultimate source of everything she has seen."

Jameson looked at Isla, who was blinking rapidly. "Now, I want you to go back and stand in front of your fellow prisoners."

Once Isla got into position, he turned the overhead lights back off and instructed the other students to once again remove their masks.

"The prisoner returns to the cave to share everything she has learned, but she is no longer used to the darkness and has a hard time seeing the shadows on the wall. The other prisoners think the journey has made her stupid and blind and violently resist any attempts to free them. Again, for the purposes of this class, a simple shake of your heads will suffice."

More laughter.

"Let's give all of our participants a round of applause."

He turned off the flashlight and turned on the overhead lights as the students gingerly made their way back to their seats.

"Plato used this allegory to explain what it's like being a philosopher trying to educate the public. And over two thousand years later, it's still being used. In fact, what if I told you a popular movie uses this same symbolic narrative?"

"Which one?" a student called out from the back.

Jameson knew the reaction his response was going to get. "*The Matrix*."

"No way!"

"Seriously?"

"That's the old movie my dad is obsessed with."

Jameson pointed to the middle of the class. "Whoever made that comment is getting an F for the term! *The Matrix* isn't old! It's not *Casablanca*."

"What's *Casablanca*?"

"Now you're just being a git."

More laughter.

Jameson continued. "People interested in philosophy have watched this movie often and can discuss it for hours. Think of Neo, going through his life, working at the computer company, selling bootleg discs until someone comes and 'drags him outside.'

In the movie, this would be Trinity, taking Neo to see Morpheus, who offers him the red or blue pill. Once Neo takes the red pill it's as if his eyes have adjusted to the light. He's now aware of the Matrix. That the world was different from what he thought. Now imagine if Neo went back to the people he sold the disc to at the beginning of the movie and tried to explain the Matrix to them?

"Even better, Cypher betraying the team—"

"Spoiler!" someone yelled out.

Jameson dipped his head in acknowledgment but continued. "You have to wonder if you can be truly comfortable in anything you know. As you live your life guided by a certain belief system, and something breaks through that's different from what you know, would you be brave enough to pursue it? Or would you stick to comfortable and familiar illusions? Who determines what knowledge is valued? Who determines what knowledge is crazy? What is the origin of knowledge? And once knowledge is attained, do you have the duty to share that knowledge with others who don't have it, even at the risk of death?"

The alarm on his cellphone trilled and he pressed the screen. "That's a good stopping point. On Tuesday, I'll expect you to have completed the worksheet and to bring any questions you have. In a few weeks we'll start reviewing for exams."

The room filled with the groans and noises of students gathering up their belongings, and Jameson did likewise. He undid the transmitter pack clipped to his slacks and the small microphone hooked to the front of his navy button-down shirt. He had office hours in fifteen minutes, followed by a departmental meeting and drinks with Rhys at the pub.

Grabbing his phone and bag from the shelf behind the podium, he headed out of the building and across the quad. It had rained earlier, but the sun was making a valiant effort to shine through the cloud cover. He stuck to the concrete footpaths, instead of crossing the grass.

The Plato's Allegory exercise was one of his favorites. Jameson knew there were many misconceptions about philosophy, including the belief it wasn't relevant in the modern world, but by its very nature, philosophy was an enduring field of study. Students who studied it learned to write clearly, think critically, and spot bad reasoning, highly sought-after skills in the current workforce. There was nothing he enjoyed more than standing in front of a class and discussing, sometimes debating, the big questions of the day. It was one of the many reasons he loved his work.

Quite unlike his *other* duties. The thought of donning his role as a member of the royal family, becoming the focus of millions of eyes and opinions, caused him to break out in hives.

He was so caught up in his thoughts he didn't notice the student coming toward him until they'd bumped into one another.

"Sorry about that," he said, stepping to the side.

The boy mirrored his movements. Wearing a cap that covered most of his face, he whipped out his phone. "Prince Jameson, the queen named you one of her Counsellors of State."

Shock held him immobile.

"Has she brought you in to detract from the public's growing dissatisfaction with the queen's job?"

Fingers tightening on the strap of his bag, Jameson watched as students and faculty slowed to ogle, their gazes fixed in wide-eyed fascination on the unfolding spectacle.

"Now that you're older, do you have a new perspective on your father's relationship with Gena Phillips?"

It felt like a long time, but in reality, the boy had rattled the questions off quickly. Jameson barely had a chance to react before security grabbed the guy. His cap flew off and Jameson noted it wasn't a student but an older man.

His chest tightened, embarrassment heating the nape of his neck and tips of his ears. He'd worked so hard to be like everyone else. To keep his unwanted royal life away from his sacred professional one. And with the presence of this rogue paparazzo, the first, but definitely not the last now that he'd tried, Jameson's efforts had been rendered useless.

News of this encounter would sweep the campus faster than the press reporting on a royal scandal.

"FUCK, MATE. SORRY you had to go through that." Rhys Barnes, his friend and fellow professor, aimed his dart at the circular target and let it fly.

Jameson shifted on the leather-topped pub stool, his fingers gripped around his second pint. "Thanks."

The encounter with the paparazzo had derailed his ability to focus. He'd rescheduled his meetings and texted Rhys, hoping to persuade him to come along for an early drink.

It hadn't taken much convincing.

He'd met Rhys during their time together at Oxford. Tall, blond, and brawny, his friend looked like he'd be more comfortable on a rugby pitch than in a lecture hall. But as a professor in the Engineering Department, his active, hands-on approach made him very popular with the students.

They sat in the back corner of their favorite pub, the Bell and the Crown. Close to the campus, it was mostly frequented by students, faculty, and staff from the uni. Which was why he preferred it. Other than a few stray glances, the patrons mostly gave him a wide berth. It was one of the few places he didn't have to keep watch over his shoulder, where he felt slightly normal.

Except today.

Today, everyone was talking about what had happened. And though he studiously avoided meeting anyone's gaze, he could feel their stares like dozens of tiny lasers.

Since the Palace's announcement of his appointment as a Counsellor of State, speculation in the media had run rampant: Why had the queen done it? What would his new role be? Was he finally taking his father's place?

Which always led to a recap of his father's affair and death.

He wasn't the only one affected by the queen's declaration. The press had begun hounding his mother again. Not as intensely as in the years after the accident, but more fervently than in recent memory. Unfortunately, despite the shocking events of the day, it wasn't the first time he'd had to deal with the invasive crush of the tabloid press in the past few weeks. But it was the first time a reporter had been brazen enough to come onto school grounds.

Rhys collected his pieces. "I wonder what would've happened if security hadn't been there."

Since Jameson hadn't been a "working" royal, he wasn't entitled to around-the-clock protection. When his father was alive, Jameson and his parents had been granted a security detail, which they'd retained for a period of time after his death. However, after the announcement, two discreet guards had shown up at the university. They never bothered or even interacted with him. They'd kept a vigilant distance. Until earlier today.

"He probably would've followed me to my office."

"You're a big guy. You could've taken him."

"Don't be daft. The thirty-second video of the takedown has already gone viral. Do you know what would've happened if I'd done it? How many trips to the palace would be involved?"

"Being friends with you takes the shine off of being fancy."

"Don't I know it."

Rhys drained the rest of his Guinness. "Some of us are heading over to Jasper's for poker night. You coming? They've been asking about you."

"Next time." He appreciated Rhys asking, and he generally got along with Jasper and the others, but he wasn't in the mood.

"Your Royal Highness."

A chill shot down Jameson's spine and he looked up to see Louisa briefly curtsying to him. Though her voice hadn't been loud, the words went into a sudden breach of sound and seemed to echo throughout the space. The crowd stopped what they were doing and openly gawked.

"Don't call me that," he hissed.

"Why?"

"Because that's not who I am here!"

"Are you sure?" she asked, glancing around at the assembly of curious stares making them the center of attention.

"That's you and your proclaiming and curtsying." He turned to the customers and attempted flippancy to diffuse the situation. "Come on. Nothing to see here."

They kept looking.

Jameson exhaled. Was there no space left for him to just be normal?

"Hello, beautiful lady," Rhys said, flashing a megawatt smile that still worked as well today as it had back at uni.

"Simmer down. She's married."

"Happily?" Rhys asked, the engineer in him approaching from a different angle.

Louisa's lips quirked. "Quite."

"Oh." Rhys shrugged.

"And she works for my grandmother."

"You work for the queen!"

More heads turned in their direction.

Bloody hell! "A little louder please. A couple near the entrance didn't hear you."

"Sorry, mate. This will require another round. Can I get you a drink, uh . . ."

And now Jameson felt like an arsehole who'd lost his manners.

"This is Louisa Collins, the Royal Household's senior events co-ordinator. Louisa, this is Professor Rhys Barnes, who I sometimes call my friend."

"A pleasure," Rhys said. "Now, about that drink . . . ?"

"No thank you. I'm hoping this won't take long," she said, with a pointed look at Jameson.

"Have a seat. I'll be right back." Rhys strode off, raising an arm to get the barkeep's attention. He needn't have bothered. The man was already pouring them a refill.

"I'm sorry you came all this way, but you've wasted your time."

Louisa perched daintily on the edge of the wooden stool. "Interesting lecture."

He started in surprise. "You saw it?"

She nodded. "Only the last ten minutes or so."

He hadn't known. Heat swept through him, though he didn't know why he suddenly felt self-conscious. "Thank you. So you also saw what happened afterwards?"

"I did. Good thing the royal protection was there."

Wouldn't have been necessary if the queen hadn't interfered in his life.

"That was over an hour ago. Did you take a tour of the campus?"

"You could say that." She placed her bag on the table. "I'm curious. Where do you see yourself, in regards to your royal duties? The ones in the cave, looking at the shadows? Or the ones outside, looking at the real world?"

Jameson glanced at Louisa. Truth was, he'd often felt the entire royal family lived inside a grand, opulent cave of their own making. But they weren't the prisoners watching shadows flickering against the wall. They held the light and took turns striding back and forth in front of it, casting themselves as larger-than-life beings. When his father died, his mother had pushed Jameson out of the cave, allowing him to live and interact with the world as it really was, and he had no interest in going back inside, as the queen was requesting.

But he wasn't keen on discussing his life, so he simply said, "It's just a lecture."

"Right." It was clear she didn't believe him, but she was a loyal employee of the Crown and not about to call him on his bullshit. Instead, she changed the topic. "You've been ignoring my calls."

"I've been busy."

Which was true.

Mostly.

But in the month since his visit with the queen, Jameson had had the time and space to think clearly. Buckingham Palace had the best home court advantage; in the presence of his grandmother's aura and the majesty of the building, he'd believed he had no choice but to comply. But he didn't want to participate in the celebration and he found it difficult to believe Marina would risk John's charitable trust over his cooperation. She knew the value his grandfather had placed on it. Turning it over to Julian was akin to dismantling it. She couldn't do that and simultaneously host a concert to celebrate him and his work.

So he'd evaded Louisa's overtures, hoping his unresponsiveness would lead to Marina forgetting about his involvement. Or better, deciding to leave him out of it altogether.

It seemed he had misjudged the situation.

"The queen has made her decision," Louisa said. "This event is going to happen."

"If that's what she wants, I'm sure it'll be a success."

"Then why have you been disregarding my calls and messages?"

"Because you don't need me," he said in a low tone, hoping she would follow his lead. "You can plan a great concert and honor Prince John, like the queen wanted. I don't need to be involved."

"But Her Majesty wants you involved," she said in a *booming* tone, either not getting his cue or choosing to disregard it.

Widened eyes darted in their direction, and he winced. Must she be so loud? "Why is my involvement so important to her?"

"She doesn't confide in me. *Why* doesn't matter. It's what she wants and it's my job to see that it's done."

Jameson bristled. "I'm sorry. I couldn't possibly do it. I don't have the time."

"My staff and I will take care of most of the particulars."

"You should contact Catherine. She'd be better suited to this than me."

Louisa's lips thinned. "Sir, I don't mean to overstep, but the queen wanted me to inform you she is not going to change her mind. You will do this. If not because you care for your grandfather and believe his life and work deserve honoring, then because she is your sovereign and she's directing you to."

The last part of her statement sealed the deal. He sighed. He'd do it for Prince John.

For the debt of gratitude and loyalty he owed the man who never would've thought to collect on it.

Given the pleasure of his grandfather's company, his unselfish counsel, and the example of what a loving husband and father could be, wasn't doing a couple of interviews and introducing a few musical acts the least Jameson could do? He'd deal with the press, the royal scrutiny, and the dredging up of his father's past scandals.

But he had demands of his own.

"I want an increase in my mother's level of protection and I want an official announcement naming me as the successor to my grandfather's charitable trust. *Before* the event."

"I'm certain that won't be a problem."

He shoved a hand through his hair. "What do you need me to do?"

Her expression never altered although her relief was evident. "A project of this magnitude would usually take eighteen months, or at least a year, to plan. I've been given *six* months. So, time is, quite literally, of the essence." She pulled an iPad from her black tote bag. "I've gotten a list of performers from other members of the royal family. I'd like to get the same from you."

"A list of performers?"

"Yes. Of musical acts to perform at the concert."

How the hell would he know?

He shook his head.

Louisa sighed. "How about a few?"

He just stared at her.

Rhys came back and placed two foaming pints on the table. "What did I miss?"

Louisa's grip on the digital tablet tightened. "One."

"One what?" Rhys asked.

"I need Prince Jameson to recommend a musical act."

Rhys shook his head. "Oh, he doesn't know music, at least, nothing popular."

He wasn't wrong.

"You're better off grabbing a random customer," Rhys said, reaching for the snacks in the bowl.

Now there was an idea . . .

Louisa pursed her lips. "In order for this event to happen on the date the queen has chosen, I need to get the invitations out by tomorrow. I have my weekly briefing with her when I get back to the palace and she will not be happy."

Rhys stopped in the middle of tossing a pretzel in his mouth. "This is for the queen?"

Jameson scanned the crowd until he saw a boy he recognized. *Perfect!* He motioned him over.

"I need your answer," Louisa persisted.

The student approached, shuffling his feet and smoothing a hand down the front of his jumper. "Sorry, Professor. I wasn't listening—"

"No, no, Alfie," he said, silently thanking Rhys for his brilliant idea. "It's all right. You listen to music? Know which artists are popular with the kids?"

As soon as the words vacated his mouth, Jameson was well aware that he sounded like a man in his dotage versus his actual thirty-two years. But it was too late to call them back and he still needed to know the answer.

Alfie's lips quirked. "Yeah. I like to think so."

Brackets formed around Louisa's mouth. "You can't be serious?"

"Any favorites?"

"I saw Of Men and Guppies in concert a few months ago. They were killer."

"Jameson," Rhys began, "I was kidding ab—"

Jameson dismissed his friend with a flick of his hand and pressed Alfie. "Anyone else?"

Alfie looked between the three adult faces. "Uhh, my mate likes

Rock Apple Brigade but they're a little too shouty and indie for my taste."

Jameson had no idea who any of these artists were. But did it matter? He just needed some names to give to Louisa so she could be on her way.

"My girlfriend has been listening to Duchess. She's cool. And bangin'," Alfie continued, a grin spreading across his face.

Duchess? Jameson straightened in his seat. "Is she a musician?"

Rhys interrupted. "I don't think—"

Alfie's brows shot into his hairline. "Oh yeah. Extremely popular."

His grandmother *would* like that. It would be kind of cheeky. Duchess.

Probably a pop singer. He'd make a note to research it later.

"Thanks, Alfie. See you in class tomorrow." Jameson cocked a brow at Louisa. "So, we're done?"

"We are?"

"Yes. Duchess. That's who I want to perform. If she's unavailable, either of the other two bands will do. You said I only needed to give you the name of one act," he said, certain he wasn't successful at concealing his smugness.

She narrowed her eyes. "Are you sure?"

"Absolutely."

She nodded once, closed her iPad, and stood. "Thank you for your time. I'll get the invitation out to her people right away."

"Great," he said, happy the meeting was finally over. He caught the barkeep's eye. "A round for everyone, on me."

A roar of appreciation rocked the room, sweeping out the royal energy and restoring order. He nodded at the chorus of thanks and pints raised in his direction. Conversations resumed and it was almost as if the last ten minutes had never occurred.

Rhys stared at him, wide-eyed and slack-jawed. "Do you know what you're doing?"

"Of course."

He didn't. But Louisa was an unwelcome reminder of his other life, and the sooner she left, taking the spectre of the queen with her, the sooner he could shift his attention back to his life here at uni.

Far away from the royal cave.

Chapter Five

*"Together united / They want to divide us / Playin' games
with our heads / But we're pushin' full steam ahead . . ."*
—Duchess, "Revolution"

Los Angeles, California

L ook up, mama."

Irritated—an almost constant state of being these days—Dani
tilted her chin and let Rhonda, the makeup artist, apply a coat of
mascara to her false lashes. As soon as the woman was done, Dani
yanked her attention back to the text from Tasha.

This is gaining traction. Remember, stay cool.

Taking a deep breath, Dani clicked on the link—which sent her
to an Instagram post from an account she didn't follow.

Against the backdrop of downtown Los Angeles—she knew this
thanks to the location tag beneath her name—Samantha Banks sat
on a half wall, gazing off into the distance. Her rainbow-colored

hair was vivid against the white sundress she wore, her cleavage taking up most of the shot.

The caption read: "The only thing that overcomes hard luck is hard work. Anger is a weakness in an insecure personality. Don't let anyone steal your light, Sparkle Sammies!"

No this bitch didn't!

The absolute nerve.

I guess it is *hard work balancing on my coattails.*

Also, the woman had one song out with nothing else in sight and she'd given her fans a name?

Miss K moved so that he and Rhonda could both work on Dani without bumping into one another. "I'm loving these long, bouncy, juicy curls. They're going to look great with that strapless Marchesa dress they're putting you in."

"It's beautiful, isn't it?"

When Dani had arrived at the mansion in the Hollywood Hills to shoot the cover for *Vibe* magazine, she'd been delighted by the outfit they'd chosen. The delicate floral creation, in varying shades of her signature red color, was a different look for her, like something you'd see on the cover of *Vogue* or *Harper's Bazaar.* A look that she was eager to embrace.

A rumble disturbed the mood.

"Damn! What was that?" Dani asked, looking around.

Rhonda touched her stomach. "Sorry. I was running late this morning and I didn't eat breakfast."

Dani glanced in the mirror, turning her head from side to side as she studied her reflection. After years in the business, she could apply her own makeup skillfully, and sometimes faster, but she had no problems letting the professionals do it. "This looks good. Go eat."

"Are you sure? I wanted to go back in and add some highlights to the corner of—"

"You can do that later." Dani laughed and pointed to the woman's stomach as it emitted another rumble. "I need you to do something about that. How am I supposed to relax with the sound of New York garbage trucks in my ear?"

Rhonda shook her head with an embarrassed giggle. "Thanks. I hope the chef made some of that bomb jambalaya again."

"You know she did. That's my favorite," Dani said, sitting back in the chair.

Now that her face was free, and Miss K could work on a bobble-head and have their hair looking fierce, Dani returned her attention to her phone.

Banks's post had over seven thousand likes!

Dani bit her lip.

Don't do it. Nothing good will come from it. You know there will be trolls . . .

She clicked on the comments.

There were the usual: "Great picture!"

"I love your hair!"

"You look so cute!"

But they didn't stay mild for long.

"Stay strong, Samantha!"

"Don't worry bout her. You're way more talented. She can't even rap."

"Slay, Samantha, slay!"

"Duchess? You mean the Queen! Bow down!"

"How are all you coming for Duchess? She hasn't done anything. She wasn't even mentioned. GTFOH!"

"Bitch please, you think we don't see what you doing? Duchess's true fans will stan her 4-evah!"

"She's trash. All she does is shake her ass and show her cunt."

Dani raised a hand to cover her mouth, stopping just short of actually touching the liner and gloss Rhonda had applied to her lips.

It had been two months since Banks posted the video, two weeks since her meeting with Genesis. Dani had wanted to believe Henry Owens was wrong and this would all blow over, but from the consistent paparazzi presence to countless Hot Topics segments on *The Wendy Williams Show*, there appeared to be no end in sight. But while the attention meant more downloads and sales, her image was still taking a beating in certain media outlets. Which meant Mela-Skin was still companis non grata. And posts like these continued to stoke the fire.

Heat seared her skin. She could hear Tasha's voice in her ear: *Don't feed the trolls, Dani.*

Fuck that noise.

Pursing her lips, she logged in to her dummy account and pulled up the post.

She typed and mumbled, "Nice mouth! You're worried about her lyrics when y—"

"Oh no you don't!" Nyla Patterson said, snatching Dani's phone and looking at the screen. Her hazel eyes widened. "Wow."

Dani stretched out her arm. "Give me my phone."

Nyla ignored her. "I can't believe you were about to respond . . . wait . . . who is @boycotttheD? You have a fake account?" she asked in the scandalized, overdramatic voice she used every week on the cable drama she starred in.

"Why not? Worked for Kevin Durant."

Nyla scrunched up her beautiful face. "Did it though?"

"Can I have my phone back, please?"

Nyla tapped on the screen several more times before handing it back.

"Did you remove the app from my phone? Have you been talking to Tasha? I can just reinstall it, y'know."

"Sure, but by the time you get to it, the urge to do something you'll definitely regret will have passed."

Dani tossed her phone on the makeup counter and sighed. "What are you doing here? I thought you were in New York for upfronts."

Upfronts were the presentations of the television networks' upcoming fall shows. They were usually attended by executives, stars, major advertisers, and the media, and were so named because they allowed advertisers to purchase commercial airtime on shows "up front," before the season began. Because she was one of the stars of a popular television show, Nyla's presence had been required the past three years.

"Girl, the old showrunner stopped by our suite, still mad that he'd been let go after the sexual harassment investigation. When he started talking about all he'd done for diversity, I knew it was time to go before I said something to get my ass fired. So, I grabbed a late flight home last night. I saw your text about the shoot and thought I'd show up and surprise you. Good thing I did."

"Yeah," Dani said, a tad calmer now. "Thanks."

Nyla was her "Oh honey no" friend, and finding that, especially in the entertainment industry, was rare. They'd met many years ago when they'd both been presenters at the Kids' Choice Awards. Nyla was the one who told Dani the truth even when she didn't want to hear it. Who always had her back, whether it was nixing the outfit she'd wanted to wear to the Soul Train Music Awards because it made her look like a thrift store floral sofa or stopping Dani from PWL, Posting While Livid.

"Anytime. And you know I mean that. How much longer are you gonna be?"

"We're just finishing hair and makeup. I haven't stepped in front of the camera yet."

"I hate photo shoots."

The tall, raven-haired beauty wore a low-necked white blouse with diamond and gold accessories that glowed against her rich pecan-hued skin tone and jeans that elongated her long legs and drew one's eye to the diamond toe ring glittering through the straps of her sexy high heels.

Dani rolled her eyes. "Yeah, you look like someone who doesn't want their picture taken."

Nyla made a face, but she placed her large Chanel flap bag on the neighboring makeup station and sat down in its chair. "How's Liam?"

"Who?"

"Liam Cooper!"

Liam Cooper had been the lead singer of the popular boy band Three Seconds from Running. With his curly blond hair and surprisingly soulful voice, he'd easily made the transition to solo pop star. They'd been introduced several years ago at an event thrown by their record label and had since performed together at a few events.

Dani shrugged. "I don't know."

"You planning to see him soon?"

Dani frowned at Nyla's too-innocent tone. "Why would I?"

"Because he's your boyfriend?"

"No he's not!"

Nyla tapped the screen of her phone and held it out to Dani. "According to *In Touch* magazine you've been dating for the past month."

Dani stared at a picture of her and Liam hugging outside of the Crypto.com Arena.

What the hell?

Then she remembered. Grammy producers had teamed them up to perform a medley of old-school hip-hop songs for the telecast. They'd been doing a sound check several days before the ceremony. She'd gone out to take a call, he'd followed to get some fresh air, and they'd entered into a discussion about their musical influences. Before they headed in, they'd hugged, not romantically, but as friends.

But a picture could say a thousand words . . . any thousand words depending on which frame was used. In this one, an amicable embrace was portrayed as an intimate clinch between lovers. The text captioning the photo, "Jay & Bey who? Are Duchess and the Prince of Blue-Eyed Soul forming a new music royalty dynasty?" only worked to sell the idea.

"Oh, for fuck's sake! Liam and I are not dating. I haven't seen nor talked to him since Clive Davis's party after the Grammys."

How had she ever believed being famous would solve her problems? This was the flip side of the Samantha Banks situation. Millions of people would see this photo, even fewer would read the story, and it would become their truth. Never mind that it was lie. And no matter how many times she denied it, they'd never believe her.

It was fucking irritating.

Though she'd attained a level of success, there were aspects of living in the public eye that could erode your soul. It took a strong person to remain true to themselves in the face of stardom's gravitational pull. To not define their worth by what others said about them.

Dani was trying, but she was still a work in progress. Exhibit A: the half-drafted comment from earlier.

As if reading her mind Nyla asked, "What are you going to do?"

She didn't need to ask what Nyla was referring to. They'd texted and talked of little else since Dani's meeting in New York.

Dani's sigh felt dragged from the depths of her soul. "I don't know."

"Are you going to apologize?"

"Hell no."

"Are you going to address it online?"

If she acknowledged the situation in any way, she'd play into Banks's hand and essentially give the singer what she wanted.

"That's the same as apologizing, and it's not going to happen."

"But if you don't, you'll lose the opportunity to work with Genesis."

Or any of the other top companies. She'd recently received a call from Andrea to say that a small venture capital firm had expressed interest in a meeting, but Dani wasn't excited by the prospect. She didn't need more investors, she needed help to level up.

"Maybe I should go away for a while. I could take a few months, jet off to a private island. Work on some new material, brainstorm new product ideas . . ."

She just had to deny Banks any more ammunition. If she wasn't around, Banks couldn't stalk her, the press couldn't get any pictures, and this situation would have to fade away.

"That could work. But it could also backfire. Banks isn't above bringing up old stuff to keep herself relevant. Or doing more of those," Nyla said, pointing to Dani's phone and referencing the IG post.

"Why doesn't she fucking get a life?"

Nyla laughed. "That's what she's doing. She's trying to get *yours*. You need some good press. The studio is always having us do charity work. You can come along to a few with me."

Dani wasn't opposed to volunteering, but she said, "That feels so forced."

"It is. But it might help."

It was time for Dani to get real. She didn't have a lot of choices. She couldn't lose this opportunity. Either she figured out a way to neutralize Banks's story, or, despite what she'd said, she'd have to apologize.

"I have a really good publicist," Nyla offered. "She works for me, not the studio, and she's cool people. Even if you don't hire her, she'll give you some good advice."

Dani pursed her lips but nodded. "That sounds great, Nyla. Thanks."

"I'll shoot her a text."

And if that didn't work out, Dani would seriously need to look into that island thing.

"Why are you figuring this out on your own anyway?" Nyla asked, her fingers flying over her phone's screen. "Shouldn't Cash be taking care of this?"

Dani rolled her eyes. "He doesn't see anything wrong with it. Jay and Nas, Lil' Kim and Foxy Brown, Biggie and Tupac . . . Beefs are big in hip-hop. And they sell records."

Dani had signed with her manager, Cash Hamad, after he'd discovered her on SoundCloud. He'd praised her potential and vowed that if she worked hard and heeded his guidance, he'd make her a star. She'd been uploading her music for several years by then, so getting the attention of someone like Cash had been gratifying. He was well known in the business and highly respected by insiders she followed. Signing with him meant taking her career to the next level.

And she had, if "the next level" meant appearances on a bunch of tracks by Cash's clients (read: men), who weren't half as good as she was. And, if said appearances were tied to a video where she put on a G-string and made her ass clap while the artist, in thick gold chains and smoking a cigar, pointed his fingers at it. Because it was *so* original the previous fifteen hundred times. As the unknown featured female rapper, she wasn't treated any differently from the video vixens who were there to be eye candy, except she had to spit her verse, too.

When one of her freestyles went viral on YouTube, Cash "promoted" her, making her the First Lady of Dirty Junky, his multiplatinum rap group. She contributed to more songs, where her verses got major attention. Next came her solo record deal with Sick Flow Records, and now her second album was rocketing up the charts. Cash, true to his name, was looking to profit from her accomplishments with a tour in the winter before getting back in the studio next year.

She should've been thrilled. She was famous, popular, and financially successful. Everything young Dani had wanted. But she wasn't making her own decisions; her career wasn't her own. It was Cash's, and he intended to ride it until the wheels fell off.

"But it's screwing with Mela-Skin," Nyla said.

"He doesn't care."

Cash wasn't a fan of her "side hustle," especially since he had no skin in that game. Instead he constantly bitched that it drew her attention away from making music.

"Alright, Duchess, we're ready for you," one of the on-set PAs called out.

Dani pushed off the makeup chair and checked her image in the mirror. "Duty calls."

Nyla stood, too. "While you handle that, I'm going to help myself to some of that jambalaya I've been smelling."

Dani laughed and headed over to the changing area, where the gorgeous Marchesa gown . . . *had* awaited her. It was gone; a red leather bikini top and matching miniskirt hung on the rolling rack in its place.

"Yo, Shaunie? What happened to the gown?"

The stylist pursed her lips. "Your manager called. He changed it."

Her hands tightened into fists. Goddammit!

She'd already had to alter her schedule because the original arrangement to shoot in Franklin Canyon Park had been nixed due to the paparazzi that hovered around her like L.A.'s infamous layer of smog. Unfortunately, the only date this house had been available was the day Dani had planned to be in New York for meetings on the rollout of Mela-Skin's newest revitalizing face mist. She'd been nurturing her annoyance since she awakened, but walking in and seeing the beautiful dress had lightened her mood.

And now this!

Nyla appeared next to her with a bowl of the steaming hot rice dish. "You need to leave Cash and get a proper agent. Someone who's going to work in *your* best interest and not their own."

"Oh, go sit down," she snapped, stepping behind the long white curtain.

"He doesn't want you to strike a deal with Genesis," Nyla called out. "He only makes money on your music."

Dani blew out a breath. Nyla wasn't saying anything Dani didn't tell herself.

Daily.

But where would she go?

Cash had great contacts in the business. He'd introduced her to everyone. And there was a long and storied history littered with the carcasses of failing musicians who'd left their first managers for greener pastures. She was grateful for Cash's initial stewardship, but it was becoming clear to her that they wanted different things for her career. And in the end, her vision should be the one that mattered.

"I know an agent that would be perfect for you," Nyla continued. "She's from my agency."

"No thanks. I actually listen when you vent. You hate your agency."

"Not that one. I left them last year for MBP. They're the top entertainment agency in the world. They represent everybody: actors, musicians, authors, athletes. The best of the best."

"I don't know."

"She's been wanting to meet you."

"I'm not ready."

"Then this is going to be awkward: I invited her to join us and she's here."

What the fuck? "Nyla!"

Standing in her underwear, Dani gripped the hanging drapery, about to tell her good friend all about herself, when she heard a new voice enter the space.

"Greetings, all!"

"Bennie! Thanks for coming."

"Nyla, you're looking lovely. I'm hearing great things about that romantic comedy you filmed last year. The soundtrack is going to smash."

"You're too kind."

Dani peeked around the flowing fabric and spied a tall leggy woman with long strawberry blond hair who looked more like a model out of central casting than an executive.

"I was excited to get your call," Bennie said. She glanced around. "Is she here?"

"She is," Dani said. Both women turned to face her. "Let me throw on a robe and I'll be right out."

"Take your time," Bennie said. "It's a madhouse out there. I'm in no hurry to experience it again."

Someone had tipped off the photographers to Dani's presence and a dozen of them had swarmed an hour after she arrived.

"I can't believe they're still here," Nyla said.

A sudden thought skidded along Dani's nerves. "Did they see you?"

"Of course not!" Bennie's voice was heavy with offense. "I took a car to get here, and I made sure the windows were tinted."

"Thank God." The last thing Dani needed was to add fuel to the fire with rumors about a split between her and her management.

At least, not until she was ready to announce it.

Dani quickly thrust her arms into the silk garment and went to meet her "guest."

"This is Duchess," Nyla said.

"I know who she is." Bennie slid her Prada sunglasses off her perfectly beat face and smiled at Dani. "You're smart, sexy, and you've rapped everyone else into irrelevancy. Why aren't you taking over the world?"

Dani tilted her head to the side. "I'm not looking to take over the entire world, just my own small part of it."

"And I'm ready and prepared to help you with that." Bennie held out her hand. "Jane Benedict, but everyone calls me Bennie."

Dani eyed Nyla before saying, "I'm not sure how much Nyla told you—"

"I didn't need her to tell me much. Everyone's buzzing about you and this Samantha Banks situation."

"Fucking kill me now!" Dani exhaled, and gestured to a nearby couch. "Let's sit down. Seriously, though, I'm about ready to go into exile somewhere until this all blows over."

"No, no, no! The idea is to counteract the negative fallout."

"I still can't get over how people are taking sides in a dispute I've never acknowledged! You can't make this shit up!" Dani snapped her fingers. "Oh, wait, that's exactly what they've done!"

"The moment you put something out into the public and ask for money, you open yourself up to their scrutiny. Sure, you could try to be 'my private life is private,' but in this day of video cameras on our phones and social media, no one's life is private. Especially not a person whose last album moved one hundred and ninety-five thousand units in its first week and debuted atop the U.S. Billboard 200."

Dani didn't disclose how impressed she was at the ease with which Bennie spouted off her numbers.

She tightened the sash on her robe and crossed her arms. "So, what do I do?"

"In the interest of showing you what I could bring to the table, I made some inquiries on the DL and there's a couple of options floating around."

"Like what?"

Bennie checked her phone. "Hosting a new reality show."

Dani arched a brow. "Excuse me?"

"Nicki did *Idol* a few years ago and Cardi judged that rap competition for Netflix," Nyla offered.

"What kind of show is it?"

"One of the major cable networks is looking to create its own dating show. They want to do it, uh"—a slight flush tinged Bennie's cheeks and she cleared her throat—"in an urban setting. They're tentatively calling it *Love in da Ho*—"

"No!" Dani said immediately.

"Oh, come on," Nyla said, her words barely audible through her laughter. "Gangstas and hood rats need love, too."

"Stop it," Dani said, pointing a finger at her friend. "Even joking, you're putting that energy out into the world."

"I figured that would be a no," Bennie said, "but I believe in bringing my clients all offers, unless they specify otherwise."

"I'm not your client."

"Not yet."

She was feeling the other woman's confidence. "Next?"

"Harper Bissette wants you to be the face of their new ad campaign."

Dani winced. She'd always considered Bissette the epitome of luxury and their signature logo handbag had been her first major purchase. The year her debut EP had dropped, she'd asked her stylist to approach them about borrowing clothes for an awards show, but word had gotten back to her they'd complained they didn't know how to dress someone so "curvy and ethnic." She'd sold the bag and never looked back, but now they wanted her curvy, ethnic ass to help sell their shit?

Pass.

"Is that it?"

"For now. I was working on short notice. I have some other calls pending."

"I'm not ready to sign anything," Dani warned.

"I understand. Give me a chance to show you what I can do."

"Nyla can give you my information. I have some time early next week."

"Perfect." Bennie opened her mouth to say something else but bit her lip instead.

Dani stared at her warily. "What?"

"I have to ask . . . You were offered the perfect opportunity to help your cause, but you turned them down. What were you thinking?"

Dani frowned. "Excuse me? If someone had come to me with what I needed to end this situation with Banks, trust and believe it would've been handled."

"The Royal Concert honoring Prince John. I know several acts that would give their right ass cheek for an invite."

"I have absolutely no idea what you're talking about."

"You were invited to perform at the Royal Concert honoring Prince John," Bennie said, enunciating every word as if Dani didn't understand English.

"Say what now?" Dani asked, her eyes wide.

Even Nyla straightened. "Prince John as in the British royal family?"

Dani was shook. She would've remembered being contacted by the royal family. Her grandmother had been a major fan, especially of Prince John. She used to say he had a kind face and she would buy every supermarket tabloid that featured the royal family. Just thinking about her grandmother's devotion caused an ache in Dani's heart.

"The queen is throwing a massive concert to honor Prince John and his work on environmental causes. She's inviting a number of the prince's favorite artists."

A royal concert? Holy shit.

"I haven't heard anything about a royal concert. No one's reached out to me."

"This one is still on the QT. They've asked us to keep it in the strictest of confidence until they announce the final list. I only know about it because our agency represents Rock Apple Brigade, and they were approached after you turned them down."

"I didn't turn them down! I didn't know about it!"

"Who would've responded on your behalf?"

She knew before Bennie finished the question.

Fucking Cash.

He hadn't even asked her. Had he been doing this all along? If Bennie hadn't mentioned it, she never would've known. How many other events had she been invited to, how many opportunities had she been offered, only to have Cash dismiss them and not inform her?

"That would've been perfect," Nyla said. "It's going to get a ton of coverage. But didn't Prince John die a long time ago? How was he a fan of Duchess's work?"

That was unacceptable. Cash had taken a chance on her and she was thankful for everything he'd done, but to confront the control he'd seized over her and her career was a lightbulb moment.

"My understanding is that she was requested by one of the younger royals."

"I see," Dani said.

Though she didn't. She couldn't imagine performing for the royal family. Which of her hits should she choose? "Profilin'"? "Holla Atcha Girl"? "Azz for Days"?

Hosting that reality show was a nonstarter, but the royal concert? That sounded . . . intriguing. The prospect of getting away for a bit, doing something no one expected? A once-in-a-lifetime opportunity with the potential to knock the Samantha Banks story out of their collective conscious?

Had she lost her shot?

"Do you think I could still get in?"

"As of this morning, Rock Apple Brigade hadn't accepted. Negotiations stalled because they asked for an honorarium. Why?" A small smile curved Bennie's lips. "Have you changed your mind?"

Dani hadn't changed her mind because she hadn't known about it in the first place. But now that she did—

"You get me back in and I'll give you a shot as my agent." Dani stood and affected a British accent. "So, guv'na, do we have a deal?"

Chapter Six

"*You are a member of the British Royal Family. We are never tired, and we all love hospitals.*"

—Mary of Teck

Two visits in two months.

Before this new reality, he hadn't been to Buckingham Palace twice in two *years*!

He'd been shown to a different room this time and recognized the blue-and-gold-silk-upholstered furniture and cream-colored wallpaper as the decor of a private family room. Releasing the buttons on the suit jacket he wished he wasn't required to wear each time he visited, he settled on the edge of a silk-damask settee and pulled out his phone to quickly check his work emails.

Twenty minutes later, the door opened, and Louisa entered, carrying her ever-present tablet and a leather folio embossed with the Palace's logo. She was dressed as impeccably as ever, although her pinched lips and furrowed brow telegraphed her pique.

"I apologize for not being here to greet you, Your Royal Highness. They just informed me of your arrival."

Irritation had long since tightened his chest and heated his skin.

He stood, rebuttoning his jacket. "The meeting was scheduled for ten A.M."

"Right. The punctuality took me by surprise."

From your family.

The words were unsaid, but her meaning was clear.

"*I,*" he said, being clear with his emphasis, "don't believe in wasting people's time."

"You'd be the first royal to believe that," she muttered, placing her items on the round marble-topped table in the center of the room. Then, as if she were remembering to whom she was speaking, her face flushed a deep red, clashing with her hair. She dropped her head. "Please forgive my impertinence, sir."

He waved away her apology. She was right. His family thought very little about how they inconvenienced others. For most, it wasn't malicious, just the natural result of growing up with your needs always met and cared for by others.

And she did have to track you down a couple of weeks ago.

"Can we get started or are we waiting for the queen? I need to get back to campus. Driving back and forth from Birmingham is playing havoc with my schedule."

She stared at him. "There must've been a misunderstanding. Your meeting isn't with the queen."

He froze. "Then why am I here?"

"I thought your being here was your decision. I needed to talk to you, but it could've been handled by phone."

He didn't know how he managed to resist throwing his head back and screaming to the impressively high ceiling in frustration. He'd had to find another professor to take over his lecture and reschedule several office-hour appointments. Adjustments he was loath to make.

"I've had the privilege of being added to the queen's schedule at ten-thirty A.M. for daily briefings," she said in a tone that expressed she considered the inclusion anything but. "That gives me twenty minutes. In the interest of brevity, I'll get right to it. The queen doesn't think a concert will be enough. She has decided to extend the celebration to a week."

"A week?" Shock seized Jameson's throat. "How many events is she planning?"

"Five, including the concert."

"The concert is in three months! How do you plan to pull that off?"

"It's the royal family," Louisa said, astonished, as if that answered the question.

And he supposed it did. Venue owners and vendors would move anything to do business with the Crown. Especially for an event of this magnitude with a worldwide audience.

"It's why I've been so busy," Louisa continued. "I need to finalize a few last-minute details. I've been granted permission to inform you that everyone we've invited has accepted. We'll unveil the event next week and announce the performers. To ensure everyone's secrecy, we've had all parties sign NDAs as part of their contracts. That way, we can control the release of the story."

"You're announcing everything?"

"Yes, and the queen wants you there."

Jameson ran a hand down his face. He'd gone from having to speak about and participate in one event to being involved in a weeklong celebration! His responsibilities—and stress!—had increased exponentially in the past few minutes.

Suck it up. You don't have a choice.

"Tickets go on sale two weeks later. We've scheduled interviews and you're going to be front and center for most of them. You won't have to do the smaller outlets, but the major ones, the international ones, are mandatory."

Jameson shoved a hand through his hair. "I do still have a job."

"By the time we're in the thick of this, your term should be over, but I'll do my best to work around it. For now. The queen wanted me to remind you that outside of your lecture schedule, this should be your main priority."

The door opened, surprising them both. His Royal Highness Julian, the Prince of Wales, the oldest of the queen's children and the next in line for the throne, strode into the room as if to his coronation.

Jameson had often thought it must be difficult to grow up appreciating the awesome responsibility that lay ahead of him. Julian's life had never been his own. From day one, he'd known that someday he would be king, and the expectations had to have been overwhelming. Julian had responded by making everyone around him suffer as much as he had.

"I heard my nephew the scholar was here for a meeting about the upcoming tribute," Julian said, his pompous attitude grating. "How's that global warming coming along? Solved it yet?"

He slapped Jameson's shoulder and made a beeline for the tea service set up on a cart. It was still morning, but Julian's flushed face and bloodshot eyes confirmed the dress shirt and slacks he was wearing were remnants from his night out, rather than his attire for the new day.

Jameson refused to rise to the bait. His uncle had always acted like that bully relative you'd rather hide away from than have to deal with at family gatherings. Except many of their gatherings took place in front of the press, so avoiding him hadn't been an option.

Considering Julian would one day be king, maybe breaking up the monarchy was the proper call. Institutions held because the people in charge respected them. Julian hadn't shown anyone that he gave a flying toss about his country's customs.

"Don't be such a wanker," Princess Catherine said, entering behind her brother and sinking onto a chair. Unlike Julian's attire, Catherine's gray slacks and pink blouse were immaculate. Too bad she hadn't been born first. She was the perfect mixture of her mother's steeliness and her father's intelligence and compassion. She would've made a stellar monarch.

"And don't you be such a kiss up, Cat," Bettina, the youngest of the siblings, said, as she entered wearing a prim yellow dress and pearls, an outfit that was modeled after Queen Marina herself. Though similar to Catherine in presentation, Bettina was closer to Julian in attitude. "We're in our fifties. Aren't you tired of being perfect?"

Brackets appearing around Catherine's mouth were the only outward sign that Bettina's attack had struck its target.

"If perfect means not making a public spectacle of myself, then no," Catherine said, referring to the recent pictures of Bettina sunbathing topless in the South of France, licking whipped cream off the fingers of her former bodyguard.

"Although"—Julian eyed Louisa—"I do enjoy having the lovely Louisa to gaze upon. You look absolutely wonderful today. Doesn't she?"

"Ravishing," Bettina said. "I'm sure Fiona would agree. Should we call your wife in and ask her?"

Louisa cleared her throat. "The queen has informed all of you that she didn't need or want you to be involved in the tribute, outside of a few public appearances."

"He was our father!" Julian said.

"You just can't stand the idea of a celebration going on without your arse being kissed," Catherine said.

"It should be kissed. Well and often. I'm the next in line. I should be the face of this. Not him!" Julian turned bleary eyes on Jameson. "What's in this for you?"

"That's not your concern," Louisa said. "The queen wants it and that's all that matters."

Julian's eyes narrowed. "You've spent a lot of time and energy pretending you were different from your father. But look who's seeking the limelight now. Maybe the apple doesn't fall far from the tree."

Jameson's blood roared in his ears and anger clouded his vision at the mention of his father. The gall. Julian was proof the apple could fall in another fucking orchard. In that moment, Jameson regretted any connection to the other man, including the paternal family tradition requiring the oldest sons share the first initial J. He didn't know how a man as good and decent as John could have sired Julian.

Julian pouted. "Maybe the people deserve to know their future king is being treated this way."

"Heavy is the head," Catherine said, pouring herself a cup of tea.

"I'm serious. This is the type of story the press would run with."

Although the tabloids were a major problem for his family, that didn't stop certain members from using them to their advantage. Some had a favorite rag they'd inform when they needed to shore up their own image or sabotage one of the others. Jameson hadn't actually believed crack investigative reporting had led to the story on Julian hunting big game in South Africa, especially since the bombshell knocked from the front pages the months-long almost daily coverage of Bettina's French escapade.

Dealing with the queen must've given Louisa some starch, because she looked at the future king and said, "I wouldn't recommend it."

Julian's blue eyes hardened. "Excuse me?"

Undaunted, Louisa continued. "This celebration is extremely important to the queen. In fact, she told me that it going off without a hitch is her top priority for the next few months. If anyone is thinking of undermining this, they should reconsider. I heard her mention stripping members of their royal duties should they choose not to act accordingly."

Jameson shared an astonished look with Catherine. He'd known this was important to his grandmother. Now he knew how important.

From the slack jaws and raised brows of Julian and Bettina, it was clear they understood, too. They recognized the import of having their duties. And what it would say to them, and the public, if the queen publicly stripped them of their responsibilities.

"Well, I should at least see who's performing at the concert," Julian said, putting his cup down and strolling over to where Louisa stood. He repositioned her iPad so he could see it. "Lester Stone, Trebles of Sheltered, Kay Morgan, Carl Page. This is going to be the most boring concert ever. Most of these people are ancient."

"They were Father's favorites," Catherine said. "What did you expect, the Pussycat Dolls?"

"You're aging yourself," Bettina slyly inserted.

"Where are the acts we suggested? I thought Mummy wanted some younger ones. Oh, wait . . . Zoey Tanner, Liam Cooper—"

"He's mine," Bettina gushed. "I can't believe he accepted."

"You mean because you've been trying to seduce him for the past few years?" Catherine asked.

"Fuck you, Cat."

Catherine arched a brow. "Don't you mean Liam?"

"Who is Duchess?" Julian asked.

Bettina's brown eyes, so like Prince John's, widened. "The rapper?"

That got Catherine's attention. "A rapper? Who chose her?"

"Prince Jameson," Louisa responded.

Julian's head whipped around to face Jameson. "*You* picked her? A rapper? For a concert to honor our father? Your *mentor*?"

He practically spat the word.

"And she's not just any rapper," Catherine said, horrified, tapping the screen of her phone. A thumping bass blared from the device and she handed it to Julian. "This is her."

"Speaking of Pussy . . . cat Dolls." Julian's prudish outrage morphed into something resembling intrigue and lust. "I definitely volunteer to be on her welcoming committee."

Jameson blinked. He'd meant to google his pick the day after Louisa had shown up at the pub. But several more drinks with Rhys and that intention had been lost. He hadn't given his pick or the concert a second thought.

Judging from Julian's expression, he liked what he was seeing.

Very much so.

And he wouldn't hesitate to act on his sudden desire. Whispers had surrounded Julian's marriage from the beginning. Apparently, the fairy tale had extended only to the wedding, not to the life after it. Post-matrimony, Julian's taste appeared to run to women who were the complete opposite of his wife. Somehow, a rapper named Duchess seemed to fit into that category.

Which meant Jameson had made a mistake.

"Don't be vulgar," Bettina said with disgust.

"Don't be jealous," Julian retorted, his eyes still glued to the screen.

"Jealous? Of an American? A rapper?" Her face contorted grotesquely with each descriptor. "You must be joking?"

Julian clapped his hands together, all signs of his previous petulance having miraculously vanished. "I'm now looking forward to this concert very much. Good luck, Jameson. You're going to need it. I'll keep my schedule clear in case I'm needed to step in."

He left with a jollier step than he'd had coming in.

Catherine and Bettina uttered sentiments suggesting their interest in the meeting had waned, and several minutes later, Jameson and Louisa were once again the sole occupants of the room.

Louisa tapped on her iPad screen. "That can't happen."

"What?"

"Prince Julian and the rapper. You can't allow that to happen," she said emphatically.

Jameson bristled. He had to add "Royal Cock Blocker" to his list of duties? "I'm not his keeper."

"She'll be here to perform. If she were to become involved with the prince and the press got wind of it, it would divert all attention from the queen's intended cause. It would be a disaster!"

Jameson exhaled audibly. "I'm not a babysitter. Besides, she'll be too busy to get into any kind of trouble with Julian."

"You'd be surprised at the trouble the prince could get into."

Heat pricked the back of his neck and he massaged the aggrieved patch of skin, thoughts of his father's liaisons flashing through his mind like unwelcome ads.

"Actually, I wouldn't," he muttered.

Louisa checked her watch. "I really must go. I need to stop by my office before my meeting with the queen. Do you have any other questions for me?"

Why am I doing this?

Why can't the queen use her own children?

Do I really have a choice?

"No."

"Splendid. We'll talk soon," she said, leaving the room.

All alone, Jameson exhaled as some of the tension of being on display left his body. This celebration, and his involvement in it, was turning into an entire production. And on top of that, he was now required to make sure his uncle and his invited musical guest stayed away from one another.

Which reminds me . . .

He pulled out his phone and searched for "Duchess." A video for a song named "Fever" was the first result that popped up.

He clicked on the link.

The same beat from earlier emanated from the device, this time accompanied by heart-stopping, eye-popping visuals. No wonder Julian couldn't take his eyes off the screen.

She was mesmerizing.

A languid heat invaded his body and settled thick between his thighs. Moisture flooded his mouth even as his heart pounded in his chest.

She wore two scraps of white material, masquerading as a nurse's uniform, which showed off an abundance of rich dark brown skin. Bending forward, while simultaneously arching her back, she slid gold-tipped fingers down slim legs encased in thigh-high white stockings, the movement giving him a perfect peek at the rounded tops of her breasts.

You look at me & I'm all you want to be
Snatched waist
Fat/thin
Face full of melanin

She flipped her long black hair back and thick lashes swept up to reveal large, brown eyes, heavily lined in black, that beckoned to him, seduced him, refused to let him go, even as she drew her thumb across her glossy bottom lip and began gyrating her body to the music.

Yo! I'm burning hot, you want what I got
bounce bounce
You see her?
My ass gives him Fever

"Fuck me."

His own voice pulled him from the trance he'd fallen into.

Good God!

This was who he'd chosen to perform for the charity concert in honor of his grandfather?

He clicked off the video and set his phone facedown next to him, as if even the empty screen would tempt him to go back and watch more.

What had he done?

Pleasure filtered from his desire, leaving anger in its wake.

It hadn't been his idea to participate in the goddamned event. His agitation, born from Marina's blindsiding, and his reluctance to submit to her emotional blackmail were the only reasons he found himself in this situation, selecting someone he hadn't thoroughly vetted first. He always did his research. Always. It was something he prided himself on. He never made a move without considering every possible consequence.

And the one time he did, it wasn't a minor blunder, like purchasing a car without the proper safety features or accepting an invitation to a party only to learn it was a setup with a daughter of one of the Tea Trust members. No, he went major, essentially inviting a stripper to perform at an official royal concert!

He'd have to keep Julian away from her while she was here.

The prospect scrambled his insides, leaving his thoughts muddy. Save one sparkling clean, pristine concern.

Forget Julian. After what you just saw, who's going to keep you *away from her?*

Chapter Seven

"Big hands, big feet / Deep pockets / On fleek / Six feet /
Plus / Coco, chiseled / A must . . ."

—Duchess, "Profilin'"

The forty-five-minute drive from London was a study in change as the sun began its descent and the landscape transformed from the urban to a more pastoral setting. Though most of Dani's previous trips here had been relegated to the city center, the scenery wasn't too different from when she'd travel from DC to Virginia.

The countryside looked peaceful, exactly what she needed. In the months since she'd accepted the invitation to perform at the Royal Tribute in Honor of Prince John, her life had gone bananas. She'd been excited when the Palace had informed her that the concert was being extended to a weeklong celebration with a series of events, including a royal ball.

Nyla hadn't gotten over that one. "Duchess is going to a real royal ball!"

But if the spotlight and scrutiny had been at a level eight before with the Banks situation, the announcement of the celebration and her participation in it had ramped the madness up to twenty.

The reveal had garnered worldwide media coverage, as did the surprise that Duchess would perform. There were the obvious headlines tying her name to royalty, but *Bossip* had come through with her favorite: "All Hail the People's Duchess Even as Clotted Cream Critics Revolt!" Late-night hosts couldn't joke enough about being surprised that she was Prince John's favorite performer.

"If video emerges of Prince John doing the 'nae nae,' I'm moving to London," one had proclaimed.

Her team had been contacted by everyone, from designers who wanted to dress her for the events to accessories brands who wanted her to carry or mention their products. Cash had been furious she'd accepted the offer.

"You went behind my back? What the fuck, Dani?"

She'd stared across the desk at the large black man, a New York Yankees cap covering his bald head, an iced-out dollar sign blinging around his neck, her own rage flaring. "I wouldn't have had to go behind your back if you'd brought the original offer to me in the first place!"

"Because you don't have time for this shit! You need to get back in the studio, work on that third album. We got to strike while the iron is hot, baby."

This was how it always was. Cash cared only about her contribution to his bottom line.

"Don't you trust me? Haven't I always made the best decisions for you?"

That was part of the problem. Dani didn't want him to make decisions *for* her anymore. She could make own decisions.

Cash pointed a finger at her. "And after everything I've done for you, you go and bring that bitch agent in on this?"

Everything *he'd* done—

It had been the final straw. She'd grabbed her Gucci backpack and stood.

His nostrils flared. "Where are you going?"

"I'm out."

"We're not done here!"

"Yeah, Cash, we are."

Something in her tone must've alerted him to the fact that she was referring to more than just their conversation.

"We have a contract!"

"And that's why I pay my lawyers," she said, throwing up the deuces on her way out the door.

She wasn't stupid enough to believe it'd be that easy. He was right about the contract, and she could face serious backlash if he decided to bad-mouth her around the industry. When this was all over, she'd set up a meeting with her attorneys and Bennie and weigh her options. But she didn't regret her decision. She was done being his finger puppet. It had been time for her and Cash to part ways.

She wished she could say the same about the press.

The paparazzi's intrusiveness had grown to epic levels. Instead of just trailing her like irritating shadows, they'd set up camp outside her houses in L.A. and Virginia.

"Are you practicing your curtsy for the queen?"

"Will you be staying at Buckingham Palace?"

"Are you going to ask the queen to make you a real duchess?"

With Dani the center of so much attention, the initial scandal hadn't receded to the background; instead, it had gotten bigger, as fans continued to take sides. But as in a game of telephone, the message had gotten twisted somewhere along the line. People were debating and supporting statements she'd never made!

Samantha Banks wasn't far behind, tweeting: "Bullying isn't just an American problem. It's a whole-world problem. We shouldn't reward bad behavior. People shouldn't be taken in by fancy titles. Love you #SparkleSammies!"

Now it was a *hashtag*?!

The press had salivated over this "new" angle to spice up their almost daily coverage of the celebration. Once again, Banks had managed to insert herself into Dani's life, and the event she'd once thought might save her with Genesis suddenly seemed like the thing to tank it by taking a small dispute and displaying it on an international stage.

Dani's nerves had been at the breaking point. When she'd begun losing her cool too often with the paps and posting from her fake IG account, Tasha had deleted the app from her phone—again— and suggested she get away.

"I will. If I can hold on for three more weeks until I leave—"

"Not three weeks. Now."

"Are you crazy?" Dani said, though she really should've been asking herself that question. "I can't leave now. I have too much to do. We have to work on the performance—"

"You can put on a great performance in your sleep."

"But this concert—"

"Forget the concert! You've got other events to worry about: a formal dinner, several social engagements, the ball." Tasha ticked them off on her fingers. "Everything you've worked for, everything you want, is riding on how you present yourself, and you're spending time debating with trolls. You've got to get with it!"

Thank God what Dani valued most in the people on her team was their competence at their jobs and not their ability to suck up to her and tell her only what she wanted to hear. But knowing Tasha was right didn't erase her problem.

"Where am I supposed to go? The moon?" Dani threw her arms up. "Social media is everywhere, the press coverage is global . . ."

"I don't know. Someplace off the grid. We'll figure it out. But you can't stay here in this environment. Blowing up on Twitter or yelling at photographers isn't a good look."

A week later, Dani was in London. It wasn't the moon, and it definitely wasn't off the grid, but it would still serve her purposes. Everything had been feeling larger than life and out of her control. She needed some time and space to get perspective.

She always stayed at her favorite hotel when she traveled to London and her team had already reserved her suite there for a block of time around the festivities, but she didn't need the British version of what she'd been dealing with back in the States. She'd secretly planned to lease a house somewhere outside of the city. When Tasha had emailed Louisa Collins, her contact at the palace and the point person for the event, to give her a heads-up that Dani would be in the country early and available if they wanted her to do any promotional pictures or advance press, Louisa had informed them she knew of the perfect accommodations and promised to take care of everything.

"My husband is the stable manager at Primrose Park, one of the royal residences, located in a village outside of London. I checked with him and a cottage on the estate will be available during that time. You can stay there."

Dani immediately pictured a small, charming bungalow like the one in the Kate Winslet movie *The Holiday*. Something cozy and full of character with exposed beams and a fireplace. She'd have time to catch up on the latest season of Nyla's show and she could finally get her bake on. She might even throw on a disguise and bike out to the village market.

Although . . . when was the last time she'd ridden a bike?

Probably when she was a kid. But how hard could it be? Wasn't that the whole point of the saying "as easy as riding a bike"?

Or was it a horse?

Either way, if she happened to lose her balance and fall, she could be caught by a tall, dark, sexy villager who came to her aid . . . and helped her achieve some toe-curling orgasms.

You're having yourself a How Stella Got Her Back Broke moment, aren't you?

Why not? If she had to lie low before the festivities, she was determined to put a positive spin on it.

"We're here, ma'am."

The driver's words pulled her from her memories of Cash, Banks, and Tasha, and back to her surroundings. They passed through a guarded, gated entrance and started down a long private road. Several moments later she couldn't contain the gasp at the sight before her.

Bordered by a lake on one side and tall trees on the other, the "house" consisted of three structures: a large three-story gray stone building flanked by two round single-story wings. Steps led up to a stately double-door entrance that appeared to be guarded by four pillars.

The driver stopped the car next to an ornate fountain in the center of the driveway, where an attractive woman with red hair stood waiting for them.

"Duchess, hello. I'm Louisa Collins, the Royal Household's senior events coordinator. Welcome to Primrose Park."

Louisa was part of the royal family's staff, but she looked like she could've been a member of the royal family. Her voice and demeanor screamed class, but she projected capability and approachability without familiarity, something Dani immediately appreciated.

"It's good to put a face to a name. And please, call me Dani."

Louisa smiled. "Dani it is."

Dani shaded her eyes from the sun glinting off the water and took in the setting. "This is beautiful."

"It's one of my favorites. In addition to the main house on the estate, there are several cottages, stables, a barn, and even a small airstrip, although it's seldom used these days. You requested privacy"—she pronounced it pre-vuh-see—"and this has it in spades."

Dani was astonished. "How large is the property?"

"The main house is eleven thousand square feet, the cottages are around three thousand, give or take. And it all sits on just over seven hundred acres."

The cottages were three thousand square feet? Including the one she'd be staying in? She had family who lived in homes about a third of that size.

"I'm looking forward to my stay."

"I'm glad. Although"—Louisa clasped her hands in front of her—"there've been some changes."

A sense of foreboding stirred the tiny hairs on the back of Dani's neck. She narrowed her eyes. "What kind of changes?"

"When the staff went to prepare the cottage for your visit, they discovered a massive leak. Unfortunately, it left the dwelling uninhabitable."

No! Dani smoothed her hands over her hair. "What about the other cottages?"

"They're already occupied."

So much for her rustic vacation fantasy. She only wished Louisa had told her *before* the long drive.

Stifling a sigh that would convey every bit of her exhaustion and irritation, Dani pulled her phone from her Dior Book Tote. "Don't worry about it. I'll have my assistant book me a suite."

A crack emerged in Louisa's composure. "No! You can't!"

Another person trying to tell her what to do? After that long-ass flight and needless drive?

"Excuse me?"

"Sorry." Louisa briefly squeezed her eyes shut. "It's important to the queen that nothing detracts from this celebration and if the tabloid press discovers you're here, we'll lose control of a carefully orchestrated narrative. We need you to keep a low profile."

"That was my plan," Dani said. What did they think she would do? Parade buck-ass naked down Oxford Street? "I just want peace and quiet. I have no intention of doing anything other than chilling and relaxing for the next couple of weeks."

"Good. Because what you've experienced in America is nothing compared to the media scrutiny here. Moreover, if they unearth your presence, you would never know a moment of the serenity you're eager to find. The tabloids have already interrogated vendors and locals for 'insider' information. The only way we can ensure the discretion of the event, and your solitude," she hurried to add, "is to keep you out of London proper."

"What am I supposed to do? You said I can't stay at the cottage."

"That's correct. But . . . you can stay here." Louisa waved her hand toward the massive structure behind her.

Here? In this castle?

Dani eyed it again. So less like *The Holiday* and more like *Downton Abbey*?

"Did you get the list my assistant sent?"

Louisa nodded. "We did. And hoping you'd agree to the changes, everything you requested is here. If you need anything else, there's a charming market town about four miles southeast. Amos will be at your service. Unless you'd prefer to drive yourself?"

"Uh, no. I've never spent enough time in the UK to get used to driving on the left side of the road and I don't think getting into an accident weeks before the event would be a good idea."

Louisa grinned. "You're right. It wouldn't."

"Then this should be perfect."

"The house has a full-time staff, but they won't disturb you. The housekeeper will prepare your meals. If there's anything specific you want, let her know."

"The staff lives here?" Dani asked, looking around.

While it was a gorgeous estate, it was also a bit . . .

Isolated.

Even more so than she'd imagined. What would it be like to be out here by herself at night? No sounds of the city, no streetlights. And the lake she'd thought was charming only moments ago suddenly gave off Jason Voorhees vibes.

"Some. The housekeeper, butler, and a few of the cleaning staff live in accommodations on the upper floor," Louisa said, pointing to the dormer windows at the top of the house. "My husband and I live closer to the city, but others, like the groundskeepers, footmen, and assistants, live in smaller homes on the property or in the nearby villages."

"Whew," Dani said, laughing with the sudden release of tension. "And what about the people who own the property? Are they here? Will they mind my presence?"

Louisa fiddled with the simple pearl stud in her earlobe. "Don't worry. We're happy you're here."

A member of the household staff exited the house and took the bags Amos pulled from the trunk.

"I kind of expected you to bring more," Louisa said with a little smile.

"For the next two weeks I'm Dani, and this is all I'll need. The wardrobe for Duchess will come when my team arrives."

"Excellent. You have my cell if anything arises. But since I expect to be furiously working on the celebration, please try to use it only if necessary." She glanced at her watch and sighed. "I was hoping he would be here."

"He?"

"Yes, His Royal Highness Prince Jameson, Duke of Wessex. This is his—"

She broke off as a black late-model luxury sedan sped up the driveway and pulled to a stop on the other side of the fountain. The door swung open and a man emerged.

Dani stared at the newcomer, her pulse booming in her ears like a thunderstorm that had formed with no warning. A shiver of pure yearning trembled through her body.

Wow.

His long, determined strides quickly brought him to them, and Dani caught her bottom lip between her teeth.

He was tall and she had a . . . thing for tall men. Not freakishly tall, like that NBA player she'd dated for a few months. No, normal-guy tall. Duchess's five-inch-high platform heels meant she rarely looked up to anyone. But in dark gray Adidas track pants, a white cropped T-shirt, and sneakers, Dani had to tilt her head back to take in the fine, solidly built specimen standing before her.

Six-three. Maybe six-four.

Heat trickled to her core.

The wind stirred the strands of his dark, wavy hair. Shades covered his eyes, but that only drew her focus to his long straight nose, his lean cheeks and chiseled jaw touched with a teasing hint of shadow, and his firm, well-shaped, really kissable lips.

Rust-colored pants covered those long legs, and his broad shoulders were cruelly concealed from view by a white button-down shirt and a navy-blue cardigan. Properly buttoned, of course. The cuffs of his shirt were rolled back over the sleeves of his cardigan and pushed up to reveal corded wrists, the left adorned with a classic Rolex. His other accessories were just as impeccable—brown, gleaming leather shoes, matching belt—their quality apparent even in their subtleness.

He looked like a sex god trying to masquerade as a mortal professor.

And that scholarly refinement, that studious veneer, made her itch to corrupt him. Tousle him up a little. Run her fingers through his hair, bite his stubbled chin, rip open that shirt—a reverse Superman—and graze her nails, promptly followed by her tongue, down his wide chest and flat belly.

Louisa dropped into a brief curtsy. "Your Royal Highness. I was just showing your guest around. May I please introduce you to Duchess?"

Dani knew none of her inner thirst showed on her face. She'd been in the entertainment game for almost a decade. Self-preservation demanded she learn how to conceal her emotions. But it took a hell of an effort.

Still, that didn't mean she couldn't test the waters.

She grabbed the end of her sleek ponytail and pulled it over her shoulder. Sliding her hands into the pockets of her pants, she swayed from side to side. "When I was told the prince had invited me, you definitely weren't what I had in mind."

He removed his sunglasses and tucked them in the neckline of his sweater.

Her knees went wobbly.

Good Lord, it wasn't fair.

His eyes were a bright cornflower blue surrounded by lashes so dark and thick it looked like Rhonda had flown in just to touch him up with some mascara.

Day-um.

"Louisa—"

Dani inhaled.

His voice.

What was it about certain foreign accents? She didn't know, but his could be bottled and sold as an aphrodisiac. Twist off the top, release the contents, and watch panties drop and thighs spread. His voice was measured, deep, and cultured. Benedict Cumberbatch mixed with Idris Elba with a dash of James Bond.

Or even better . . .

She was in the presence of her very own Mr. Darcy.

Macfadyen, not Firth.

He continued, and, like most men, when he opened his mouth, he ruined it.

"—if this is your idea of a joke, you need to reassess your bloody material!"

Chapter Eight

"I count him braver who overcomes his desires than him who conquers his enemies; for the hardest victory is over self."

—Aristotle

When I was told the prince had invited me, you definitely weren't what I had in mind.

Her voice, sweet and husky with a slight southern drawl, rained over Jameson like a hot shower, on a cold evening, after a long day.

She was here.

The woman who'd starred in his fantasies numerous times over the past couple of months was now standing in his drive.

In the flesh.

It was surreal. His mind had conjured and brought her forth.

Her, but not her.

Irritation had been his constant companion from the moment he'd received Louisa's voice mail informing him that Duchess was arriving today at Primrose Park. He'd been finishing up some research at his office, but he'd jumped in his car and raced home, trying Louisa's cell the entire way. He didn't know what the woman, or his grandmother, had planned, but he wanted to make it clear that under no circumstances should they expect him to entertain the rapper.

His initial and continued explosive reaction to her meant he needed to keep his distance. She was too dazzling, too tempting, too . . . inappropriate.

He wasn't going to be the second prince in his direct lineage to lose all sense of propriety because of a woman.

Pulling up, he could see he'd been too late. Louisa was there with a woman who was clearly familiar to him, but who looked different than he'd expected.

Oh, it was her. Duchess. Same creamy brown skin he'd trailed his fingers across in his mind. Same big brown eyes he'd lost himself in. Same body that could bring a man to his knees. And had. In one of his fantasies, Jameson had been prostrate behind her, his hands gripping her small waist, his lips pressed to a rounded derriere that had made him eager to be christened an "ass man."

But if Duchess's online persona was an eleven, in person it was more muted. Like an eight. It didn't detract from her beauty. If anything, she was more enticing without the distraction of her usual outer trappings.

Blood rushed to his cock and Jameson prayed the tailoring of his pants would successfully hide his lack of control. He firmed his jaw and forced himself to discard those thoughts. He didn't care how she looked or how vibrant she was. It didn't change the fact that she was an American rapper who roused him like no one else ever had and she couldn't be here.

"Excuse us." He steeled himself against her obvious dismay and gestured for Louisa to follow him. He moved several yards away and kept his voice urgent but low. "What is going on? I thought she was staying in one of the cottages."

"A leak. And since you're her host—"

"For the celebration," he clarified. "Her host *for the celebration.* She's early."

"I know. But she needed to get away."

Needed to get away? That sounded like a vacation, and Primrose Park wasn't some hotel or bed-and-breakfast.

"The celebration doesn't begin for another three weeks."

"Very well. But if she stays in London, how long do you think it'll take the press, not to mention Prince Julian, to find out?"

Jameson slid his hands into his pockets and stared out over the lake.

He'd give it less than a day. And the moment Julian was alerted to her presence?

Julian had brought Duchess up often, telling the press he was "most excited" for her performance. Her being here early would shift the focus away from the purpose of the celebration. That was the last thing Marina would want.

Or Jameson himself, for that matter.

John had done important work, during a time when others weren't interested. He deserved everything this celebration promised and shouldn't be upstaged by an American entertainer and her possible affair with the married heir apparent.

Duchess joined them, narrowed eyes and a pinched expression replacing her earlier teasing openness. "Is there a problem?"

"No—"

"Yes—" Jameson said, irked with himself for his inability to ignore the seductive sway of her hips. "This isn't going to work. I did not agree for you and your entourage to take over my home for three weeks!"

Duchess's brows rose. "Entourage? Dude, you act as if I'm rolling ten deep with my homegirls. Look around. I'm the only one here.

And, just so you know, this is as much a surprise to me as it is to you!"

Dude? Did she just call me Dude?

Her full lips had tightened, color had blossomed on her cheeks, and she'd jammed her hands onto those delectable hips.

Damn, she was sexy!

He hated that he noticed.

And had responded.

"Your Royal Highness," he said, crossing his arms over his chest.

Duchess waved a hand. "You don't have to call me that."

"Not you. Me. You should address me as 'Your Royal Highness.'"

He ignored Louisa's incredulous stare as well as the prickling of unease at the back of his neck. He wasn't one to require people to address him formally. Hell, he usually went out of his way to avoid it. But something about her was stoking powerful urges within him, upsetting his usual equanimity. At least if she was irritated with him, she'd keep her distance, making it easier for him to keep his.

Duchess cocked her head to the side. "Excuse me?"

"Of course," he said, nodding his head graciously, purposefully mistaking her statement.

Her features didn't shift, but her eyes? Fuck, they were amazing. Rich, molten dark chocolate, they sparked to life. She was furious. He imagined all the things she would say to him, the energy radiating from her enough to power the small village nearby.

And as if he were some bloody masochist, awareness and heat shot straight to his already engorged, throbbing cock.

A tiny smile curved the corners of her lips, though he wasn't fooled into believing it contained any warmth.

Come on, Duchess. Give me all you've got.

"Your Royal Highness," she began, the words emerging garbled, as if from gritted teeth.

He waited, anticipation skipping up and down his spine.

"I—" She closed her eyes. Exhaled. Opened them. "I . . . understand. I wouldn't like it if someone showed up on my doorstep uninvited, asking to crash for two weeks. I'll get my bags and be on my way. I'm sure my team can still get my suite at the Baglioni."

She headed to the steps leading up to the house.

Jameson stilled. That was . . . unexpected.

Louisa eyed him quite urgently. "Do something!"

He shrugged, trying to decipher his own disappointment at her easy acquiescence. "What do you want me to do?"

"Amos, I need your help," Duchess called to the driver standing next to the car.

Amos glanced over to him and Louisa for clarification. Apparently, Duchess had thrown them all for a loop.

"Never mind," Duchess said, grabbing the large Louis Vuitton overnight bag and walking back to the car.

"The queen will not be happy about this," Louisa promised.

Jameson sighed. She was right. If Louisa had arranged for Duchess to stay here, it was done with the queen's knowledge and approval.

He gestured to Amos, who took the bag from Duchess and started up the steps to the house.

"Hey! Give me back my—"

"Please—" Jameson said.

She turned to look at him and he was struck again by her beauty. He'd thought the woman on the video was stunning, but the one before him took his breath away.

He cleared his throat. "I'm sure we can work something out, Ms.—"

He looked to Louisa for the missing information. He didn't know her real name and he couldn't call her Duchess . . .

"You can call me Duchess."

He frowned. "Is that your given name?"

She blinked. "It's the name I'm giving *you*."

Cute.

"As a member of the royal family, I'm not allowed to address anyone with a royal title if they don't hold one."

"And as a person, I'm entitled to be addressed by the name I choose. I never said I was *a* duchess. It's my name. If you want to speak to me, I suggest you start there."

"Very well . . . Duchess. I don't think London will be necessary. I'm sure we can find something on the grounds. What about Primrose Cottage?" he asked Louisa.

Primrose Cottage was the estate's small guesthouse. At one time or another it had been used by various members of the royal family who'd wanted a private place to stay. Muriel Spark had even used it to finish a novel. Although part of Primrose Park, it was on the other side of the property. It would provide Duchess with privacy and they'd never have to see each other.

"Occupied," Louisa said, dashing those hopes.

"By whom?"

"Not sure," she said, "but it's not available."

"How about one of the properties closer to the villages?"

"Look, you can both stop. I refuse to stay anywhere I'm not welcome. Not anymore."

Jameson frowned at the last two words. *Not anymore?* What did that mean? Had she been made to not feel welcome somewhere?

Why do you care? You're doing the same thing.

He didn't like the way that unbidden thought made him feel.

Spurred on by Louisa's withering glare, and his own burgeoning shame, he said, "Duchess . . . Please accept my apology. Between the tribute and the media coverage . . . it's brought back some difficult memories and I haven't been handling them well. But none of that is your fault. I'm truly sorry. It would be my honor to host you at Primrose Park."

She tilted her head to the side and eyed him for a long second before nodding. "Apology accepted."

Relief acted as a release valve for his tension. "Thank you."

With his clear permission granted, the staff sprang into action, hurrying down the steps, grabbing her bags, and carrying them into the house.

"I'll have them place your things in the Celestial Bedroom, in the east wing. You'll have all the privacy you need. Although there's nothing exciting around here. Nothing showy or popular for you to post online."

"You been checking out my Insta?"

Heat crisped the tips of his ears. Ignoring her question, he continued. "I only meant this isn't the environment for a young person who's used to an active social life."

"Because I'm an empty-headed rapper who only cares about partying and her image?" She frowned. "Don't worry. I won't go live and announce a party here. At least, not tonight."

"That's not what I meant."

She pursed her lips. "If I'm in the east wing, where will you be?"

He'd apologized. But in his effort to self-deprecatingly describe their isolated surroundings, he'd unintentionally offended her.

Smooth, Jameson. "The west wing."

"Of course. Well, I appreciate you allowing me to stay. If we both try hard enough, we can avoid seeing each other while I'm here."

YOU SHOULD ADDRESS me as *"Your Royal Highness."*

Seriously?

Dani tossed her tote on the bed. The nerve of that man! Why should she call him her royal anything? He wasn't *her* prince. He needed to read a history book. America won the Revolutionary War. She wasn't required to bow down to him or anybody else.

Bitches bowed down to her!

She'd conceded only because her grandmother would roll over in her grave if Dani had acted like the stereotypical class-less American when meeting one of her beloved royals for the first time. Everything was riding on the positive coverage of her participation in this once-in-a-lifetime event. How she was seen, how she was received, needed to boost her image in Genesis's eyes. She had to make this work. And if that meant abiding by his rules and protocols, because she was in his country, then that's what she would do.

Plus, she could hear Nana saying, "You're staying in his house. Act like you have some home training."

So, she'd done it. She'd given him his "Your Royal Highness." With a smile that she hoped looked pleasant, because it felt tight as fuck on her face.

How had she gotten in that situation to begin with? She couldn't remember the last time her first interaction with a man hadn't led to him eating out of her palm. Even if she didn't like them, she knew how to deal with them. She'd noticed how the prince had reacted when he'd first seen her. Even when she was dressed down, she knew the reaction most men had toward her. She'd acted as she usually did, flirting with him, attempting to get him on her side.

But he hadn't taken the bait. He'd treated her and her presence as if she were unwelcome.

So, you got all up in your feelings because he wasn't feeling you?

Nyla also didn't have to be here for Dani to hear her voice.

"It's crowded enough in there. I don't need all of you giving your opinions!"

Dani's voice was loud in the quiet space.

Oh right. Because she was in a bedroom. In a castle. By herself.

Despite her dark mood, she recognized that the accommodations were luxurious, with light-colored walls and dark wood furniture. The king-sized bed, clearly the focal point of the room, had a large headboard and a sumptuous duvet piled with sky blue and gold pillows that looked like a cloud, hence its name. To her left was a small sitting room, with a chaise lounge upholstered in the same fabric as the pillows. It didn't have an en suite bathroom—she'd passed one on the opposite side of the hall as she was shown to her room—but the view . . .

She headed over to the French doors and stepped out onto the balcony that overlooked the property. It was incredible; even in the dimming light there were rolling green hills for as far as the eye could see.

She pulled out her phone and took a picture, texting it to Nyla.

Sunset is God saying nighty-night to his Sparkle Sammies.

Several seconds later, her phone buzzed, and her friend's face appeared on the screen.

"You are a mess," Nyla said, laughing. "And that's some view for a cottage on a country estate."

From the lighting to the fact that Dani could see Nyla's profile as she ran a makeup brush over her face, she could tell her friend had called using her iPad, while sitting at the vanity in her bathroom.

"Turns out there was a leak at the cottage, so now I'm staying in the main house."

"It's gorgeous," Nyla said, nodding approvingly.

Dani leaned over and propped her elbow on the stone balustrade. "What are you up to today?"

"Heading out to have lunch with one of the producers from the show. He wants to pitch me this idea on my character's . . ."

"Hmmm," Dani responded, her brain still puzzling over her interaction with, and reaction to, the prince.

"You didn't hear anything I just said!" Nyla finally faced the screen, her skillfully drawn brows arched, her tone breaking through Dani's fog.

"Of course I did," Dani protested. She hadn't. "You're having lunch with a producer."

"That was like two topics ago. Plus, I can see your face. You ghosted." Nyla narrowed her eyes. "What's wrong with you?"

"Nothing."

Nyla didn't say anything. Just continued to stare at her.

"Fine! It's the prince."

"Who?"

"Remember Bennie mentioned a young royal had invited me? Well, it's him. This is his house. And he'll be staying here. With me."

"What happened?"

"He acted like a straight-up jerk! Like my presence would stain his precious royal ancestral home."

"Why don't you leave?"

"I can't. The goal is to stay under the radar for the next few weeks." She sighed and looked out at the green vastness. "This isn't just under the radar. It's buried. Forget the east wing. I'm up in Rapunzel's tower."

"East wing?"

"Yeah. I'm in the east wing. Far away from him in the west wing."

"You're in separate *wings*?" Nyla asked, her voice full of humor. "Then it should be easy to avoid him, right?"

"I guess so."

"Which prince was it?"

"Prince Jameson. Why?"

"The really hot one?" Nyla grabbed her phone off the vanity top. Dani straightened. "Don't—"

"Holy shit!" Nyla breathed, staring at the screen in her hand.

She turned the phone so Dani could see the photo of him wearing a dark gray suit and standing next to a blond woman, his head bent toward her as if listening to what she said, an intense expression on his face.

"I know what he looks like, Ny. I was just talking to him."

And she was also aware that the photo was a pale imitation of the man in person.

"Why do they insist on keeping him in hiding?" Nyla continued to stare transfixed at the phone.

Considering how he'd acted, the Palace must've known what they were doing keeping the prince out of the limelight.

"Did he have bad breath?" Nyla asked suddenly.

"Uhhh . . . I don't think so. It's not like I was trying to sniff it or anything," Dani said with a laugh.

"Has he lost a lot of hair since this picture was taken?"

"Afraid not." His hair was actually shorter in the picture. Dani preferred its current wavy length.

"Well, something had to be wrong with him. To be that good-looking, rich, and an actual prince? So he suffers from asshole-itis. He's hardly unique in having the condition."

"True."

"And you have experience from dealing with his fellow sufferers."

Dani nodded.

"Then keep that in mind and do what you went there to do. It's unfortunate, but you need him more than he needs you. You're doing this for Mela-Skin and the next phase of your life. Be nice. I've seen you do it. Better than most when you put your mind to it."

"You're right," Dani said, thankful her friend had seen her text as the cry for help it was. She needed to be cool. To be smart. To use a little Duchess honey to get what she wanted.

"Of course I am. Now, you go back to being in the separate wing of the magnificent castle you're staying in and I'll head to Cecconi's to have brunch with a producer whose breath actually does stink." Nyla rolled her eyes. "Sometimes I hate my life."

"No, you don't."

"Says you. Oh, make sure you send that pic of the grounds to Tasha so she can post it on your IG," Nyla said, before blowing a kiss and ending the call.

Dani braced her palms against the railing and inhaled the air. With a little time and distance, it was hard to fathom how she'd let the prince get under her skin. Sure, when he'd shoved a hand through his hair and stared off across the lake, lust had dampened her panties. The man had actual chiseled features! But it was the jet lag. It had to be. She'd get some rest and she'd feel better.

Even if it fucking killed her.

Chapter Nine

"The force of the blow depends on the resistance. It is sometimes better not to struggle against temptation. Either fly or yield at once."

—Francis H. Bradley

That could've gone better.

After Louisa had left—with a tersely uttered "Fix this or I'll have to inform the queen!"—Jameson had given instructions to his staff about their new guest, then shut himself away in his office. The large room had always been a sanctuary for him, the mahogany-paneled walls, navy blue area rug, and floor-to-ceiling shelving the epitome of a gentleman's study.

Coming home to a household in turmoil was not how he usually ended his day. He preferred a quiet evening with papers to read and grade followed by a few fingers of scotch.

Tonight, he'd skipped the papers and gone straight for the alcohol.

He leaned back in his desk chair, resting the tumbler of amber liquid on his chest.

Two weeks with Duchess in his house.

She hadn't been what he'd expected, and he should have known better. After all, he was aware that the glitz, glamour, and fairy tale the public saw rarely collided with the reality. But he hadn't applied the same consideration to her. He'd expected a full-blown diva, complete with fur coat, full hair and makeup, and an entourage.

Instead, she'd been stunningly casual in jogging bottoms, a T-shirt that showed off her toned midriff, and trainers.

The furthest thing from a diva. One might almost mistake her for a regular person.

Almost.

He took a sip of his drink. Choosing her to perform at the concert had been a mistake. All his fault. Because he hadn't taken the queen seriously and failed to do his research. But it was done now. The best he could do would be to get back into his routine and keep his distance. It shouldn't be difficult. Once the celebrations began, they'd all be too busy to have anything but the most cursory interaction. In a month, she'd be on a flight home never to be seen or heard from again.

With that thought, he straightened and set his glass on the desk. There were emails he needed to check for work, grades he'd planned to enter. Maybe the rote academic tasks would be enough to calm him so he could finally put that disastrous encounter behind him.

He opened his laptop and clicked his email icon. Sure enough, several messages were waiting, including two from students asking permission to submit late work and one informing him of an upcoming department meeting. He bypassed those and clicked on the message from *The British Journal for the History of Philosophy* about the manuscript he'd submitted. They'd accepted it for publication the following year but had a few notes for him to address.

Splendid. He enjoyed his field of study; it required a concentration and attention to precise language and intent that he usually took pleasure in providing. Working on this article was just what he needed to end the day on a positive note.

Except . . . he couldn't focus. He was unsettled. Agitated. His blood simmered just beneath his skin.

As though they had a mind of his own, his fingers engaged his search browser and typed in "Duchess."

Because of who and where he was, he was immediately bombarded with results for royalty.

Margaret, Duchess of Strathearn.

Simon, Duke of York.

Charlotte, Duchess of Richmond.

Right. The last time he'd searched her he'd been on his phone. He narrowed down the options by adding "rapper" to the search query, and there she was, her image all over his screen. Most of the photos showed her the way he'd expected: wearing different glamorous outfits, posing on various red carpets; there were even several stills from performances.

In some she was slightly more casual—jeans, over-the-knee rhinestone boots, a fur-lined hood on her jacket, her face hidden behind shades and large hats. Her head was usually bent as if she knew she was being photographed by paparazzi.

But none had her looking the way she had earlier. Very few showed her with another man, romantically, but there was a search result that hinted at having information about her personal affairs.

"Here's the Tea on Duchess's Dating Life."

It's none of your business, Jameson. You don't need to know who she's screwing to have her participate in the celebration.

He clicked on the link and read.

She wasn't married. There were rumors she was dating a fellow rapper, but she was also linked to a pop singer . . .

Online sites were notorious for getting stories wrong or simply fabricating them. He'd do well to put little stock in anything he discovered there. Why, then, did the weight on his chest ease? As if he'd gotten good news about a situation he hadn't known he'd cared about?

There was a row of thumbnail video images about her. Most of them seemed to be official music videos and performances, although one headline jumped out at him, grabbing his attention:

"Why Duchess Is the Sexiest Entertainer on the Planet."

He didn't even waste his mental breath talking himself out of clicking on that result. It started with a young black man who spent several minutes talking about hitting buttons and subscribing to his channel. Impatient, Jameson scrolled through until the screen flashed with different images of her performing.

"—commands the stage, her words daring you to step to her, her moves making it impossible not to—"

Jameson's heart stuttered to a stop before galloping back to life. She was a vision, strutting across the stage in sparkling rhinestone high-heel boots and what amounted to a bikini, her curves on display. And that was before he heard the lyrics:

Thigh-long python, so big it makes me blink
Don't believe the hype / It's real? Bitch, send the link
Turn it down, walk away, let his hopes sink?
Fuck no, I like a challenge, put it in and hope it shrinks.

He leaned back in his chair, aware that he was in some kind of a fugue state as the blood left his brain and journeyed to his willing dick, which stiffened in his pants.

"Add in a face full of grace and a body made for sin."

A close-up of her face filled the screen, her luminous dark brown skin looking as if it had been dusted with particles of gold. Extremely long lashes framed those beautiful brown eyes that seemed to stare into his soul. And a wide mouth with glistening full lips pouted.

His heart pounded in his chest as he stared at the face of an angel walking on Earth.

"—it's no wonder Duchess has men and women aged nine to ninety bonkers over her. Thanks for watching and as a treat here's some raw footage from her video 'Holla Atcha Girl.' Enjoy!"

On a four-poster bed surrounded by white gauzy drapes and wearing very little, Duchess arched her back and cupped her breasts. She rolled to her side and dragged her hands along the curve of her hip before gracefully swinging her legs behind her and rising to her knees. All while staring into the camera, her eyes wide and seductive, her lips calling to him.

Come on, Jameson. You know you want me.

He wasn't even aware when he'd begun stroking himself. Through the fabric of his trousers, his cock throbbed heavily against his lower belly. Uncomfortably so. He should turn the video off, but he couldn't tear his eyes away from the screen. From her on all fours crawling across the mattress.

And it had been so long.

The abrasion of the rough fabric against his cock felt unbelievably good. Giving in, he undid the button and zipper and slipped his hand inside, pulling his cock out of the opening of his boxers.

Pre-cum was already leaking from his head, so he used it as lubrication, one hand gripping the base, just above his balls, the other rubbing up and down his shaft.

So good . . .

Her skin.

Those gorgeous eyes.

Her lips.

He sped up his strokes, his cock throbbing in his fist, the feeling so intense his hips lifted off the chair to meet his palm.

Stroking the end of her sleek ponytail.

Her rounded, swaying hips.

That voice . . . *you definitely weren't what I had in mind.*

Sizzling bliss enveloped his entire body, zipping through each extremity and concentrating in his dick. His balls tightened and he couldn't contain the loud groan as he came, his pulse sprinting, stars bursting in the darkness of his closed eyes.

Slowly, sounds came back to him, the smell of sweat and sex permeated his senses, and the stickiness of his cum coated his hand and shirt.

Son of a bitch!

Disgust wasn't far behind as he yanked several tissues from the box he kept on his desk and cleaned himself up. He stood and refilled his tumbler with scotch.

The depths he'd sunk to, having a wank to videos of the woman staying in his house.

He was no better than his father.

THE FOLLOWING MORNING, Jameson sat at the dining room table and cradled a cup of hot tea in his hands. He kept his eyelids almost closed, the weak morning light beaming in through the windows too much for his splitting head to endure.

If this was his punishment for last night's actions, so be it.

"Can I get you anything else, sir?" his housekeeper, Margery, asked.

Jameson sent an unsteady smile up at the woman who'd been with his family since he was a young boy. Although his mother had left Primrose Park years ago to move into an apartment at Kensington Palace, he'd be forever grateful to her for allowing Margery to remain here with him.

"This is fine," he said, looking at the platters of fried eggs, sausages, bacon, mushrooms, tomatoes, and fried bread placed on the table in front of him and trying not to vomit. "It's more than I usually eat, but there's something to be said for variety."

"I made a little extra for our guest."

A *little* extra? There wasn't much missing from a traditional English breakfast.

"I didn't include blood pudding. She just arrived. Didn't want to scare her off."

He pressed the back of his hand to his lips. Thank God Margery hadn't added that fare, though not because it might have appalled Duchess.

No, he'd handled that all by himself the day before.

"I have no idea what she likes," he said, his lack of hospitality on display.

What did they eat in the States? He'd detected a slight southern accent. Wasn't their cuisine culturally specific? Lots of carbs, like pancakes and pastries? Or did she live in Los Angeles? Maybe she'd want that god-awful avocado toast everyone seemed to rave about.

If his mother were here, she'd know what to do, but she was off on her annual trip to Monaco. And he was glad for it. The press had been relentless in dredging up the story of his father's affair and subsequent death. The Palace had kept their word and provided protection for her, but that meant only that the photographers couldn't physically touch her. It didn't stop them from following her car when she left palace grounds or accompanying her in a throng when she went shopping, shouting shameful and embarrassing questions.

It wasn't as if Jameson hadn't been taught about entertaining company, but he'd never cared about his lack in that area, until now. Having a houseguest might not have been his choice, but that wasn't Duchess's fault. She'd shown up expecting quiet and privacy for two weeks. Instead, she'd walked into his self-flagellation over his unprecedented lust.

He looked at his housekeeper. "What would you suggest in this situation?"

She smiled. "How about I talk to her and find out what she likes?"

"That's perfect. Thank you."

Margery would take care of ensuring his guest's comfort while he took care of his raging hangover and got himself under control. The next time he saw Duchess, he'd be levelheaded and composed.

Coolly distant but pleasant.

Not nauseous with a semi-stiffy anytime thoughts of the night before whispered across his brain.

"Good morning."

Duchess's husky voice caught him off guard, especially since he hadn't anticipated hearing it for a while.

The last bite he took lodged in his throat and set up camp, causing him to choke.

Margery gasped and moments later took to battering his body.

The housekeeper had strong hands. Great for homemade bread. Not so much for his aching back.

Bloody hell.

As his face burned and his spine smarted from its unwanted adjustment, tears streamed down his face. So much for making a better impression.

He felt like a fucking idiot.

"Is he okay?" Duchess asked, distress discernible in her tone.

"He will be," Margery said, her prior pounding dwindling to

soothing circles. "Can you bring me some water? The pitcher is on the counter in the kitchen, through that door."

"Of course."

And then Margery was pressing the cool glass into his hand.

"There, love," she murmured. "Slowly."

He was once again that little boy who'd come into the kitchen for his snack and hit his knee on the chair because he hadn't been watching where he was going, his head forever in a book.

The tidal wave of his embarrassment threatened to pull him under, but he fought it, focusing instead on taking sips of water and breathing in through his nose until his vision cleared. Recovered, he wiped his face with a napkin and forced himself to look up.

Duchess stood across from him, lovely in soft pink joggers, a matching jumper that fell teasingly off one shoulder, and her hair in big soft ringlets. Her hands gripped the top rail of the chair, her expressive eyes worried and cautious.

"Pardon me."

She waved a hand. "You don't need to apologize. Are you sure you're okay?"

"Great." Save his bruised ego. He took another sip of water. "What are you doing here?"

The concern fled her face. She pursed her lips. "Even from my banishment in the east wing tower, I can smell the delicious food."

"Banishment?" Margery asked, her expression undergoing a transformation similar to Duchess's. She gave him a censorious glance.

Would he ever wake up from this nightmare where he constantly did and said the wrong thing?

"This is Margery, my housekeeper. If you need anything, she'll be happy to attend to it. Margery, this is Duchess."

Margery smiled. "Welcome to Primrose Park."

"Thank you." Duchess smiled. She gestured to the food on the table. "You certainly have your hands full. Does he eat like this every day?"

Jameson bristled. "No, *he* does not. She made this for you."

Duchess shook her head. "Oh please. I wouldn't want to put you through too much trouble."

"Nonsense. It'll be nice to have someone other than Prince Jameson to cook for again. Do you have a specific menu you'd like?"

"No, I'm pretty easy—"

His cock threw off its "semi" status and hardened fully.

"—plus, I like to eat the cuisine of the places I'm visiting. I'm open . . . except for blood pudding. I have no interest in trying that."

"Understood," Margery said, her eyes twinkling.

"Oh, and I know that tea is the national drink, but I'd prefer coffee, if you don't mind."

"That can be arranged, Du . . . is it Duchess? Or the Duchess? Your Grace?"

Duchess pulled the chair away from the table and sat down. "Actually, you can call me Dani."

"Dani," Margery said, a smile blossoming on her face, before hurrying back into the kitchen.

His gaze flew to meet hers.

Dani.

Such a sweet, simple name for a woman who invoked feelings in him that were anything but.

"I didn't mean to be rude earlier," he said. "Of course you should be here. I was surprised you were awake. I expected the jet lag to fell you."

She unrolled the cloth napkin and placed it in her lap. "It's always better to get on your new time zone as soon as you can. I may be sluggish the first couple of days, but if I spend that time sleeping, it'll make it more difficult to get acclimated."

He nodded. Margery came over, placed a cup in front of her, and began pouring the steaming hot brew into it.

"Thank you."

Margery beamed and placed the coffeepot on the table. "Help yourself. And if you'd prefer something other than what's been prepared, let me know."

"I'm good. This looks wonderful," Dani—the name so perfectly fit the woman before him that he couldn't think of her as anything else—said, adding some of the bacon, eggs, and mushrooms to her plate.

Jameson didn't know why he was surprised to see her doing something so commonplace. He didn't know quite what he'd expected, but this normality wasn't it.

Without pausing from what she was doing, Dani said, "Don't worry. I only wear my thong to dinner."

He dropped his fork. "Pardon?"

"You're looking at me as if you thought I was going to eat while hanging upside down from a stripper pole," she said.

That image immediately seared itself on his brain. But in the fantasy that began running on a loop in his mind, the pole was in his bedroom and he was the only one there to enjoy the show.

Unaware he'd been staring, and annoyed he'd been caught, he frowned. "Such vulgarity isn't necessary."

He sounded like a rigid prick, but he couldn't help himself.

"Maybe you should tell yourself that," she said, before taking a bite of her food.

The sound of pleasure she made shot straight to his dick. Once again, his gaze flew to hers, except this time, the tiny twitch at the corner of her mouth let him know she'd made the sound on purpose.

"This is delicious, Margery," she said.

"Thank you. I'm glad you're enjoying it. If you have time when you're done, I'd like to discuss what you may want for lunch. Prince Jameson is usually only home for breakfast and dinner."

Irritation filled him. He knew Margery was referring to him by his official title because they had company, but he needed to tell her it wasn't necessary.

"Of course," Dani said. "But there's not much on my agenda."

Another thing he hadn't considered.

He picked up his fork, then placed it down again. "What *do* you have planned for today?"

She shrugged. "Nothing. I haven't had a true day off in about four years. My iPad is full of downloaded books, movies, and TV shows I've missed because of work. I figure I can find a few secluded nooks to just hang out and relax."

"Feel free to make yourself comfortable anywhere."

"Except the west wing?"

She wanted to make herself comfortable in the west wing? Near his office? Or his bedroom?

"Like in *Beauty and the Beast*?" she attempted to clarify.

He shook his head, unsure of what the layout of his house had to do with a French fairy tale.

She sighed. "Never mind. I will. Thank you. And what are you going to do with your day?"

"Work. We're administering exams." Which meant his hangover wouldn't be the same hindrance as if he actually had to give lectures. "At the University of Birmingham. Where I teach. Philosophy."

Yes, rambling. That would impress her.

"Must be interesting."

"It is."

Unlike his responses. Bloody hell!

He made a quick decision. "I probably won't be home until late."

"Don't worry about me. I've been watching after myself for a long time," she said.

He was sure she had. The problem was Jameson's body wanted to take over those duties for her.

Chapter Ten

"Normal is an illusion. What is normal for the spider is chaos for the fly."

—Charles Addams

Jameson flipped his pen on the desk and leaned back in his chair. His day was over, and he'd be hard-pressed to give anyone specifics on what he'd done. During exam periods, he offered extended office hours for any of his students who had questions before his test. He also needed to copyedit his paper for the journal, but his mind was preoccupied with his new houseguest.

Duchess.

Dani.

He needed to leave. He'd run out of credible excuses to be there an hour ago and the cleaning staff had already walked past his office several times. They were ready for him to go so they could do their job. Granting their wish, he shut everything down and retired for the evening. In the staff parking garage, he nodded to his protection detail before backing out of his space. He wanted nothing more than to grab something to eat, get a hot shower, and relax with the latest issue of his favorite academic journal.

Pulling into his driveway, he was somehow relieved to see everything looked the way it usually did.

What did you think, there'd be a dozen cars, streamers, and loud music denoting a party?

Of course not. But maybe he'd expected some outward manifestation of the chaos she was causing inside of him. Something that explained why he felt the way he did. But of course, there was nothing. Because he was being ridiculous. After parking, he grabbed his crossbody bag by the handle and headed inside his house.

The pungent scent was the first thing he noticed.

What the hell? Was something burning?

"Margery?" He dropped his bag by the door and hurried toward the kitchen. As he got closer, plumes of smoke joined the acrid smell, bolstering his conclusion. Panic surged through him and he pulled his phone out of his pocket intending to call 999. There were so many people inside the house, even at this time of night. He hoped he'd be able to notify everyone in time.

He burst through the swinging door and skidded to a stop at the sight. Had a bag of flour exploded?

White powder covered every available surface: the wide butcher block of the island, the hardwood floors, even the forest green walls. Cracked brown eggshells littered the countertop. A rolling pin covered in beige gunk was precariously close to falling on the floor. A glass bowl containing that same beige glob sat on top of various pans in the sink. A loaf of sunken bread was on the stove top, next to caved-in rolls and a pan that looked like halfway through baking the batter had tried to escape and ended up looking like a phallic appendage. The oven door sat ajar, and smoke drifted, accusingly, from it.

It was a bloody horror show.

He turned stunned eyes to the only occupant in the room. "What the fuck is going on here?"

Dani spun around and stared at him, shock and apprehension all over her features. Flour dusted her curls, smudged her cheeks, and blotched the front of her jumper.

"Shit!"

That wasn't from Dani. His gaze slid to the source of the sound and saw what had previously been blocked from his view by her body: an iPad propped against some books. And not just any books . . .

"Are those my first editions of the works of Locke, Hale, and Newton?"

"Oh! I don't know. I needed something sturdy so I grabbed them from the library."

Something sturdy?

Those were three rare treatises by some of the forefathers of philosophy. First editions, one with its original cover, two rebacked to period style and with their original ownership bookplates. It had taken years and a considerable amount of money to find and acquire the books and she was treating them as if they were no better than a twelve-quid tablet stand from Amazon?

Anger flared within him, burning through any mindfulness or solicitude. "Of all the bloody idiotic . . ."

The dismay slid from Dani's face, leaving a closed, blank tableau behind.

She shrugged. "We're just doing a little baking."

A glop of batter from the stand mixer's paddle plopped on the floor, landing next to her bare foot.

"Margery bakes several times a week and the kitchen never looks like this!"

"She's probably better at it than we are."

"We? Oh no. I'm not a part of this," said the stunning woman on the iPad screen.

"My friend Nyla," Dani said.

"Your . . . friend," he said, grinding his teeth so tight his jaw ached.

"Hi, Your Royal Highness," Nyla said, waving. Her smile dimmed when he didn't respond.

Instead, he gingerly maneuvered around the mess on the floor, trying not to touch any contaminated surface, until he reached his books. Rescuing them, and not caring one bit when her tablet fell flat on the counter, he shook his head in disgust at the flour and batter clinging to their spines.

He opened the drawer next to the stove and pulled out a hand towel. "You can't bake?"

Pausing in the act of repositioning the device, she seemed startled by his question. "I have the ability to bake, obvi. I'm just not good at it."

He delicately attempted to clean the book. "Then what in the hell possessed you to start now?"

"*The Great UK Baking Championship!*" she and Nyla said at the same time, although Dani said it with a "duh" tone while her friend's intonation was more resigned.

He knew the show; one couldn't live in the UK and not be aware of it.

"Bread week. It really is a fucking bitch," Dani said, picking up a miraculously unscathed champagne flute and drinking from it.

A bag of flour wasn't going to be the only thing to explode in this kitchen.

He knew he needed to calm down. He never let himself get this worked up. Over anything. But this woman had the uncanny ability to affect him like no one else.

"Where is Margery?"

He'd send his housekeeper to the store to get Dani any kind of bread she wanted if it meant this wouldn't happen again.

"Don't be mad at her. She offered to make this for me or even stay and watch, but I told her I wanted to do it myself." She bit her lower lip. "That might have been a mistake."

"You think?"

"Maybe I'm better at tarts? I'll see if Margery has any tips for me beforehand."

"Tarts?"

"Yes, that's what I'm making tomorrow."

Tomorrow?

A hiss followed by a gurgle emanated from the oven. He returned his gaze to her. "You plan to do this again?"

"Of course. Baking is one of those things you have to practice to actually get better at. Who knows when I'll have the time off again to do this? And it's such a nice kitchen."

He looked at the mess all around his "nice kitchen" and groaned. His life was being wrenched upside down. The queen was shoving him into the limelight and forcing him to host a woman he didn't know, a woman who couldn't be left to her own devices and who seemed intent on tearing his quiet, orderly existence into pieces. He was actually going to have to babysit her . . . if he wanted the house, which had been standing since 1774, to survive her visit.

Never mind that he had his own responsibilities.

His grumbling stomach reminded him that he was starving. How was he going to find something to eat in this mess?

The silence must've gone on for longer than was polite because Nyla piped from the tablet, "Don't worry, Your Royal Highness. Dani will clean this up."

She didn't have to keep calling him that. But she was American. He couldn't expect her to know the proper protocol.

Dani turned an incredulous look at her. "Excuse me? I don't clean."

"You don't bake, either, but that didn't seem to stop you," he said, before he could help himself.

She narrowed her gaze on him, and although irritated, he couldn't ignore the awareness that skimmed through him at her look.

A flush settled on her cheeks and she cleared her throat. "Fine. I'll take care of it."

"Wonderful. If only that solved my current problem," he muttered, turning away.

"What does that mean?"

"It means that it's going to take you a long time to clean this up and make it suitable for Margery to use. And I haven't eaten."

"Couldn't you just order something in? Get it delivered?"

He was surprised he hadn't burst a blood vessel. "No, I can't just have something delivered. In case you haven't noticed, we're not in the middle of London! We're out in the country."

In solitude, which he'd always loved.

Before now.

"I was just asking," she said, flicking her gaze upward.

"Quit playing, Dani. It's enough," Nyla said. "Your Royal Highness, your housekeeper left you a plate in the refrigerator."

Bless you, Margery. And Nyla.

Scowling, he crossed the room, staring at the charred mess through the oven door in distaste. Opening the refrigerator, he spied a plate on the shelf with a sandwich and a side of his favorites, truffle chips.

Grabbing it, he nodded his thanks to Nyla. He couldn't resist a glance at Dani, who was looking at him with a pained expression, but the moment she caught him staring, her back straightened and her mouth twisted.

She toasted him with her champagne. "Enjoy."

His jaw tightened and he left the kitchen, the sound of her sultry laughter following him.

"WHY WOULD YOU do that?" Nyla asked, an incredulous look on her face.

"I don't know," Dani said, her posture slumping as soon as it was clear he wasn't coming back.

She exhaled, the rush of breath actually blowing a curl off her forehead and distributing a puff of flour. She looked around at the mess. Nana would kick her ass. This man had allowed her to stay in his home, albeit begrudgingly, and she'd destroyed his kitchen.

She hadn't done it on purpose. Not that it was an accident. One didn't make this type of wreckage by accident. Rather, she hadn't done it maliciously.

It had taken Dani approximately three hours to run out of things to do.

She'd had good intentions. She'd taken a self-guided tour of the castle and marveled at the beautifully decorated rooms with their gorgeous furniture and museum-quality art and the number of staff she spied, both in the house and in the elaborate gardens.

Finding a lovely room filled with sunlight, she'd planned to while away the morning hours diving into the new memoir of one of the hottest pop divas in the game. Everyone had been raving about its realness and how the superstar finally answered the many questions about her infamous 2015 pool party, where it was alleged that all four members of her girl group had gotten pregnant.

By their personal trainer!

She'd given up after the first three chapters.

She'd tried to watch a few of the movies she'd downloaded, but they couldn't hold her attention, either. Why did men insist on writing women either as vapid boob carriers, constantly getting into trouble and requiring saving, or manipulative boob carriers out to break men's hearts or double-cross them? That's, of course, when they chose to write them at all.

She'd played some games on her phone, applied a face mask, even downloaded an app that promised to teach her Italian in fourteen days—!—but by lunchtime she was seriously considering a walk to the nearby village.

A walk!

What was she, sixty?

Around the time she began to ponder asking Margery for some cards or a puzzle, it had occurred to her that maybe the reason she hadn't taken a vacation wasn't that she was too busy but that she didn't know *how*. She'd been working, in some capacity, since she was thirteen years old. To save up money for herself or to lessen the time she spent feeling unwelcome in others' houses. Her work ethic was her one constant. It was all she knew.

And it was going to take more than declaring herself "on vacation" to make it so.

That's when she remembered she'd planned to use this time to work on her baking. Nana had been an incredible baker and she'd wanted to pass her knowledge on to Dani. But Dani had always put her off, assuming she'd have plenty of time later for those lessons.

She'd never regretted anything more.

On the rare occasions she found herself at home with a few free hours, she always put on an episode of her favorite baking show and attempted to make something similar to the contestants' creations, though she was absolutely terrible at it. At anything involved in the preparation of food, really. But something about the whir of the mixer and the kneading of dough always calmed her.

And suddenly all she'd wanted to do was bake bread.

Margery had set her up with the ingredients, shown her where the appliances were stored, and offered to stay and help. Dani had waved her away, knowing the other woman had several errands to run in town. Instead, she'd FaceTimed Nyla and roped her friend into the "adventure." Between the spirit of Nana and the recipes of Peter Nashville, the bread king, Dani was certain *this* time she'd create the bread, rolls, and muffins that would make Nana proud.

What she hadn't accounted for was how different it was over here. Back home, her kitchen was bright, airy, and spacious, like a set from a Nancy Meyers movie, which was the exact look she'd been going for. Here, though the house was large and lovely, the same emphasis wasn't placed on the kitchen being a showpiece. It was extremely functional, just smaller than she was used to. And the baking temperatures were Celsius not Fahrenheit. She knew that but had forgotten. The measurements were slightly off, the terminology kept tripping her up—cookie, biscuit, muffin, all different! Plus, maybe the flour?

Whatever the reason, nothing turned out the way she'd planned. Recipe after recipe, she'd followed the instructions to the letter—give or take—but instead of beautiful buns with chewy golden crusts and pillowy soft crumb, she'd ended up with burned, flat, dense projectiles of death.

Oh, and a mass that looked like a dick with a loaf-shaped ball sac.

Nothing that would earn Nana's respect.

And she'd ruined her host's kitchen in the process.

"Straight up, I thought he was going to have a heart attack," Nyla said, a smile breaking out on her face.

"I know, right?" Dani giggled. "And that muscle in his jaw started ticking like the turn signal on an old Chevy!"

They both burst out laughing, the amusement lightening the tense atmosphere.

"He had every right to be upset. Look at what you did to his kitchen."

"I know. I know." And Dani did. "Something about him just . . . aggravates me."

"You mean the way he doesn't fall at your feet like most men?"

"Well, I wouldn't say that," she huffed.

But it was true. He was aware of her, but he didn't let it affect his decisions. Instead, he continued to treat her as if she was a bother.

Maybe that's what bugged her. She knew that look. Had been on the receiving end of it often while growing up. Forced to stay with relatives and friends of her nana who barely had enough time, attention, space, and food for their own families, let alone a plus one. She'd come to despise that feeling of being unwanted. It was the one thing that drove her. That kept her going. The idea that she would never be made to feel that way again.

And here she was, a successful entertainer and entrepreneur and she was *still* getting served side-eye for being somewhere she wasn't appreciated.

"I mean, I get it," Nyla was saying. "Those pictures didn't do him justice. Even through the screen, I could sense it. The intensity. That man is fine with a capital, bolded, and italicized, thirty-six-point-type-size F!"

"Enough! Fuck. You think he's hot. Message received."

Nyla pursed her lips, but she continued. "You gotta think about this from his perspective. People don't live out there because they're extroverts. He's not used to having people foisted upon him and invading his home. You're the same way. How many people have actually been inside your places?"

Not many.

But Dani didn't want to consider the things she and the prince might have in common. She'd admitted her mistake. That was all she was willing to concede at the moment.

Nyla winced. "Despite what you told him, you're not doing this tomorrow, are you?"

"No." It was best to save her future forays into baking for when she was back in familiar surroundings.

"What are you going to do?"

"I don't know." But she needed to figure it out. Boredom wasn't her friend. "I'm really sad that one pastry didn't turn out, though. It looked so good on the show."

"Yours was worse than Sally's, and she came in last and got kicked off."

"Thanks."

"Anytime, sis," Nyla said cheekily. "You know, you could just ask Margery to make it for you. She was a sweetheart. I'm sure she wouldn't mind."

"*I* wanted to do it. And I will. This has to be the bottom. It can only get better, right?"

"One would hope."

Dani pushed away from the counter. "I should start cleaning this up."

"That's a good idea," Nyla said, moving her head as if trying to see the entire tableau through the screen. "It looks like it'll take you a while."

"Want to keep me company?"

"Uhhh, no. I've got better things to do than watch your tragic version of black Cinderella. Peace!"

Nyla threw up the deuces and disconnected the call.

Dani looked around. Some vacation this was turning out to be. She'd really lost her damned mind. This was a lot. Even for her.

She took a fortifying sip of champagne, donned the heavy-duty yellow rubber gloves, and started by tossing everything she'd baked into the trash. No one should be subjected to noxious nibbles.

Not even her host.

Probably.

The sink was filled with glass and ceramic mixing bowls of various sizes and discarded pans, all sacrificed on the altar of her baking ambitions. She removed everything from the basin, rinsing each item in hot water and setting it aside for proper cleaning later.

"'Tragic black Cinderella.' Good one, Ny," she muttered, laughing beneath her breath while she gathered the tools and cooking utensils she'd dirtied.

A scraping sound startled her and she almost dropped the bundle she held. Turning, she found Jameson standing there.

Scowling.

She inhaled several calming breaths to soothe her panicked heart, then carefully placed the pile next to the sink. "Come to yell at me some more?"

"No. Although I could." He motioned around the room. "But I thought you could use some help."

Was he for real? Or was this all part of his diabolical plan to get revenge by lulling her into a false sense of gratitude and then changing his mind?

"Why? I made the mess; I should have to clean it up."

"I know." Still, he grabbed the broom leaning against the wall, and started sweeping.

For a long time, the only sounds that filled the space were the skimming of bristles across the wooden floor, running water, and the clang of glass on glass.

You know what you have to do.

She sighed deeply and faced him. "I'm really sorry. I shouldn't have done this. I have no excuse except I was bored and still a little pissed at you."

When he didn't immediately respond, she turned back to the sink and grabbed the sponge, scouring the unlucky bowl with such ferocity she thought she'd scrub through the enamel.

He didn't have to accept her apology, but it was the polite thing to do!

"I haven't been a gracious host," he finally admitted. "In fact, I've been a right ass. I invited you to stay in my home and then behaved as if it were an imposition. This was between me and my grandmother. None of this was your fault. And I apologize."

Her mouth actually dropped open. She hadn't expected that at all. "I accept your apology."

"And I accept yours."

More sweeping and washing. Skimming and clanging.

Unable to resist any longer, she stole a look at him. Even doing chores, he was mesmerizing. She wondered if there were YouTube videos of hot guys doing mundane tasks. Folding towels. Making lists. Sweeping. Preferably shirtless.

She'd have to look into that.

Jameson's entry would be very popular. She was certainly getting tingles from watching him work. But his technique was a little off. He held the broom and dragged it toward him like . . . someone who'd never done it before!

Was this his first time?

He glanced up and halted midmotion. "Are you laughing at me?"

"Who, me? Nooo," she said. Though she definitely had been.

"If you'd rather do this yourself, I can—"

"No, no, no! You're doing a great job. Please continue."

She bit her lip and returned her attention to her own tasks, genuinely touched he was helping her when he didn't have to.

"You mentioned being bored," he said. His technique was jacked up, but his approach was methodical, moving the debris from the perimeter to a central pile. "I thought you came early to relax before the celebration?"

"I did. But I've been working since I was thirteen years old. It's a lot harder to turn it off than I thought."

"I know exactly what you mean," he muttered, bracing an arm on top of the broom and shoving a hand through his hair.

"Really? You've been working since you were thirteen?" she asked, not hiding her incredulity.

"Since I was born, technically. And I've never managed to fully turn it off."

That sounded dreadful! She guessed you could never make assumptions about someone else's experiences.

"I know the area seems remote, but one of the neighboring estates is open for tours, the village has some nice shops and pubs, and Birmingham isn't too far. There's plenty to see on campus."

She sprayed all-purpose cleaner on the stove top. "Sounds promising."

"The Palace would prefer you keep a low profile, but if you get bored enough that the thought of attempting those tarts seems appealing, I give you permission to risk it."

Dani laughed. "I'll keep that in mind. But I can assure you I'd have to be going stark raving mad to attempt anything in this kitchen ever again!"

"I'll tell Margery to keep watch for any wild eyes or twitching."

Their shared laughter cleared the air, leaving a companionable mood behind. "Good call."

"Can I ask you a question?"

Dani finished wiping off the stove top and bent to run the rag over the oven door. "Why not?"

"This may seem impertinent but . . . how did you get batter on the ceiling?"

How did she *what*?

She looked up and sure enough . . .

"Oh my God! If my nana saw that . . ." She moaned and straightened, covering her face.

"Your nana?"

"My grandmother. She raised me. My sad attempts at baking are a tribute to her."

"I'm sure she'd give you high marks for effort. You should ask her for tips when you get back home."

"I wish. She passed away when I was younger."

"Oh. Well . . . I'm sorry." He resumed sweeping. "If she raised you but died when you were younger, what happened next?"

Grief lodged itself in her throat. She swallowed. "Other family took me in."

She saw more questions forming, questions she had no desire to answer. In an effort to preempt the coming inquisition, she removed her gloves and tossed them next to the sink. Channeling

Simone Biles, she braced her hands on the island and hopped up onto the counter.

Jameson watched her warily. "What are you doing?"

"I can't leave it up there. I've got to try and wipe it off."

"The staff can take care of it tomorrow."

She wasn't a stranger to having household help, but the number of people he had working for him was mind-boggling. Butlers, maids, footmen, dishwashers, valets . . . If she needed someone to wipe her ass, she was sure some unlucky person held that position, too.

And that was just inside the house.

When she'd asked Margery about it, the housekeeper had first informed her that Jameson actually kept one of the *smaller* staffs in the royal family and, second, explained that the term "household," when discussing royalty, actually referred to the administrative departments that supported members of the royal family, like their private secretaries, personal assistants, and communication secretaries. Some members lived where their household was based, but many did not. As the Duke of Wessex, Jameson lived at Primrose Park and chose to base his household here.

Listening to it all, Dani found it impossible not to feel a little like Alice falling through the rabbit hole into Wonderland.

"Oh, so *now* you offer up your staff?" she joked. "No, I can get it. I feel bad enough. I don't need them to know how much I sucked."

"We're in such a good place, I hate to ruin it by telling you the staff is already talking about it."

Great!

"They would never say anything to you, of course."

"No, but they might spit in my food."

"Never," he said, looking scandalized.

She laughed. "I've got this. It shouldn't be that hard."

She squinted up at the splotch. When she reached for it, the tip of her middle finger barely grazed the hardened batter. She rose up on tiptoe.

"Christ! Duchess—"

She heard the broom clang on the floor, then felt his hand haltingly touch her thigh. Where his skin met hers . . . an explosion of sparks that sent goosebumps down her leg. She shook the affected limb, not to dislodge his touch but in response to the unexpected sensation. Still, it had the effect of the former. Balanced on one foot, with no support, she felt herself flailing.

"I've got you!"

One strong hand squeezed her upper thigh and the other took a firm hold on her ass. She froze and her pussy spasmed in anticipation.

He's squeezing your butt. Big deal. Not like it's the first time that's *happened.*

She licked her lips. "Thanks."

"My pleasure. I mean, glad I could help. Here." He held out a hand and helped her down.

They both broke contact the moment it was physically safe to do so.

She looked around, trying to ignore the awareness hovering thick between them. "I think we got a good amount done. I can handle the rest."

"Are you certain?" Solicitous words even as he was already backing toward the door.

"Yeah. Thanks for coming back to help . . . and for the conversation."

"Of course. Well"—he picked up the broom and propped it against the wall—"good night, Duchess."

"Good night."

He turned and left the kitchen. She slowly counted to twenty, and when he didn't return, she sagged back against the island and fanned herself with her hands.

A sexy prince who's a prick?

Easy to resist.

A sexy, considerate one who looked at her as if he wondered what she tasted like?

Damn, she was in trouble.

Chapter Eleven

"Under the light of awareness, the energy of irritation can be transformed into an energy which nourishes."
—Thich Nhat Hanh

Jameson had been so angry after he'd come home last night to find his kitchen ruined. It was like some twisted version of the rock star stereotype. Instead of destroying hotel rooms with sex, drugs, and alcohol, she'd decimated his kitchen with flour, baked goods, and attitude.

But it hadn't taken him long to recognize he'd acted like a prick. Sure, she'd made a mess, but he didn't have to respond the way he had. So, he'd gone back to apologize . . . and had gotten more than he'd bargained for. His anger hadn't diminished his attraction to her. If anything, the encounter took his feelings a layer deeper, because he'd gotten to know a little more about her. As a person and not just a performer.

When he'd come downstairs that morning to find Margery making his breakfast, he wouldn't have been able to tell a baking holy war had broken out the night before if he hadn't been there to witness it. His kitchen was spotless. The countertops gleamed, the floor and walls were clear, and there were no dishes in the sink.

There was a brisk knock on his partially opened office door and Rhys stuck his head in.

"Heading to a meeting, but checking to make sure you're still coming to the faculty party tonight?"

Jameson frowned. "The faculty party?"

Rhys's brows rose in surprise. "Yes. It's been on the calendar for a month."

"Right." Jameson massaged his brow and nodded. "Sure."

"That was convincing." Rhys stepped in the office. "How's your houseguest settling in?"

"Making herself at home," he said, regaling Rhys with an account of the night before.

Rhys laughed. "I would've given my left sac to see your face when you walked in. Nix that. I wouldn't. But I bet it was hilarious."

"I can assure you, at the time, it wasn't."

Rhys scratched his cheek. "Destroying your kitchen was unexpected, but she was bound to do something after the way you greeted her. You told her to call you Your Royal Highness."

Jameson winced. It sounded even worse than he remembered. He wished he hadn't felt the burning need to share their initial interaction with his friend.

"I thought you had a meeting to attend?"

"They can start without me. I'm sure you're not following the coverage—"

"That would be the correct assumption—"

"—but your family has been getting a lot of praise for inviting Duchess to perform. They're marveling at the queen's inclusion and the notion that the royal family may be catching up with modern times." Rhys eased into a chair.

Bullshit.

"What's funny is that none of you had any idea what you were doing."

Jameson shook his head. "That can never come out. Do you understand?"

Rhys straightened. "Whoa! Mate! I know. I would never. You know that, right?"

Jameson did know. Now. But in the beginning, he'd kept Rhys at a distance as he'd learned to do with everyone else in his life. He'd subjected the other man to all the usual loyalty tests, and Rhys had never let him down.

One night, over a pint, Rhys had turned to him and said, "Enough. I don't want to hear any more about your secret skill making your stomach do weird belly rolls or that the toes on your left foot are webbed. Whether it's true or false, I'm not going to the press. I want to be your friend, but I'm not going to stick around and be bloody tested all the time!"

And that had been that.

Jameson nodded and Rhys relaxed, tension easing from his body. His brown eyes lit with interest. "What's she like?"

"That wasn't in the coverage?"

"Fuck off. You know what I'm asking. Is she as hot in person as she is in her videos?"

Just thinking about Dani's videos and what he'd done to himself had Jameson fighting for control.

He cleared his throat. "I guess."

"You guess? Did you see the one where she stuck out her tongue and licked the screen?"

Jameson swallowed. He hadn't and he wasn't sure he should.

Rhys narrowed his eyes. "What's wrong with you?"

"Nothing."

The other man leaned forward and studied him. "You're look-ing a little peaked. Your eyes are bloodshot, and you have shadows beneath them. Have you been drinking already?"

"No! I may not have been getting enough sleep."

"Because of her?"

"Why would it be her? I barely know her."

"I can't imagine a man alive who would have her staying in his house and not use the chance to get to know her."

Jameson exhaled and ran a hand through his hair. The woman was so . . . present. She was one small person, but she somehow managed to take up a large amount of space. She was everywhere, which made her impossible to ignore.

"Is the attraction mutual?"

"Who said I was attracted to her?"

"I mean, you're not hideous," Rhys continued, as if he hadn't heard Jameson. "You've made the unofficial listing of hottest pro-fessor every year you've been here."

Jameson scoffed. "That's a low bar to hurdle. My only competi-tion is Benton, Stolberg, and you."

"You didn't answer my question."

He remembered the way she'd looked at him. *When I was told the prince had invited me, you definitely weren't what I had in mind.*

"Maybe. But it's irrelevant. You know why I'm doing this. Be-sides, I've been given a separate mission to keep her away from Julian."

"One way to do that would be to get involved with her yourself."

One way, but not the best way. Though his body liked that idea very much.

"It's only been a couple of days and she has you bothered. She's going to be at Primrose Park for two weeks. Secluded. Alone. Just the two of you—"

"And a house full of staff."

Rhys waved that off. "What are you going to do?"

"Keep my distance, as much as possible. Once the festivities begin, it won't be a problem."

"And is that why you're like this?" Rhys gestured to him. "Because you wish you'd made another decision?"

Sometimes Rhys was a little more perceptive than Jameson wanted.

"No. This is about being forced to host someone in my space when I wasn't expecting to. You know I'm not good at being social."

Massive understatement.

"Between our blowout in the kitchen last night and yesterday morning—"

"What happened yesterday morning?"

He winced. "I insulted her over breakfast."

Rhys looked at his watch. "Dammit. I have to go. But I want to hear that story. Save it for tonight."

"I'm glad my trauma provides you cheap entertainment."

Rhys laughed and opened the door in time to see a young man and woman stop right outside.

"This is it. Professor Lloyd's office." The student adjusted his backpack. "Is there anything else I can do for you?"

A hood hid most of the young woman's face. Her hair was in two thick blond braids, and large black eyeglass frames couldn't hide her light brown eyes and full lips . . .

There was something very familiar about her mouth.

"No. This is good," she said, in an accent that was sort of British and an appalling mixture of different areas, most notably Birmingham and Wales with a touch of RP. "Thank you."

Rhys shot wide eyes at Jameson over his shoulder and mouthed,

"Dude has no chance!" before taking off with a cheery "See you tonight!"

Jameson rose and approached the door, his attention back on the couple. The young woman was heading toward him when the young man reached out and snagged the strap of her bag. Her eyes met Jameson's and he saw something like impatience flicker in their depths, but she looked away.

Heat settled in his midsection and his cock hardened. What the fuck? He wasn't some teenager. He didn't get uncontrollable erections. In fact, the only time it had happened to him recently had been with his houseguest. But—

"Can you do something for me?" the young man asked her.

"What?"

"Can I have your number?"

She laughed. "You're cute. Where are you going now?"

He knew that laugh. Had heard it the night before in his messy kitchen.

Dani?

"Meeting some friends at the Guild."

"After I talk to Professor Lloyd, I'll come find you."

"Cool." The guy took a step away and then turned back. "Are you sure we haven't met before? You seem so familiar to me."

"You say that to all the girls, don't you?" She waved off his denials. "It's fine. I have one of those faces."

"No you don't," he blurted out before realizing what he'd said. He paled and began backpedaling. "Yeah, I'll be over . . . no rush . . . take your time . . ."

Jameson hated him in that moment. Hated that this boy was also affected by her. Because it meant he wasn't anything special. She caused a stir in everyone when she set out to do so.

Dani turned back to him. "May I?"

He stood back and gestured for her to enter. She passed and his body tightened.

It *was* her. His body had recognized her before his brain did.

Shutting the door, he went around his desk and took a seat. His office wasn't large, but he'd been fortunate to obtain one with a window. The sun broke through the clouds and brightened the space. Or was it just her presence?

She sat in the chair Rhys had occupied and crossed her bare legs, the chunky motorcycle boot on her left foot dangling.

He frowned. "What do you think you're doing? You shouldn't be here. What if someone recognized you?"

Dani pulled the hood off her head. "Do you think this is my first time at the rodeo?"

Her fake accent had disappeared as quickly as it had come on. She removed her glasses, and even with the different hair and eye color, and the makeup that hinted at a change in face shape, it was her. Still gorgeous, just slightly different.

"I don't know what that means."

"It means I know how to disguise myself. I do it all the time."

"You do? Because there are hundreds of pictures of you out and about."

"First my Insta and now you're looking me up online?" she asked with a coy smile and a dip of her lashes.

"Of course. Did you think I'd invited you to perform without doing my research?"

"I give the paps those pictures so they think they're actually doing their job. But most of the time when I go out, it's in one disguise or another. I like them."

Members of the royal family didn't engage in disguises. It was part of the unspoken pact between them and the people.

"What are you doing here? Is there something you needed?"

"Not really. I was bored and since you pretty much banned me from baking, I knew I needed to get out of the house. You mentioned the campus last night and I wanted to check it out, so I had Amos drop me off." She toyed with a stack of papers on the edge of his desk. "You're very popular."

It was nice to hear. He worked hard to make his lectures fun and informative. He really wanted his students to see philosophy the way—

He frowned. "How do you know that?"

She shrugged. "I may have asked around."

"How long have you been here?"

"Long enough. Of course, it doesn't hurt that they think of you as Sexy Wexy."

He winced. He hated that nickname. And it wasn't even his. The press had first used it to refer to his father, who was given the title Duke of Wessex when he married Calanthe. As pictures surfaced of Jameson when he'd come of age, some enterprising reporter had unearthed the dreaded moniker. He'd thought it was starting to die down, but if she'd heard it . . .

"I don't bring my royal life here. I've tried really hard to not let it affect my work."

"I understand. Trust and believe."

She had this habit of saying a phrase as if it were an entire sentence or thought that he would understand.

"You shouldn't be here."

"Why?"

"You know why. If you're discovered—"

"I won't be. Chill. People see what they want to see. I promise you no one expects to find Duchess at a British university in the middle of nowhere."

"Are you really going to the Guild?"

"The what?"

"The Guild of Students. The student union building over by the main campus entrance. You told that guy you would meet him there when you were done here."

"Oh. No."

"But you told him you would."

"So? How would you have me handle it? Give him my actual number? Give him a fake number? Tell him no and embarrass him in front of you? I won't show up. Big deal. I'm just one of thousands of girls on this campus."

Nothing about her was like anyone else, but he didn't plan on telling her that.

"Just steer clear of that part of campus and you should be fine."

"Not a problem."

"Anything else?"

"Are you trying to get rid of me?"

"Yes."

A smile teased her lips. "Do you tutor athletes?"

"What?" She scrambled his brain.

"The guy who was in here when we showed up."

"That wasn't a student. That was a friend. Professor Rhys Barnes."

"If I knew college professors looked like you two, I might have attended."

"You didn't go?"

"School wasn't my thing. I needed to be a success immediately. College was going to take too long."

Needed not wanted. Interesting.

Her nail scraped the arm of her chair. "I guess you were expected to go to college."

"Not traditionally. In the past, we were expected to begin royal duties after school. But I've always wanted to pursue higher education. I'm sure my grandmother thought I'd do my four years and be done with it. She never expected me to stay."

Her laughter jolted his pulse. "It's so weird to hear you refer to the queen of England by something as normal as 'grandmother.'"

"It's weird that I'm more comfortable thinking of her as the queen of England and not as my grandmother."

When her brow furrowed and her smile dimmed slightly, he realized he'd revealed too much.

"I chose a different path, one that allowed me to follow my passions. And for that forbearance I have my mother and my grandfather to thank."

"Prince John. You must've been extremely close. Are you looking forward to the celebration?" she asked, her gaze open and curious, indicating she was genuinely interested in his response.

But he wasn't ready to share. Even if he found himself enjoying their conversation.

"We all are," he answered, noncommittally. He toyed with a stack of books on his desk. "Is there anything else? I do have some exams I need to grade before I leave."

"Yeah." She put her feet up. "What are you and Professor Thor doing tonight?"

The Norse god of lightning? A pretty apt description of Rhys.

"We have to attend a faculty get-together."

"A get-together? Like a party?" she asked, her hybridized British pronunciation appearing again.

As a natural-born Brit and a member of the royal family, he couldn't encourage the use of that accent. It wasn't right.

He stared at her.

"Damn. You're no fun." She let her feet fall with a thud and straightened. "Look, I didn't mean to bother you. I just needed to get out and be around people."

"Weren't you looking for privacy and time to unwind?"

"I was. I am. I mean, it all sounds good in theory, but . . ." She heaved a sigh and stood, smoothing a hand down the scrap of patterned fabric masquerading as a sundress. "I'll go."

"Duchess?"

She turned. Was she aware of the heart-stoppingly stunning figure she made, framed in his doorway, centered in the sun's spotlight?

Of course she was.

"The Botanical Gardens are on the other side of campus. Many find them charming, with footpaths, bridges, and tunnels that visitors enjoy exploring. If you're looking for tranquility, it's the perfect spot."

"That sounds lovely. I'll check it out."

He cleared his throat. "Yes, well . . ."

Their gazes met and held for one, two, three heated moments before she glanced away.

"Have fun tonight." She hefted her bag on her shoulder. "I'll see you when you get home."

Unexpected warmth suffused him at her use of the word "home."

He extinguished the warmth before it gained any traction.

Chapter Twelve

"*Leave that good girl on read / Fantasize / Spread those thighs / Watch me bob my head . . .*"

—Duchess, "Azz for Days"

Dani tugged the pillow closer and shifted on the surprisingly comfortable love seat, reaching for the nearby flute of bubbly. The laptop screen, situated on a delicate table she'd pulled from the other side of the room, was showing the fourth and final wedding.

"Wait, Hugh, you're going to marry *her*? What are you thinking? You're just giving up?"

"Duchess? Are you in here? Who are you talking to?"

She froze at the sound of Jameson's voice coming from somewhere behind her.

Shit!

Uncurling her legs and pushing the small blanket to the side, she neatened her shirt and ran her fingers through her hair.

What are you doing? Stop primping. He doesn't care. He's made it clear he doesn't find you the least bit attractive.

Which was fine. Actually, it was better than fine. It was perfect. She didn't expect anything to happen. But she could still look great while nothing happened. Because, though she would never admit it to another soul, she hated that he didn't seem to respond to her the way other men did. Just once, she wanted him to want her . . . so she could reject him.

Be like "In your face, Princey!"

It was a childish but accurate representation of her feelings.

"What's going on? I thought I heard voices?"

She tapped the track pad on her laptop, pausing the movie. "No, it's just me. Margery and the rest of the household staff retired hours earlier."

"I see you found the old drawing room."

She had. When she'd first come upon it during her tour the day before, it had been the closest thing to a room at her house that she could find. Large, with three floor-to-ceiling bay windows, the high ceilings and light wall coloring meshed beautifully with the vibrant patterns, sturdy, gleaming antiques, and dark wooden floors.

She shifted to glance at him over the back of the sofa and involuntarily sucked in a breath. Even with his face in the shadows and wearing dark jeans, a chambray shirt, and an ivory cardigan, he was headier than the champagne she'd been drinking.

Dani had admired the way the fabrics sat on his frame when she'd visited the campus that afternoon. Without seeing the labels, she could tell his clothes were impeccably made. At the beginning of her career she hadn't known shit. Hell, the only way she could tell an item of clothing cost a lot of money was if it was a brand name or had a logo on it. If the jeans didn't have something conspicuous that proclaimed what maker they were from, she assumed they were "no name." The kinds of clothes she'd worn most of her childhood. The ones that never quite fit right, irritated her skin, or subjected her to cruel teasing.

With money came stylists and designers dressing her, and she began learning there was more to quality than a label. In fact, some well-known brands used inexpensive fabrics and slapped their high-end markers on them for the higher profit margins. Quality was about the fit and feel of the fabrics, the way they draped on the body. There wasn't a label in sight on Jameson's clothes, but she could tell from the way the cardigan hugged his broad shoulders and his jeans rested on his hips and cupped his ass, they were some of the best-quality clothes money could buy.

In the ongoing silence she realized he might be waiting for a response.

"I didn't know it was 'old.' Is there a newer one I should be using?"

"No. This actually is the drawing room my mother used."

"Pretty big space for arts and crafts."

He laughed. "Drawing room, as in a sitting room for the lady of the house to use while visiting with friends or intimate acquaintances."

Why in the world would her face heat at the thought of this room and the term "intimate"?

He leaned against the doorjamb and shoved his hands into his pockets. The change in his stance allowed the soft light from the hall to illuminate his features.

She narrowed her eyes. His lids were slightly lowered, his dark hair was tousled, and his posture wasn't as rigid as usual. In fact, he looked—

"Are you drunk?"

He frowned and wrinkled his nose, as if her question offended him. "Of course not. I don't get drunk. But I did have a few drinks."

Ahhhh . . .

He straightened and strolled farther into the room. When he reached the back of the sofa where she was sitting, he stroked his chin and leaned forward to stare at the screen and the image frozen upon it.

"Is that *Four Weddings and a Funeral*?"

Embarrassment crawled over her. He could tell that, just from four people standing outside of a stone church?

She should've closed the damned top.

"No," she said, reaching out to rectify that situation.

"Don't shut it." He came around and plopped down next to her. "And, yes, it is. This is the scene where his brother interrupts the wedding."

The love seat that had been the perfect size for her to sit with her legs curled beside her seemed far too snug and cozy when shared with his large frame.

Her skin tingled and butterflies fluttered awake in her belly.

This would not do! She wanted him to be affected by *her*, not the other way around.

"Spoiler alert," she teased, trying for that duck-above-water calm.

"Sorry. Have you never seen this movie before?"

"No. But Nyla mentioned it when I told her I was coming to London. Said I'd enjoy it."

"I'll let you in on a secret." He lowered his voice and leaned toward her. His fresh masculine scent tinged with the heavy sweetness of whisky wafted over her, and she shivered. "You don't have to wait until you're in England to watch British movies. I'm pretty sure this is available in the States."

"Ha ha. Very funny." She dislodged a pillow and hit him with it. "This isn't my first trip here, y'know, but usually when I come, it's for work. I'm basically in and out. I don't have the time to sit around and watch movies."

He nodded toward her computer. "Are you enjoying it?"

"I am. It's funny to see a young Hugh Grant. I know who he is, of course. I watched him in that one series on HBO and the Padding-ton Bear movie. Here, he's so bumbling and cute. I can see what the fuss was all about. But dude needed a haircut."

"You should see pictures of some of the royals during that time. Julian attempted that look. Claimed it got him laid."

Dani glanced at Jameson sharply. No one would ever set their mouth to call her a prude, but hearing him say "laid" felt outrageous. Sinful and decadent.

She looked away from him and lifted her hand to her neck, the pads of her fingers noting the rapid beat of her pulse.

"Speaking of hair, Andie MacDowell's curls are gorgeous! But he should've gotten together with Fi. They're way more appropriate."

"Really? Why?"

"The American—what's her name? Carrie—is too different. But he and Fi had a lot in common. They had a great connection and they'd been friends for years. She knew the good and bad of him and still loved him. Carrie was too flighty. Plus, who is she? We get to know almost nothing about her. I don't know whether to blame her acting choices or the screenplay."

"You mustn't say that in public. The screenwriter is beloved by many here," Jameson said. "Have you seen some of his other films?"

Dani liked movies, but she wouldn't call herself a movie buff. She didn't go around collecting information like who directed this movie or who the cinematographer was. "I don't know. What's he done?"

"*Notting Hill, Love Actually*—"

"Dang! *Love Actually* is my jam! I watch it every year!"

A smile curved his lips. "You have some very amusing sayings. 'Dang.' What is 'dang'?"

She laughed, the sound of his posh British accent saying "dang" too much for her to handle.

"Dang is a noncurse-word way to say 'damn.'"

"Why not just say 'damn'?"

She shrugged. "I don't know."

But that wasn't true. She *did* know. She'd been lulled into comfort. For a second she'd been Dani and not Duchess.

He shifted and draped an arm along the back of the sofa, the fabric of his jeans bunching on his thighs. His fingers brushed her shoulder in a leisurely, unhurried motion that blazed through the material to brand her skin.

Moisture flooded her mouth.

"I've listened to your songs. You don't have a problem saying curse words."

"No, I don't," she said, mesmerized by blue eyes that appeared to gleam beneath lowered lids.

He reached over and swiped his thumb across her lower lip. "There are times I find it inconceivable that those words would come out of *this* mouth."

The action, so carnal and . . . baller, was at odds with the man she'd thought he was.

Heat settled seductively between her thighs.

"What words?" she asked, her breathing growing shallow.

"Curse words. Profane words. Dirty words."

"Don't I look like someone who would say those words?" she whispered, surprised by the effort that simple act took.

"Yes. And no."

Confusion shaded with anger and threatened to burst the sensual bubble. "What does that mean?"

"When you're dressed in a red leather corset with garters and fishnets, strutting around onstage, you definitely look like a woman who can say and do exactly what she wants."

Her heart stuttered in her chest. That was the outfit she'd worn for the Billboard Music Awards. He'd watched her performances. And from the tone of his voice, he seemed to have liked what he saw.

Pleasure flamed her insides.

"But," he continued, "sitting here, with your hair falling around your shoulders, wearing leggings, this unbelievably soft jumper, and tucked under a blanket, you don't look like someone who would say those words."

"I don't?"

He shook his head. "No. Although you do look like someone I'd like to do those things to."

Her breath abandoned her.

"What are we going to do?" he asked.

"About what?"

He moaned low. "Us. This . . . thing between us."

His words left her dazed. Jameson was a professor and a real-life prince, yet he had Ja Morant on the court-worthy moves. This man, with his cardigans and rare philosophy books, shouldn't have the power to stoke her thirst to dehydration-level like this.

She leaned away from him. "I don't know what you're talking about."

"Yes, you do. Aren't you tired of fighting it?"

She was, but she didn't like the fact that he'd caught on to what she was feeling. Or that he'd spoken the words out loud.

"But you're probably used to it. Because most men respond this way to you, so this . . . ache is nothing new?"

Dani shook her head. "You don't know me."

"You're right. I don't. But it doesn't matter. Because when you're near I can't think or focus or—"

He cupped the back of her head, pulling her close, and she didn't fight him, her gaze on his firm lips.

Not as full as she usually preferred.

But when they touched hers, all rational thoughts boarded a nonstop flight back to the States. Light brushes and delicate nips that evolved into a panty-drenching lip-lock, his kiss was the perfect balance of curiosity and audacity. Like a man given an exquisite treasure that he revered but knew he sure as hell deserved.

His tongue slid across the seam of her lips, and, as if calibrated to his particular pressure, she opened for him, granting him access. A moan rent the air and she couldn't tell which of them had made the needy sound. She lifted trembling fingers to the dark strands nestled at the back of his head and let them delve into the silky richness.

Her heart pounded in her chest with bruising force and her pulse thundered in her ears. He tasted so good. So sweet. And his tongue? It could be certified as a pleasure stick. She tangled with it, sucked on it, as if it was all that stood between her and the loss of sustenance.

What could he do with that tongue between her thighs?

Her clit pulsed as if interested in the answer. *Yes, bitch, let's find out.*

Aching to be closer, she pushed aside the blanket and scrambled onto his lap, straddling him. This time he was the source of the sound of pleasure, his hands hot as they caressed her back and pressed her into his chest.

He was so goddamned strong, his arms like bands of steel encircling her. And that hint of brute power, so at odds with his scholarly demeanor, sent a primitive flood of wetness to her core—

To be met by the hard ridge of his erection thrust against her.

The frenzied fog of passion in her mind coalesced into one clear, crystalline, overriding thought.

I need him inside of me.

As if he'd heard her intention, and to foreshadow what might come, he cupped her ass and squeezed, lifting his hips to grind his cock in the crevice between her thighs. She threw her head back, Technicolor stars bursting behind her eyelids. His lips traversed the column of her neck, leaving tiny rises of ecstasy in their wake.

"God, you feel amazing." His warm breath tickled her ear.

She shivered. "And we're just getting started."

He trailed his fingers along the skin at her waist before lifting her shirt over her head and tossing it aside. He buried his face between her breasts and inhaled. "I've been aching for these for so long."

Say what now?

Had she heard him correctly? He'd been aching for *her* breasts? What did that mean? And for how long?

But then he took one pebbled peak into his hot mouth and nothing else mattered except chasing the sensation to its inevitable conclusion.

Liquid heat wound its way to the hub of all desire at her core. Following that heat, he slid a hand into her elastic waistband, between her thighs, and inserted one long, elegant finger into her. She arched her back, forcing her nipple farther into his mouth.

"You're so wet," he murmured against her skin.

She was and she wanted . . . "More."

He slid a second digit into her, and she rode his fingers the way she hoped to ride his cock.

"That's it, love. That's it . . . Do you like that?" he asked, his tone raw and wanton.

"Fuck yeah."

His eyes darkened and he took her mouth in a hard kiss that threatened to splinter her soul.

"You still want more?" he panted.

"Do you have more?" she breathed.

"Fuck yeah," he said, tossing her words back at her.

Her pussy throbbed at his response. Leaning back, her breathing frantic and driven by a mind-numbing, all-consuming passion she hadn't experienced in a long time, she tackled the button on his jeans. "Condom?"

The fingers gripping her hips flexed. "What?"

"Do you have a condom?"

He stiffened. "No."

Button undone, she pressed her lips to his neck and inhaled. He smelled so good. Damn. Her lashes fluttered as lust ripped through her with dizzying speed. She needed to be closer, wanted to curl her body around his like a python claiming its next victim. "I didn't mean here. Up in your room?"

He shook his head and sagged back against the love seat. "No. I don't have any. It's been . . . a while."

Through the haze of her longing, she finally caught the clue being lobbed in her direction.

No condom? No sex.

Fuck!

Lifting her head, she shifted until she was sitting on the cushion next to him, her legs still sprawled across his lap. He draped an arm over them and threw his head back.

She stared at him. It should be a sin to be that gorgeous. His cheeks were flushed and his lashes hid his eyes. This wasn't how she'd wanted things to end. She'd hoped sex would ease the attraction she felt. Instead she was left with a dissatisfied ache she'd have to satisfy later on her own. What was worse was that the interlude had only heightened her taste for him.

And her thirst for more.

He exhaled audibly. "I'm sorry."

The heat of his hard cock burned against her skin. She swallowed. "It's okay."

"No. I shouldn't have . . . Excuse me."

He gently moved her legs and stood, stuffing his cock back in his pants, and leaving the room.

What in the fuckety fuck?

She couldn't believe this was happening. Earlier today, the way he'd tried to get rid of her, she'd thought he hated her. And now . . .

He could still hate you. But this proves he isn't as immune to you as you thought. He's, in fact, like every other guy.

A frisson of disappointment shot through her at the notion, and she didn't understand why.

Chapter Thirteen

"A traitor is everyone who does not agree with me."

—George III

Even an early-morning summons from the queen couldn't pull Jameson's attention away from what had happened with Dani.

His cock stirred thinking about last night. The feel of her. The smell of her. Her taste.

He'd been imagining it since the first time he saw her, and if he were honest with himself, he had to admit the craving had intensified with each encounter. But now, his need had been assuaged. He'd kissed her. Touched her. Breathed her in. He'd satisfied his curiosity and could get back to normal, making her remaining time here much easier to tolerate.

He'd tried to approach it with her before he left for the palace.

"About last night," he began, clearing his throat.

She hadn't even looked up from her phone. "We don't have to talk about it. We made a mistake. Thankfully, it didn't go any further. No reason to make it more than it was."

It was exactly what he'd planned to say. More or less. And yet he didn't like hearing it from her. Instinct urged him to argue with her.

Be quiet, you git. You got what you wanted with no histrionics, no issues. How often has that happened for you in the past?

Never. He didn't engage in one-night stands. He dated. But he always found it challenging to separate those who were interested in him from those who were interested only in his title. The relationship would be going well and then the woman would start dropping hints about meeting the family or asking to accompany him to certain high-profile events. One woman even contacted the media, offering herself as a source since she was "the girlfriend of Prince Jameson."

But he was good now. The situation with Dani was settled.

"Her Majesty the Queen," the footman announced.

Jameson smoothed a hand down his thigh and glanced at his watch.

Why did he continue being on time when no one else in this blasted building offered him the same courtesy?

He stood and bowed deeply as his grandmother entered, dressed more casually than before, in a long black pleated skirt, white blouse, and light blue cardigan.

"Things are going well," she stated as she took a seat.

On its face, a very benign statement, but Jameson could see the glint of excitement in her eyes.

And she had every right to be elated.

The coverage about the tribute celebration had been exceptional, from excitement about the various events to glowing reviews of the concert's lineup and stories about Prince John and his history of charitable giving. She couldn't have orchestrated a more positive response from the media or the public. Any stories about royal children's screwups or turmoil amongst the queen's siblings had been buried by an avalanche of agreeable press.

He settled across from her. "The reception has been affirming."

"I'll say. During my weekly meeting with Hammond, he didn't make his usual unsubtle digs about the uselessness of the monarchy. He even admitted that the upcoming celebration was bringing a favorable light to all things British."

A slight smile while mentioning the Prime Minister? Jameson had never seen the queen so giddy.

It was unnerving.

"My plan is working. Now more than ever, it's important we keep this momentum going. This entire celebration has to go off without a hitch."

If Louisa's persistence and doggedness in dealing with him was any indication, it would.

"I've been thinking of other ways to celebrate Grandfather, and I'd like to create an award in his honor."

His grandmother blinked and stared at him for several long moments. "Tell me more."

"It would be an annually awarded monetary prize for work in the field of environmental studies, aiming for the prestige of the Nobel Prizes. It's a lofty goal but achievable, especially since there is no current Nobel category for environmentalism."

"I like it, and I think John would have, too. Keep me updated."

"I will."

So far, so good.

"The celebration isn't the only thing getting rave reviews. Your first few interviews have been praised by everyone."

Once he'd accepted he would have to participate, Jameson had approached his duties with the same intensity and attention to detail as he did his work at the university. He didn't enjoy the production or the scrutiny, but since his name and image were going to be used, he'd give the celebration his full effort.

As expected, his profile had increased more than he was com-

fortable with. In response, the Palace had dispatched additional
security to cover his estate and the campus and to accompany him
when he traveled in the city. It was as if all the years he'd worked so
hard to maintain an uninteresting persona had been undone.

Stories about his father were in heavy rotation but now they were
spun to reflect positively on Jameson.

"The Better Wessex? Will Jameson Prove He's Royal Material?"

"From His Father's Ashes: A Prince Is Born!"

"Here Comes the Bride? With Imogen Itching to Get Hitched,
Will This Wessex Settle Down?"

Fortunately his mother was at the tail end of her travels. She'd
been subjected to a marked rise in interactions with the tabloid
media while abroad, their obscene innuendos designed to provoke
her for a more salable picture or video, but it was nowhere near
what she'd be facing when she returned to London. The Palace had
promised more protection would meet her plane when she landed.

"I've been doing my best."

"You're succeeding. And the . . . entertainer you chose? How is
she settling in at Primrose Park?"

Though her tone remained pleasant, his grandmother's gaze
sharpened.

"We've managed to make it work."

"I have to admit I was surprised when Louisa informed me of
your choice."

So was he. But he knew he should probably keep that tidbit to
himself.

"When I'd suggested picking younger acts, I was thinking of one
of those girl singers or maybe a boy band. There's been some concern about the propriety of her inclusion; however, the response
has been mostly positive. Interesting that someone like her would
garner such praise."

He bristled at the distaste evident in her voice.

Why? You thought the same thing. And you were worse, because you essentially said it to Dani's face.

The door opened and Louisa breezed in with a curtsy. "Ma'am. Your Royal Highness. I apologize for my delay. I was in a meeting with the executive director of Bloom Urban."

Marina waved a hand. "I was informing Jameson about the response to his rapper."

"Yes. Her approval rating is through the roof with the young crowd. There has been some pushback about her image and whether she's an appropriate role model for women, but for the most part, people think it's exciting that the monarchy has chosen someone so popular yet edgy." Louisa grinned. "They've been saying there may be hope for the royal family."

A slight tightening of her expression was the only indication of the queen's displeasure with that response.

"We could use that to our advantage. She offered to make some pre-event appearances. We should set something up. The press is eager for anything that has to do with her."

Jameson brightened. If the Palace agreed to use her for press events, keeping her whereabouts a secret would no longer be necessary. She wouldn't have to remain at Primrose Park, and he'd be spared the sweet temptation of her presence.

But what about Julian? And keeping Dani out of his clutches?

He couldn't concern himself with his uncle. It was an issue of self-preservation.

What happened to things getting "back to normal, making her remaining time here much easier to tolerate"?

Oh, sod off!

But the queen shook her head. "I want the press focused on John. I won't have him, or his achievements, eclipsed by the goings-on of some common entertainer. Keep her out of sight. When the festivities begin, she'll be just another face in the crowd. Like the other musical acts."

It was clear his grandmother had never met Duchess. If she had, she'd've known there was no way the rapper could ever fade into the background.

"Is there anything else?" he asked.

"No. Louisa will be in touch with your updated schedule of appearances."

He nodded, knowing a dismissal when he heard one. Another two hours of his day in exchange for a fifteen-minute audience.

"Oh, and Jameson?"

Almost to the door, he turned.

"I've always admired you for your insistence on being judged by your own actions and not resting on the royal family's laurels. God knows, your aunt and uncle could benefit from a similar mind-set. But in the end, we are all defined by our membership in this family. Who we are, where we come from, our prestige, our very position in society, is built upon that association."

He stared at her, unsure of her meaning or where she was leading to.

"I can't say it enough: this celebration is important. It's possible the future of the British monarchy depends on it. I won't let my children's antics sully it. And now that you're the face of the event, I won't allow you to, either. Your father couldn't control himself when it came to beautiful women who traded on their sexuality. Don't give in to any genetic compulsion pulling you in that direction."

Shock almost felled him. Was she saying what he thought she was saying?

"Excuse me?"

"She's in your home, but she does not belong to you. Keep your hands to yourself. I will not allow hurt feelings or bruised egos to mar this event. The last thing I need is another salacious scandal involving a prince of the royal family."

With that nuclear edict deployed, his grandmother returned her attention to Louisa, leaving him alone to deal with the toxic emotional fallout.

JAMESON STRODE INTO the house, irritation simmering beneath his skin.

Who had he offended? Had he kicked a kitten or stolen a kid's toy? Was that why karma insisted on punching him in his bollocks?

He headed straight to his office and poured a drink. He'd been minding his business. Keeping to himself. Doing everything the queen had initially praised him for.

And yet he was the one shouldering a disproportionate amount of responsibility for something that had nothing to do with him and hadn't been his idea.

She's in your home, but she does not belong to you. Keep your hands to yourself.

Did the queen know what she was asking? He'd like to see her bloody well try it!

He took a sip of whisky and savored the burn. He knew what he was supposed to do, and he'd do it. After all, his sovereign had issued the order. There was no other viable choice. Plus, he could help thousands of people and do his part for the environment, as his grandfather would've wanted.

He just needed to keep his desires—and hands!—to himself.

On the desk, his phone buzzed. He glanced over, surprised to see Dani pop up on the screen. Though Louisa had ensured they'd had each other's information after Dani's arrival, this was the first time she'd actually texted him. He took another swig before swiping to see what she wanted.

DANI: Can you do me a favor?

Frowning, he responded: That depends.

DANI: Wow! This explains what everyone says about
British hospitality.
JAMESON: What do they say?
DANI: Nothing. That's the point.

Fighting the urge to smile, he typed: What can I do for you?

DANI: I'd poured myself some champagne but left it in
the kitchen. Can you bring it to me?

Was she serious? She couldn't come downstairs to get her own glass of champagne? Which person was he dealing with: the superstar or the houseguest?

JAMESON: A member of the staff would be happy to
accommodate you.
DANI: This is not something I'm comfortable entrusting
to staff.
JAMESON: I'm in my office in an entirely different wing
from you. It'll be easier for you to get it.

Three gray dots and then: Are these original hardwood floors?
Wha—

JAMESON: Of course.

DANI: And how would they respond to water and bubbles?

Water and bubbles . . .

She was in the tub? And there were bubbles?

His cock throbbed to life. He typed: Don't move. I'll be right there.

DANI: *smirk face emoji* See you soon!

He left his office and headed to the kitchen. Along the way he tried to steep himself in his annoyance. Use it as armor to protect himself from thoughts about her naked and wet.

In a bathtub full of bubbles . . .

The image was explicit enough in his mind. He didn't need to actually see it. He would leave the glass outside the door. And the bathroom floor was tile. It would be fine.

As expected, a bottle of champagne and a filled flute sat on the counter. He grabbed the glass but thought, What were the chances she'd be texting him again when she wanted more? He should take the entire bottle.

When he saw the distinctive royal blue label, with the family's crest, his eyes widened and he froze.

No, no, no . . .

Decades ago, Prince John had collaborated with a specific producer to create his own vintage champagne. When Jameson turned twenty-one, John had gifted him a crate of the rare bubbly with a promise that they'd enjoy a bottle each year on Jameson's birthday. The following year, his grandfather died. When he went to toast his grandfather on his thirtieth birthday, the sight of only two bottles left had hollowed out his chest. He hadn't been able to engage in the tradition the last two years, wanting to hold on to those bottles for as long as possible. Another way to preserve the memory of the man who'd been like his father.

Margery would never have given Dani this bottle. Which meant she'd helped herself to one of his most prized possessions. Out of all the bottles in his wine cellar, over twelve hundred, *this* was the one she chose?

Why hadn't she asked?

Why hadn't you shown her, like a proper host would have?

Ignoring that thought, he marched out of the kitchen, across the foyer, and up the stairs to the east wing of the house. When he got close to her bathroom, he was struck by the sound of singing. Was that her? He didn't know she was a singer, too. She had a lovely voice, a smooth alto that caressed his ears like warm honey.

Which he may have appreciated any other time. But not now. Not after what she'd done. Forget leaving the glass in the hallway and slinking away—

He flung open the bathroom door.

Bubbles.

She was surrounded by bubbles, looking like the wettest of all wet dreams, frothy lather sliding down one raised shapely leg—

Thank God for his anger.

"Who gave you permission to open this bottle?" he asked, clutching it by the neck.

Her eyes widened and her head jerked back, but she quickly recovered. "Excuse me?"

"Do you know what you've done?"

She sat up and her leg disappeared—to his regret—beneath the water's surface. "You told me to make myself at home and Margery said I was free to explore the wine cellar and pick something to drink. No one said, 'Here, enjoy any bottle you want . . . except this one!'"

His heart pounded so loudly in his chest he barely heard her. "This was given to me by my grandfather. It's one of two bottles left! You like champagne? You could've taken any other bottle. The 1989 Krug Collection, the 1997 Louis Roederer Cristal, the 1990 Dom—"

He flinched as something wet hit him square in the chest.

Openmouthed, he stared first at the colorful ball of mesh on the floor and then at the soapy mess sliding down the front of his shirt. "Did you just throw your sponge at me?"

She pursed her lips. "You needed to cool the fuck down."

"It's hot water."

"It served its purpose."

What in the hell was happening to his life? In the space of a few days, his quiet, orderly existence had been turned upside down by this American rapper who had him ricocheting between annoyance, fascination, amusement, irritation, and mind-altering lust.

And the queen wanted him to stay immersed in the chaos!

Forcing himself to take a calming breath, he carefully set the bottle of champagne on the nearest vanity. He pulled his shirt from his trousers and began unbuttoning it, already disgusted by the feel of the sodden fabric against his skin.

Water sloshed. "What do you think you're doing?"

How many sponges did she have?

He glanced up. "Don't you dar—"

The admonition died on his lips. The sound he'd heard wasn't her preparing to launch another soap-soaked missile. She'd risen from the tub, her body dripping, glistening, and perfect. Her breasts were high handfuls that topped a long flat torso, tiny waist, and lush round hips. All of it was covered in glistening bubbles that slid, in stark contrast, down her brown skin.

Raising his eyes, he found hers half lidded, a flush staining her cheeks. He remembered that look. Had seen it on her face right before he sank two fingers into her snug, heated depths.

He wanted to see it again. This time his cock would do the honors.

His first steps were halting, giving her time and the opportunity to stop this. Say something. Tell him no.

She remained quiet.

He reached the tub and waited.

She inhaled sharply, then arched a brow.

Never breaking their visual battle of wills, he slipped out of his oxford shoes and stepped into the water. She launched herself at him and wound her arms around his neck. Her soaked body pressed into his and their lips met in a bruising, fiery kiss.

The feel of her slick, slippery skin short-circuited his senses. He was aware only of her. Of the breathy moans he swallowed, the faint floral scent that teased his nostrils. The lushness of her ass.

God, her *ass*—

He palmed the fleshy globes, unable to contain the rumble of raw appreciation that boomed in his chest.

He'd spent weeks fantasizing about this woman, visions so vivid he'd awakened with a rigid cock and the tormented realization that he wasn't actually balls deep inside of her. And after last night, he knew nothing he'd ever dreamed had prepared him for the reality.

When he could no longer ignore his need for air, he broke away, but an invisible force drew him back. He trailed kisses along her neck and glided his tongue across the sharp protrusion of her clavicle. She clung to him, her head thrown back, her springy curls soft against his arm.

"I'm sorry about the champagne." She gasped. "I didn't know."

"What champagne?" he groaned, before capturing her mouth again.

She was a sensual blaze in his arms and he was stunned at how good it felt.

How natural.

How right.

Why should the bubbly suds be the only lucky ones? Bending, he took a dark-tipped nipple into his mouth. She hissed and clutched his head tight to her. His heart hammered inside his chest and he laved the bud, alternating between long, deep pulls and lightning-fast flicks with the tip of his tongue. She writhed in his arms, her sounds causing his cock to swell with need.

Always one to bring meticulous attention to any task he undertook, he focused on the other nipple, using his tongue and fingers to worship it with the same care and devotion he'd showered on its twin. Her gasps and hitches of breath nearly drove him insane, and a tidal wave of urgency caught him unawares.

He dropped to his knees, and the rose-scented bathwater sloshed onto the floor. It didn't matter. Nor did the fact that his clothes were now drenched. Her unabashed responsiveness was something he hadn't known he craved until that moment and he needed more. He gripped her hips and pressed openmouthed kisses across the taut flesh of her lower belly, loving when she bucked against him and plunged her fingers into his hair, tugging sharply on the strands.

He smiled at the slight bite of pain and swirled his tongue into her belly button.

She shivered.

He licked a path from her left hip bone to her right before going lower and nuzzling the smooth skin and the strip of crisp curls above her core. "Can I taste you?"

She stilled and stared down at him from beneath lowered lids.

He waited, holding his breath in anticipation.

She nodded.

Dizzy with relief, he slid his hand into the warm water and wrapped his fingers around her ankle. Lifting her leg, he placed her bare foot on the lip of the tub and groaned as her glistening pink flesh was bared to his gaze.

"Beautiful," he breathed.

He hooked an arm around her raised thigh and leaned forward, putting his mouth on her.

Her quads quivered, but he held her steady and explored her swollen labia, tugging on the flared lips, and sucking on her engorged clit. She cried out as her taste exploded on his tongue. He had the perfect vantage point to watch her, her head thrown back, eyes closed, mouth open.

She was so fucking gorgeous he couldn't breathe.

She palmed the back of his head and ground her pussy into his face.

"That's it, love," he murmured. "Fuck my mouth."

He took it all. Holding her to him, he fluttered his tongue against the silky moist skin she smashed against his cheek, his nose, his chin. Her fevered whimpers drove him mad. And still he needed more. He trailed his middle finger to her anus and rimmed the opening. When she didn't tense or move away from his touch, he gently inserted the tip of the digit inside.

"Damn, baby," she breathed and pushed back against it, depriving him of her flavor but filling his palms with an abundance of ass. He finger-fucked the puckered entrance while moving his face closer to recapture her clit. He sucked on the nub of pleasure.

"Ahhh, that's it, baby . . . right there . . ."

With a scream and a shiver he felt ripple through her slick body, she came, gasping and arching her back, her fingers digging into his shoulders.

Without a delay, he lifted her in his arms and stepped out of the tub, careful to make sure he landed on the rug and not the wet, slippery marble. In two strides, he reached the tufted bench beneath the window and laid her on its upholstered surface.

His hand delved between her legs, his fingers gliding through the folds of her outer lips, his thumb finding her clit.

She raised up on her elbows and gripped his wrist. "Wait, stop!"

He froze. "What?"

He was breathing like he'd run a marathon. Had he done something wrong? Misread the situation? Moved too fast?

Her eyes were hazy and her tongue darted out to lick her lips. "I want to. Really. But . . . Damn, this is embarrassing."

He couldn't imagine anything distressing enough to stop what they were doing. "What is it? You can tell me."

"I need to moisturize my skin."

He blinked. Had he heard her properly?

He hadn't voiced the question out loud, but she must've read his expression because she said, "I know. I know. But if I don't do it now, I'll get itchy and I won't be able to enjoy this. Damn, Jay, I never expected you to throw it down on me!"

He laughed, torn between relief that she still wanted him and incredulity at finding himself in this situation.

Skin moisturizer. Right.

"Where is it?"

She pointed at the vanity, where he saw several brightly colored bottles and jars. "The blue one."

He grabbed a large jar labeled "Mela-Skin Body Custard" and brought it over to her.

She held out her hand. "I'll be quick."

"I don't want that word associated with anything we're doing." He wanted to savor this experience. It would be the only one they had. "May I?"

One corner of her mouth curved upward. "Okay."

Twisting the lid, he dabbed a small amount of the rich cream on his palm.

She giggled. "Don't be afraid of it. You'll need a little more than that."

He scooped out a dollop. "Is that better?"

"Much," she said, her low tone deliciously husky. "This bodes well for us, Jay. You take direction nicely."

He rubbed the lotion between his hands. "Where do you start?"

"My arms."

He started at her shoulder and smoothed the cream into her skin. Her breath hitched in her throat, but otherwise she didn't make a sound. Her skin was velvety soft; he could spend hours touching her. He held her wrist in one hand and stroked his other one over her upper arm, her elbow, and her forearm. Then he repeated the ministrations on her other limb.

"Next?" he forced out of a mouth gone dry.

"My body," she said thickly.

God grant him strength!

Replenishing his supply from the jar, he turned to face her and drew in a shuddering breath. Reclined against the bench, one foot braced on the cushion, her hair a poufy cloud of curls, her naked skin dewy and flushed, she was an irresistible temptation.

He pressed his hands against her breasts.

"Fuck me!" he groaned as the hardened peaks scraped his palms.

Her lashes fluttered and her head fell back. He stared at the long, graceful column of her neck, then swallowed and massaged the custard into her chest, taking his time and savoring the weight of her breasts, the silkiness of her skin, the way she arched into his touch. He slid hands shaking with need down her belly, making sure he didn't ignore the sides of her torso.

He cleared his throat. "I guess that leaves your legs."

She slid to the edge of the bench and put her feet flat on the floor. "It does."

He dropped to his haunches before her and, gripping her knees, spread her thighs wide.

It was his turn to lick his lips as he took in the sight of her bare pussy and he couldn't resist leaning forward and pressing a kiss to the glistening folds.

Straightening, he dipped his fingers into the jar and spread a dab of lotion on each thigh, shin, and instep. Then he rubbed it in, thoroughly but quickly, certain it wouldn't take much more before he came in his pants.

"Are you good?" he panted, holding on to his control with a willpower he hadn't known he possessed.

"You better believe it," she said.

Her quip lessened the tension long enough for him to rise to his feet and discard the rest of his clothes. More than his cock swelled at the frank admiration on her face as she watched.

She crooked her finger. "Come here, Your Royal Highness."

He took a step, then cursed. "We still don't have condoms."

Goddammit! He was a stubborn idiot. When he'd stopped at the chemist's near the campus this morning, he'd purposely avoided that aisle, believing not purchasing some would prevent this very scenario from happening.

You bloody arse!

"No worries." Languidly, she uncurled her body and glided over to the vanity. Reaching into a glossy black leather pouch, she pulled out a gold foil wrapper and tossed it to him. "I hate being unprepared even more than I hate being denied something I want."

He eased on the protection and she pushed him down on the settee, but when he reached for her, she shook her head. She turned around and he barely had time to appreciate her luscious, ripe ass before she backed up between his thighs, gripped the shaft of his cock, and slid down his aching length.

Holy fuck!

His eyes rolled back in his head. She felt unbelievable. Her pussy gripped his cock in a viselike bear hug, the pleasure a step removed from pain. He trailed his hand down the middle of her back and grasped her hips, her silhouette an erotic composition that threatened to shred to pieces his earlier vaunted willpower.

Once fully seated, Dani hissed and shifted in his lap, the movement sending spasms of ecstasy zipping up his spine. Bracing her hands on the settee, she peered at him over her shoulder.

"Hold on tight and try to keep up."

Chapter Fourteen

"You don't know his friends / Late night texts / Tit pics on request / Look in the mirror and ask / Is any man worth that lack of respect?"

—Duchess, "Infinite Rage"

Jameson groaned and fell back onto the mattress. "Jesus, woman, what are you doing to me?"

Dani was wondering the same about his effect on her.

She kissed his chest and snuggled close, throwing her leg over his thighs. "If you don't know then I must be doing it wrong."

He gathered her to his side and trailed his fingers along her body. "No, you're doing everything right."

He bent his head and their lips met. His kisses were divine. Slow, languid, thorough. As if he had nothing better to do and nowhere he needed to be. As if discovering the planes, textures, and ridges of her mouth were his all-consuming life's work.

"What I meant," he said, when they'd finally pulled apart, "is that I don't do this. I don't make out in the old drawing room and I definitely don't accost women while they're taking a bath and have my way with them."

"You don't hear me complaining, do you?" she asked, stroking the hairs on his chest.

If someone had told her that several days into her trip she'd be loved up with a prince at two in the morning, she'd have asked them what cush they were smoking and whether they could procure some for her.

And yet, here she was.

Last night had been crazy good. And not because it had been so long, cobwebs had tried to reconstruct her hymen, but because she hadn't expected what she'd gotten. Who'd known the prim and proper prince could do what he did? And say what he said? She'd thought it would be a little more . . . vanilla. More missionary, beneath the covers with the lights out. Which would've been fine. Instead, it had been flip her over, smack that ass, and make her scream his name.

She had loved every moment of it.

And while the "prince" part would be enough for some women to get off on, it did nothing for her.

What did?

His body.

He was tall with the kind of physique people wouldn't expect when they heard its owner was a professor of philosophy. Jameson wasn't ripped like many of the entertainers and athletes she knew. He spent his time teaching, not in a gym or with a professional trainer, but things were still tight, proportionate, and just yummy.

And her admiration wasn't confined to the way his frame looked. She adored what he could do with it. He may say he didn't do this often, but he knew what to do with his hands, his fingers, his tongue, his teeth, and his mouth.

And his cock.

He must've been blessed with natural-born gifts.

And she wanted to explore those inherent talents further.

She traced one gold-tipped fingernail around his nipple and smiled when he shuddered.

"When's the last time you got some?"

"Excuse me?"

The shock in his voice tickled her. Despite his skills in bed, he was so prim and proper outside of it that a part of her got off on being crude.

"Fuck, Jay. When's the last time you *fucked* someone?"

He stared at her. "About five minutes ago?"

She hit his chest. "Before me?"

He sat up. "It's been a while."

She frowned, since the movement dislodged her from her comfy position. "But you enjoyed what we did, right?"

He scooted back to rest against the headboard, then pulled her against him. "If you have to ask, then clearly *I'm* doing something wrong!"

She nestled into his side. What a waste of one of Britain's natural resources. Although—

"If you had fun and I had fun, how about we *enjoy* ourselves a few more times while I'm here?"

He tilted her chin and stared down at her. "Just sex? With no strings attached?"

She shrugged. "I don't mind a little rope play . . ."

"No strings attached as in claims of pregnancy or threats to spill to the tabloids if we don't get married or pretend to be dating for at least a year?"

What the— "That's happened to you?"

"A few times."

She didn't know why his revelation was such a bombshell. People seemed to lose their moral compass when it came to trying to secure money and power. She'd seen both men and women do some shady shit to live the lifestyle without the hard work.

She rolled away from him and reached into the top drawer of the nightstand next to the bed. Finding what she sought, she placed it next to the lamp and curled back against his side.

"I'm working on a major deal that will require my full time and attention for quite a while. Trust and believe, I'm not looking to get pregnant or married. Why would I want to be your princess? I'm my own Duchess."

A smile tilted the corners of his lips. "Okay. I'll . . . trust and believe."

In one quick, smooth motion, she slid her thigh over his and straddled him, nestling his cock in her folds and rubbing her clit against his length. "Are you making fun of me?"

He hissed in a breath and gripped her hips. "I would never. Just a little teasing." He raised his thumb to her lips and pushed it inside her mouth. "I thought you liked my teasing."

She moaned around the invasion, laving it with her tongue. "I do. I love it."

He pressed the digit, wet from her saliva, against her clit. "Good. Tell me, what's that?"

She threw her head back and ground against it, the pressure so . . . fucking . . . amazing. "What's what?"

"The fabric you took from the drawer. Who's tying up whom?"

Tying up? Fabric?

All thought processes had ceased to function as the blood left her brain and set up camp in the tiny nub of pleasure between her thighs.

From the drawer? Oh.

"That's . . . my . . . SLAP."

He stilled. "Pardon?"

"My satin-lined cap." When he didn't resume his ministrations, she sighed. "I wear it at night to protect my hair."

"From what?"

The utter bafflement on his face sent her into spasms of laughter so intense, she fell back, ass in the air, to land in a graceless pile next to him.

"Oh my God," she heaved out.

"What's so funny?" he asked, adorably grumpy.

"You've never dated a black woman, have you?"

"Of course I have," he said, a muscle ticking in his jaw.

"Okay, okay." She scrambled to a sitting position. "Let me rephrase. Have you ever gotten to the point in a relationship with a black woman where she slept over?"

"No."

"Then don't worry about it. I'm not sure it's even worth having the 'black hair 101' discussion if this is only going to be for a few weeks."

"Do you wear the cap every night?"

"Yes."

"Then I want to know about it."

She stroked her fingers along the stubborn set of his jaw, gratified when it relaxed into her touch.

"Later. There's one more thing I want to put out there."

"I'm all ears." He shoved his hands behind his head, an unstudied gesture that would've brought millions to their knees if it had been captured on a screen.

Her sensitive core throbbed in response.

Focus, Dani. This is important. "Let's keep this just between the two of us."

"I have no intention of running to the press."

"Not the press. Everyone. The staff, your friends, my friends. Loose lips and a thousand ships and all that. Neither of us wants to deal with the fallout from that little bomb dropping."

"Agreed."

If only all of her negotiations had been so easy.

Or as fun.

"Thank you," she said, kissing him, allowing her tongue to briefly tangle with his before releasing his lips.

She worked her way down his body, grazing his nipple with her teeth, pressing kisses along his hip bone, until she reached his cock, which stood tall and proud before her. She gripped its warm steely strength in her palm then pressed it against her cheek, overcome by a dose of affection remembering the pleasure it had given her. She licked the tip and he groaned. "Duchess!"

She glanced up at him. "Jay?"

"Hmmmm?" His moan was low, guttural.

"I think you can call me Dani now."

DANI TILTED HER head to the side and tapped a nail against her bottom lip. "I was wrong. It *is* bigger than yours."

Jameson winced. "Even for a prince with a healthy . . . ego, that's something no man ever wants to hear."

She laughingly slapped his arm as she stared at the large house in front of them. After several days of fucking until her body hummed, she'd thought she would've had her fill of him. But when she saw him, she'd imagine all the things he'd done with his hands and mouth the last time they were together, heat would pool between her thighs, and before she knew it, they'd be at it again.

It was an intense, sensuous fuck cycle.

"It's one of the country's most beautiful privately owned parks," Jay was saying. "Over fifteen thousand acres. The Baslingfield family has owned this estate since the late seventeenth century."

He'd taken her for a drive in the country to an estate called Baslingfield Court. She couldn't even fathom owning that much land. Or having something in her family for that long.

He shepherded her toward the large front door. When he went to walk in, she pushed against him. "What are you doing?"

"Don't you want to see the inside?"

"Sure, if we're not committing a breaking and entering."

He held out his hand. "We'll be okay."

She studied the gesture, recognizing the implicit trust accepting it required. Heeding her gut, she slid her hand into his and followed him into the house.

In the first room they came to, the largest rug she'd ever seen covered the gleaming dark wooden floor. The same wood shrouded the walls, carved into an exquisite, intricate design. The amount of work it must've taken to complete this room, large as some apartments, would've been insane. And when she looked up, she was stunned by the masterpiece of elaborate composition on the ceiling.

It was a spectacular place.

"It must be awe-inspiring to live in something that qualifies as a work of art," she breathed, staring out at the magnificent view framed by windows dressed in luxurious draperies, made from a glimmering floral fabric.

"You've seen one drawing room, you've seen them all," he said, hands in his pockets, the picture of casual elegance.

"Are you kidding me?"

"No. It's nice, but there's a space like this in many country homes. I spent much of my childhood in rooms like this one."

Wow.

Her smile held little amusement as she turned away from him and strode over to the large floor-to-ceiling, eighteenth-century fireplace. In only a week, she'd come to see him as Jay, this smart, sexy British professor whose mouth, whether it was his accent or his tongue, scrambled her insides.

But he wasn't Jay. He was Prince Jameson. Of course he'd seen lots of places like this one.

"We had entirely different upbringings. The only time I would've seen anything like this would've been in a museum."

The privileged ennui slid from his face. "I must sound like a right prat. I'm sorry."

She waved his words away with a nonchalant gesture. Maybe he'd been experiencing the same thing she'd been. Seeing her as Duchess, but forgetting she'd grown up as Dani.

In the States, and by her fans, her upbringing was pretty well known. And if it wasn't, they would've correctly assumed part of it, believing "real" rappers only came from poverty.

A discussion for another day.

But Jay had seen the outer trimmings and thought this was how she'd always lived.

Another difference between them.

"Was it difficult for you? Your childhood?" he asked.

She stiffened, automatically anticipating the morbid fascination that usually accompanied that question.

"Sometimes. But I wouldn't change anything. It made me who I am today."

His bark of amusement jarred her.

She flinched. "Seriously? You find my pain amusing?"

"Of course not," he said with a knowing look. "But while our experiences were different, our public response to it is the same."

"Excuse me?"

"I recognize a canned answer when I hear one. On the rare occasions I am forced to grant an interview and am asked what it's like growing up royal, I say"—he cleared his throat—"we're like most families in that we have our share of eccentricities, traditions, and family disagreements. Ours happens to capture the interest of millions of people, instead of just our neighbors."

She stared at him and they both burst out laughing.

She pressed her palms to her aching cheeks. "It's really ridiculous, isn't it?"

"It is. No one wants the real truth."

"They don't," she agreed. "At least not from me. If I were a man, they'd want to hear about my gangsta background, about slinging rock or shooting people. Since I'm a woman, they want to know if I was a stripper or abused drugs or tied to some dude who gave me a chance."

"Is that what happened?" he asked softly.

"No. I'd own it if it did. I was a kid who liked to read who had the misfortune of being born to people who weren't old enough and didn't want to be parents. I was then blessed to be taken in by a grandmother who loved me and, later, other family." Though they weren't as nurturing. "I took a job at a music studio when I was old enough to get it and a chance meeting led to all of this. If you go back far enough, you'll see me attempt to explain that in earlier interviews. But that reality wasn't as satisfying as their fantasy, so I eventually stopped trying."

Jameson nodded. "I understand. As royalty, people want our lives to be glamorous. They imagine their childhood and what they believe would've made them happy, and that's what they want to hear. They want us to have had our own bedrooms and servants and never had to do chores. They want the circus and elephants and cotton candy and enormous fun all the time."

"And it wasn't?" she asked, channeling his tone from earlier.

"It was. Sometimes. I would never stand here and tell you it was horrible. I didn't have to worry about lodgings or food or the love of my mother. But the experience was also lonely, confining, and sometimes scary. And after my father died—"

He glanced away from her.

Was she much different from those other people? There was a part of her who assumed the very thing he said. Not that his life had been perfect, but that it certainly had to be better than hers. Watching him studiously avoiding her gaze, she recalled the saying that a gilded cage was still a cage.

She went over and wrapped her arms around him. "I didn't know about your father. Or the rest of it. I'm so sorry, Jay."

"Me, too."

They stood that way for a while and she attempted to transfer, from her body to his, as much sympathy, compassion, and understanding as she could. He shifted against her, tilting her head up with pressure against her cheek, and lowered his lips to hers in a kiss that stole her breath. Their tongues tangled and she clutched a hand in his sweater as an unexpected tender emotion threatened to overwhelm her.

From far away, Dani heard someone clear their throat.

"Your Royal Highness?" A short young man with light brown hair stood in the doorway.

She broke their kiss and buried her face against his chest. She would never call herself shy, but she'd been unprepared for the intimacy of an embrace that went beyond satisfying sexual hunger to the giving and receiving of care and consolation.

This can't be happening. We decided this was a temporary thing. Now is not the time to be catching feelings!

She moved away from him and forced a laugh. "I didn't know drawing rooms were such a turn-on for you."

She kept her voice low, though their interloper was yards away. "Neither did I."

She grabbed his hand, anxious to return to a surer, more physical, footing. "Let's go back to your house and take care of it."

He reeled her close and whispered in her ear, "Looking forward to it, I promise. But not yet. I have another surprise."

His proximity sent delicious curls of arousal throughout her midsection. "You do?"

The person who'd initially interrupted them stepped forward. "If you'll follow me."

"Do you know him?" Dani asked, complying with the young man's request.

"He's the son of one of my groundskeepers."

Just like Downton Abbey. "People stick to their station here, right?"

He bristled. "Pardon?"

"I'm just saying that in America, you can grow up to be anything you want to be."

"So, America's better? Save the lack of universal health care, exorbitant costs of basic human services, and institutional and structural racism?"

She stopped and put a hand on her hip. "You want to go there? Right now?"

He leaned close and kissed her. "No, I don't."

Good, because she didn't want to, either. And it wasn't the point she was trying to make.

"What I meant is that over here, with the way I grew up, I'd probably be the one leading us around instead of on your arm."

"Then thank God for America," he said, with a quick kiss.

They traveled down several hallways lined with the occasional pieces of antique furniture and large oil portraits of past relatives until the young man reached a door that he held open for them.

"Thanks, Tom. And remember, not a word."

The young man nodded and hurried away.

Jameson stepped back to let her precede him. In the growing dusk, Dani gaped at the sight of an enormous inflatable movie screen and a large crowd assembled on folding camping chairs or blankets.

"What are you doing? Hanging out with about eighty people is not keeping things on the down low."

"No one will see us."

He led her away from the group to a tent hidden so strategically by landscaped bushes that they could view everything without being observed. Inside, a small, raised platform had been constructed and topped with a love seat, colorful pillows and blankets, and an assortment of refreshments.

"This is incredible!"

"They host this event twice a summer, but I've only been a few times over the years with friends. I thought it would be fun, with the added bonus of getting us out together, without being noticed."

"It's perfect."

He nuzzled her briefly. "Have a seat. I'll get you something to eat and drink."

She smiled at him. "You thought of everything. Do you know what's showing?"

"I do."

A man strolled in front of the huge screen. "Welcome to Open Air Cinema at Baslingfield Court!"

As everyone clapped and cheered, Dani leaned forward, swept up in the palpable excitement, heady with the feeling of being a part of everything, but still private.

Like she and Jameson were in their own little world.

"We're so glad you could make it out this evening. Tonight's feature, *Pretty Woman*!"

More whistles and applause.

The man laughed. "Excellent. We knew you'd love reliving this classic rom-com. And as a special treat, for this evening only, a double feature. Trust me, if you don't stay it'll be a, say it with me—"

"Big mistake! Huge," the throng said in unison.

"Exactly. The second film is another Julia Roberts classic, but shot in our backyard. *Notting Hill*, with Julia, Hugh Grant, and that iconic blue door!"

Notting Hill? Hadn't Jay mentioned that movie the other night as another one written by the *Four Weddings and a Funeral* guy?

He settled next to her on the love seat and she turned to him in surprise. "Did you do this?"

"Me?" He popped an olive in his mouth. "What makes you think I have that kind of power?"

"You're a prince!"

"Not an important one. We just got lucky."

She wasn't sure she believed him. "Serendipity or planned, thank you."

He draped an arm along the back of the sofa and she settled into her favorite nook, resting her head against his shoulder as the opening scene projected onto the screen.

"I'm so excited. This is going to be great. Ha! That magician palmed that coin. It was so obvious. Oh my God, Costanza! I forgot he was in this."

Jameson shifted. "Are you going to talk through the whole movie?"

"No!" She pouted. "Well, maybe a little. I have opinions."

"Yes, you do." He kissed her and whispered, "But we're trying not to draw attention to ourselves, right?"

Fine.

She'd do her best, but she wasn't going to make any promises.

I could get used to this.

The thought unfurled from nowhere. She jerked forward in her seat.

"Everything all right?" Jameson asked, eyes, she was thankful to see, still on the screen.

"Uh-huh."

She sat back. It would be.

Once she remembered why she was here.

And it definitely didn't involve getting hung up over a prince who didn't fit into her plans.

Chapter Fifteen

"*Love is a canvas furnished by Nature and embroidered by Imagination.*"

—Voltaire

A week later, Jameson held Dani close, one hand on her hip, the other on her arm. "Are you peeking?"

Dani touched the front of her blindfold. "No! I told you I can't see shit!"

"Good," he said, continuing to move at an unhurried pace while he guided her to their secret destination.

"Jay! Dammit, where are you taking me?"

Despite the demand of her words, the apprehension he sensed in her tone and her frame tugged at his heart. Two weeks ago he didn't know her, but now he was as familiar with her body as he was with his own. He'd learned her shivers of delight, her moans of pleasure, the hitch of breath right before she came.

And he appreciated that there was so much more to the woman than the persona. So much so that he was ashamed of what he'd previously thought about her, how unfairly he'd judged her without even knowing her.

Seeing the blinding white structure up ahead he said, "We're almost there."

"This had better be good."

It would be and he hoped she liked it. It had taken a few phone calls and he'd pulled some strings he didn't know he had, but in the end, it had all come together.

"This is it. I'm going to take off your mask," he said, undoing the ribbon. "But keep your eyes closed."

"This may have worked in bed the other night, but I don't like it in public."

He couldn't contain his smile remembering the fun they'd had engaging the different senses. How had he ever lived without having a—what had she called it?—peppermint fatty?

A young woman stepped out of the structure. "Everything's ready."

Dani jumped. "We're not alone? Did she hear me?"

"No. It's okay."

Stuffing the black satin mask in his pocket, he moved to stand beside her. "Open your eyes."

Her lashes fluttered and she took a moment to acclimate herself. She frowned. "Where are we?"

Anticipation and excitement merged within him as he cupped her shoulders and turned her around.

She immediately recognized the white tent. "Wait a minute. Is this—? It is! It's *The Great UK Baking Championship* tent!"

Her obvious joy—evidenced by her jumping up and down, laughing and clapping—charmed him more than he'd expected. As did his continued pleasure in doing things for her. Seeing her happy made him happy.

She flung her arms around his neck, and when their lips met, the familiar languor, which only she caused, invaded his body. Her taste, her smell, her feel. He wanted more. More of her. More of this.

More of everything.

"Sorry," she said, pulling away, breathless.

Her eyes were hazy, her lips moist. He loved how she didn't hide the effect he had on her. Especially because he couldn't.

"You never have to apologize for your kisses."

"Good to know," she murmured. She rubbed her thumb over his bottom lip. "I probably shouldn't have done that outside."

Probably not, but they hadn't left Primrose Park and security officers discreetly patrolled the borders of his property. The only people around were his usual estate staff. They should be fine. But in the future and off his property, he simply needed to be more careful and keep his head about him. Which was difficult when being with her led to an intoxicating scramble of his thoughts.

She turned back to the tent, her brown eyes wide, her fingers touching her parted and less glossed lips. "Am I going to be on the show?"

He raised a brow. "Do you really believe you bake well enough to be on this show?"

"Good point."

He laughed and took her hand. "Come on."

Inside was bright and airy with a peaked roof and zippered window walls. Along the back of the structure, a long bright turquoise counter was littered with bowls, glass jars, and small appliances. Amongst the open shelving was a fake half-moon window with illuminated letters that spelled out the word "cake." A light purple prep island with a wooden countertop was centered in the space.

"Oh," she said, frowning. "There's only one station."

"Is that a problem?"

"Every other detail is perfect, but there's usually two rows of workspaces lined on each side," she said, moving around the area to demonstrate her point, "with refrigerators placed every few stations."

"Hmmm . . . that does seem odd. But what's that on the counter? Maybe it'll give us a clue about what's going on."

It was a testament to her genuine excitement that she hurried over to the island instead of giving him the eye roll he deserved. He was a horrible actor.

On one side was a flat, black, glossy surface he'd been told was the cooktop. On the other side was an assortment of utensils and small appliances used for baking. And in the middle was a mysterious pile covered by a red-and-white gingham cloth.

Dani's smile was wide. "This is exactly how it looks when the contestants are getting ready to do a technical challenge!"

"A technical challenge?"

"When the bakers have to make something the judges choose, under strict time restraints and with very few instructions on how to do so."

"So you *are* a true fan of the show," a voice said, and a short blond woman wearing a blazer and jeans walked out to stand in front of them.

Dani clutched his arm. "Oh my God! That's—"

"You're excited to meet *me*?" Melody Lucas said, a huge smile on her face. "I can't believe Duchess watches the show!"

Dani hurried forward to shake her hand. "You are too funny. I wasn't sure I was going to keep watching, you know, after all the changes and the new hosts, but . . ."

"You absolutely should," Melody said. "I enjoyed my time on the show immensely. And when I received a call from Prince Jameson asking me to participate in this surprise, I was honored."

Dani turned shining brown eyes in his direction. "You're amazing," she mouthed.

His heart shifted in his chest.

"Okay," Melody said, briskly clapping her hands together. "Get into position."

Dani's expression shifted into one of firm determination. She gave a curt nod and hurried to stand behind the sole counter in the middle of the tent. Shrugging, Jameson followed her.

She eyed him. "What are you doing?"

"Working with you."

Dani shot a look at Melody, who nodded and said, "You'll find aprons in the cubbies of your station."

Once they were situated, Melody threw her arms wide and said, "Welcome to the Royal Team Technical Challenge. Usually, I'd say something witty and tell the judges they'd need to leave, but today, it's just us, so I'll get on with it. In case you were wondering, it's bread week."

Dani gasped in horror, and it took everything Jameson had to keep his lips from quirking.

"For your technical challenge, you're going to make that most simple of British biscuits, the scone. You are to make twelve identical treats, because as part of my contract, I'll be taking some of these home to have with tea tomorrow. You have one hour. Ready. Set—"

"Bake!" Dani exclaimed, before whipping off the gingham cloth and staring at the ingredients. Her expression fell. "This is going to be a disaster. I don't know how to bake these. *You* don't bake at all. And the instructions they give say things like 'Put ingredients in a bowl. Mix together. Put in oven. Bake.' How much of each ingredient? What do I bake it on? How long do I bake it? Those important pieces are usually missing. We're screwed!"

"Let's see what the instructions say." He reached for the laminated, printed sheet next to him.

Dani peered over his arm. "There's a proper ingredient list! And it says to preheat the oven to 220 degrees. These aren't the typical instructions!"

"You think I'd leave that to chance? Clearly, the horror you left in my kitchen affected me more than it did you."

"With these instructions, we can totally do it. Scones, here we come."

"Your tongue is marvelously talented with a lot of things, including butchering English terms. It's scones."

"That's what I said."

"No, you said 'scone,' rhymes with 'bone,'" he said, giving his American accent a try. "It's 'scone,' rhymes with 'gone.'"

He'd barely gotten the last word out when a dusting of flour landed on his chest. He shouldn't have been shocked, considering the bathtub incident, but he was.

He lifted his gaze to her grinning face. "You didn't just—"

More flour landed.

When her hand went for the bag again, he moved quickly and snagged her around the waist, carrying her away from the flour. Her delighted shriek was loud in his ear, but he didn't care. He tossed her over his shoulder, swatting her backside in the process.

"Put me down!"

"No."

"Jay!"

Melody popped her head back in. "Ummm, I just wanted to remind you that the clock is still running. You now have fifty-four minutes."

If the queen could see him now.

His Royal Highness Prince Jameson engaged in a food fight!
In public!

But she's not here. And you've been careful.

He had been. He'd tasked his staff with replicating the set of the
show and made sure Melody Lucas signed a nondisclosure agree-
ment. He was allowed to have some fun!

He hurried back to their station and put her down.

"You're going to pay for that later," he said, his eyes narrowing.

"Oh, I hope so," she said, tossing a grin over her shoulder. "Now
stop playing around. We have scones," she said, with the proper
British pronunciation, "to prepare."

LATER THAT AFTERNOON, Dani set the basket of baked pastries on
the kitchen counter in the main house. "That was crazy fun. So
thoughtful. And caring. I can't believe you re-created the show! No
one has ever done anything like that for me before."

He stood next to her. "I find that hard to believe. I'm sure your
past boyfriends showered you with gifts."

"They did."

He didn't like the acidic feeling blazing in his chest. "For example?"

"Cruises on private yachts, trips to glamorous destinations
around the world—I dated an NBA player who rented out his arena
for the night so we could have dinner and he could give me a private shooting lesson."

Unclench your jaw, Jameson. You shouldn't be surprised.

He wasn't. She was a beautiful, exciting, and accomplished
woman. Many men would do whatever was necessary to be with
her. He couldn't expect his little gestures to send her heart soaring.

"And yet what you've done for me, the outdoor movie and the baking show today, have been two of the most darling gifts anyone has ever given me."

He blinked. "They were?"

"Uh-huh. With my past boyfriends, you could've taken me out and dropped any other girl into the same situation. Because those other gestures weren't really about me. They were about the guy trying to flex and show me how important he was. But your outings? You chose them with me in mind."

He had. Lately, she'd claimed more than her fair share of space in his brain.

She moved close to him, their bodies touching. "Jay, I like you."

His pulse thundered in his ears and his heart pounded in his chest, like it wanted to burst free and merge with hers. "I like you, too, Dani. A lot."

The words, though innocuous, held the weight and reverence of so much more.

"Oh my. That was the sweetest thing I've ever seen," his mother said, shattering the intimate moment.

Dani froze and Jameson whipped his head around to stare wide-eyed at the woman standing in the doorway, wearing a powder blue sheath dress and matching jacket, her dark hair twisted into an elegant bun. "Mother! What are you doing here?"

"Your starring role in Marina's latest PR scheme starts soon. Where else would I be?" Calanthe said, accepting his kiss on her cheek while trying to peer around him at Dani. "I hope I'm not interrupting."

"Of course not." He took her elbow and steered her over. "May I present Dani Nelson? Dani, this is my mother, Her Royal Highness Calanthe, Duchess of Wessex."

Bowing her head, Dani slid her right foot behind her left, bent her knees, and slowly descended before rising. "Your Royal Highness."

He raised his brows. "Oh, I see. My mother gets a proper curtsy, while I get smart retorts?"

Dani's eyes widened, their murderous intent clear, even as she shook her head. "That's not . . . exactly true."

"Don't listen to Jameson," his mother said. "That was lovely, dear, but not necessary. A handshake will do. And you may call me Calanthe."

"It's a pleasure to meet you, Calanthe. That's a beautiful name."

"Thank you. It's uncommon these days, which can be a benefit and a curse." She smiled. "Two Duchesses in the same room. Usually a cause for concern."

Dani touched a hand to her chest. "You know who I am?"

"I do. I was brought up to speed as soon as I got back."

"The Tea Trust, no doubt," Jameson murmured.

"We like to keep each other informed."

"You mean you all like to gossip," Jameson said.

"My grandmother was the same," Dani said, a pained tint dulling her expression. "She had a similar group of friends in our neighborhood. She used to say if it took a village to raise a child, then the entire village needed to be informed."

"Sounds like a wise woman," Calanthe said.

"She was." Dani exhaled audibly, her smile a bit shaky. "It was lovely meeting you, ma'am. I'll head up to my room and leave the two of you to catch up."

Jameson reached for her. "You don't have to go."

"No, no," she said, gently squeezing his hand. "You should spend this time with your mother."

"He's right, Dani, there's no need for you to leave. We're going to talk about you, so I might as well get my information from the source. Tea?"

Should he be nervous? Jameson wasn't sure, but he didn't try to fight his mother. When she was determined, nothing got in her way. "Margery is not here."

"I can make tea. I'm the one who trained her."

As his mother began working in the kitchen, he pulled out a chair for Dani at the small table in the corner.

"Royals! They're just like us!" Dani said, a bemused look on her face.

"Pardon?"

"A feature from an entertainment magazine in the States where they catch celebrities doing things like pumping gas in their car or drinking a Venti Vanilla Bean Crème Frappuccino from Starbucks or, horrors, grocery shopping."

"From your tone I can tell you've been spotlighted in this feature and you didn't like it."

"Whether I like it or not is irrelevant. It sells."

He understood that sentiment far too well.

"They wouldn't do stories like that here. Not about *my* family."

"Why not?"

"Because everyone is invested in us *not* being normal. It's part of our unofficial contract with the public. We remain on a slightly elevated pedestal, high enough for them to look up to us, but not so high that we're seen as unsympathetic or unlikable."

Divots furrowed Dani's brow.

Too much, Jameson. She doesn't want to hear your poor little royal boy screed.

Forcing a carefree smile, he said, "But that's never stopped my mother. No one can keep her out of the kitchen. She's always been that way."

"He's right," Calanthe said. "It's the reason he's managed to live a relatively normal life. Unlike his spoiled aunts and uncle."

"Mother!" he said. He cleared his throat and attempted to get their conversation back on track. "How was the South of France?"

"Marvelous, as usual. The weather was superb and the company . . ." A becoming flush tinged her cheeks. "But don't change the subject. Are you sure you want to do this celebration?"

What choice did he have?

"It's not as dire as you're making it out to be. She wanted to do something to honor Grandfather. She knows how close we were and thought I'd want to be a part of it."

His mother eyed him sharply. "She also knows how much you hate being in the public eye."

"You do?" Dani asked.

"Ever since he was a little boy. One time he went on a volunteer mission to Chile with Bettina and some of his distant cousins and the Palace had set up a press conference on their return. You should've seen him. A tall, gangly teenager. So serious. A hint of what he'd become. His expression was so clear that he felt it was all a waste of his time."

"Really?"

"It's true." Calanthe spotted the basket of scones on the counter. "What are these?"

Dani stood. "You don't want those."

"Maybe I do."

"Margery didn't make them. We did."

"*We?* Jameson . . . baked?"

"He surprised me by setting up a scene from *The Great UK Baking Championship* on the estate!"

Calanthe slid him a look. "Did he?"

He yearned to extinguish the knowing expression on his mother's face.

Don't make a big deal of this.

"He set it up so we had to complete a challenge. Bake scones." Dani pursed her lips. "You look shocked. That's not something he'd normally do?"

"No, dear, he wouldn't."

Dani slid a considering once-over his way before continuing. "They only look halfway decent because of his efforts. I'm not a cook at all. That was my grandmother. I should've spent more time with her in the kitchen, learning all of her recipes and soaking up her knowledge when it was offered."

"Your grandmother is a chef?"

"No. Just a really good home cook. She passed away about fifteen years ago."

"I'm sorry, dear. Unfortunately, that's something you and Jameson have in common. He also lost his father when he was younger."

He stiffened. What was his mother doing?

Dani touched a hand to her throat. "I knew he'd passed away, but Jameson didn't tell me the circumstances."

"It was hard for him. Not because they were particularly close, but because of the scandal surrounding it."

The sound of his molars meeting was loud in his ear. "Mother—"

"The scandal?"

"Jameson's father died with his mistress."

Her words hit him with the force of an arctic wind, slamming into his chest, making it harder to breathe. Had his mother actually brought up his father? They never talked about it between themselves, let alone in front of a stranger.

Dani seemed dazed. "Oh."

But Jameson couldn't respond because he'd been transported back to an encounter with his father, two days before the accident. He'd been trying to discuss his decision to attend uni instead of joining the military as Richard had, but his father had been busy and preoccupied.

"I'm disappointed in your decision, but we'll talk more when I get back," Prince Richard had said, rushing off to undertake an official engagement on behalf of the queen before leaving on a "special" trip.

It was the last time Jameson had seen or spoken to his father.

Then came the swarming horde of reporters, the flashing lights, the rhythmic clicks of cameras. Everywhere he went they followed, shouting invasive queries about how he was handling his emotions and whether he'd known about his father and Gena Phillips.

Nor had his mother been spared the focus of their lenses. They hounded her wherever she traveled. And when she'd put herself between him and the voracious throng, she'd been subjected to their cruel and hurtful questions. It was callous and relentless, and he'd been brimming with impotent rage because he couldn't protect her. He could only stand by and watch the person he loved most in the world suffer at the hands of the greedy, entitled press.

Jameson had vowed then and there to never be like his father. To never have his actions be the cause of her having to endure that torture for entertainment.

He never had.

And he never would.

"It's not a secret, dear. Everyone knows."

Dani's eyes went liquid with concern, and he hardened himself against it. "It was a long time ago."

"It was," Calanthe agreed, her tone gentle, "and with different circumstances. But you both had to deal with the death of an important parental figure."

"Why are you telling me this?"

"From that moment I witnessed, my son trusts you. He let you in. And he doesn't do that with a lot of people. I have faith in his judgment." The easygoing manner suddenly slid from Calanthe's face to be replaced with a maternal fierceness. "But if we're both wrong, just know there's no place on Earth where you would be able to hide from me."

Jameson held his breath, wondering how Dani would react. This could get unpleasant quickly. He'd seen her in fight mode.

But Dani surprised him by nodding. "He's lucky to have you."

The pressure in his chest eased. Crisis averted. Though, if he'd thought about it, he would have realized that Dani and his mother had more in common than their monikers.

Something vibrated against the table and Dani picked up her phone. "I need to respond to this. It's an SOS from my assistant about arrangements for her arrival in a few days. Would you two please excuse me? It was a pleasure meeting you, Calanthe."

"You, too, dear." His mother smiled. "I'm sure we'll be seeing more of one another."

Dani stood and squeezed his shoulder before leaving the room, her phone already to her ear.

Jameson turned back to his mother. "Is there anything else you'd like to share with her? My childhood crush on Scarlett? My first pet? Want to break out the old home movies? Look at my primary school report cards?"

"I haven't seen that look on your face . . . ever."

"What do you mean?"

"That sparkle of excitement a person gets when they meet some-one they sincerely care about."

"I've dated women I've cared for. What about Imogen?"

"Lady Harrington? She's a lovely young woman and perfect on

paper, but she doesn't affect you like this. You look positively electric. And that's why I mentioned your father. I did that for you," Calanthe said.

"For me?"

"Yes, because you weren't going to."

"Why would I tell Dani about my childhood and our family?"

"Because it's important for you to open up when you're in a relationship."

"Mother, I don't want you getting the wrong impression. Dani and I are not in a relationship. It's not serious. She's leaving when the celebration is over."

"And you're just going to let her go?"

He didn't answer her. "For someone who's usually more guarded, I'm surprised you said as much as you did."

Calanthe looked at him with a tenderness he remembered from his childhood. "When I saw the two of you together, admitting how much you liked each other, it was more intimate, more touching than watching the vows at Lord Portwith's wedding last year."

He scoffed. "You're exaggerating."

"You may have started out convincing yourselves it's not serious, but I don't think either of you believes that anymore."

He tried to laugh off what she was saying, but the chuckle stuck in his throat.

"I hate to burst all of your romantic notions, but it's not in the cards for us. We enjoy spending time together. That's all. And in two and a half weeks, she's going home, and I'll never see her again."

Calanthe stared at him before nodding. "Then I apologize. I got it wrong. Probably for the best anyway. If Marina thought there was the possibility of you being in a relationship with an American entertainer . . . she'd hit the palace roof."

He shook his head. "Technically I'll need her approval to marry, but she doesn't have a say in who I date."

"My darling, you have no idea how important this is, do you? Marina loved two things in this world: the monarchy and John, and with John's passing, it's all on the Crown. Her children are a disaster, save one, but Catherine can't take the throne. It's going to be that ridiculous Julian. And now with whispers about abolishing the monarchy or, at the very least, reducing the amount the public spends on them, she will do anything to ensure that doesn't happen on her watch. And you're the key to that. She needs you. And if you get caught up in a scandal and ruin her chance to save the House of Lloyd . . ."

She reached out and covered his hand with her own. "Just promise me you'll be careful. I don't want you to be flattened in service to Marina's ambitions."

Chapter Sixteen

"Commandin' you thru the screen / A virtual dom / Steady blowin' up your spot / With straight style and aplomb . . ."
—Duchess, "Who You Gon' Tell"

Over the next week, Primrose Park shifted from the idyllic, secluded space she and Jameson shared to Operation Duchess Goes Royal. Dani had always planned on relocating to the Baglioni once her team arrived, but she'd been shocked by her reluctance to leave Jameson behind. She wasn't ready. So when he suggested she stay, even offering to turn an old barn on the estate into an impromptu rehearsal space for her use, she eagerly jumped at the opportunity to delay their eventual separation.

The first morning he'd come up behind her as she stared out the window. Wrapping his arms around her and pulling her against his chest, he followed her gaze to the various cars and passenger vans that had accumulated overnight. Between the workmen, who'd brought in floors and mirrors, and the dancers, who were walking around in various forms of workout gear, it was a hectic sight.

"Now *this* is an entourage," she said, referring to his accusation when they'd first met.

"You don't let anything go, do you?"

"Nope. The dancers got in last night and we're starting our first rehearsal."

"Will I see you this afternoon?"

"Probably not. I have back-to-back meetings with my team."

"Dinner?"

She shook her head. "I can't."

He frowned. "Is this what it's going to look like for the next week?"

She winced. "Imagine that this is the calm before the storm."

And she'd been right. Between meeting with the venue manager and the lighting director to finalize their idea on the presentation for the space they had, doing last-minute wardrobe and costume fittings, and practicing the choreography for the performance, Dani's schedule kept her busy.

And as her work life intruded, so did Jay's. He was either in his office, meeting with Louisa, or doing press interviews about the upcoming celebration. They met only in the evening, falling into each other with a hunger that showed no sign of diminishing.

"Okay!" The shout from Gabrielle, her choreographer, brought Dani out of her reverie. "Let's run through this again!"

Six background dancers stood in two staggered lines in front of her, reflecting a beautiful range of skin tones. She wasn't just putting on a good show; the performance would also serve to showcase the beauty of black women and women of color to highlight the importance of Mela-Skin.

Multitasking, bitches.

The beat boomed through the speakers and Gabrielle yelled, "Five, six, seven, eight . . ."

In unison, their bodies moved to the music, pelvises thrusting, hips popping, arms twirling. Attitudes on point. Some of the steps would be familiar to anyone who'd watched the video, but they'd made some changes. Dani wasn't interested in movements solely to titillate, as had been the intention with the first video, but rather in emphasizing feminine power and sexual enjoyment.

Her head bopped to the song as she ran through the moves under her breath.

"Shoulder, hip, sway and sway, turn, pose . . . Wait!"

She jumped from the chair she'd been sitting on and strode over to the dancers, who stilled, their chests expanding and contracting as they inhaled and exhaled deeply. She adjusted the waistband of her black leggings and slid into position before the bank of mirrors.

"I know we said shoulder, hip, sway and sway," she said, executing the move, "but I don't like the way it looks. You see?" She repeated the steps. "I want to change it."

Gabrielle crossed her arms over her chest and jutted her hip to the side, considering Dani's request. "What if we add in the sequence from the Grammy performance two years ago?"

Dani mentally recalled the moves then swiftly did them. Joy bubbled in her chest. "Ooh, yes. That's it! Do that!"

Gabrielle smiled then lifted her arm in the air and rotated her index finger in a circle. "Let's take it from the top."

The women began again and easily inserted the new steps. And it looked better.

"Grab some water and we'll move on to the next song," Gabrielle said.

Three hours later, Dani ended rehearsals with an exhausted smile on her face. "I think we're done for today. That was perfect! Tomorrow you'll go to the arena and practice the choreography there. The next time I see you, we'll run through the entire show."

"This is going to be lit," Tasha said, coming over to her with a bottle of water.

"I think so," Dani said, taking off her heels and flexing her feet. "Oh my God, why do I always do this?"

"Do what?"

"Go all out on rehearsals, as if I'm a member of Alvin Ailey." She leaned back in the metal folding chair. "Probably because I'm excited. When we start rehearsals, I know a performance isn't too far behind."

And she loved the performing aspect of the business. There was nothing in the world like the energy she got back from the crowd. It was the best high ever.

"Are you happy with the direction of the show so far?" her assistant asked.

Dani swallowed and nodded her head. "I am. I'm particularly happy with the set list."

"A few of us were talking about going out tonight. You want to come?" Tasha asked.

Dani wanted to. She missed doing stuff like that. In the beginning she'd enjoyed turning up and turning out. But Samantha Banks wasn't the first person to try to make a name or get some coins by coming for her.

"Thanks for the offer, but you know I can't."

"C'mon, we're on a different continent! We can make it safe! Throw on a wig, change your appearance . . ."

"I'm good."

Tasha frowned. "I expected to find you going crazy out here in the country."

Dani finished her water. "It's not as bad as I thought it'd be. Turns out, it was just what I needed. It helped clear my head."

In more ways than one.

"I can see that. You seem better than you were before you left the States."

She was. The time she'd spent here had given her a perspective that was difficult to have in her normal life. And of course, there had been Jay. She hoped she could find a way to take this peace back with her.

You mean, find a way to take him *back with you.*

Dani smiled. "You guys go and have a good time. But be careful."

"Trust me, when you're not with us, no one cares who we are. It's like we go around with our own invisibility cloak."

"Must be nice. I need to get one of those."

"Do you need me to get you anything before we leave?"

"Nope. I'm going to run through the set one more time and lock it in."

After waving good-bye to everyone and thanking them for all of their hard work, Dani looked at her discarded shoes. Nah. She'd work on the movement now and worry about dancing in the heels later. Looking at her reflection in the mirror, she smoothed her ponytail and retied the knot on her T-shirt, then padded over to her phone on the large speaker and cued up her first hit. The song they were starting the show with.

You look at me & I'm all you want to be
Snatched waist
Fat/thin
Face full of melanin

She said the lines right before her entrance and began to move. There were certain iconic steps that fans expected to see when she performed this song, but she also wanted to give them something new and exciting. Not to mention, she was going to be exposed to an entirely different audience with this performance.

She wanted to wow everyone.

It wasn't every day a hip-hop act was invited to participate in a true-blue royal celebration. And not just a hip-hop act, but a female artist. Despite her popularity, she was aware that women made up only a small percentage of the industry. She never truly represented just herself; she represented her genre, women in her genre, black people, and then black women. Society saw a lot of bodies behind her, like those mirrors in a fun house. And if she messed up or made a mistake, it wasn't her own folly. It reflected on all of them. It was hella unfair but that's the way it was.

She needed the good publicity and press from this trip to overshadow the scandal with Samantha Banks. She couldn't risk losing Genesis's interest. This was more than a performance. This affected the rest of her life. And she couldn't let anything derail her, not even the delicious prince who'd been taking up so much real estate in her brain she should be charging him rent.

She just needed to focus. Preferably on remembering the new sequence of steps. Every time she got to this part, her body wanted to do the old choreography. The choreography she could do in her sleep.

Like she just did!

Fuck!

She scrubbed her hands through her hair, threw her head back, and looked up at the ceiling.

"Rough day?"

She started, surprised to hear Jameson's warm, cultured tone. Despite her pep talk to herself, heat suffused her body at his appearance.

"Not anymore," she said, pausing the song.

Then she was in his arms and his lips were on hers and everything was right with the world.

"I see everyone's gone?" he said, when they finally drew apart.

"Yeah, you just missed the last of them. They're headed back into the city to hit some pubs."

"And you didn't want to join them?"

"Why would I, when I have all the entertainment I could ever want right here?"

"Good answer." He nipped her bottom lip. "What were you working on when I came in?"

"We tweaked the choreography for one of my songs and my head is having a hard time remembering the changes."

"Yeah, I can see how that would be difficult."

"Except I don't have time for this to be an issue."

"Come here," he said, settling on a chair. He pulled her down on his lap. "Maybe I've never seen you in work mode before, but you've been really intense this past week."

"This is important."

"Why?"

"What?"

"Why is this so important to you? The concert. This event. Don't get me wrong. This is important to me, too. But you don't need this or us. You're one of the most popular performers in the world."

"Googling me again?"

"You're not going to distract me this time, though you're very good at it."

She sighed. "Have you heard of a singer named Samantha Banks?"

"No. Should I have?"

She laughed. "She thinks so. She's this up-and-coming pop star who's decided to take me on."

"What does that mean?"

"She's been using me as a come up, picking a feud to get more publicity."

He smoothed his thumb over her furrowed brow. "I understand about people trying to use you for their own purposes, but what does some singer I've never heard of have to do with you doing the concert?"

"It's not about her. Not really. It's about me, my brand, and a deal I'm working on. I can tell you, but you have to promise not to tell anyone."

"Hmmm, that might be difficult. Since I talk about you and us all of the time, it's guaranteed to come up—"

"Okay." She took a deep breath. "Several years ago, I started a skin-care company called Mela-Skin to provide natural skin-care products to women of color."

"I didn't know that. That's wonderful."

"I thought you looked me up."

"I never got past the pictures and videos."

She smiled wryly. "The company has been doing well and we were recently approached by one of the world's largest cosmetics companies interested in acquiring us."

"That's amazing," he said.

"It is. This is a major deal, Jay."

"I can tell. But it's about more than the money, isn't it?"

"I told you a little about how I grew up, right?"

"You were raised by your grandmother and when she died, other family members."

"I know I was lucky to have family who could take me in. But those years after my grandmother died . . . The lack of stability is hard for a kid. No matter what we might say, we crave structure. There would be times when I'd go to school from one relative's house and come home to a different person. There was no rhyme or reason to where I'd be and who'd make decisions for me. And I didn't like it. I swore that one day I'd be in control of my own fate. It's the guiding principle of everything I've done with my life and career. And while being a rapper is great and has given me lots of opportunities and exposed me to people and places I wouldn't have known otherwise, I was wrong in thinking it would allow me to call my own shots. I answer to more people now than I did as a kid."

"I understand. It's partially why I'd resisted being a public part of the royal family for so long. With the family, there is no self. Only the Crown. The queen expects us to live, move, and breathe in service to the monarchy."

"Part of what Genesis gets if it purchases Mela-Skin is my brand. And this thing with Banks is diminishing that. We thought some positive press would help."

"Like performing at a tribute concert for one of the most popular royals of all time?"

"Exactly."

"And dating a young, handsome royal? Would that help?"

She jerked back. "I don't know. Are you offering?"

Suddenly subdued, he stared at her, a thoughtful cast to his features. Her own stomach churned as she waited for his answer. When had their jokes shifted into something more serious?

Finally, he shook his head. "No."

She released a trapped breath. In relief? Or disappointment?

"I wish I could. I truly do."

"It's okay." She smoothed her hand down the front of his shirt.

"This is my business. I appreciate you wanting to help, but I can handle it on my own."

He leaned forward and rested his chin on the top of her head. "Being a part of this celebration is the closest you'd ever want to come to being tied to my family."

"Oh, I don't know." She wriggled in his lap. "I enjoy being tied up and coming with you."

"I'm serious, Dani. This family is fucked up. I'd never want to subject you to them. And if there was even a whisper of the two of us being involved, the Palace would insert themselves in a major way."

Insert themselves— Why was she thinking like a horny teenager?

"They could try."

"They wouldn't just try. They'd succeed."

Her heart twisted at the concern and conviction glowing in his eyes. She recalled some of the comments his mother had made and her tone when talking about the queen and others. His family had really done a number on him.

"It doesn't matter. None of it is going to happen. I'm going to kill it at all of the events next week and smash my concert performance. The coverage will be so spectacular that all of the companies who originally bowed out will come crawling back."

"You had interest from more than Genesis?"

"I did."

"That's incredible."

"It was. And that's why me being here is so important and why this has to work. I can't lose this deal."

"It's that important to you?"

"It's the most important thing in my life."

"Even more than music? Are you planning to stop performing?"

"Eventually. I'm good at rapping and I enjoy it, but it's not my passion. I'd still like to be involved in some way, but on my terms, whatever I choose those to be."

He hugged her. "You're a woman of many talents, Dani Nelson."

She decided to share another piece of herself with him. "Danielle. My first name is Danielle."

"Danielle Nelson," he breathed, as if inhaling her name into his soul. "You're divine. I'll do everything I can, behind the scenes. If you charm everyone else a fraction as much as you've charmed me, by the end of the week they'll be saying, 'Samantha who? We want more Duchess!'"

"I didn't know Dame Maggie Smith was a fan," she said, laughing at the crazy voice he'd pulled out of thin air.

"Why wouldn't she be? I am."

This celebration was about *his* family and he was concerned about how she'd do? Was it possible for her chest to contain a heart that had doubled in size?

Staring into his beautiful, earnest face, she knew he would always have her back.

No, not her.

The lucky lady who'd earn his heart. He'd make a wonderful husband and partner.

To that woman.

Smiling weakly, she pushed off his lap and grabbed a nearby bottle of water to wash the suddenly sour taste from her mouth.

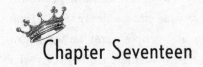

Chapter Seventeen

"It is not for the people to give laws to the prince, but to obey his mandate."

—Frederick I, Holy Roman Emperor

The queen wants to see you today. She has a spot open at three thirty."

Jameson curled his fingers into a fist on the desk. Why hadn't he heeded his initial instinct and not answered his phone when he'd seen Louisa's name flash on his caller ID?

Because she still would've found a way to get him. The Royal Household's senior events coordinator had proven she was nothing if not tenacious.

He glanced at his watch. "That's in two hours."

"Then you'd better hurry, sir," Louisa said, before disconnecting the call.

He sighed, looking down at his trousers and jumper.

After changing into a dark suit, he left the main house and headed over to the barn to find Dani. She was surrounded by dancers, as was usual lately, but he only had eyes for her. He was certain he wasn't the only one.

Throwing her arms in the air and waving them from side to side, she dropped down into a squat and spread her thighs, bringing them back together and sensuously rolling to a standing position.

Moisture fled his mouth. Was anyone else suddenly sweltering?

Jameson was intimately aware that people weren't always how they appeared. That there was a distinct difference between who or what people presented to the public and who they truly were. It was a way of life for royals and it was why he'd been happy to limit his time in the spotlight, so he wouldn't have to take part in the farce.

And yet he'd fallen into that same trap by making assumptions about Dani. He'd assumed she was the same as Duchess. And he'd learned she was so much more. He'd known she was smart; one only had to have a conversation with her to glean that. But she was also enterprising. In addition to her music, she'd started a company that was doing so well, Genesis was interested in purchasing it.

He'd done some research on Mela-Skin after she told him about it. She'd recognized an area of the market that wasn't being served and had stepped in to fill the void. The reviews for her product were stellar, and the business world appeared in awe of what she'd accomplished.

And these last few days had educated him on how much went into being Duchess. The rapper persona was a part of her, but an exaggerated version. It took a lot of work, and a substantial number of people were involved. He understood why she hadn't taken a vacation in years. The success of two multimillion-dollar companies rested on her petite shoulders. His respect and esteem for her had grown. Dani was an exceptional woman.

Refocusing on the present, he met her eyes in the mirror and her slow knowing smile sent the blood racing directly to his cock.

Who was he kidding? His blood had set up residence down there the moment he'd first seen her.

Another few seconds and she was done.

"Everyone, can you take a moment and thank the prince for his hospitality," she said with a twinkle in her eyes he could see from across the room.

He was suddenly the focus of applause as thank-yous rained in his direction. Going for stoicism, he nodded, although he couldn't prevent the heat from settling on his cheeks or the tips of his ears.

"Duchess, can I speak with you for a moment?"

She said something to a woman standing near the front before moving toward him, shapely and lithe in the leggings and T-shirt that appeared to be the dancer's uniform.

"You look great," she said when they'd stepped outside. "Do you have another interview?"

"No. A summons from my grandmother."

The teasing smile dropped from her face. "Does she have to summon you before you can go to the palace? I mean, can you just drop by and spend time with your grandmother?"

He hadn't taken such informal liberties with his grandfather and he'd been much closer to Prince John.

"I can visit the palace whenever I choose, but to see the queen, it's generally accepted that one must make an appointment."

Dani stared at him. "Wow. I know it's your family, but that's crazy weird."

He could see how it appeared that way. But—

"It's how things are done."

"How close are you to the queen?"

"Uhhh, not very."

"No. Like, how close are you to being king?"

He laughed. "Why? Does the thought of that turn you on?"

She tilted her head and swayed side to side. "Depends on your answer."

"Uhhh, not very."

"Perfect. Because as much as I love the royal vitamin D you've been giving me, I'm not interested in turning over control of my life to anyone, and that includes abiding by antiquated notions of propriety to keep a monarchical system of government in place."

Just as he'd said.

Smart.

He stared down at her. Many unlikely occurrences would have to happen before he could ever ascend to the throne. He ignored the twinge of his conscience that warned if she were a permanent part of his life, those notions of propriety would go into effect immediately. Becoming king wasn't a requirement.

"Then you should be ecstatic to learn you have nothing to worry about."

"Delirious." She grinned, leaning toward him before she caught herself at the last minute. "Well, tell her hi for me. Or bow or whatever it is that people do."

He ached to touch her but knew they couldn't risk it. Too many people around. "I'll be sure to do that. Enjoy the rest of your rehearsal."

She gave him a two-finger salute and backed away from him before turning and heading into the barn.

"Alright, let's run through it again and make it sexy!"

THIS TIME IT was the Green Drawing Room.

He'd been coming to the palace since he was a baby. He didn't need the color wheel tour of the drawing rooms, but it seemed that was the experience he was getting, whether he wanted it or not.

Marina sat in an emerald and gold upholstered chair. "You're ready for next week's events?"

"I am."

He'd gone over the schedule multiple times, confirming where he was going to be, when he needed to be there, and what would be required of him at each appearance.

"And the award?"

"It will take some time until it's ready, but I'm going to announce it at the ball. I thought it would be a fitting way to close out the celebration."

"Excellent. So it appears I was correct to believe you were the right person to carry out this responsibility."

"It appears so."

Her gaze hardened. "Then how do you explain this?"

Jameson started at the slap of a manila folder landing on the table. The impact caused several glossy photos to slide out onto the burnished mahogany. With narrowed eyes, he picked them up. Shock chilled him from the inside as he stared at images of him and Dani from the past few weeks. Of them at Primrose Park, their evening at Baslingfield, their afternoon in the baking tent.

The pictures were innocent, portraying the two of them walking around the estate, watching the movie together, laughing as they attempted to bake scones.

Anger misted his vision. "Where did you get these?"

"Don't question me!" she rebuked, her posture ramrod straight. "What were you thinking?"

"I wasn't thinking anything. Because there's nothing going on."

"That's not how I would describe these pictures. I can see the way you're looking at one another. That is not nothing."

"She's a guest at Primrose Park, with your approval. I was being hospitable and keeping her occupied so she wouldn't go into the city, get discovered, and have the focus shift away from the celebration. Isn't that what you wanted?"

The queen shook her head. "I wish I could say this was the first time I'd had this conversation. I never thought I'd be having it with you."

She tossed several more photos onto the table, and Jameson winced when the top one showed him and Dani kissing after the screening at Baslingfield. He'd been caught up in the magic of the evening and captivated by how beautiful she'd looked sitting next to him. Thinking it was safe, he'd pulled her behind a tall hedge and pressed his lips to hers, not wanting to wait another minute to taste her.

The other pictures had probably captured similar incidents. Moments when he'd been unable to control himself.

"I expected this type of thing from Julian. He's never been able to resist a pretty face and an easy manner. Have you watched her videos? My private secretary showed me one. She's practically offering herself on a silver platter."

The distaste in her voice was quite different from the public statement the Palace had put out taking credit for Duchess's participation in response to the praise surrounding her inclusion.

"But you, Jameson? I thought you were better. You're a man of intellect and great thought. Like my John. I couldn't have anticipated you would be the one ruled by your baser instincts."

His hand fisted by his side.

"And do I need to mention your father? I loved my son, but his weak character and selfishness almost ruined us. It certainly led to his death. I thought, of any of the family, you would be able to do the right thing."

Resentment choked him at the mention of his father.

"Do you remember what it was like after he died? The scandal? The press? How it affected your poor mother?"

He hadn't forgotten the toll it had taken on Calanthe. The lost look in her eyes, the despair. Holed up at Kensington Palace because it was the only place she was safe from the constant swarm of paparazzi.

"And despite what she was going through, she still thought of you. Your welfare. You inherited responsibilities that day. You inherited the Wessex duchy, but you shouldered none of the responsibility. Even after you turned twenty-one, you didn't have to step fully into that role. It is by my grace that you've been allowed to live in your ivory tower."

He swallowed past the burning in his throat and forced himself to speak. "And I've always expressed my gratitude for your benevolence."

"You owe me. You owe your mother. You owe this family. Your father put his desires over royal duty. You will not do the same."

"This isn't what you think it—"

"I got those from the *Daily Express*."

A British tabloid had taken those pictures? He'd thought Marina was having him followed. But the media . . . this was much worse. The tabloids would dredge up Richard's death and turn Jameson's relationship with Dani into something lascivious.

Like father, like son.

The coverage had the potential to devastate Dani's business. Getting swept up in a royal scandal wouldn't be the type of good press she wanted to generate.

No one would emerge unscathed.

All because he'd been unable to curb his impulses when it came to her.

Fuck!

He shoved a hand through his hair. "When are they going to be printed?"

"They're not."

He narrowed his eyes. "I don't understand."

"It took a lot to keep them from going with this story. But I've promised them exclusive behind-the-scenes coverage of the celebration. It was distasteful, but it's what I had to do. And they know I'll keep my word. Much has gotten out about this family, but it's only a fraction of what it could've been."

Comprehension dawned. His mother had been right.

Marina loved two things in this world: the monarchy and John.

And in her eyes his actions had the possibility of tarnishing both.

He had underestimated what his grandmother was willing to do to preserve the monarchy.

"What do you want?"

"For you to do what I've asked from the beginning: serve as the face of the family during this celebration. Give the press, and the world, a good royal to focus on. And stay away from her." She tipped her head toward the photos of him and Dani.

"And if I do, you'll make sure the tabloid doesn't release those pictures?"

"The tabloids aren't an issue. I told you I've taken care of it. My job is to safeguard this family. Allowing those photos to be released would only hurt us."

And Dani.

He didn't say that out loud. His grandmother didn't know what was on the line for Dani, and Jameson wanted that to continue, realizing Dani might need his protection in a way he hadn't considered.

Marina substantiated his concern when she said, "Of course, these photos *could* get out in the American press along with unconfirmed rumors of her setting her sights on a royal against the wishes of the family. It may not mean anything to her fans, but Louisa mentioned a situation she was involved in. I'd imagine a big conglomerate, focused on her brand, wouldn't be too eager to sign a contract with someone involved in a salacious scandal."

Her words were like a physical blow. Jameson had always known that as queen, and ruling monarch, she had worries and responsibilities he could never comprehend. But she was still his grandmother, and his grandfather had adored her. She and Jameson weren't close, but the knowledge of his grandfather's feelings for her had imbued her in his eyes with a warm, loving glow she hadn't been entitled to.

Marina was ruthless. He needed to remember that.

"This is important for all of us, Jameson. I want you to take over John's charitable portfolio and continue overseeing his award. I know your grandfather would've liked nothing more. But I will not let you or anyone else ruin this celebration. Focus on your duties. And stay away from that American!"

"HEY!"

Jameson glanced up from his desk to find Dani standing in his doorway. He'd seen the cars and heard the music when he drove past the barn an hour ago. Considering what had happened during his meeting with the queen—and his resulting piss-poor mood—he hadn't wanted to disturb her, so he'd continued to the main house and holed up in his office.

"I was looking for you," she said, crossing her arms and leaning against the jamb. "I thought you'd stop by on your way home."

"I was tired. And I could tell you were still working." He gave her a thorough once-over. Even in black leggings and a cutoff T-shirt, with no makeup and her hair in a ponytail, she was radiant. But then, she always struck him as stunning. "You look good."

She rolled her eyes. "Right."

He stood. "You do."

"Thanks. But don't get too close," she said, when he came around the desk. "I'm all hot and sweaty."

"I can see that. Half the work is done for me."

Her laughter turned into a sigh when he pulled her into his arms for a kiss. He'd heard his grandmother's warning, but she'd misunderstood the situation. What he and Dani had was casual. They weren't hurting anyone. She wasn't a danger to the monarchy. Jameson could fulfill his duties and continue seeing Dani. They'd just have to be more careful.

"Mmmm, do I get this after all of my rehearsals?"

He led her over to the sofa and pulled her onto his lap. "I'd be happy to oblige."

She swept a lock of hair off his forehead. "How was your meeting with the queen? Did it go well?"

"I wouldn't say 'well.'" He dropped his gaze and picked at a stray thread on her thigh. "It wasn't what I expected."

"In what way?"

He should tell her. About the pictures and Marina's warning that she could have them published in the States. But this was his fault. Dani hadn't done anything wrong. Marina had made this threat because of him. It was his issue. He'd handle it and keep her safe.

"I thought it was something new, but it was more talk about the celebration."

"Why is she sweating you so hard?"

He arched a brow.

She laughed. "Bothering you. Why is she constantly bothering you?"

He sighed. "The monarchy has a serious PR problem and there's been talk of abolishment."

She gasped. "Is that possible?"

"Some countries have done it. It could happen here, but it would take an unprecedented act by Parliament or a public referendum. However, the fact that she's worried is troublesome."

"Is that what's really behind this celebration?"

"Partly. Her love for my grandfather and wanting to celebrate his life is genuine. But the positive exposure it'll bring to the family is key."

"You know I get needing some positive press." She laughed. "What I don't understand is why she drafted you to be the face of it. And why you agreed."

He sighed, suddenly not wanting to discuss this. "How about we both grab show—"

"No, don't shut me out. Your mother said you never wanted to be in the spotlight. Why now?"

He gripped her hips and squeezed. "My grandfather gave his life to his causes. To see them in the hands of a drunken philanderer doesn't sit well with me."

Dani wasn't fooled. "Try again."

He huffed out a laugh. "This isn't the easiest family to grow up in."

"Yeah, I believe we've established that."

"What's ironic is to avoid a scandal the queen is using the person who's the product of one." At her questioning look he elaborated. "My father, Prince Richard, was eighteen when he got my mother pregnant. She was seventeen and from a well-regarded aristocratic family. As you can imagine, those things aren't done. My grand-mother forced them to wed. To—"

"—avoid the scandal," Dani completed his sentence. "This is like a soap opera."

"It's much worse. Fiction can't compare to our actual history. No one would believe it."

"You were saying . . ."

Right. "My father was the more gregarious sort. Outgoing, charming, athletic. He had certain ideas about what a prince should be and how a prince should act, and they weren't matched by a slight, studious son who was more comfortable with books than blokes."

She arched a brow and leaned away, eyeing him. "There's nothing slight about you."

"Now," he said, the back of his neck heating. "But I was what you'd call a late bloomer. My first year of uni, the year after my father died, I grew six inches and put on a little weight."

"That explains it."

"Explains what?"

"Why you don't act like most men who look like you do and have what you have."

"Thanks, I think."

She flattened her palms against his cheeks and kissed him lightly on the lips. "It's a compliment."

He touched his forehead to hers before continuing. "My mother did her best to shield me, but my father was a man of extreme passions and appetites. My existence had cost him his youth and I was a disappointment. But my grandfather was kind and compassionate. He was the prince consort and could be charming and outgoing, but he was also an academic.

"After Father died, I knew what would happen. I'd have to abandon my interests and assume his duties. And I was furious. I'd have to give up what I loved and be forced into a role I didn't want, because he couldn't exert a modicum of self-control."

"But that didn't happen."

"No, because Mother and Grandfather stood up for me. They went to the queen and pleaded my case and she listened. Because of that, I never had as much exposure as my aunts and uncle and my younger cousins. Thus making me the ideal fresh face to sacrifice to the wolves in service to the throne now."

"Not the wolves." She laughed. "And not this face. It's too pretty."

She was adorable.

"I am not pretty! As for why I agreed . . . I didn't have a choice. She named me a Counsellor of State. By law, if she asks me to carry out an official duty for her, I'm required to do so. But I owe my grandfather so much. This is how I start to pay him back."

"Okay," she said, wrapping her arms around him. "I got it."

"Now you know the real reason behind the celebration and why next week is important. The eyes of the world will be on us; everything has to be perfect." He took her hand and kissed it. "And we have to be careful. No one can find out about us."

"I thought we'd already discussed that. I'm on board. We can control ourselves in public."

"Are you sure?"

"You're not *that* irresistible."

"Right. But you are," he said.

She rose from his lap, then knelt on the floor in front of him. "We're just talking in public though, right?"

He nodded, unsure of where she was going.

"We can still do what we want in private," she said, running her hands up his thighs.

His lashes fluttered as tingles suffused him. "Absolutely."

"Good." She licked her lips. "Because I've been thinking about this all day."

She reached for his belt and made quick work of the buckle and the button on his trousers.

His chest expanded in gratitude as he realized how close he'd come to never having known her. How had he gotten so lucky? Why? After their first encounter, she'd had every reason to never speak to him again.

"I'm glad I didn't know. I wouldn't have wanted this picture in my head while meeting with my grandmother."

Dani gazed up at him, her eyes soft and shining, her lips slightly parted. "Speaking of head . . ."

She reached inside his fly and wrapped her fingers around his thickening cock, applying the perfect amount of pressure as she stroked his shaft from the base to the tip.

He dug his nails into the cushions of the sofa and lifted his hips, thrusting into her grip.

A bead of cum formed on his tip and she licked away the evidence of his arousal before she hollowed her cheeks and engulfed the entire cap in her mouth, the suction a sweet torture that blew his mind.

He almost came apart. "Oh God, love. You're killing me."

She glanced up at him. "You taste so fucking good, baby."

The rhythmic rasp of her tongue caused shivers to rack his body. And that was before she turned her attention to his balls.

She locked her arms around his knees and pulled him forward until his ass was near the edge of the sofa. She cradled his sac in her hands. Her touch was amazing. Her tongue was even better. She ran it along the space between his balls and pulled one into her mouth.

He jerked off the seat. "Fuck me."

"I'm about to," she said, drawing the other one in and rolling it with her tongue.

He was holding on to his composure by a gossamer-thin thread when she released his balls and flicked wet kisses up his shaft.

"Did you like that?"

She had no idea. "I can't take much more."

"You'd be surprised what you can take when you have to."

Without warning, she wet her lips and pushed his cock through a seam pressed so tight it felt like he was sliding into the snuggest of channels.

Oh fuck! Oh fuck! Oh fuck!

If this kept up, he wouldn't last. And it couldn't end soon. It felt too good.

In the effort of trying to dampen down the overwhelming urges surging through him, it took several seconds for him to notice she'd stopped.

His eyes flew open. "What's wrong?"

"Jay. Baby. Let go."

"I am."

"You're not. You're holding yourself back. Don't. You want to fuck my mouth? Fuck my mouth. I can take it."

Once again her lips consumed his cock. And this time he gave in to it. He drove his fingers into her hair and bucked his hips upward, thrusting into her hot mouth over and over, claiming all the gratification he could. He trusted her, trusted she knew what she could handle. That she'd stop him if it became too much.

Euphoria coiled at the base of his spine and he curled his toes in his shoes. "Dani, love, I'm close."

The wetness of her mouth was replaced by her hand.

"You want to come on my tits?" she asked, stroking him fast and hard.

He opened his eyes and found she'd managed to discard her top. The erotic action intensified his arousal. The sight of his pale cock in her brown hand, the bare expanse of her chest, her perfect breasts with her dark stiff nipples . . .

"Fuck yeah."

He stared into her eyes, felled by the emotion he saw in their depths. A desire that matched his own and something else. Something intense and all too real, but unnamed. The potency of those feelings drew him in, secure in the knowledge that she'd accepted him for himself.

Not for his titles. Or for what he could do for her.

In spite of them.

"I got you, Jay," she whispered. "Let go."

His balls tightened and his cock stiffened almost to the point of pain. Body on fire, and with a palace-rattling roar, he came, gazing at her while spurts of his fluid coated her chest. As he drifted back from the rapturous climax she'd given him, Jameson vowed he'd do everything in his power to protect Dani from his grandmother.

No matter the cost.

Chapter Eighteen

"I'm god of all I survey / You don't own me / Knocking bitches out the way / Like Showgirls, Nomi . . .*"*

—Duchess, "Don't Try This"

D uchess, who are you wearing?"

"Duchess, would you collab with Samantha Banks?"

"Duchess. Duchess! Over here!"

Dani had been invited to some lavish and extravagant events. The Met Gala, the *Vanity Fair* party after the Oscars, and Diddy's White Party in the Hamptons, just to name a few. But nothing could've prepared her for the spectacle she was experiencing.

The blinding flashes from cameras, the cacophony of voices calling her name—it was a bit overwhelming and it took her back to her first days walking the red carpet. She thought she'd never get used to it, but a publicist had taught her to not look frazzled, inhale a calming breath, and, taking her time, start at the beginning of the row of cameras and slowly move her eyes along to the end. Doing so would give each person enough time to get several angles, since their cameras could take multiple shots in a second. It had required practice, but now she was used to it.

Stand tall. Chin up, shoulders back. Show off the gorgeous gold and sequined dress.

Hair toss or hand on hip.

Microsquint for soft eyes and scan the crowd of photographers, looking just above them.

Move on.

And then she was inside.

The East Gallery was unlike any gallery she'd ever seen in her life. It was a large hall with an alcove at one end. In the middle of the room, against the left wall, was a fireplace, carved in white marble. Above it hung a full-length portrait of someone royal flanked by several others. Crimson silk covered the walls, a striking contrast to the ivory and gold carved ceiling, from which large gold chandeliers hung. Waiters circulated carrying glasses of champagne.

"Duchess!"

Several heads in the room turned at the shouted greeting, but because of the man moving toward her, Dani knew that she was the one who'd been addressed.

Lester Stone reached her and grabbed her shoulders, going in for the two-cheek greeting. "You look gorgeous."

Dani ran her hand down the iridescent sequins covering her skirt and floor-sweeping train. "Thank you."

"I couldn't believe it when I heard you were invited. Thank God. I was afraid I was going to be surrounded by old fuddy-duddies."

Lester Stone was a legendary rock star, and though he was pushing seventy, he would never include himself in that category. He was one of the bestselling music artists of all time, having sold over 250 million records worldwide. While she didn't geek out over his band's music like most of the world did, she recognized his talent.

That recognition didn't entitle him entrée into her pants, though he hit on her every time he saw her. She'd googled pictures of him from when he was younger and she could definitely see the appeal. But between the years of hard partying and the plastic surgery to counteract them, he was this startling mix of leathery under-the-scalpel-a-few-too-many-times alertness that was initially off-putting. It was clear he thought he still looked thirty-five. Or he coasted on his celebrity. Either way, it wasn't going to happen. And after a couple of meetings, she'd made that clear.

But despite that, she liked him, so she wasn't offended when his hug lasted a little longer than normal and his hand somehow grazed her ass.

"I was honored to be invited," she said.

"It shows the royal family has some good taste that I hadn't thought they possessed. Come on, we're all over here."

She placed her hand on his proffered arm and followed him, although she looked around for Jameson as she went. He was nowhere to be seen.

Her pussy still tingled from his marathon eating-out session that afternoon, after which he'd left to get ready at the palace and carry out tasks with the queen and the royal family. This had all started with them both intending to scratch an itch or as a vacation fling. But Jameson was more than she'd expected. They were so different, she never would've thought they would have anything in common, let alone enough to sustain a relationship. But she was now at the point where she was willing to give it a try. She just knew that the thought of saying good-bye to him at the end of this week was entirely too painful. Almost unfathomable.

When they reached the small group on the other side of the room, Dani had to resist pinching herself.

Do you realize where you are? The small girl from Hampton, Virginia, is at Buckingham Palace surrounded by musical—and actual!—royalty.

The people standing before her made up the Who's Who of music. They'd all been inducted into their music's Hall of Fame, had numerous number one albums, and had performed sold-out shows all over the world.

And little Dani Nelson.

Not Dani Nelson.

Duchess.

That's who you are. That's what got you here. And just like these people, that's what you're here to represent. So get it together and give them what they're paying for.

Like standing beneath a waterfall, she let the persona flow over her.

"Hello, I don't think we've met in person but it's nice to finally meet you," a petite woman garbed in a flowing navy blue gown, with long silver-blond hair, said in her distinctive voice. "I'm a big fan."

Kay Morgan, one of the most successful and influential rock stars on the planet, and the woman who'd won the most Grammys to date, was a fan of *hers*?

"Likewise," Dani said to the superstar. "It's a pleasure to meet you."

"Hello, Duchess," Carl Page, a Motown legend, said. "We met backstage at the AMAs a few years ago."

"We did," she said, leaning forward and greeting him with the two-cheek kiss. "It's good to see you again."

She recognized Bobby Worth, a British rock and pop star from the eighties and nineties, but they'd never met, and he only gave her a brief nod before turning back to the person at his side and resuming his conversation.

Looking around, she gave a charming grin. "So, what brings you all here?"

They laughed.

A playful voice behind her said, "How's the other half of music's newest royal couple?"

"Liam!" she exclaimed, giving him a genuine hug. She shook her head, smiling slightly. "What are you talking about?"

"According to *Us Weekly*, we're dating."

"I thought it was *In Touch*?"

"*Us Weekly* has actually confirmed the rumors."

"Oh well, if *Us Weekly* confirmed it . . ." She laughed. "How have you been?"

"Merely existing until I saw you. You look stunning, as always."

She smiled at the appreciation in his hazel eyes. "I'm sure I'm not the first woman you've said that to this evening."

"No," he admitted. "But you're the first one I've said it to that I actually mean it."

"You know I'm immune to your charms, right?"

"That's because you haven't spent enough time in my company. I've got all week to change that."

"Good luck."

"Do I need luck? Especially if Grandpa Stone is my only competition."

She slapped his arm. "Don't say that. At least not out loud."

"So, despite the fact that he made a beeline for you the second you walked in and the way he's glowering at me right now, you're not together?"

"Are you out of your mind? He's an old white dude. Totally not my type."

"What about young white dudes? Can we try?"

His suggestion wasn't that outrageous. *Us Weekly* and the article

Nyla had mentioned wasn't the first time they'd been linked. It would almost be easier if it was true. Liam Cooper understood her world and the role the media would play in it. He'd get what she needed to do for her image.

She slid him a look. "Judging by the number of female glances I'm getting, I think you're going to be too busy."

Lester appeared by her side, inserting himself back into their conversation. "I heard your latest single. Is the video coming soon?"

"I filmed it a couple of months ago. It went up last week."

"The video won't be the only thing coming when he sees it," Liam said under his voice.

She elbowed him in the side.

But she had to admit she was grateful when someone else claimed Lester's attention.

"Looks like the money they used to renovate the place paid off," Kay said, taking a sip from her drink and glancing around.

"You've been here before?" Dani asked.

"Plenty of times. Especially when Prince John was alive. He was a great guy. Smart as a whip. And sensitive. He really cared about the environment way before it was popular to say so. That's why I was happy to participate when they asked me."

"Things were definitely different back then," Bobby said, joining their conversation.

"He didn't mind being in the background. And he was all about the children. None of that fragile male ego bullshit," Kay said.

Dani loved her for saying that and for the fact that she said it not even caring that most of the people they were currently talking to were men.

"I don't know what he would do about Julian and Bettina," Bobby said. "It's not like they were angels, but they knew better than to act out in the press like this."

Kay nodded. "They're too old for this shit. John wouldn't have stood for it."

A woman who'd been standing next to another musician—Mona maybe?—said, "I heard the queen was even considering passing over Julian in favor of abdicating to Catherine."

"That's why they were desperate to do this," Bobby said. "This is probably the most consistent, best piece of press the Firm has gotten in a long time."

"The Firm?" Dani asked.

Bobby nodded, a hint of condescension on his face. "It's the little name they've given themselves. Only for those in the know."

"Smart of her to have Jameson front and center," Mona said, a blush breaking through her heavily made up and contoured cheeks.

When she heard Jameson mentioned, Dani's heart began to beat in her chest.

"If it was one of the others, the press would be too busy asking questions about their numerous scandals," Kay said. "They'd never be able to focus on the prince's good works and all of his causes."

"And this new one is so fresh I can see the dew on his skin," Bobby said, definite interest in his voice.

It was like that *Seinfeld* episode. Her worlds were colliding.

Dani suddenly realized that though she knew who he was, she'd been thinking about him as hers. Her smart, sexy, funny professor, who just happened to be a member of the royal family. But he wasn't just hers.

God, she was selfish. She'd been thinking about this event and how it would affect her. What it was going to do to her life. But what about his life? She knew how he felt about the spotlight. Now he would be soaked in it. And it would only get more intense this week. Suddenly, she worried about him.

She knew why he was doing this. But did he know what he was getting himself into?

An actual trumpet blared before a string quartet, set up on a dais she hadn't noticed earlier, began to play.

"Speak of," Mona murmured.

A man wearing black and white garb straight out of a historical novel appeared in front of a microphone and stand.

"Ladies and gentlemen, may I present Their Royal Highnesses the Prince of Wales . . ."

A striking man, his dark hair tumbling over his forehead, walked out and stood behind him.

"The Princess Catherine . . ."

A woman with a serene, regal bearing, her strawberry blond hair in sleek waves over one shoulder, wearing a maroon gown and a ruby and diamond tiara, joined him.

"The Princess Bettina . . ."

A blond woman in a long black dress, with a stunning diamond and sapphire tiara, came to stand at the end of the line.

"And your hosts for tonight's dinner, His Royal Highness Prince Jameson . . ."

Jameson strode into view and Dani lost her breath. He looked gorgeous in his formal black tie, tailored to perfection across his broad shoulders and a navy blue and gold pocket square. So tall and strong. And as she covertly looked around, she noticed all the admiring gazes he received.

Look all you want, bitches. I'm the only one here who knows what those lips and fingers taste and feel like. Who's screamed his name as he fucked her into the wee hours of the morning.

"And Her Majesty the Queen."

The queen appeared to glide and stand in front of everyone, a vision in an emerald green gown that contrasted beautifully with her pale skin and matched the awe-inspiring tiara nestled within her snow-white curls.

Wow. They were a gorgeous group of people. Gazing up at them, they looked like what one would imagine a royal family, of a majority-white nation, would look like. And in that moment, Jameson had never seemed so far away from her.

"Duchess. Mr. Cooper. Are you ready to meet the queen?" Louisa asked, appearing at her side in a simple black gown that looked gorgeous against her red hair.

"Now?" Dani asked, surprised.

"Yes. The queen asked for an introduction to the performers and those speaking during the events. The rest of the guests will head into the State Dining Room and take their seats. But you all"—at this she motioned to the other musicians—"should follow me."

Liam offered Dani his arm, and she took it, trailing Louisa and the others as they crossed the hall toward the double doors at the end of the room. They'd been opened to showcase a long table exquisitely set for dinner, surrounded by several smaller round tables that were equally beautifully dressed.

A majority of the guests had been seated at their tables and the royal family had been positioned between the two rooms. She and Liam joined a line of people waiting to meet their hosts.

"My first royal meet and greet," Liam whispered, referring to paid VIP preconcert opportunities for fans to take photos and chat with the artists.

"How much you think the queen charges for a selfie?" she asked, laughing.

She looked up and caught Jameson's gaze on her. She bit her

lower lip and smiled but his jaw tightened, and he looked away, refocusing his attention on the person in front of him.

Ouch.

When she reached the beginning of the receiving line, a white-gloved hand halted her progress. Only when Kay was several royals ahead of her did the hand disappear and she was allowed to proceed.

She executed a curtsy to Princess Bettina, who stared down her nose at her before murmuring, "How do you do?"

The princess had barely uttered the last word before her gaze shifted to Liam. Then her eyes lit up and her lips curled in feminine interest.

Even princesses weren't immune to Liam's charm.

Next Dani met Princess Catherine, who, though polite, eyed her curiously.

Prince Julian, the one who'd been announced as the Prince of Wales, stared at her as if each time he blinked, he could see through another layer of her clothes. He held out his hand and when she took it, he pulled her close. The moment caught her off guard. As did his comment.

"You look like a delicious chocolate treat wrapped in gold. Do I get the chance to unwrap you and see if you taste just as sweet?"

Holy fuck.

Her eyes widened, trying and failing to contain her shock and disgust at his come-on. It wasn't the first time a man had made such comments to her. It wasn't even the most vulgar. It was the most unexpected, though. Because she hadn't thought it would happen here.

Aware that she'd caused a slight holdup, she forced a smile and pulled her hand out of his grasp. "I don't think so, Your Royal Highness. Some chocolate can be too rich even for you."

Asshole!

She exhaled and tried to catch her breath, forcing herself to calm. Because Jameson was next, and she was truly looking forward to this experience.

They'd previously discussed how they would act, considering he'd been the one to officially invite her but they also wanted to keep the change in their relationship secret.

"Your Royal Highness," she said, finally offering him that perfect curtsy.

"Duchess," he said.

She'd gotten so used to him calling her Dani, that hearing his delicious voice using her stage name sent tendrils of heat through her.

He held out his hand. "You look lovely this evening. Thank you for being here."

"It was my pleasure," she said, squeezing slightly and stroking her finger along his palm.

His eyes darkened, his nostrils flared, and she knew that look. Knew that he was remembering the pleasure he'd previously given her.

There he was. There was her Jay.

She released his hand and he held on for a fraction of a second before letting go.

Thank God for the padding in her dress. Her nipples were so hard, she was pretty sure they'd be visible through the metallic fabric.

Which was not the impression she wanted to give the queen.

"Your Majesty."

The queen scanned her from head to toe, her blue eyes sharp. "I must admit, you're not what I was expecting."

What the hell did that mean?

She hadn't expected Dani to be the artist Jameson chose to perform?

She hadn't expected someone who looked like her to be called Duchess?

But any answer to these questions, even if forthcoming, would have to wait, as another white-gloved hand motioned for her to move into the dining room, so as not to back up the line.

Again.

She was directed to a seat at the long table, only two spots from the head. If the queen sat there and Jameson near her, that would put Dani close to him for the evening. She wondered if he'd had a hand in the seating arrangement.

"Intense, right?" Liam said a few moments later, sitting next to her. "I thought meeting the president was intimidating."

"Not all of us have had that pleasure," she said.

"Trust me, after this, that will be a walk in the park. Princess Bettina gushed all over me. And what was up with the young one, Prince Jameson? I half expected him to summon the guards and throw me in the dungeon! He looked as if he wanted to murder me."

Dani's heart stuttered in her chest. "He did?"

"Yeah. Maybe his teenage girlfriend had a crush on me or something."

The music started, and around them everyone stood, so Dani followed suit. The royal family walked in and took their seats at the main table. When she saw the final seating, Dani understood the folly of her earlier thinking.

The queen was placed at the center of the table, with Jameson on her right, Prince Julian on her left. From her vantage point, Dani could see Jameson, but they weren't seated close enough to talk, nor could she hear what he was saying. He was seated next to a beautiful woman in a pink gown, her blond hair in a chic bun, who seemed very familiar with him. Actually, the woman seemed familiar to Dani, too. She said something to make him laugh, leaning so close their shoulders touched.

"Maybe second time's the charm," Kay, seated on her other side, said.

"Excuse me?"

She nodded toward Jameson and the blond woman. "The prince and Lady Imogen Harrington. The two of them dated a few years ago. Maybe she's trying to rekindle that old flame?"

She was the woman in the internet picture with Jameson that Nyla had showed her! He nodded at something Lady Imogen was saying, her hand resting comfortably, proprietarily, on his shoulder.

They're in public. They're old friends. He can't be rude.

But that didn't prevent Dani's anger from growing, even as she knew it was irrational for her to be so upset. She engaged in small talk with the people near her but couldn't keep her eyes from straying back to the two, who made a striking couple.

Who looked like they belonged together.

Liam reached over and put his hand on hers. She shot him a look, then realized he was removing the knife she'd been clenching.

"I know, this is totally not our scene. But it'll be over soon," he said, misinterpreting the reason for her distress. "Perhaps I can convince you to join me for a drink."

She smiled noncommittally and took a sip of water. *Get yourself together, Dani.*

"You know," Liam continued, "wherever we go, we're usually the ones who are fawned over. But in this situation, they're the rock stars and we're just commoners. I never thought I'd ever be in a position when I'd say that someone was out of my league. But these royals are in a class of their own."

Dani looked back over at Jameson just as Lady Imogen placed her hand over his on the table. Hints of red tinged the edges of her vision and she reached for her glass.

It was going to be a long night!

Chapter Nineteen

"Always go to the bathroom when you have a chance."

—King George V

Between bouquets of pink and white flowers and the gold candelabra centerpieces, Jameson watched Dani throw her head back and laugh at something Liam Cooper said. Jealousy reared its acidic head, burning a path straight to his heart. It wasn't a polite chuckle in response to required chitchat. It was throaty and genuine. And he recognized it because it was the way she'd laughed with him.

The night before, he'd been the one inside her, clutching her lush body against his, breathing in her scent as her pussy gripped his cock when she came. And now they were separated, forced to talk to people they didn't want to.

You can't speak for her. She seems to be enjoying herself.

True. When he'd first entered the room, his eyes had swept the crowd until he found her. She'd stood out, not because she was one of the few black people in the room, or because of what she was wearing. It was because of her essence. Her aura. She exuded this energy that was magnetic and drew him like a traveler of old following the North Star.

But upon locating her, he saw another man standing so close he could've been an additional appendage. Jameson's first instinct had been to go over there and claim her. Let everyone know she belonged to him.

Where had that possessive streak come from? That wasn't like him at all. He'd never been the jealous type.

But then, he'd never been with someone like Dani before. For the first time he understood how others must have felt dating a royal. Someone the world believed belonged to them, too. Everyone knew her. Hell, most people had seen her almost naked.

And that put him in a vulnerable state he hadn't anticipated or known how to navigate.

None of this had been helped by Julian's behavior during the receiving line.

"There she is," Julian had said, jabbing his elbow into Jameson's side. "Bloody hell, I thought her videos were sexy. She looks fucking unbelievable in person."

Jameson's hands had balled into fists. He could picture the drool falling from Julian's mouth as they both watched Cooper place a hand on her waist and lean forward to whisper in her ear. A roaring noise filled his ears. If he'd been holding a champagne flute, he would've broken the stem. But he couldn't say anything. To do so would give himself, and their relationship, away.

"Do you think he's fucking her?" Julian whispered.

"What?" Jameson said, choking on his disgust and anger.

And jealousy.

"Of course he is. If her songs and videos are anything to go by. As a prince, I'm sure to get in there."

God, his uncle was a piece of shit.

Jameson glared at Julian. "She's here as our guest. You don't want to piss her off before she's scheduled to perform."

"I don't need you to tell me that," he huffed before conceding, "You're right. Mother would blow a gasket if that happened. Maybe afterwards ..."

When Dani had reached Julian, the prince had clasped her hand and practically undressed her with his eyes before making a tasteless, inappropriate remark.

Jameson's vision of the person in front of him had narrowed to pinpricks and he'd turned, ready to smash his fist into his uncle's face, consequences be damned.

But Dani had handled the crown prince well. He knew she was angered by his comment, but she'd disentangled herself with a smile and a tart comeback before moving on.

And then she was before him.

His vision had cleared. His breathing slowed. And his heart steadied in his chest.

Mine.

A fact that had been reinforced when he'd taken her hand and felt their instant connection.

A wicked smile had tilted her luscious mouth and she'd looked up at him with brown eyes that promised everything he could handle and more.

But then she'd curtsied, addressed him by his title, and moved on. And the juxtaposition of her visual tease and prim actions made him harder than anything he could remember in a very long time.

If Dani was always by my side, I wouldn't mind attending more of these formal events. Having her near would make them bearable.

The unbidden thought popped into his head, leaving him shocked by the desire it revealed.

They'd agreed this was temporary. Neither had mentioned the possibility of their affair enduring beyond her time here. But he was clearly considering it. Which was folly. These events were the countdown to her leaving. And like Cinderella, when the ball ended in a week, she would disappear.

You're being a tad dramatic.

Fine.

She wouldn't disappear. She'd go back home and jump into her new business venture. But the outcome would be the same.

She'd be gone.

The pain that lanced through him at that unwelcome reminder would've felled him had he not been sitting.

"Everyone is excited for this celebration. It's all anyone has talked about for the past few months," Imogen said, snapping him from his thoughts and bringing him back to his immediate surroundings.

He smiled and nodded, which was enough for her to keep going.

That was uncharitable, Jameson.

Lady Imogen Harrington was a nice woman and he'd enjoyed their time together when they'd briefly dated two years ago. Their coupling had been looked upon with favor by the Palace. But Imogen had been looking for someone who was more than a royal in name only. They'd parted ways cordially and had maintained an amicable relationship. Any other time he would've enjoyed being seated next to her.

Unfortunately, at this moment, he only wanted to sit next to Dani.

She's a lovely young woman and perfect on paper, but she doesn't affect you like this. His mother had been right about Imogen.

He risked a glance down the table to find Dani holding court with the guests seated on either side of her. His eyes couldn't quite decide where they wanted to focus. On her face, or on her cleavage, tantalizingly displayed by that incredible dress.

She'd shown him the dress before he left for the palace. The liquidity of the material had looked inviting on the hanger, but—

"No one else will be dressed like this."

"Don't you like it?"

"I love it."

But it was so . . . flamboyant. All eyes would be on her.

Pressure tightened in his chest. "Maybe you should choose something more like what Catherine or Bettina will wear."

"Why? I'm not a member of the royal family or of British high society and I'm not trying to be anyone else but me."

And she'd been right. She was a peacock in a field of wrens, a ruby in a bag of colorful glass, an orchid in a bouquet of carnations. On her body, the dazzling dress should've been outlawed. From the bodice the liquid gold fabric seemed to fit her as if it had been painted on, flaring out just above her knees to allow her to walk. When she'd crossed the room, the material had flowed behind her like a pied piper, her curves a lure that had been difficult to resist.

Blood engorged his throbbing cock and he shifted in his chair. He hoped he'd be able to make it through the event at this rate.

Cooper ruined the picture, leaning over and whispering in her ear.

"Is everything all right?" Imogen asked.

"Of course. Why do you ask?"

"The expression on your face. As if you've seen something that's displeased you?"

Yeah, fucking Liam Cooper appears to have issues with personal space!

"No. Everything's fine."

"Lovely. Because I was wondering—"

His gaze was once again drawn to Dani. This time their eyes met. She winked.

That one gesture was like a release valve on everything pressing against his chest. He didn't know how she had the power to make him feel better, but even across a table her influence was palpable.

Smiling, he turned his head and found his grandmother staring at him. Her eyes flicked briefly to Dani and though her expression never altered, a cloud of displeasure formed and hovered overhead, before she looked away and began talking to Carl Page, an entertainer Prince John had loved.

Dread tightened in Jameson's gut.

That wasn't good.

AFTER DINNER, THEY headed back into the East Gallery, where the orchestra played and several couples took to the constructed dance floor. Out of the corner of his eye Jameson noticed shimmers of gold. Turning, he saw Cooper escorting Dani out amidst the growing crowd.

Beside him, Imogen sighed. "They make a great couple."

Though it pained him to admit it, she was right. Dani and Cooper looked great together. In the same way that Dani wasn't dressed like any of the other women here, Cooper looked completely different from the other men. He wore a royal blue tuxedo with a black satin shawl collar, a striking contrast to his curly blond hair. Together, they were magnificent.

They were from the same world and understood the same challenges. Maybe Cooper was a better fit for her.

"I didn't even know who she was," Imogen said. "I don't listen to her type of music. But when I saw her videos I worried that she might turn up here dressed like that! I guess we should be thankful she didn't. I actually heard a few of the guests say she was very charming."

Jameson pursed his lips. The snobbery of this crowd sickened him.

"Now, this is the music I prefer. It's Strauss. And perfect for dancing . . ." She trailed off wistfully.

The protocols and traditions of the British aristocracy. Imogen wanted to dance but she couldn't ask him.

Dani never had a problem telling him what she wanted.

Jameson held out his hand. "Would you care to dance?"

Imogen beamed. "I'd love to."

As the orchestra moved into the next song, he led her out onto the floor and pulled her into the proper hold. He may have been able to forgo most of his royal duties, but his attendance and attention had still been required behind the scenes. He'd endured years of lessons in dance, etiquette, and comportment. He may not have as many opportunities to utilize his skills—fortunately!—but the movements were ingrained in him. He maneuvered her around the floor with ease.

When the song ended, Lord Croft approached them. "Your Royal Highness. Lady Imogen, may I have the honor of the next dance?"

Imogen looked at him, but when Jameson tilted his head, signaling it was her choice, her smile tightened, and she turned back to the other man. "Certainly."

Jameson bowed. "Thank you for the dance, Lady Imogen."

Unable to help himself, he searched for Dani, and found Julian stalking toward her like a heat-seeking missile.

Knowing what might happen, Jameson hurried across the floor, beating Julian by a couple of seconds.

"Dance?" he asked, slightly breathless from the exertion.

She stared at him, her eyes wide. "What are you doing?"

"Isn't it obvious? I'm asking you to dance."

"I thought we'd agreed to keep our distance in public."

He glanced around. Several people were covertly watching

them, including Julian, whose eyes had narrowed and face had reddened.

"At this point, it would be easier for you to accept than for us to stand here and have this conversation."

Finally aware of the scrutiny, she placed her hand in his and followed him onto the floor.

He slid an arm around her and cupped her upper back while she placed her hand on his shoulder. He wished he could drop his hand lower, pull her closer, and press his cheek against her hair, but this was the best he could do and have them both remain scandal-free. Their bodies fell into the perfect off-center position, and he led her in a standard waltz around the space.

One, two, three.

One, two, three.

They moved together effortlessly, and after a few moments everyone else faded away until it was just the two of them and the music. Her hair had been styled in an updo, with tendrils framing her face and feathering against her neck and bare collarbone.

"You seem to be enjoying yourself," she said, her gaze over his right shoulder.

He inhaled. She smelled amazing. "I do?"

"Yes. With Lady Imogen. Were you reminiscing about old times?"

"No. We discussed the celebration."

"How long did you two date?"

The soulful cocoon he'd imagined vanished.

He frowned. Why were they talking about Imogen? Especially when he'd spent most of his time with the other woman thinking about Dani. "Six months, maybe."

He wished she would look at him, but she insisted on focusing on some point over his shoulder.

"Why did you break up?"

His chest tightened. What was with the bloody third degree? "For the same reason I imagine many people do. We wanted different things in life."

At that, she looked at him. "What did—"

"What about you?" he asked, his reservoir of patience tapped out. "Did you know Cooper before today?"

Her brow furrowed. "Liam? Of course. We're with the same label and we've performed together several times."

"And did you date him?"

"Why would you ask me—" She broke off and took a deep breath, her breasts pushing against the confines of her bodice. "No, we never dated, although the tabloids have suggested we're dating now. We were just talking. Being polite. It's what you do at dinner parties."

"Polite? When I came in earlier you two were very chummy."

"Because we know each other. And we're both out of our element and it's good to see a friendly, familiar face."

The tension in his chest eased. "That's how it was with Imogen."

"Oh no, that's different. I never dated Liam, but you dated Imogen for six months."

They needed to continue their conversation somewhere private. "Let's—"

The music stopped and Louisa handed Marina a microphone.

Dani's withdrawal was tangible. She crossed her arms. "You're up."

Goddammit!

Meeting Louisa's eye, he nodded, but he squeezed Dani's elbow and said, "Don't go anywhere. Please. I won't be long."

He couldn't risk looking to see if she'd granted his request. Not with everyone in the room watching him. Flicking the cuffs of his jacket, he strode over to where the queen stood on a slightly raised dais and took his place next to her. Then she began to speak.

"Thank you all for joining me to celebrate my beloved John and his lifelong passion for charity. As you all know, my husband was an early adopter of the environmental cause. When we were first introduced, in 1965, I was trying to get to know him and he was trying to convince me that the Palace needed to reimplement recycling protocols closer to World War II standards!" She paused for the laughter. "He died far too soon for my liking, but then that was John's modus operandi. He was way before his time in a lot of ways."

The queen took a moment to compose herself before continuing.

"And I couldn't think of anything he'd love more than a week focusing on his favorite charities along with a concert featuring some of his favorite acts. The proceeds from all of this week's events will go to John's charitable trust. So I will thank you in advance for your generosity. And I couldn't be more pleased that his work will continue influencing and benefiting generations to come, thanks to our grandson Jameson. You'll be seeing and hearing more from him this week, as I've named him the Crown's representative for these celebrations. He's the future of this family and we couldn't be prouder."

There were gasps of surprise and then an enthusiastic round of applause. He nodded and smiled tightly, but his attention was on one person.

Dani.

He scanned the room and found her speaking to a footman on the far side, away from the guests gathered near the platform. Giving in to the primal need to be near her and fix the tension between them, damn the consequences, he excused himself . . . only to find his way blocked by Julian. The crown prince's features were flushed, and his hair was a bit disheveled.

"How does it feel to be up there and have my mother fawning

over you?" he asked, his words slurring as he lifted his glass to his mouth.

"Sober up, Julian," Jameson said, attempting to move past the man and follow Dani.

"It won't last," Julian said. "You're only in her good graces because she needs you. But once she doesn't, once you, heaven forbid, disappoint her, you'll be on the discarded heap like the rest of us."

What were they, two boys in school fighting over the same girl?

"The difference between the two of us is that would be fine with me," Jameson said, before walking away.

He approached the footman, distinctive in the palace's uniform of black tails with a red and gold vest. "Where did Dani go?"

"Your Royal Highness?" the young woman asked, confusion and a touch of panic coloring her expression.

"Duchess. I saw you talking to her. Where did you send her?"

"Oh. Uh—"

"Yes?"

"Well, sir, I—" Heat flooded her cheeks.

Impatience was getting the best of him. This need for her was clawing in his chest.

"Spit it out!"

She flinched. "The lavatory!"

He blinked. "The lavatory?"

"I can't believe I just said 'lavatory' to Prince Jameson," the footman uttered before composing herself. "I'm sorry. There was a line at the one we're supposed to direct guests to, so I sent her to the one near the Royal Closet. I know I shouldn't have, but she's Duchess. It's not like she's a regular member of the public . . ."

"It's okay," he said, gentling his tone. "You're not in trouble. You did the right thing. Just don't send anyone else."

Relief flooded her face. "Thank you, sir. And I won't. I promise."

He exited the ballroom and hurried down the long hall to the room that didn't hold fur-lined mantles, crowns, and scepters as the name might suggest, but was actually where the royal family assembled before official state ceremonies. Coming across the door he sought, he slipped inside and closed it behind him.

Small, by palace standards, the room was similar to many others in that it was lavishly appointed, with a magnificent fireplace, antique chairs and tables on an enormous Aubusson carpet, and paintings from many of the world's great artists adorning the wall.

It was also empty.

Several moments later, the mirror-backed door on the other side of the room opened and Dani emerged, smoothing a hand down the front of her dress. His audible exhalation was loud in the space, and she froze, glancing up with wide eyes.

"Jay! You scared me."

A montage of emotions altered her features. Relief. Warmth. Hurt. Anger.

She began walking. "Are you planning to meet your girlfriend here?"

Instead of answering, he met her in the middle of the room, clasped her nape, and dragged her close, sealing his mouth over hers and claiming her lips.

There was no resistance at all as she melted into him. She tasted of champagne and sweets and the thing that was totally her. That had him addicted. He wrapped his arms around her waist and pressed his body against hers. She moaned and he kissed down her throat, wanting to claim her. Wanting to taste all of her skin.

As if he hadn't done exactly that in the past three weeks.

He brought his lips back to hers and lifted her in his arms. Frantically looking around—why were there so many bloody figurines and vases covering every inch of usable surface!—he backed her against the only bare space on the wall, next to the fireplace. Her legs clamped around his waist. He dragged his lips and tongue across the cleavage he'd been studying earlier. She hummed and pressed his head tighter to her body, ruining his prudently styled hair.

He didn't care.

He slid one finger inside of her and his eyes rolled back in his head at her wetness. He added a second digit, thrusting in and out of her snug heat.

"Yes . . . baby," she keened, holding on to him and riding his hand.

Rotating those fingers, he crooked them upward and massaged the hard nub of her G-spot.

"Fuck! Jay! Baby!" She exploded against him.

He kissed her to muffle the sound and undid his zipper, allowing his erect cock to spring free. Gripping its base, he plunged it into her pussy. They both groaned at the joining and her forehead fell forward onto his shoulder. Then there was no finesse, no slow loving. His hips pumped as he slammed into her. Unable to check the need to claim her. To let her know how much he wanted her.

Using his body and one hand to hold her steady against the wall, he used his other hand to force her head up and back until they were staring at each other.

"You're everything. You're everywhere. Your scent teases me. Your taste taunts me. Your skin is the smoothest. Your ass is incredible. And you feel amazing. It's all I ever think about. All I want. Do you understand?"

"I do, baby. I do," she whimpered.

Pleasure zipped up his spine and he both welcomed and dreaded his impending release. But it was inevitable, as was falling for the woman in his arms. As he came, to stifle the bellow that wanted to tear from him, he sealed his mouth around the pulse in her neck. When she joined him, several moments later, one hand clutched the front of his shirt and she slapped the other one over her mouth.

They both were breathing heavy and he took a moment to gather his thoughts.

"Look at me," he said quietly, wanting her to see the truth of his words.

She did, with lust and satisfaction in her beautiful eyes. But even now, some of that satisfaction was ceding to her earlier hurt. He wouldn't let that happen.

"I have duties as a royal. Especially as the face of this event. But I'd much rather be with you. Here or anywhere else. Doing this or not. We could've watched a movie, played a game, or simply read. As long as I was with you."

He searched her gaze, hoping she believed him.

"I know that. I do. It's just . . . This wasn't part of the plan," she said, in a weighty whisper. "What are we doing?"

If only he had the answer.

Chapter Twenty

*"Don't let the name fool you / I'm the queen in this bed /
Get it right / Make it tight / Or it's 'Off with his head!'"*
—Duchess, "Hunting Hoes (Dirty Junkie f. Duchess)"

Another day, another crop of flashing lights trying to blind her. The sun was bright as Dani stood on the London sidewalk. With its businesses mixed in with attached row homes, the streets filled with bicycles, café tables, and sidewalk signs, the neighborhood wouldn't have been out of place in any city in the States.

Or it wouldn't have been if people had been allowed to move freely as they progressed through their day. Instead, on either side of the street, large crowds of people and photographers were secured behind heavy-duty steel barricades, arms holding phones raised, the sounds of cheers and applause deafening as a group of celebrities and one better-known-by-the-hour royal held court in front of a white four-story building. Police, in black with neon yellow vests, and personal protection, including her own bodyguard, Antoine, strolled the perimeter, heads on a swivel.

Louisa, lovely in a green floral dress, was introducing Jameson to several people. He smiled and nodded, casually sexy in sandy-colored slacks and an open-collar, dark blue button-down that matched his eyes. Dani inhaled as heat coursed through her. Would there ever be a time when she wouldn't want him? Even when she was annoyed with him, the way she'd been at the dinner, one kiss from him had her spreading her legs, already wet in anticipation.

The opening event last night had been their first public outing as Duchess and Prince Jameson, two people who knew each other but definitely did not fuck.

It hadn't gone the way they'd anticipated.

Neither had known how they'd react to seeing the other in their element, outside of the bubble they'd created at Primrose Park. It had been challenging for both of them. They needed to do better.

A short white woman wearing jeans and a yellow top blushed and ducked her head when he shook her hand.

Dani resisted the urge to roll her eyes. She was starting to realize he had that effect on everyone.

Louisa moved to stand in front of the bank of microphones. "Good afternoon. May I present His Royal Highness Prince Jameson."

Jameson flashed a smile that was no less devastating for being affected.

"Thank you all so much for coming. My grandfather was the patron for hundreds of organizations, though it was no secret environmental causes were his passion. Today, we're here at Bloom Urban, a charity that was near to his heart. Established in 1994, its mission is to help urban areas become sustainable through corporate partnership drives and grassroots environmental campaigning. Here to tell us a little more is Katie Fielding, Bloom Urban's executive director."

The blushing woman in the yellow top scooted forward. "Thank you, Your Royal Highness."

Jameson ceded the floor to her and stood with his hands clasped behind his back, which only emphasized the breadth of his chest. Dani dragged her gaze away from it to find him staring at her. He winked and she struggled not to allow her lips to curl upward, even though her insides were acting as if she was seeing her favorite group in concert for the very first time.

Tearing her attention away from him, she tried to refocus on why she was here and what the woman was saying.

"Rapid urban development is exacerbating our environmental problems and Bloom Urban is tasked to change that. We want to make our communities sustainable, leaving a healthy environment, prosperous economy, and vibrant civic life for generations to come. Prince John and his input were invaluable, and we were beyond grateful for his patronage. And as we've gotten the time to speak with Prince Jameson, it appears we will transition into very capable ha—hands," she stammered, another bright blush staining her cheeks.

Jameson moved to stand next to her. "I'd planned to disclose this at the end of the week, but because this place was so important to my grandfather, this is the perfect opportunity to announce the royal family will be instituting the John Foster Lloyd Prize for Environmentalism. It will be awarded annually to individuals and or organizations for work in the field of environmental studies. We'll release more information in the coming months."

Katie clasped her hands together. "That is certainly exciting and we're honored you chose to reveal it here. Now, we have an interesting morning lined up for you. We'll start with a tour of the Bloom Urban offices and look at some of the initiatives Prince John worked on as well as some of the projects currently in development. So, if you'll follow me—"

Jameson looked as if he wanted to wait for Dani, but with Katie lingering expectantly, he gestured for the other woman to precede him.

Dani swallowed her disappointment. It was just as well. As much as she wanted to spend time with Jameson, she needed to keep up appearances.

"Shall we?" Liam asked, holding out his arm for her.

She smiled up at him. "We shall."

Liam was also on the receiving end of a lot of attention. Dressed in dark jeans and a green V-necked T-shirt, with a beanie covering most of his blond curls and his sunglasses tucked into his neckline, he looked every inch the magnetic pop star who'd earned his place on countless lists of the sexiest musicians of all time. As she took his arm, they joined the queue of people ascending the steps into the building.

A scream broke through the crowd and she thought she heard "—Duchess!"

Reflexively, she turned to see where the sound came from. There was a commotion happening to her left, but security seemed to have it in hand and Antoine wasn't involved. She shrugged and continued up the steps.

D to the A to the N I
You wanna know why
Dudes go sky high
When I say jump—

Was somebody shouting the lyrics to her song?

Eyes wide, she turned and spied a group of four teen girls on the far end of the crowd, leaning over the barricades. Two security officers stood in front of them, their arms outstretched.

When Dani stopped, the girls began jumping excitedly. "Duchess!"

"I told you it was her!" one of the girls said.

"Yo, it's really her," a boy said, running up to join the group.

"Move back now!" the security guard said.

Lips tightening, Dani touched Liam's arm. "Go ahead. I'll be there in a minute."

She hurried down the steps and across the street to the area where the security forces were trying to contain the growing group of kids. As she got closer the teens got even more frenzied.

"Duchess! Duchess! Duchess!"

While one girl continued rapping the lyrics to "Sky High," a couple of the kids provided a stripped-down beatbox to accompany her, and Dani couldn't help bopping her head and grooving her shoulders to the impromptu flow.

"That's all they see of me / My femininity / They think they have the key / Silly little guy . . ."

Dani jumped in. "You could never see / What I'm meant to be / I belong to me—"

The entire crowd finished with her. "D to the A to the N I!"

"Yeah!" The group of kids clapped and whistled.

Dani laughed, joy filling her at their love. Ironically, although they were calling her Duchess, it was the first time since the events began that she'd felt more like herself in public. Like Dani. To see their brown faces, bright shining eyes, and wide grins took her back to who she'd been before all of this happened. To when she would've been on that side of the barricade with them.

"Hey, guys! What's good?" she asked, reaching out to take the hands being waved in her direction.

"Yo! Watch yourself," Antoine said, when one of the boys tugged on her hand. He moved to stand between her and the kids.

She smiled. "It's okay."

He gave her the look that told her he wasn't budging.

"He got a little excited. I promise to keep my distance, but I don't want to stand apart like I'm better than them. Like I've forgotten where I'm from. Please."

After a long moment, Antoine nodded and stepped from in front of her. But not before he aimed a look at the group to indicate he wouldn't tolerate any shit. Several wide eyes and low murmurs signaled his message had been received.

She refocused on the kids. "How are you guys doing?"

"Great, now that we got to see you," one girl said.

"What are you doing here?" a boy asked.

Dani gestured behind her. "Right now, I'm about to take a tour of this building."

"She's here for the Prince John tribute concert, idiot," another teen said.

"Wait, you are?"

"Yeah," Dani said.

"Prince John was cool for a royal. My big sister met him once when he came to her after-school program."

"He was," a young girl said. "Now all they do is get drunk, do stupid stuff, and then whine about their problems. Like we care."

Dani raised her brows. Jameson may have had a point about the royal family having a PR problem.

"Are you coming to the concert?" she asked the group, her eyes flickering over their young faces.

"You takin' the piss, mate? The tickets are bare pricey. We don't have the Ps for that."

She laughed. "Run that by me again."

"We can't afford the tickets," another girl translated. "Even the ones that haven't sold out are hella expensive. I heard they're going for over a hundred quid!"

"And no offense, but I wasn't keen to pay that much to see some old-timers. But you and Liam? That'd be sick!"

"You like Liam, too?"

"Of course." One of the girls practically swooned. "Did you see the way he moved in his last video?"

"Yeah!" Some of the girls shouted and gave each other high fives before breaking into lyrics from his newest release. "Don't walk away, baby / I was wrong / You were there, beside me / All along / Give me just one more chance / And I'll do my part / 'Til it's my name (my name) / That's engraved on your heart!"

So cute.

"Now that's what's up!" Dani bit her bottom lip. "Give me one sec."

She hurried back across the street, intending to go into the building to grab Liam, only to stop short when she reached the bottom of the steps and saw him standing where she'd left him, his hands shoved in the back pockets of his jeans, an indulgent smile creasing his face.

"Looking for me?" he asked, cocking a brow.

"You got a moment to come over and meet some friends of mine?"

"For you? Of course," he said, taking his time to descend the steps, his gaze never leaving hers. When he reached her he said, "After you."

The group started going crazy again when the two of them crossed the street.

"Guys, this is Liam."

He waved a hand. "What's up?"

A couple of the girls in front actually screamed.

He playfully covered his face and turned away. "Oh no. They hate me."

"No, we don't! Don't go!"

He laughed and straightened. "I'm just playing."

He reached out to shake some of the hands and the clicking of cameras caused Dani to glance over her shoulder. Instead of going inside the building, a swarm of press was now standing outside, their cameras and phones trained on the little impromptu gathering.

"Are you guys coming to the concert?" Liam asked.

Dani shook her head. "Apparently the tickets that are left are quite expensive."

She hadn't thought about how much tickets would be going for or who would have access to the concert or even be able to see the show. Which seemed like a shame. She understood the plan was to donate the money to the prince's favorite charities, but Dani thought the point was also to celebrate Prince John. At that price point, only certain people would be able to demonstrate their support or take part in the festivities.

"You know what? How about I donate thirty tickets? That should cover everyone here, right?"

"Oh my God, seriously?"

"Of course."

A cheer rose from the crowd.

Liam smiled down at her before adding, "I'll donate an additional thirty. Everything's more fun with a friend."

He moved closer to Dani and slid an arm around her waist.

She resisted the urge to roll her eyes. She knew better than to take him seriously. He was an American entertainment magazine editor's wet dream, with the constant parade of women. And while he was attractive and there was a time when she may have tested those waters, it wasn't an option now.

Because of Jameson.

But she and Jameson weren't for public consumption. They still hadn't defined their relationship, but whatever it was needed to be kept private. Anything she could do to ensure that, she would.

Which was why she didn't slip from Liam's embrace.

"Is Duchess your girlfriend?"

Liam smiled and his hold tightened. "I'm hoping, but she's making me work for it."

"As I should," she said, playing for the cameras. "Take note, ladies, don't give yourself or your heart away too easily. If a man wants you, make him work for it a little, okay?"

"Ooooooooh!"

"I'm available, Duchess, if you change your mind," a young boy said.

She winked and blew him a kiss. His face brightened in wonder and several of his friends started pushing and shoving him.

"Please! Why would she want your ashy ass when she can have Liam? He's totally fit," another girl said.

"Did you hear that? I'm 'totally fit.' They're on my side," Liam said, pressing a kiss to her cheek.

Again, the flashes went off and the crowd went crazy.

Dani slid him a look. "You are such a flirt."

A smile tilted his lips, but his gaze was steady. "You think I'm teasing. I'm being serious."

Was he? She'd thought their banter was playful and easy. As

much as she liked Liam and enjoyed his company, she didn't want to lead him on or send mixed signals.

But then his expression lightened, and relief eased her worries. Of course he wasn't being serious. Flirting was as instinctive to him as breathing.

"Whatever," she told him. Turning back to the crowd she said, "You guys are the best welcome party any girl could ask for and I hate to break this up, but"—jerking her thumb over her shoulder—"I gotta get back to work."

"Can we trade jobs?" a boy in the crowd asked.

She placed a manicured nail against her lip as if she were considering it. "What do you do?"

"I wash dishes at the Bird in Arms. It's a pub down the street."

She scrunched up her face. "Hell no, dude!"

Everyone laughed and she and Liam waved and backed up.

"Thanks, Antoine," she said to her bodyguard.

The big man nodded.

With his hand on the small of her back, Liam led her across the street. As they neared the building, the press saw their opportunity.

"Are you and Liam an item?"

"How long have the two of you been dating?"

"Do you think the concert tickets are priced too high?"

"Do you think the Palace should've offered cheaper tickets?"

"What did you enjoy more, the formal welcome reception or your time with these kids?"

"Has the queen not made you feel welcome, Duchess?"

Shit.

"Keep walking and don't answer," she told Liam.

"I know the drill."

Another voice shouted, "Hi, Duchess! Surprised to see me?"

As bad as the press was, this was even worse. Anger and irritation coursed through her, and she turned to see Samantha Banks, dressed in a short white skirt and bright pink shirt, standing to the far right of the crowd. She knew when Antoine spied the other woman because he moved to put himself between them.

"Hey, it's Samantha Banks!"

"Samantha! Samantha!"

The clicks and flashes were frenzied as the press focused on the interloper.

"Welcome to London, Samantha!"

"Did Duchess ever apologize?"

"Come on." Liam's words penetrated. "You don't want to be a part of this."

"I can't believe she's here. Scratch that. Yes, I can. She's like my fucking shadow."

Did this girl's audacity have no limits?

"Samantha, did Duchess invite you?"

"Are you performing at the concert, too?"

"I'm not performing," Samantha said, propping a hand on her hip. "But if Duchess asks me to do a song with her, I would. That would be the proper thing to do, right?"

Dani saw red.

"You can't engage with her. If you do, you're giving her what she wants."

"Fuck it, I know that, Liam."

She did. And he was right, she needed to leave the situation. Now. The eyes of the world were on her. Genesis's eyes.

"Get her inside," Antoine yelled over his shoulder.

Taking a deep breath, she took Liam's hand and continued up the steps.

"Duchess! You can't keep ignoring me!" Samantha called out. "I won't let you."

The press jumped on that.

"Are you ignoring her, Duchess?"

"Why are you ignoring her?"

"Samantha Banks, you a stalker," one of the girls in the group she'd spoken to earlier said.

"Yeah. You said nobody invited you. Why are you here?"

"I didn't say nobody invited me," Samantha shot back. "I said Duchess hadn't."

Wait, what? So, someone wanted her to be here? Who?

"Leave Duchess alone," a young boy shouted.

"Yo, Banks, you need to go bye-bye!"

"Signed D to the A to the N I," a girl chimed in.

The crowd laughed and started chanting:

"You need to go bye-bye / Signed D to the A to the N I!"

All of it was being caught on phones and cameras. It wasn't the image she wanted and she knew the royal family wouldn't be pleased.

"Let's go." Liam escorted her inside the building.

The first person she saw was Jameson. She wanted to run to him and throw herself into his arms. Tell him that bitch Samantha Banks had followed her over here. She was certain he would listen and understand how she felt, but one look at his tightened jaw and furrowed brow disabused her of that notion.

"I hope we weren't holding things up," she said, telegraphing with her eyes for him to stay cool.

I'll explain everything later.

"They've moved on to the gallery. I just wanted to make sure you hadn't gotten lost."

"No. Just saying hi to some of my fans."

"And that required both of you?"

"I grabbed Liam when I realized they were fans of his, too."

"Don't worry, Your Royal Highness," Liam said. "I had my eye on her the whole time."

Jameson's brow lifted, but he didn't say a word. He pivoted on his heel and headed into the offices.

Fuck.

Chapter Twenty-One

"Jelly like a mofo / You know . . ."

—Duchess, "You Know"

From her position in the third row of the Royal Box, Dani looked down at the most famous tennis court in the world. The alternating lighter and darker lawn stripe pattern, the crisp white lines of the court, the stewards standing by the exits, ball boys and girls scurrying back and forth, and the almost fifteen thousand people filling the stands. She resisted the urge to pinch herself.

I'm at Wimbledon!

Flicking aside the long asymmetrical skirt of her Prabal Gurung floral dress, Dani leaned forward and braced her elbow on her bare knee, resting her chin on her curled fingers.

Technically, she wasn't. Wimbledon was the name of the tournament; the venue was the All England Lawn Tennis and Croquet Club. And the tournament wasn't scheduled to be held for another week. Still, the two were irrevocably linked in her mind.

Not because she knew anything about tennis. She barely knew the rules and had held a racket only once in her life! But that didn't matter to most black women she knew if Venus or Serena was playing. And that interest, that instinctive rooting value for the black female tennis players that followed, was one of the Williams sisters' biggest legacies. It's how Dani had been fortunate enough to meet Yolanda Evans, a rising star in tennis who'd won the U.S. Open two years ago.

Yolanda had also been the one to school her on the history of the club and tournament. How black people hadn't been allowed to play at the club until 1951 and that the tournament didn't even pay men and women equal prize money until 2007.

And now my black ass is at Centre Court sitting up in the Royal Box for everyone to see.

Fucking surreal.

"It's quite something, isn't it?" Liam's smooth voice poured into her ear.

She smiled. "It certainly is."

"Do you play?"

She turned to look at him, her "Are you serious?" expression mostly hidden by the oversized Gucci sunglasses she wore. "No."

"I played when I was a teenager. I was pretty good, but once the band took off, there was no time to devote to it."

"That's amazing. I had no idea. Do you still play?"

"I have a court at my house. You should come over and play with me sometime." His lips curved. "I have a wicked serve."

She tilted her head, and curls tumbled over her shoulder. "I bet you do."

He grabbed one of her curls and tugged on it.

Immediately she could hear the incessant click of shutters and flashes of cameras followed by "Smile, Duchess!"

Dammit!

A gaggle of photographers was camped beneath them, in the perfect spot to get pictures of the match but also pictures of the celebrities in the box and crowd. No doubt they'd caught that moment.

And she was conflicted by that. Yesterday's incident at Bloom Urban had been covered by every media outlet in the world. While the organization and the upcoming concert had gotten some coverage, it had been widely overshadowed by her interactions with various parties.

For the most part, it had been positive for her. She'd been praised on how she'd handled Samantha Banks, with some in the media questioning the propriety of Banks showing up.

"Why is she there?" a woman had asked her coanchor.

Dani still didn't know the answer to that one. She kept expecting the singer to pop out and challenge her to a game of tennis.

Some stories focused on Duchess's interaction with the kids and her offer to buy concert tickets for them. That action was also praised, but it turned into a jumping-off point for a discussion about the price of tickets.

But the biggest story had been about her and Liam, and speculation about the nature of her relationship with the pop star.

Sure, *Bossip* had topped everyone's headline with "Duchess Snacking on That Tasty, Curly-Haired Vanilla Cake?"

But *People*, *Entertainment Weekly*, *TMZ*, *Radar*, *Daily Mail*, and others had all asked some version of the same question: Were Liam and Duchess ready to reign as music's new power couple?

It wasn't true, but she couldn't deny the coverage helped her case with Genesis. The possible secret romance between two music stars would win out over a one-sided feud. And, as an added bonus, if the press was focused on that relationship, they wouldn't be attuned to anything going on between her and Jay. She'd vowed to get him to understand that when she called him, but she could tell by his voice that he'd been tired and not in an understanding mood.

After the charity event yesterday, Dani had headed to the concert venue for a full dress rehearsal. The show was two days away and they'd needed to make sure everything would run smoothly. Apparently, Jameson had spent that time with his grandmother.

The queen hadn't been happy with the press coverage. The incident with Samantha Banks had overshadowed Jay's announcement of the prize honoring Prince John and the work Bloom Urban had been doing. Dani hadn't been happy because she knew how important the prize was to Jay and how much it meant to him to honor his grandfather. And Jameson hadn't been happy because of all the speculation about Dani and Liam being a new couple.

"But it's not true. And if it keeps the press off us, isn't that a good thing?" she'd asked him during their FaceTime call.

"I get it," Jameson had said, shirtless in bed, his expression tense. "But I don't like it."

"I know. But you like me, don't you?"

"I do like you, so show me some of the things I like most," he'd said.

Which had led to a very hot and satisfying mutual masturbation session.

Even though it had ended "happily," the call was the first time she'd understood how their goals might be in opposition to one another.

But she didn't blame him. Because she didn't like it, either. Lady Imogen had been a part of the select group invited to these events, and though Dani knew there was nothing going on between her and Jameson, it was still painful to see them together.

Which was why she'd been avoiding looking down at the court, where Jameson stood talking to Louisa and Imogen.

What that man could do to an ordinary outfit . . .

On anyone else, the suit would look classic and pedestrian, but

Jameson filled it out quite nicely, the light bluish gray color and slim fit giving it a younger, more modern feel that attracted many a gaze.

Don't worry about it. He's not interested in her. He's with you.

Except it looked like he was with Imogen. The same coverage that harped on her and Liam couldn't help but comment on Jameson and Imogen.

How great they looked together.

How long their families had known each other.

How she would make a great duchess.

That one hurt.

Dani didn't do jealousy over a man. But she was feeling some kind of way about Jameson.

Not that she didn't trust him. She did. But she also wanted to claim him. To go down there, grab the microphone, and let everyone know he belonged to her.

"Are you okay?"

Liam's hand rested on hers, causing her to realize she'd curled her fingers into fists. She flexed her hand, disrupting his hold.

"I'm good. Getting a little impatient, I guess."

"Don't worry. It'll start soon. Until then, I'll have to do better to keep you entertained," he said, sliding an arm around her shoulder. She started and looked at him, surprised to find his face only inches from hers.

More shutter clicks and flashes.

This is a good thing. This is a good thing.

She'd keep saying it until she believed it.

"Duchess?" A young page stood at the end of her row. "There's someone who wanted to say hi."

He gestured up to the entrance into the box.

Recognizing the woman, Dani hopped up and waved her down.

Excusing herself, she stepped past Liam and made her way to the end of the row.

"Stephanie!" She hugged the young woman. "Oh my God, it's been a minute! What are you doing here?"

Stephanie Evans, Yolanda's younger sister, smiled. "Hoping to run into you! You look amazing."

"So do you. Wait." Dani turned to look down at the court. "Is Yolanda here?"

Stephanie nodded. "Yeah, she's playing."

Dani wrinkled her brow. "I thought they had a British player and someone from France."

"They did. But Caroline tweaked her knee and she wanted to rest it up for Wimbledon, so she pulled out at the last minute. Since Yoli was already here preparing for the tournament, they asked her to step in and she agreed."

Dani smiled. This was going to be more fun than she'd initially imagined.

Noting Liam's interest, she turned and touched his shoulder. "Stephanie, have you met Liam Cooper?"

"No, I haven't."

He smiled and took her hand. "It's a pleasure. And I'm a big fan of your sister's, as well."

"I'll make sure to tell her that . . . after the match. Don't want to distract her." Stephanie laughed. "I have to go. I just wanted to come up and say hi."

"I'm glad you did. Please tell Yolanda I'll be up here cheering her on."

"Will do. It was so good to see you. And nice to meet you, Liam."

"I didn't know you knew Yolanda Evans," Liam said, once Stephanie had left and they'd retaken their seats.

"Yeah, we met at the ESPYs several years ago," Dani said, referring to the annual ceremony that recognized outstanding achievement in sports but was attended by celebrities from all fields.

"She's really good. I was looking forward to seeing her play at Wimbledon this year," he said, the genuine interest in his gaze different from the almost customary flirting he'd been doing with her.

Interesting.

There was a movement on the court. To her left, two rows of young boys and girls strode out and stood.

"Ladies and gentlemen, it's time for the event to begin," a female voice said from the intercom. "Please welcome onto Centre Court His Royal Highness Prince Jameson."

Jameson strode onto the court to meet a young woman holding a microphone. Though Dani knew how much he hated these events, he looked incredible, possessing a sophistication and ease that was as natural to him as breathing. Other men might try to perfect that air, but with Jameson, it just was.

"On behalf of Her Majesty the Queen and the rest of my family, it is my honor to welcome you here today. Prince John loved tennis, especially Wimbledon. He never missed a finals. It only seemed appropriate that as we honor him this week, we include something he enjoyed. I want to thank the players who took time out of their training mere days before Wimbledon to thrill and entertain you for a good cause. Join me in welcoming Pauletta Cornet and Yolanda Evans."

The two players walked out of the club, through the rows of boys and girls, and the crowd went wild. Dani clapped when she saw her friend and when Yolanda looked up at the Royal Box and waved, Dani surged to her feet and waved back. Liam stood with her, and only after she stopped did she look around and realize they were the only ones standing. With a playful grin, she sat back down.

"I also want to thank our guest musicians up there," Jameson said, gesturing to where she and the other musicians sat.

The applause was deafening, but when their eyes met, she couldn't hear anything but her own beating heart. Heat flowed through her. Was there any hope for them? Should they just end it now and spare them both pain?

When the applause died down, he looked away, severing the connection.

"Because of your generosity, more money has been raised to honor Prince John's lifelong work on environmental causes." Jameson smiled. "Now, let the game begin."

THE SMILE SLID from Jameson's face the moment the double doors closed behind him and he was back in the clubhouse.

"Where was Julian?"

As president and patron of the All England Club, a role he'd inherited from Prince John, Jameson's uncle was scheduled to be with him during the event today.

"He called right before you went out. Said since the queen had entrusted you to be the face of the family, you should be able to handle it."

"Great."

Louisa exhaled. "She isn't happy,"

"Tell me something new," Jameson said, shoving his hands through his hair.

"I'm serious."

"So am I. I'm doing everything she's asked me to do."

Louisa eyed him. "Except controlling Dani."

"When did that become a part of my job? In fact, the last time I responded to my grandmother's summons, she told me to keep my distance."

Jameson had been clear on what her directive had been. That's the reason he was in this current mess.

"Did you see the headlines this morning?" Louisa asked.

Jameson sighed and began taking the labyrinthine walk to the Royal Box.

Louisa fell into step next to him. "*The Telegraph*, *The Times*, *Daily Mirror*, *The Sun*—"

"I saw them." Most of them. "Bloom Urban got some nice coverage."

"The few times they were mentioned! The majority of the coverage centered on Dani and either her feud with this singer Samantha Banks or her relationship with Liam Cooper."

He was well aware. He'd been tormented by those images. Of Cooper standing too close to her. Gazing at her. Touching her. They certainly looked like two people attracted to one another. Even to him. And he knew better.

This past week, their days had been filled with events, which meant her evenings were filled with her preparations for the concert. They didn't have the time to spend together, and he was missing her terribly.

Seeing the coverage of her and Cooper hadn't helped his mood, but he'd known how distressing it must have been for her to see this Samantha Banks show up. All he'd wanted to do was hold her and reassure both of them it would be okay. He'd had to settle for a phone call.

"You have nothing to worry about," Dani had told him.

"I'm not worried."

At least, not the way she thought he was.

"I'm not interested in Liam. But the media thinking I am . . . it's a good thing, Jay. If they're focused on that romance, then *you* and I can remain a secret. And that's the plan, right?"

It was. Except he didn't know if that's what he still wanted.

Louisa was venting about the situation. "The media is also running with this idea that the tickets are too expensive."

"Dani didn't say that."

"She didn't dispute it, either." Louisa exhaled and massaged her temples. "It's all added up to a difficult morning."

"I'm sorry, Louisa."

"It's fine. This one was easy. Introduce the match. Watch the match. No opportunities for anything to be said or done to take attention away from the event and the concert tomorrow evening. Nothing to tarnish the family's image."

"You care about the family's image?"

"The queen does. And her feelings about the event are also directly related to her opinion about my job performance and whether I'm given another high-profile assignment."

The weight of everything lay heavy on his shoulders. So many people depending on him. He wished he could go back in time to when he was the only one affected by the decisions he made.

But had that ever been the case?

Louisa pushed through the double doors that led out to the seats. "You should go watch the match."

He wasn't particularly excited about the event before him. It would be like torture. He'd wanted to spend time with Dani in public. Now he was getting his chance, albeit not as he'd intended. He should be able to keep everything professional and aboveboard. And if he was there, maybe she wouldn't always feel a need to talk and laugh with Cooper.

"I had them save two seats for you up in the Royal Box."

"Two seats?"

Louisa cleared her throat and gestured ahead. "The queen invited Lady Imogen to join you today."

Jameson's head turned and he saw Imogen waiting for him at the entrance to their section. She smiled and wriggled her fingers in a wave.

This keeps getting better and better.

He knew what his grandmother was doing and he hated the pressure it put on him and the hopes it gave Imogen. He wanted to be friendly and polite because they'd known each other a long time and their families were close, but if her being here bothered Dani as much as seeing Dani with Liam did him, he'd have to rethink how he handled the situation.

"They just told me you arranged for us to sit together. How sweet! Why didn't you tell me earlier?" Imogen said, kissing his cheek.

Why indeed?

He shot a look at Louisa, who'd already turned and headed back to the clubhouse. "I just now learned it was a done deal."

Imogen smiled and squeezed his arm. "It doesn't matter. I'm happy to be included and to get more time to spend with you."

Bloody hell. Damn Louisa. And damn the queen for putting him in this predicament.

"After you," he said, gesturing for her to precede him. "Have you met our VIPs?"

Though there was only one VIP he was interested in. Her and *her* VIPs—Very important Parts—that he'd spent the previous evening lusting over through a screen.

Calm down, Jameson. This isn't the time or the place.

Following Imogen, he climbed the steps and entered the private box. He saw Dani and Cooper immediately, sitting in the third row. His eyes were always drawn to her. If he was in a room with her, he sought her out. And if she wasn't present he found himself looking around, hoping for a surprise . . .

She was stunning in a red-and-pink-toned floral dress, her hair a mass of curls that tumbled down the crown of her head.

"Your Royal Highness! Are you joining us?" Bobby Worth asked.

At the singer's question, everyone in the box turned to them, including Dani. Pleasure glowed in her expression before Cooper reclaimed her attention.

Bollocks.

"I've heard these are the best seats in the stadium and you guys are the wittiest crowd."

He shook hands and spoke with the members of the box as the page led Imogen to their seats. When he finally joined her, she was settled next to Dani.

"The last time I was in this box, I was farther back," Imogen said, beaming.

Jameson's smile was tight, but he leaned over and finally allowed himself the opportunity to drink in the sight of Dani. It had been days since he'd been this close to her in person.

"Duchess. Cooper. I hope you're enjoying yourselves?"

"We are, Your Royal Highness," Cooper said, slinging an arm around Dani's shoulders.

Jameson watched the motion and thanked his royal British upbringing for allowing him to keep his emotions safely hidden. He met Cooper's gaze and saw through the glossiness of his image to the man beneath. The singer knew what he was doing.

"And have you both met Lady Imogen Harrington?"

"I haven't, although it's been difficult not to notice you," Dani said, the picture of wide-eyed innocence.

Jameson couldn't prevent his lips from twitching at the remark. He let his gaze float to hers and was reassured by what he saw.

"Enjoy the match," he told them.

"We will."

They settled back as the contest began. Ordinarily, he enjoyed watching tennis, and though this promised to be a good match, he was cognizant only of Dani, sitting less than five feet away from him. He caught her shifting in her seat and crossing her legs, the fabric of her dress drifting open to reveal gorgeous brown skin that appeared to have a slight shimmer. He was also aware of Cooper leaning close to her, whispering in her ear. Of Dani laughing at what he'd said.

"It looks like it might be true after all," Imogen whispered in *his* ear.

"What might be true?"

"Liam Cooper and Duchess. They've been together all week. They might truly be an item."

Don't look over. Don't look over.

He did and almost popped a blood vessel. The muscles in his body tensed.

He needed to get ahold of himself. He was acting possessive and jealous, and that wasn't like him. He couldn't seem to control his passions and it was driving him insane.

His weak character and selfishness almost ruined us . . . Your father put his desires over royal duty. You will not do the same.

Jameson tightened his jaw. Was he more like his father than he'd thought?

Feared?

Chapter Twenty-Two

"Thousands in crowds / Yellin' my name / Give a shit 'bout you joining / After you came . . ."
—Duchess, "Holla Atcha Girl"

Exhaustion weighing on her limbs like a snow-laden branch, Dani tied the sash on her robe and padded into the living area of her suite. Until twenty minutes ago, the room had been filled with everyone from her beauty team to wardrobe to her tour people, going over last-minute details before the concert tomorrow. Between the tennis match that afternoon, the full-dress rehearsal, and meeting with the recently departed crew, she wanted nothing more than to dive onto the bed and hit up Mr. Sandman for a visit.

That's a lie. You do want more. You want Jay to be here with you.

She settled for curling up on the white sectional.

Dani sighed. It was true. She couldn't deny loving his company, even when she had to experience it with other people. At the tennis match they'd found little ways to share private moments, either by catching the other's eye or sharing a smile at a comment or joke. All while remaining appropriate with their companions *and* in the face of relentless media scrutiny, photographers spending more time with their lenses pointed at the Royal Box than on the exhibition occurring on the court.

Risky behavior for people with so much to lose if they were caught. Yet those flashes of intimacy hadn't been enough. She'd wanted more. For it to be her and Jameson with no plus-ones to entertain. To revel in his large hand holding hers as they whispered their impressions to one another and openly snuggled when he draped an arm around her shoulders.

But that would never happen.

She and Jameson? Together in public? Officially?

The black Rapper and the white Prince.

Who was she kidding? The press coverage would be constant. Intrusive. Overwhelming. Some of it would be positive, but Dani was savvy enough to know it would also be rife with racist under- and overtones.

Jameson would hate it. It would remind him of the vicious, frenzied scenarios he and his mother had survived after his father's death.

And what about her? How would the storm of media attention affect Mela-Skin and Dani's plans for her future? A story about her and Jameson would make the situation with Banks look like high school hijinks. Would the messaging help or hinder her chances to take her company to the next level?

And that was before they considered the practical implications. Busy schedules, wildly different time zones, long flights for short visits. She'd found it challenging to date bicoastally, but bicontinentally?

What if it was nothing more than a vacation fling? Did they want to risk blowing up their lives for something that could be attributed to two attractive people being forced into seclusion together?

In their intimate, cloistered bubble at Primrose Park everything had seemed so easy and the opportunities endless. The past week had given her a taste of what a romance between them in real life might entail. And she wasn't sure either of them was ready for it.

Despite all that had happened, Dani's coverage had been incredibly positive. Bennie had called to inform her that stories about Duchess conquering the UK (#DuchessWatch) led all the entertainment and satellite radio shows. Producers from *The Tonight Show*, *The Real*, and *The Kelly Clarkson Show* had reached out to book an appearance.

More important, Barbara from Genesis had been encouraging in her feedback. If Dani killed at the concert and had a great showing at the ball, she could head back to the States having achieved what she set out to do.

And that *was the purpose of your visit. Not getting sprung on one very fine royal.*

When her doorbell rang, she wanted to ignore it. She wasn't in the mood to deal with anyone. But Tasha had mentioned having room service send up a protein smoothie before bed. Pushing to her feet, she shuffled over to the door and opened it to find Jameson standing there, still dressed in his clothes from earlier, minus the tie, jacket slung over his arm.

Giddiness tingled through her, only to be snuffed out by apprehension.

"What are you doing?" She grabbed his arm and pulled him inside. "Get in here before someone sees you."

He headed straight to the couch, sitting down and leaning his head back.

She took her time following and settled next to him. "You look awful."

"Thanks." He reached out and touched her cheek. "And you look gorgeous as always."

Gorgeous? With her hair tied up and no makeup? If she'd had any doubts before . . . "Are you crazy? What if someone saw you?"

"It's after one in the morning. Even paparazzi have to sleep, right?"

"Do they? They're soul-sucking creatures. They may not need as much sleep as us mere mortals." She smoothed hair off his forehead. "Seriously, Jay. You shouldn't be here."

"I know. But here I am nonetheless." He shifted his body to face her. "I've missed you."

Her heart melted. "I know. I've missed you, too."

"Really? Because you've been looking really cozy with Cooper."

She drew back, as if stung. She wasn't in the mood for this shit. Not tonight.

She crossed her arms over her chest. "I'm surprised you even noticed considering Lady Imogen's been hanging off your arm like a rare Birkin."

They sat there, the silence loud.

"What's a Birkin?" he finally asked.

"What do you want, Jay? I'm exhausted. And, in case you've forgotten, I have a big performance tomorrow. I should be in bed."

"Then let's go."

She put a hand on his arm.

He sighed. "I'm sorry. I know what we said. And it makes sense. It truly does. In a few days you're going home, hopefully to good news about your business."

"And you'll begin work on the new award you created to honor your grandfather and take over patronage of his charities."

"Yes."

She bit her lower lip. "I don't know what your grandmother told you, but you're not going to be able to go back to teaching. You know that, right?"

The world had gotten a taste of him. There was no way he could return to hiding his light on a college campus. Whatever deference the school and the press had given him before would be over. He'd never be treated as just one of the faculty again.

He sighed. "I hope that's not true."

"But if it is you'll begin your full-time duties as an official working member of the royal family."

They'd dictate his life: what he did, where he went, who he could see.

Jameson closed his eyes and shook his head. "This can't work."

"This can't work," she agreed, even as her heart was breaking.

"Then why do I want you with a fever that never cools? Why does your absence, both actual and perceived, cause an ache in my heart nothing short of your presence can alleviate?"

His words were so fucking intoxicating. "Oh, baby."

"I need you, Dani. And that need isn't governed by notions of time, familial duty, or patriotism. It's about you and me and being as close as two people can be. I don't know if I'll be able to let you go."

"Then don't."

Their lips came together, fusing more than their bodies. But what started out frantic and wild settled into something deep and lingering. She took her time, slanting her mouth over his, caressing him with her tongue, grazing his jaw with her teeth. She savored the experience, like sipping a vintage bottle of champagne or listening to a great album. As if it was the last time she'd ever have the pleasure.

Because it was the last time she'd ever have him.

She worked her way down to his chest and her hands shook, fumbling in her need to unbutton his shirt. Getting it done, she scraped her nails over his taut torso. He trembled and gripped her hips.

She wanted to be closer. She crawled onto his lap, rotating her hips and grinding against him. He threw his head back and moaned as his cock thickened and lengthened beneath her. She took in his sexy sounds, saved them to revisit later.

"My turn," he rasped, flipping her onto her back. Reverentially, he spread open her robe and audibly inhaled at her bareness. "Jesus, Dani, there are no words to describe how fucking beautiful you are."

He stuck his thumb in his mouth before massaging the moisture into her tightly budded nipple. She hissed and arched into his touch.

"Hmmmm," he moaned, the sound low and needy and sexy as fuck.

He sucked on his thumb once more, this time rubbing the wetness on the tight nub a little farther south. A shudder rocketed through her body.

"Do you have any idea what giving you pleasure does to me? How it feels when you respond to my touch?" he asked, his lids so low they were almost closed, a flush high on his cheeks.

She pulled her lower lip between her teeth and leisurely released it. "Why don't you show me?"

"Planning on it." He undid his pants, then reached into his pocket and produced a condom.

She smiled. "Came prepared, did you?"

"Quite right," he grunted, before sliding into her.

She cried out, reveling in the rightness of it. His cock stroked her inner walls and flirted with her G-spot, the friction impossibly good. Faster than she wanted, but still not soon enough, pressure coiled tight in her lower belly and every insertion and withdrawal shot shards of pleasure along her limbs.

Fuck! His whip appeal game was potent. She clenched around him. He growled and increased his pace, the strength of his strokes powerful enough to push her body along the cushions, save for the arm he'd slid around her lower back, pinning her in place.

"Look at me, love. Open those beautiful eyes."

She did and they stared at one another. Time slowed and sounds faded until all she could hear was their combined panting breaths.

And words.

". . . goddamned tight . . ."

"Right there, baby—"

". . . this my pussy?"

"Fuck me . . ."

Tingles crept up her body, and she pressed her thighs against his hips and urged him faster, harder, deeper.

"So . . . close . . . ," she whimpered. "Almost . . . there . . ."

"That's it, Dani. Fuck, give it to me!"

"Jay!" she screamed, before she lost the ability to do anything other than surrender to sensations consuming her.

When their breaths finally returned to their bodies, he lifted her in his arms and strolled into the bathroom. Soaping and rinsing her from neck to toe—he knew better than to get her hair wet!—he dried her off, applied lotion to her damp skin, then carried her to bed, where he pulled her back against his warm, naked chest.

"You need your rest. Go to sleep, love."

And she did.

THE STADIUM WAS sold out. Almost 95,000 people came to remember Prince John, learn about his causes, and enjoy the musical acts. Jameson hadn't been sure they'd sell the remaining tickets, but the events of the past week had imbued the show with a fear-of-missing-out energy that allowed them to sell out, despite criticism over the price.

Aided by the global press coverage, they'd also made a deal to sell the worldwide distribution rights for the concert to a popular streaming network. The increased interest meant they were able to command top dollar. The money they'd made would be put to good use, funding the Lloyd Prize and supporting the charities his grandfather had loved. Additionally, opinion about the royal family was at an all-time high. It appeared his grandmother's plan had worked.

Jameson had opened the show with a speech followed by a video montage celebrating the life and legacy of Prince John. Then Julian, Catherine, and Bettina had each come out to share a personal anecdote about their father. Carl Page was the first act to perform, and each successive performer had been introduced either by the royal who'd personally invited them or by a video package of Prince John. Kay Morgan was finishing up and then it would be Dani's turn.

Music by the performers and the din of the crowd flowed backstage, making it difficult to hear and be heard, while equipment, cords, and boxes made traversing the area dangerous. But there was a hum of excitement. Of anticipation. It showed in the flushed faces, bright eyes, and hurried movements.

This was Dani's world. And he was eager to see her shine in it.

As he made his way to the part of the arena set aside for the performers, he marveled at his current situation. A month ago, if someone had told him that he'd engage in a passionate, potentially life-altering affair with an American rapper, he would've suggested they seek the guidance of a mental health professional. But it had happened. And now that it was over, he was left dissatisfied and oddly bereft.

He'd awakened her before sunrise this morning, kissing down

her soft, warm body, inhaling her scent, and tonguing her pussy one last time, attempting to imprint her flavor on his taste buds. After she'd come, it had taken everything he had to leave her bed, but it had been the right thing to do. They'd both agreed it was folly to imagine a future between them. A clean break would be best.

Or as clean as it could be considering they'd need to interact for another day and a half.

Reaching the door to her waiting area, he took a deep breath, adjusted his cuffs and the sport jacket he was wearing, and knocked. A woman who looked vaguely familiar opened it.

"Your Royal Highness," she said, executing a proper curtsy. "It's nice to meet you in person. I'm Nyla, Dani's friend."

Right. She was the face on the iPad who had watched his kitchen row with Dani from the safe distance of her home in L.A.

That seemed like a lifetime ago.

"Hello." He held out his hand and she shook it. "Please forgive my behavior that day. I can claim no good excuse except shock at what I'd walked into."

"Don't worry about it," Nyla said, nonchalantly waving an elegant hand. "Duchess brings out . . . strong emotions in people. It's all water under the bridge."

It was clear Dani and the woman were close. He didn't know what Dani had told her friend, but she must've mentioned the change in their relationship. They stood there taking each other's measure, two people who cared about the same person recognizing a like-minded spirit.

Nyla nodded—whether in approval or to signal the end of the perusal he didn't know—and stood back. "Come in."

Black leather couches and chairs were positioned in a welcoming arrangement near a buffet table piled with drinks, snacks, and platters of fruit, cheese, and veggies.

He waited until she closed the door behind her. "Dani didn't mention you were coming."

She smiled. "I managed to pull some strings and get an invitation."

"If I'd known, I would've taken care of it. Will you be attending the ball?"

"Dani talked to Louisa and it's a go."

"Good. I'm sure Dani is happy to have you here. How is she?"

"In performance prep mode." She motioned with her head toward the back. "She's over there."

Curtains separated the large area they were currently in from another zone. He stepped through the fabric divider and into a bevy of action and commotion. Dani was surrounded by people applying makeup, styling her hair, and adjusting her clothes. Her back was to him, but he caught a glimpse of her reflection in the mirror. He swayed, suddenly light-headed.

She wore a long-sleeved red top that made her look like she was covered in airy clouds. It stopped just beneath her breasts, leaving her midriff and belly bare, except for a thin diamond chain that glowed against her skin. Red leather shorts barely covered her round sumptuous ass, and thigh-high stiletto boots, in the same crimson color, completed the outfit.

Her wide eyes were heavily lined, her lips popped with the same bright red color, and her black hair was slicked into a sleek fall down her back. Tendrils curled around her forehead and temples, and large diamond hoops swung from her ears.

She was a sexy flaming siren. Untouchable. Something to stare at and adore from afar.

Her expression was tense and focused, causing her to look more like Duchess and less like Dani.

But then, her gaze met his in the mirror and she smiled.

There she is.

"Hi."

"Hi," he said, able to see that his grin looked as goofy as it felt. He cleared his throat. "Kay is almost done with her set and then they'll redo the stage for your performance. I just wanted to make sure you're okay before I head out to introduce you."

"We're good." She switched her gaze to the group around her. "Can y'all give us a moment? I'll meet you outside."

And then it was the two of them.

"You look incredible."

She struck a pose. "This old thing? Just something I threw on."

He laughed, as he knew she'd intended. He took her hands in his, raising his brows at her long red nails. "Americans and their weapons. Do you have a permit to carry these? They're dangerous."

"Goes with the look. And they can cut a bitch should Stalker Samantha show up."

He decided not to tell her the singer had indeed tried to get backstage earlier. After the stunt at Bloom Urban, Jameson had discussed the possibility with Louisa, so they'd ensured security and workers at each backstage entrance had the pop star's picture and ordered that she wasn't to be allowed access. Dani didn't need to worry about "Stalker Samantha." Her only concern should be putting on the best show she could.

He squeezed her hands once before releasing her. "You'll do great."

She shrugged. "I'm not worried about my performance."

"You're not?"

"No. I'm a little nervous because this is a slightly different audience, but I love performing live. It's a high unlike anything else. The energy you get back from a crowd is indescribable."

"Well, I'm looking forward to it."

"You've already seen some of it, when we were practicing in the barn."

Mentioning the barn brought back memories of the time they'd spent together at Primrose Park. And emphasized that she would be leaving soon.

"How long are you staying after the ball?"

"A day. Two at the most."

He swallowed past the sudden obstruction in his throat and nodded. "So, this is it?"

She tugged on the collar of his shirt. "I'll see you at the ball tomorrow."

"I know. But it won't be the same."

A month ago, this had seemed easy. They'd been wildly attracted to one another and the sex had been off the charts. What was the harm in them getting to know each other and having some fun? A summer fling. And yet what he was feeling now couldn't be described as easy or carefree or fun. It was deep, and soul stirring, and complicated as hell. And giving it up, letting her go, was turning out to be harder than he'd ever expected.

"Dani—"

"Jay, I—"

They laughed. He motioned for her to continue. "You go."

"What if—"

A knock on the door and then someone called, "Time to go, Duchess!"

Bloody hell.

"'What if' what?" he asked.

"What if . . ." She closed her eyes and he waited, barely breathing, not knowing what his response would be, only hoping she'd say it.

But then her lips tightened and she shook her head. "Nothing. It was stupid."

Disappointment lanced through him.

She leaned forward and softly kissed him. "Later, Your Royal Highness."

"Bye, Duchess."

And then she walked away, disappearing behind the curtain.

He took several moments to get himself together and calm the chaos of emotions boiling inside before making his way back to the stage. The general buzz of the concertgoers morphed into cheers and hollers as he strode over to the microphone.

"The one, the only. Duchess."

The lights flashed and the crowd erupted. A thumping beat blared from the speakers, and the tall video screen at the back of the stage flickered to life. Five women, dressed in white, danced against a black background in time to the music. On the screen, Duchess emerged, her red figure striking against the neutral backdrop.

The audience went wild.

She executed the same moves as the dancers, her graceful body stirring all kinds of feelings within him. And then everything went dark.

When the lights came back up, the image that had been on the screen was in person on the stage.

The crowd got louder.

"Duchess is here!" she called.

"Bitches better bow down!" came the response.

"Yeah." She smiled, like she had a secret. "What's good, Wembley? How y'all feeling?"

A chorus of answers pelted the stage.

Dani tilted her head in a movement he'd seen in several of her videos. "I want you to do something for me. Throw your fists in the air / And pump them like you just don't care / If you're a bad boss bitch / Who rocks with Duchess / Somebody say, 'Hell yeah!'"

"Hell yeah!"

She was a powerhouse who commanded the stage and the attention of every person in attendance. Her videos could never properly illustrate how immensely talented she was or how much work went into what she did. She glided across the stage, dancing, rapping into the mike, not missing a single cue. One song, two songs, three. They all got her at one hundred percent maximum effort. And she did it all while wearing four-inch heels.

He couldn't tear his gaze away from her.

After the third song, she took a break. One of her dancers walked over and handed her a towel and a glass of water.

"Thank y'all for coming out tonight to remember Prince John and support his charitable causes. I've gotten to know a lot about him lately and the more I've learned the more I wished I could've met him. He must've been a wonderful person to inspire such love and respect."

Dani glanced over to where he was standing. Their gazes met and tangled for a brief second, during which her expression seemed to soften before she broke their visual connection.

"He was a firm believer in sustainability—not just working to protect our environment but focusing on how, as a community, we live, work, and play so we don't deplete our natural resources for future generations. And you don't have to be rich or royal to do your part. Activism on this issue needs to be affordable and inclusive. It's our planet, too! So, when you leave here today, think of one small, sustainable thing you can do and incorporate that into your life. Imagine the impact we could have if everyone in here made one small sustainable change. I think Prince John would approve!"

His heart hammered in his chest. He'd mentioned his grandfather often, but now he knew she'd actually listened. And remembered. The stinging prick of tears burned behind his eyes.

Don't make a spectacle of yourself.

He dropped his head and pinched the bridge of his nose.

This woman would be his undoing.

The audience clapped and yelled their approval.

Dani returned the glass to her dancer. "I was having such a good time I forgot that I brought a friend along to help me, in case I got scared or nervous. Is it too late? Do you guys mind if I bring him out?"

A friend? Who?

Jameson turned to see Liam Cooper striding past him and onto the stage.

Bloody hell!

The crowd erupted as the singer took her outstretched hand.

"Hey, Duchess!"

"You know Liam Cooper, right? Liam was kind enough to agree to help me, but you guys have been so great, I don't think I need him anymore."

"I was watching. You were awesome. Wasn't she?" Liam asked the crowd.

They looked fantastic together. Like they truly belonged up there. And their chemistry was palpable. When she went back home, would she start dating Cooper? The media would be into it. And it could help her company . . .

"But I feel so bad," Dani was saying. "We did all that work."

Liam nodded. "It's true. We did."

"Maybe we can still show them. You guys don't mind, do you?"

A song began that he didn't recognize, but the crowd did, because they went insane. Dani started rapping and when Liam sang his first lines, Jameson wanted to hate him, but he couldn't. His voice was impressive.

"Fuck! It seems no one is immune to Duchess," Julian said, coming to stand beside him. "You see how she moves? Can you imagine all of that riding your cock?"

Jameson balled his hands into fists. His uncle was asking for it. "Take your vulgarity elsewhere."

"Relax. You don't have to pretend. Mother isn't here. Besides, I'm introducing the next act."

"But that doesn't require us to converse, does it?"

"You've managed to pull this off so far, but the celebration isn't over yet. In some ways, it's just beginning."

With a smirk and a dip of his head, Julian wandered off.

What did that mean? Now he had to worry about what his uncle was planning?

The song ended and Liam kissed Dani's cheek, sending the audience into raptures. Then he waved and ran off the stage.

"Wow, the crowd is stellar! I hope they stay pumped for my set," Liam said, coming to stand next to Jameson.

"You were good."

Onstage, there was a record scratch and the music changed to another beat that got the fans going.

"Let's end on a banger, shall we, Wembley!" she yelled into her microphone. "D to the A to the N I / You wanna know why / Dudes go sky high / When I say jump—"

"Thanks. How can you help but be great when you're with her? She makes you give everything, requires you to have your shit together. It's one of the things I love about her."

Liam accepted a towel from a stagehand and walked away.

Jameson turned to watch Dani, the singer's words reverberating in his mind.

. . . one of the things I love about her.

. . . I love about her.

. . . love . . .

His stomach plunged and his pulse boomed in his ears, louder than the music and the voices of the audience singing in unison. He stumbled back a few steps and reached out to brace himself on a piece of equipment when his knees threatened to buckle.

He loved that about her, too.

Because he—

Loved—

Her.

Chapter Twenty-Three

"*The swerves of my curves / The dip in my hip / This is me, naturally / Call me thicc with 2 c's . . .*"

—Duchess, "Fever"

A crowd of people milled around the Approach Gallery, the space that led into the ballroom. The ceiling was vaulted in the shape of a barrel, the night sky slightly visible through the engraved glass. Floral tapestries adorned the wall above chaises and large porcelain vases. Up ahead a queue of people waited to descend into the ballroom.

"Are you ready?" Nyla asked, channeling Cinderella's older, sexier cousin in a stunning strapless, pale blue sheath.

Showtime.

Dani pasted on a smile. "Don't you know? Duchess stays ready."

Nyla gave her a knowing look and took her hand. "And Duchess looks amazing."

Dani was actually confident on that score. She loved the gown made for her by Aurora Kerby, an up-and-coming black designer who was doing impressive work but hadn't broken out yet. Nyla had worn the designer to the Golden Globes last year and had raved about the experience. During her time in New York, Dani had met with Aurora and had liked what she saw. And when she'd been notified about the calendar of events for the celebration and informed she'd need a ballgown, the choice had been a no-brainer.

The dress was a dramatic A-line gown crafted of black tulle; the sleeveless bodice had a deep-V halter neckline that bared the smooth, tantalizing stretch of skin from the base of her neck to her waist. Sequins had been sown strategically throughout the fabric of the full, floor-sweeping skirt to give the impression of a starry night against a vast, dark sky. Miss K had replicated that sparkle in her hair by using diamond clips to arrange a partial updo of curls that brushed her face and flowed down her back. Large ruby drop earrings and a ruby and diamond cuff on her upper left arm completed the sensual but romantic look.

"The prince will love you in this."

"I didn't wear it for him," Dani said, with a nonchalance that didn't fool either of them.

"But that doesn't mean you don't care what he thinks."

Dani sighed. Facts.

When she'd seen him backstage at Wembley, looking more polished than usual in charcoal khakis, a light blue button-down shirt, and a navy blazer, her knees had buckled. But it had been the unguarded hunger infusing his expression as his gaze skimmed over her in the mirror that had been her undoing. She'd actually considered suggesting they continue seeing each other beyond her time in the UK. But then the universe interceded, snapping her back into reality.

God looked out for children and fools.

Since she'd waved good-bye to twenty-five a couple of years ago, she knew where she landed in that metric. Thinking she and Jay could be together was the epitome of foolish. But seeing him, being with him, put those thoughts in her head. Had her thinking the impossible could be made possible.

"I must've done something momentous in a past life to be lucky enough to escort the most beautiful ladies here tonight," Liam said.

"Thank you." Dani smiled and eyed his classic tuxedo. "You look handsome."

"And yet no one will be looking at me." He turned to her friend. "Nyla! Good to see you!"

Nyla accepted his kiss on her cheek. "You, too, Liam."

Dani slid Nyla serious side-eye. She hadn't mentioned they knew each other. "You've met?"

"Like everyone in entertainment, we've seen each other around," Liam said.

"I always thought *our* world was tiny and exclusive," Nyla said.

"Nothing like this." Liam held out an arm for each of them. "Shall we?"

Dani scanned the crowd. It might be stupid, but she was hoping she'd see Jay. Maybe find a way to walk in with him. But he was nowhere to be found.

You're going all in on the insane, aren't you? After all of your talk about keeping your relationship a secret, he'd be an idiot to actually escort you into the closing event of the celebration.

Dani threw her shoulders back and curled her hand around Liam's bicep. "Let's do this."

The trio joined the line of others waiting to enter the ball. When they arrived at the top of the stairs, Dani gasped at the sight.

The first thing she noticed was the height of the ceiling. Soaring, even from her perspective, it gave the room an imposing feel. Carved open rosettes adorned the plaster, from which large gold and crystal chandeliers hung.

Below, it was like a scene in a fairy tale come to life. Men in black tie and women in neutral and jeweled tones, both sparkling and muted, dotted the enormous space. A throne canopy, in a rich red and gold, sat on a dais on the far end of the room beneath the prominent display of the crest of the House of Lloyd. Chairs covered in a matching fabric were situated on either side of the area, providing guests places to sit down during the festivities. Standing golden candelabras dotted the perimeter, the flicker of their candles adding an otherworldly glow.

Dani had thought the splendor of the celebratory dinner had been impressive. This made that event look like her high school prom. The ballroom at Buckingham Palace was simply spectacular.

The footman standing next to them announced, "Duchess and Miss Nyla Patterson escorted by Liam Cooper."

Although the activity on the far side of the room continued, those closest to them turned to watch as they made their way down the grand stairs.

Don't trip. Don't trip. Please don't trip. Be graceful. You've done performances on slippery stages in stiletto heels. You can do this.

Her eyes skimmed the crowd, her breath catching when she saw him. If ever a man was made to wear white tie . . .

He was magnificent in full royal regalia. His tailcoat was expertly tailored to emphasize his broad shoulders, slim hips, and long legs while the navy sash, multicolored ribbons, and medals lent him a regal stature and gravitas. He looked like a dream come true. A dream she'd never known she wanted until him.

Until that moment.

Across the breadth of the room and the people in between, their eyes met and held. Her vision narrowed until she could see no one else.

After tonight you'll never see him again.

The thought swept through her, leaving her chilled and bereft.

She shivered and that slight loss of focus caused her to stumble. She steadied herself, tightening her grip on Liam's arm.

Were they being rash? Did it have to be all or nothing? They were two people with means and influence. They could find a way to keep their travel secret, avoid high-profile places and events, employ more disguises. If they wanted to, they'd make it work. They had to. Because the thought of never seeing him again was unbearable. She wasn't ready to let him go.

When she, Nyla, and Liam were almost to the bottom of the stairs, she lost sight of him. While the footman introduced the next couple, they were swarmed by fellow attendees.

"That was a dazzling performance," a woman on her left said.

"The concert was incredible. I think Prince John would've been proud."

"I really enjoyed the two of you performing together. Serious chemistry," Kay Morgan said, her iconic style on display in a black flowing topcoat and dress, her grayish blond waves piled in a messy knot on top of her head.

"Thank you," Dani said. "I caught your set on the monitor. You were wonderful."

"Getting them ready for you." Kay winked.

A cleared throat made Dani laugh. "Kay, this is my friend Nyla Patterson."

"It's a pleasure," Nyla said, shaking Kay's outstretched hand. "I'm a fan."

"Thank you. Are you a musician, too?" Kay asked.

Dani shook her head. "She's an actress."

"I'm afraid I don't watch much TV or movies these days. Tell me something you've been in."

As Nyla started to run down her IMDb page, Liam touched Dani's elbow. "How about some champagne?"

"A man after my heart! Yes, please."

He excused them and led her to a roaming waiter and his loaded tray.

"Thanks," she said, accepting the drink Liam handed her.

"You're welcome." His smile rivaled the sparkles in their flutes. "I've really enjoyed this week."

"Me, too. It turned out well, I think."

"I've especially enjoyed my time with you. When we get back to the States, we should hang out more."

The interest in his gaze caught her off guard. Hold up. She thought he knew the score. They'd been playing it up for the cameras. It wasn't real. She hadn't taken it personally or him seriously.

"Liam, I think you're great, but—"

"Ahh, dagger." He closed his eyes and staggered back, pressing his hand to his chest. "You wound me."

"I'm sorry. I didn't think you meant any of it."

"It's cool. Not that I'm not disappointed. I think we'd be great together. But your interest is clearly elsewhere."

She arched a perfectly sculpted and gelled brow. "What are you talking about?"

"I knew from day one he had his eye on you," he said, nodding over to where Jameson stood with Lady Imogen and Princess Catherine.

Fuck. "I don't think that's true."

"What I didn't know was if his feelings were reciprocated. Until the tennis exhibition."

This wasn't good. She thought they'd been careful. She shook her head. "You're mistaken."

"Don't worry. Your secret is safe with me." He stared at something over her shoulder and sighed. "I'm being summoned. Save me a dance, beautiful."

He kissed her cheek and strode off. Dani watched several heads twist in his wake, following his progress.

Did she need to worry about that? He said he'd keep the information to himself, though she hadn't confirmed it, but still . . .

"I think he really likes you," Nyla said in her ear.

Hello, Echo.

Dani twisted her bottom lip. "I know. And he knows about Jay."

Nyla shrugged. "He won't say anything. If only to preserve his shot with you."

"Shot denied."

"Who knows what might happen when you get back to the States?"

"I know. Nothing."

"You've been getting some great press and it's clear you and he vibe. Maybe—"

"Nyla!" Agitation sharpened Dani's tone. "Let it go!"

Nyla closed her mouth and tilted her head to the side. She studied Dani with narrowed eyes, then said—

"You know it's not going to work, don't you?"

Dani should've played it down or played it off, but she couldn't. Her feelings and her own concerns were too close to the surface. "Why? Because I'm an American? A rapper? Black?"

"Yes," Nyla said, her blue-shadowed eyes wide. "Look, I get it. Prince Jameson is smart, compassionate, and good-looking, if you like the tall, dark, square-jawed type. But he's a member of the royal family. And after this week, his profile has been raised dramatically. They will expect him to choose a certain kind of wife, one who will help him in his royal duties. Are you willing to give up your life and your work to be here with him?"

"I'm not marrying him!" Although the thought of that imaginary wife caused a knot to tangle in her belly. "We're still getting to know one another. You know . . . dating."

Nyla moved closer and squeezed her forearm. "You grew up hearing your grandmother talk about the royals but you never listened to her, did you? I'm your friend and I'm only saying this because I love you. What do you think will happen if this story gets out?"

"It's not going to—"

"You've tempted fate and gotten lucky, Dani! But if you continue seeing each other, it's only a matter of time. Do you really think the Palace isn't going to have something to say about it? That the press won't get involved to a level that'll make the Banks situation seem like a slow media day? Are you ready for the things they'll say about you? Because, look around! There are a lot of faces in here and only a handful look like you or me. And you're talking about joining the whitest of historic institutions."

This wasn't breaking news. On some level, Dani knew Nyla was right. She'd told herself the same things minus Nyla's bluntness. Still, when she weighed her friend's wisdom against the dread that enveloped her at the thought of letting Jameson go . . .

"This was supposed to be a fling. He was hot, available, and even I could see the sparks from L.A. You were consenting adults who were thrown together in an unusual circumstance. There was no harm in it. But you're trying to turn a fuck into forever. And I don't think you've considered that being with him means diluting who you are. If they let you in, you know that control over your life you've been striving for? They'll take it. And there will be nothing you can do about it."

And there it was. The marble that did more than balance the scales of justice; it gave the advantage to the side of Nyla's home truths. Had Dani worked her ass off and come so close to having everything she wanted only to cede the authority to dictate her life and her choices to others?

Hell to the no.

But Nyla was being extra. It didn't have to be that serious.

Dani nodded. "I'm good."

Nyla's smile was tinged with sadness. "Of course you are. And don't worry, we're going to have a great time. We'll enjoy this exquisite champagne, laugh, dance, and provide bomb pictures. And when the night is over, you'll say good-bye and walk away with your dominion and dignity intact. You take a moment while I go get us some refills."

Dani turned away from the crowd, blinking back the unexpected tears Nyla's words had brought. Rhonda would be pissed if she messed up her makeup, and Dani would be damned if she let these people see her cry.

"Well, you look different!" Rhys Barnes said, coming to stand next to her.

Jay's friend was incredibly handsome in his tails and white tie, though the formal wear did little to rein in his untamed energy. In fact, it only emphasized his brawniness.

Get it together, girl. Fake it now, fall apart later.

She tossed her hair back and grinned. "Professor Thor."

"Pardon?"

"The tall Viking god thing you're rocking. Jay didn't mention that's what I called you?"

"No, he didn't." Rhys laughed. "But I'll make sure to ask him about it."

"You do that. It's nice to finally meet you. I've heard a lot about you."

"Same." He peered closely at her. "I know it was you at Birmingham, but I still can't see it. Top-notch disguise."

"Thank you. I learned from some of the best."

"I hope you taught our Jameson some tips. It would be nice for him to have a way to take a break from being hounded by the press that doesn't involve his hibernation."

Our Jameson? Hardly.

"Will you be staying around for a while?"

He'd asked the question in the same jovial tone as the rest of their conversation, but fine lines deepened at the corners of his eyes as his gaze sharpened.

"I'm scheduled to fly out in two days."

"Oh. I hope you reconsider. You've been just the tonic. I must admit I like the Jameson that's been influenced by a Duchess."

"Dani, I went too far. If you want to go for it, I'll support y— Oh!" Nyla stopped short, the abrupt motion causing champagne to slosh over the rims of the flutes she was carrying. Her gaze landed—and lingered—on Rhys. "I didn't mean to interrupt."

"You're not. This is Professor Thor, Jameson's friend. Nyla Patterson."

"A pleasure. And you can call me Rhys." He took the glasses from Nyla and placed them on the tray of a passing waiter. Pulling the handkerchief from his breast pocket, he dabbed the spilt liquid from her hand.

"The pleasure is all mine," Nyla said, sounding dazed and disoriented. The skin above her strapless bodice flushed and her tongue darted out to lick her lower lip.

The gesture drifted from chivalrous to intimate in two seconds flat! Dani fussed with the skirt of her gown, adjusted the cuff on her arm, anything to avoid spying on the moment.

Oh, for fuck's sake! Get a room!

The soft strains of classical music merged with the babble of conversations as the string orchestra began to play.

"Can I get you another drink?" Rhys asked Dani, though his gaze remained on Nyla.

"No, thank you."

Rhys folded the square of his handkerchief and returned it to its home. "Ms. Patterson, would you care to dance?"

Nyla's eyes glowed. "I'd love to."

"If you'll excuse us . . ."

As Rhys led Nyla to the designated area for dancing, she turned back and mouthed, "Oh my God!" before she was swallowed up by the sea of guests.

In spite of everything, Dani laughed. She knew Nyla's earlier words hadn't been said to hurt her. Dani had no doubt that her friend had her best interests at heart. Nyla was beautiful and single. Why shouldn't she have her own fling? And without all of the drama and complications of the royal family.

"You look stunning."

Dani's breath caught in her throat. His words whispered along her skin and nourished her soul. She turned and there he was.

"You look like a real-life Prince Charming."

Color tinged his cheekbones and he smiled. "And you look like a piece of heaven, sent down to tempt me."

When he said shit like that, how was she supposed to resist him?

He reached out and touched her earrings. "Those are beautiful."

"Thank you. I love rubies. They're my favorite gemstone."

"I'm not surprised. They're flawless, hot, and passionate. Just like you."

She inhaled and her nipples beaded and brushed against the fabric of her dress. She shot a furtive look over his shoulder, and while most people weren't paying attention, several were eyeing them with speculation.

"We're being watched."

"I don't care."

So sweet . . . "Yes, you do."

His blue eyes bore into hers. "I don't want this to be over."

She knew how she felt, but she hadn't imagined he'd been having his own second thoughts. She blinked. "You want to keep seeing me?"

"More than anything in the world. Do you want to keep seeing me?"

Pleasure bloomed in her chest. All caution and concern melted in the face of his smile. "What if I meet you at Primrose Park after the ball? I can delay my departure for several days and we can discuss everything? Figure this out away from nosy eyes and ears?"

He stepped closer to her. "I want to kiss you so bloody badly."

"I want that, too." She recalled what Nyla had said. "Later. You need to walk away now. We haven't been caught. We don't want to press our luck."

"There she is! The woman of the concert." Prince Julian came to stand beside Jameson.

Seeing them standing together, side by side in similar dress, the family resemblance was striking. But there was nothing about the elder royal that attracted her at all.

"I'm not sure that's true, but thank you," she said, civilly.

His eyes swept her from head to toe, pausing to focus on her chest area. "I believe the ladies are acquainted with one another, but Jameson, allow me the honor of introducing Samantha Banks, a singer from the States."

Dani's eyes widened as the pop singer joined their group, delicate in a floor-length, cap-sleeved, chiffon gown, color-blocked in shades of teal, dark blue, and violet that actually managed not to clash with her hair.

It didn't matter how she looked. Pretty faces could hide evil minds.

"Your Royal Highness," Samantha cooed, holding her hand out.

Anger barreled through Dani like a wildfire, obliterating the contentment she'd managed to claim for herself just moments ago. She was so fucking tired of reacting to this woman and playing by her rules. Dani wanted to have it out, end this shit once and for all. But she was acutely aware of where she was, the growing interest around them, and everything she had to lose if she wasn't smart.

Woosah, bitch!

"What are you doing here?"

Samantha curled her lip. "Why should you be the only one with royal connections?"

Dani's black-and-red-ombré stiletto nails pricked her palms. Long acrylics were not conducive to throwing a punch. "This isn't a game or stirring up trouble on social media. This is my life. My business."

"Did you bring her here?" Jameson asked his uncle, his hand resting reassuringly, protectively, on the small of her back.

"I think Miss Banks has a lot of talent. If you could invite Duchess, I don't see why I couldn't invite her. Especially given the things I've been reading about Duchess. They haven't been very complimentary."

Dani stiffened. Prince Julian was the reason Samantha was here? Why would he invite her? What did he have to gain?

"Did you know this when you suggested her?" Julian tsked and shook his head. "If Mummy knew, I don't think she would've approved of your choice."

"Julian—"

"Excuse me," Louisa interrupted. In a simple sage green gown, her usual cool composure was marred by the lines of tension bracketing her mouth. "Her Majesty would like a word."

"Am I going to meet the queen?" Samantha breathed.

"No," Louisa said. The dismissive disgust in her tone would've made Dani laugh if she wasn't furious.

"This will be the perfect opportunity to tell Mummy what I've learned. I knew appointing you as the face of this event would be a bad idea. Your judgment is obviously skewed."

"Not you," Louisa said. "Only Prince Jameson and Duchess."

Julian's face registered his indignation. Dani glanced at Jameson, but he'd gone expressionless. He dipped his head and motioned for her and Louisa to precede him. Pressing her lips together, she followed the other woman. People stared, parting to allow them to pass, and she schooled her features to not give away her inner turmoil.

The queen sat on the dais at the far end of the room. She looked regal and elegant in a white dress and a blue sash. Dani wondered if she was aware that her hand rested on the arm of the empty throne next to hers instead of her own. Though there were close to two hundred people in attendance, on the dais under the canopied throne, they had a privacy Dani hadn't anticipated.

"Your Majesty," Dani said, dropping into a curtsy.

"Everyone is talking about your performance," the queen said, in the cultured voice Dani remembered from the dinner.

Dani didn't know how to take that comment—was it a compliment or a complaint?—so she answered in the same neutral vein.

"I was honored to be invited."

"Yes, well, Jameson clearly saw something the rest of us didn't."

There was no ambiguity of meaning in *that* statement.

The queen looked out over the large assembly of guests. "It's been quite a week."

"It has."

"I'll admit I wasn't sure about you in the beginning, but you proved to be very popular."

First Samantha and now the queen. Dani'd had to bite her tongue so often, she was surprised the thing hadn't fallen out of her mouth.

It doesn't matter. You know what you have to do.

"Thank you," she managed through gritted teeth.

"Your presence brought the attention of . . . well, let's just say, a *new* segment of society, to a cause that was meaningful to my John, and for that, I'm grateful."

A new segment of society? Which one would that be?

Don't cause a scene.

"It's an important issue. We all have a part to play."

The queen finally "gifted" Dani with the full force of her scrutiny. "Excellent point. We all have a part to play. Including Jameson. This week was significant for him, as well."

"He was a gracious host"—eventually!—"and he's done a wonderful job representing your family."

"Indeed. We have big plans for his future."

Dani pursed her lips. This was more than casual chitchat.

"I don't know why you're telling me this, ma'am."

"Oh, I think you do. You've managed to not get caught again, but any thoughts the two of you have about prolonging this entanglement need to end now."

Get caught?

Again?

Dani briefly eyed Jameson, who, like the guards in the furry black hats stationed outside the palace, stood still and quiet.

Except for the muscle ticking furiously in his jaw.

"With all due deference and respect, you can't tell me who I can be involved with or how to live my life."

The queen sighed and her perfect posture appeared to relax. Slightly. "You may not believe this, but I admire you. You're a hard worker, with apparent musical talent and a head for business."

Dani's surprise must've shown on her face because Marina said, "Oh, yes, I know about your company. And I know you're on the precipice of turning it into a very successful venture. You must understand that when you're in charge, you have to make the best decision for your organization, even if it's unpopular. You are a beautiful woman, adored by millions. You can have your choice of anyone or anything in the world."

The queen straightened, and that brief moment of kinship disappeared from her expression.

"But not Jameson. Not this family. I won't allow it."

"Grandmother! That's enough!"

Louisa gasped. "Sir! You forget yourself!"

But Dani barely took notice of Jameson's attempt to defend her. The queen's harsh words rocketed her back to her childhood, mired in feelings of being unwanted, unloved, and uncared for after Nana's death.

We don't have room.

You can stay here a week but then you need to move on.

I can let you have this couch. What you gonna let me have?

Bile burned the back of her throat. What was so wrong with her?

She'd played stages and venues across the globe. She had money, accolades, and awards. Women wanted to be her. Men wanted to fuck her. Everyone knew her name.

But what did any of that matter when she was still being rejected?

Without a word she gathered the voluminous fabric of her gown in one hand and hurried down the dais steps.

"Dani—"

She heard him behind her, but she didn't stop. She could feel the tears welling. She couldn't save Rhonda's gorgeous work from being marred, but she'd be damned if she started its ruination here.

There was no way she'd climb that giant staircase in time. Scanning the large space, she saw a door near the platform where the orchestra played. She had no idea where it led, but it had to be better than this.

"Dani? Hey!" Liam grabbed her hand. "What's going on?"

"I'm fine. I just need a minute."

"You're not fine. Wait, where are you going?"

"I'm sorry, I can't," she said, pulling away from him.

She moved quickly, avoiding people when possible, muttering apologies and nonsensical excuses when she couldn't. That door was her lifeline. She just needed to get to it.

When she finally reached it, she walked into a small storage closet. Not the most luxurious of accommodations, but it was empty and that was her only requirement. She closed the door behind her and locked it, cloaking herself in darkness. She reached on the nearby wall for a light switch and, finding one, turned it on to see chairs, covered in the same red and gold fabric as the seating and the throne, stacked inside, along with a few tables and antique decor pieces.

She dropped into a vacant chair and pressed fingers to her forehead. What had she been thinking?

She hadn't been. She'd been caught up in hormones and feelings. Everyone knew a relationship between her and Jay would never work. The two of them were the only ones who thought they'd had a chance.

A knock sounded. "Dani?"

"Go away!"

"No," Jameson said, his voice tense even through the door.

"Look, I just need some time to get myself together. I haven't forgotten what I'm supposed to do. I'll be there in a second."

"I don't give a damn about what you're supposed to do. I want to talk about what happened."

"There's nothing more to say to each other. The queen was right."

"No, she wasn't." The handle jiggled again. "Dani, people are already staring. If you don't open this door right now, I'll call a page over to go find the key. Which will alert any number of people to what's going on."

He would. She heard it in his voice. He'd morphed into the professor, the one she hadn't talked to in weeks although it felt like months.

Relenting, she rose and unlocked the door. Jameson stood there, pissed off, and sexier than any man had a right to be.

"Why did you run from me?"

"I didn't," she said, bristling at being called out for her mad dash.

"Yes, you did." He entered the space farther, making it seem smaller than it was.

"What does it matter? You heard her. Your grandmother made it clear how she feels about a relationship between you and me." *Not Jameson. Not this family. I won't allow it.* "I refuse to be anywhere I'm not wanted. Never again."

"*I* want you. And she can't tell me who I can be with. Or love. She doesn't run my life."

"Who are you trying to kid? Me? Or yourself? That woman runs her children's lives, your life, this whole fucking country. But not me. I didn't sign up for this! I'm outta here."

"Dammit, Dani," he said, pulling her close and crushing his mouth to hers.

She opened up and the kiss immediately deepened. Their tongues tangled, rasping against one another, and she moaned, curving her hands around his broad shoulders, shivering at the raw male strength flexing against her palms. He smelled incredible and tasted even better. Never experience this again? It was unthinkable. She didn't want to leave his arms. She couldn't imagine ever tiring of his kisses.

But they did have to breathe.

He raised his head and focused on her with feverish eyes. She couldn't look away.

"This. You. Us. That's all I care about." Inhaling harshly, he leaned his forehead against hers. "Say you believe me."

She cupped his cheek. "I do."

"Say you feel it, too," he demanded.

Her heart pummeled her chest. She pressed a soft kiss to his lips. "I do."

Someone gasped . . . and it wasn't either of them.

Dread churned her belly.

"Shit!" Jameson muttered.

In unison, they turned to find a small crowd watching them from the open door.

Chapter Twenty-Four

"Shall they be a family in name only; or shall they, in all
their actions, be true to the name?"

—Plato

If Jameson had a moment's doubt they'd been discovered, it was
alleviated when he saw the expressions on the faces of the guests.

Shock from Imogen.

Resignation from Liam Cooper.

Approval from Kay Morgan.

Disgust from Countess von Habsburg.

Almost immediately, several phones shot up, pointed in their direction. Members of the press, beneficiaries of the elite invitation,
hurried over, cameras at the ready.

He clenched his jaw, frustrated by his circumstances. He hadn't
asked for this. He was simply a man who wanted to be with his
woman. Why did the world care?

After the concert, he'd headed back to Primrose Park, but instead of reveling in triumph after a rewarding celebration of his
grandfather's life, he'd felt lonely and steeped in sorrow. There'd
been a time when driving down the long driveway and seeing the

familiar structure of his ancestral home had given him immense satisfaction. Not anymore.

In fact, since Dani had relocated to her hotel in London, taking her sparkle and vibrance with her, the place hadn't held its usual joy for him. Memories of her permeated so many spaces: the kitchen, the old drawing room, his office . . . the thought of never seeing her again, of never touching her or hearing her laugh, left him hollowed out.

Had he really fallen in love with her?

No! Impossible. It was too fast. A month ago, he hadn't even known her!

But in the past few weeks he'd been happier than he could ever remember being. He couldn't imagine going back to a life without Dani in it.

Did she feel the same?

Their situation was complicated, filled with duty, work, and obligations that required a great deal of focus and attention. But if she cared for him, he'd do anything to convince her to give them a shot. What they'd discovered was special. They deserved the opportunity to explore it: in their own way, on their own timetable, and outside of the spotlight.

This wasn't what he'd had in mind.

In the midst of the crowd, Jameson made eye contact with Rhys, who was standing next to Dani's friend Nyla. The actress was watching her friend, worry creasing her brow. With a sharp nod, Rhys barreled his way to the front of the throng and closed the door.

"Move along," Jameson heard Rhys say over the sounds of complaint.

"What is he doing?" Dani demanded. "We can't stay in here."

He sat on a nearby chair. "I need a moment to think."

"About what? They saw us. They know."

It wouldn't be long before the story got out. He imagined the juicy tidbit making its way through the ballroom, like a note emitted from a musical instrument.

"It's going to be fine. We just need to come up with a plan on how we're going to handle this," Dani insisted, standing over him.

Even worse, it wouldn't be long before it was all over the internet.

His mother!

Fuck!

The last thing he ever wanted was to have her blindsided by a story involving him. He'd promised to never cause her to have to endure what she'd gone through with the press after the death of his father.

The door opened and he stood, tensed and ready for battle, only to exhale when he saw Roy, one of his protection officers.

"Sir, come with me."

Jameson nodded, then held out his hand to Dani. She took it, and her firm grasp grounded him. They needed to get someplace private where they could talk and figure this out. Together.

He turned to his PPO. "Can you find my mother and bring her to me, please?"

"Your mother? Jay, it's not that deep."

"Dani, please. Trust me."

"Yes, sir," Roy said. "But first, let's get you out of here."

In minutes the gathering had increased threefold, but the invited press and guests were way too polite to carry themselves like a mob. Still, their heightened curiosity was palpable as he and Dani followed Roy through a concealed exit out of the ballroom and down several hallways to one of the family's private sitting rooms.

Passing through the door held open by the guard, Jameson stopped short when he realized they weren't going to be alone in the spacious chamber. The queen, his aunts and uncle, and Louisa waited. Then he noticed the yellow silk draperies and the oil portrait hanging on the wall.

The Den of Despondency. Perfect.

Not liking this turn of events, he warily eyed his grandmother where she sat on the same ornate yellow chair as during their first visit, all those months ago.

Julian rushed Jameson, his face flushed. "Now I understand why you got an attitude when I mentioned fucking her. You were already doing the deed. It appears you're a chip off the old block after all."

Dani's grip on his hand tightened.

"Say another word," Jameson said, anger overriding his usual decorum, "and I will kick your bloody ass, heir to the throne or not."

"That's enough," the queen said, her voice cutting through the tension. "This isn't helpful to anyone right now."

"He's lucky we're not back in the States," Dani said. "I know people."

"Why is this necessary? I was looking for Liam Cooper before I was summoned," Bettina said. "Only a few people saw them. Easy to contain."

"Are you really that stupid?" Julian spat. "Everyone saw, including the press and staff. It's only a matter of time until it's beyond the walls of the palace."

"It's going to go viral before that happens," Louisa said.

"Is this what you meant by your family inserting themselves?" Dani muttered beneath her breath.

"This is only the beginning."

Dani huffed out a laugh and rolled her eyes.

"What?" Jameson asked.

"Genesis won't have to worry about me and Samantha Banks now! I wished it was for how I conducted myself this week, but I'm pretty sure this will blow both of those stories off the front page."

Julian ceased pacing. "That's it! Her true motivations have been revealed."

She eyed the crown prince with the same disdain Jameson had once seen her give his pint of Guinness, before saying, "I should probably call Bennie."

"Who?"

"My manager."

"Absolutely not," the queen said. "I haven't made a decision."

"I'm not stopping you," Dani said. "Although . . . where is my clutch?"

"What decision?" Bettina asked, still managing to pout and look confused. "She's leaving. That's what you always want from the men I'm with."

The queen glared at her. "That's why we're in this situation. You, Julian . . . Calliope, Alcott! Your horrible judgment and indiscretions!"

"That's not fair," Julian said.

"You take this for granted, living as if it will always be here. Nothing is guaranteed. There has been serious talk about abolishing the monarchy. Where will all of you be then?"

Julian, Bettina, and Catherine exchanged startled glances, and Jameson frowned. So, he'd been the sole recipient of that significant information? Why?

"In exchange for your lives of privilege I only asked that you keep your lapses private. Instead you parade around moaning about how difficult your life is and act surprised when the people resent you for it. The same people who start to wonder if we're too expensive or perpetuate outmoded values." She shook her head in disgust. "I never thought I'd ever say this, but thank God John isn't alive to see what you've become."

Bettina's mouth dropped open, the color drained from Julian's face, and Catherine pressed a shaky hand to her chest. Dani looked at everyone as if she couldn't believe this was happening.

He'd warned her about his family.

But he'd never heard the queen speak to her children in that manner. It was a testament to her heightened emotional state. Which meant she was capable of anything.

And that could be catastrophic for him. He needed to talk to Dani. Alone. He had to tell her what his grandmother had threatened to do. She should hear it from him.

Because she was right. As much as Jameson hated it, the revelation of their involvement would obliterate any story in its path, including the events of the royal tribute. His grandmother would be furious. And someone would bear the brunt of her displeasure.

The queen managed to channel the composure that had benefited her since she'd assumed the throne. "I have worked too hard to have it end this way. And I will not tolerate John's memory and life work being ruined. We're going to fix this."

Catherine finally entered the discussion. "What do you suggest?"

"The only thing that might temper it. We confirm the two of them are dating. Lean into the fairy tale. It worked for Julian and Fi."

"This is bullshit!" Julian erupted, his pale skin reddening. "First you inform us of this celebration for our father but tell us we'll only have minimal involvement. Then you bring him in and parade him in front of us as our replacement—"

Catherine held up a hand. "Julian—"

"Stay out of this, Cat! Everyone knows you're enjoying this."

"You're sick," Catherine said, crossing her arms and stalking over to a window.

"Why do you have to address anything? I'm sure I'm not the first woman Jay has dated. Did they all require press releases?"

Jameson curled his lip. "We are not making an announcement about our relationship. This is not a publicity stunt in service to the monarchy. This is our lives. Our private lives."

"But you didn't keep it private. And now we have to address it."

"It's okay, Jay. I guess the fact that I'm black is newsworthy." Dani rolled her eyes, then patted his arm. "They can put out a statement. Bennie will probably want to, as well. Just a simple 'we're enjoying each other's company,' yada, yada, yada . . ."

He shifted to look at her. "Dani, you don't understand—"

"At least one of you sees reason," the queen said. She tilted her chin. "Louisa, set her up for etiquette and comportment lessons and a meeting with the press office. We'll need to begin incorporating her into Jameson's schedule—"

Dani's head jerked to the side. "Say what now?"

"What schedule?" Jameson asked, confused.

"Your new schedule as a senior working royal," the queen said, continuing without missing a beat. "And we'll need to figure out how to deal with her music and videos. We can't have that sort of image associated with the prince's girlfriend."

Dani shook her head as if the motion would resolve her confusion. "What's going on? What are you doing?"

"Exactly what I said. The Palace will issue a statement confirming your relationship, and you'll act accordingly until you're no longer needed."

Blood thundered in his ears. "That's out of the question!" he said.

Dani stared at his grandmother. "You're crazy if you think I'm agreeing to that."

"I've made my decision. You don't have a choice."

"I always have a choice. And I'm not giving that up because you have a PR problem."

"As if there's nothing in it for you," Bettina sneered.

Dani cut her eyes at the woman. "Really? You want to come for me?"

Bettina blanched and stepped back.

"Public relations?" The queen's fingers gripped the arms of her chair. "I'm trying to save centuries of tradition! We embody our country's values. We represent an ideal. We will survive this and you will do what I say."

"Wait a minute!" Dani finally let go of Jameson's hand, and he felt the absence. Keenly. "I don't care what you expect from them, I'm not a member of your family or one of your subjects. I'm not doing it. I've been dealing with the press for over ten years. My team can help us with this."

Catherine stepped forward. "I'm really sorry this is happening to you, but you have no idea what you're going to face. The tabloid press is very different on this side of the Atlantic. Especially when it comes to us. Our being funded by the public leads to a feeling of ownership. They believe they're entitled to all of our lives, and they're not particularly welcoming to anyone who comes into them. They can be ruthless. We've been prepped on this since birth. Nothing you've dealt with can prepare you properly. We can't allow you to deal with this on Jameson's behalf. He's a member of the royal family. We must be involved."

"Nyla was right." Dani turned to him. "I'm leaving and you should come with me."

He wanted to. Was this what he'd signed up for? What he had to look forward to until Julian's children were of age?

"What is it about the men in this family?" the queen asked, laughing to herself. "You're provided with women who would be perfect for you and yet you just can't stay away from these . . . spirited ones. I told you this would happen. And I warned you that if you couldn't do what was right and stay away from her, I might have to take matters into my own hands."

He froze. *Fuck!*

Dani stopped and turned around. "What is she talking about?"

"I'll explain later. Let's go."

"He didn't tell you?" the queen asked. "About the pictures?"

Dani pulled against him. "What pictures?"

Jameson glared at his grandmother. "Don't do this."

She arched a brow. "You didn't, so I will."

"Jay!" Dani poked her finger in his chest. "Don't talk to her. Talk to me. What. Pictures?"

Not now. Not like this.

"I took care of it."

"You weren't being as careful as you thought," the queen informed her. "A tabloid captured the two of you kissing during your little jaunts around the countryside."

"Jesus Christ," Julian said.

Dani focused on him, refusing to acknowledge the queen. "And that's a problem why? What are you not telling me?"

Jameson stared down into her beautiful eyes, dreading the moment when the confusion would turn to disappointment, betrayal, and then rage. "The story wouldn't be about two people who met and are 'enjoying each other's company.' If I didn't stay away from you, she threatened to send the pictures to the press in the States and plant the idea that the relationship wasn't approved by the family."

Dani physically recoiled, her expression pained, as the information sank in. Tabloid photographers had taken compromising pictures of them. The queen had known about them before tonight. And he'd known about all of it, because the queen had threatened to smear Dani's reputation in the States if he didn't stay away from her.

And he hadn't done that, either.

"You knew this all could jeopardize Mela-Skin and you didn't tell me?"

He could feel her withdrawing from him, mentally and emotionally. In desperation, he pulled her into his arms. "I didn't want to worry you. And I handled it."

"I don't need you to handle anything for me. That's my job. I've been taking care of myself since I was fourteen years old."

He hated that. She didn't have to be alone anymore. He was here. He wanted to help her. "I was trying to protect you."

She pushed away from him. "No. You were more interested in continuing to get your rocks off. You knew how important this was for me. If there was a chance something out there could've derailed it, you should've told me. I had a right to know."

Her anguish crushed him. He couldn't believe how quickly everything had fallen apart. "I know, love. I'm sorry."

Dani shook her head. "This is too much. I don't want any part of it. I'm going home. You can stay here. Problem solved."

She backed away from him, each step drawing her closer to the exit.

He couldn't let her leave. Not on these terms. If he could only explain. "Dani—"

"No, Jameson. I'm done. Leave me the fuck alone!"

She yanked open the door and bumped into his mother, Rhys, and Nyla standing on the other side. He wasn't sure she recognized them.

"Great!" Julian threw his hands in the air. "Are we to have no privacy? If anyone can have access to our private quarters, why not start charging for tours? That should help to support us!"

"Oh give it a rest," Catherine said.

"Excuse me," Dani said, proving the truth of his thought since she failed to acknowledge her friend as she hurried from the room.

"Dani?" Nyla called after her, then scowled at Jameson. "What did you do?"

Jameson shook his head. "You should go after her."

Her lips tightened until they practically disappeared, but she did as he suggested. When he saw Roy, he started, "Can you—"

"On it," the officer said, closing the door behind him.

Although every fiber of Jameson's being screamed for him to chase her and beg for her forgiveness, he had to handle a few issues here. Starting with his mother.

"Are you okay?" he asked.

Calanthe, elegant in a simple yet dramatic burgundy caped evening gown, crossed the space and took his hands. "I'm fine, but I was worried. Everyone's buzzing about you and Dani. Thank God Roy came to fetch me."

He inhaled deeply. "It's probably going to get worse before it gets better. And I'm sorry. I never wanted to put you through that again."

"Jameson, this is not your fault. You fell in love, my darling. You did nothing wrong."

"Calanthe," the queen called out.

His mother brushed a hand against his cheek before greeting her monarch with a curtsy. "Ma'am."

"I'm glad you're here. It's time for your son to finally put his duty to this family over his personal interests."

Calanthe clasped her hands loosely in front of her. "It's my understanding that's what he's been doing."

"Not this week." The queen dismissed his efforts during the tribute with the wave of her hand. "I'm talking about with regard to this woman."

"This isn't only about her or Jameson," Bettina complained. "It affects all of us. The tabloids will shove recorders in my face everywhere I go. And after I'd just drawn them off my back."

"So you *did* give the tabloids the story about my hunting trip in Limpopo!"

"Shut it, Julian!" Bettina returned her attention to the queen. "None of this would've happened if you'd just left him in the library where he belongs, instead of bringing him here as if he was the answer to your problems."

"I didn't want to be here," he exploded, his chest rising and falling. "You seem to be under the impression that I came here and asked to play a role in this tribute. I did not. I was happy back at Birmingham, teaching my classes." He didn't mention that if he hadn't been drafted, he never would've met Dani. He didn't think they deserved credit for the one good thing to come out of all this. "I did what was asked of me. I held up my end of the deal."

"You call this holding up your end?" the queen retorted. "No one will be praising John or his work. Everyone will be too busy gossiping about you and your rapper."

"You mean the press coverage won't benefit the monarchy, like you wanted," Calanthe said.

His mother was right. The queen had been annoyed at the amount of attention Dani had received all week. Not because of them. No one had known about them. But because of who Dani was. Her enthusiasm, her joy, her ability to relate to people. It was the same presence his grandfather had. One that his grandmother lacked.

The queen set her jaw. "You *will* do this, Jameson."

"No. Dani doesn't want to be involved. And I'm not going to force her to do anything she doesn't want to do."

And he'd make sure she understood that . . . as soon as she started speaking to him again.

"Then I'm going to do what's necessary to protect this family." The queen turned to Louisa. "Issue a statement: 'It has come to our attention that rumors are circulating about His Royal Highness Prince Jameson and his involvement with an American entertainer known as Duchess. The Palace denies the existence of such a relationship, nor would such a union meet with the Royal Household's approval. Any claims to the contrary can only be seen as the machinations of someone desperate to haul herself into the ranks of British society.'"

Hurt and anger hardened into a knot in Jameson's stomach. That statement would allow the Palace to wash its hands of the whole affair and maybe even appear like a victim, while putting all of the blame and suspicion on Dani.

It was diabolical. And brilliant.

"So you're willing to ruin her life? For what? The people don't even want us anymore. And that's with you in charge." Jameson shot a disgusted look at Julian. "You're doing all of this to save a monarchy you'll turn over to Julian. A son you didn't even trust to host a week of events celebrating his father?"

"Fuck you!"

"No thanks. I don't know where you've been."

"We all know where you've been and it's—"

Jameson punched him. Everyone gasped and Julian cried out, grabbing his face. "I think he broke my nose!"

The pain radiating up Jameson's arm was intense, but the satisfaction was immeasurable. Well worth it.

The queen rose from her chair. "Not for Julian. For the family.

For our legacy. Our bloodline has ruled for over a thousand years! It will not fall apart on my watch!"

He shook his head, suddenly realizing how ridiculous this all was. Selling his soul and his happiness wouldn't help this family. And it certainly wouldn't honor his grandfather, who'd encouraged him to make his own way. He wouldn't want this for Jameson.

"Maybe it should."

The queen's nostrils flared and her body trembled. In a low, cold voice, she commanded, "Louisa, get that to the press office. Tell them I want it issued first thing in the morning."

"You can't do that!"

Rumors about them kissing, the statement by the Palace, and the pictures—which he was certain would now get leaked—would turn this into a media frenzy of epic proportions. Dani would be painted as an attention-grabbing, social-climbing hussy trying to seduce a member of the royal family.

And it would kill any opportunity she and Mela-Skin had of attracting an offer from a major company.

"Pledge your cooperation and I won't."

He looked to Louisa and could see the conflict on her face, but it wasn't fair of him to put the burden of his mistakes on her. His hands curved into fists at his sides and his eyes darted around the room as he struggled to think. *Use that glorified brain of yours!* He couldn't let her get away with this!

But what could he do?

He was facing his own moment from Plato's Allegory of the Cave. His entire life, he'd believed in the sanctity of the royal family, even as he ran away from it. But Dani, so different from anything he'd ever known, had broken through. Showed him there was something more. Would he stay here and do his duty? Retreat back into his shell at Birmingham?

Or would he dare to be brave?

Would he be willing to leave the familiarity and comfort of the cave and step into the sun?

Calanthe took his hand. "Jameson, do you love her?"

He nodded. "More than I ever could have imagined was possible."

"Fair or not, you're a member of this family, and for you, the personal and the public will always be in conflict. But you can stay true to who you are, to the man I, and your grandfather, raised you to be. You love her? Go to her. You should decide together what you're both willing to do. I told you, you don't have to sacrifice your happiness for the Crown. I would never want that for you. And, even with his faults, neither would your father."

"You're making a mistake, Calanthe."

"I don't think so, ma'am. Richard and I had a lot of problems, but on this, we would have agreed."

Rhys, uncharacteristically quiet up to this point, came over and dropped a set of keys into Jameson's hand. Clapping Jameson on the shoulder, he confided in a low voice, "I'm parked in that space you showed me you used when you wanted to avoid security and your parents. And Nyla messaged me they were heading to the airport. Good luck!"

"Thanks."

"Jameson!" the queen called to his back. "Don't you leave. We're not done here!"

He hugged his mother, kissed her cheek, and made his escape.

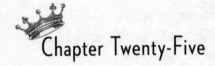

Chapter Twenty-Five

"Ooh, baby, what you do to me / Love me right, grind it
slow on me / Busy bitch with things to do / But you got this
bitch chasing after you . . ."

—Duchess, "Mind Games"

At night, Farnborough, a full-service private airport outside of London, was breathtaking, with a glowing green light that illuminated the far end of the award-winning sculptural design. But Dani wasn't in the mood to appreciate its beauty. She sat in the cream leather club chair of the private plane she'd chartered, snuggling beneath the blanket she'd been given and waiting to take off. The sooner she could get out of this fucking country, the faster she could put everything behind her and get her life back on track.

Across from her, Nyla ended a call. "I told Bennie what was happening. She and a publicist are going to meet us at your house in L.A. tomorrow afternoon."

"Thank you." She flashed her friend a grateful, if wan, smile.

Nyla had caught up with Dani as she'd been wandering around the behemoth palace, frantically searching for an exit.

"Why in the fuck does this place exist?" she'd raged, after backing out of a space just like the one she'd stumbled upon moments before. "Who needs this many fucking rooms?"

When Jameson's bodyguard appeared, she'd been ready to fight, believing he'd come to take her back to that condensed, modern-day version of *Game of Thrones*. But he hadn't. He'd escorted her and Nyla out of the palace, ensuring they avoided any guests or members of the press, and provided them a car and driver who'd been instructed to take them anywhere they wanted to go.

Dani had meant it when she told Jameson to leave her alone, but the fact that he didn't even try to come after her . . .

"Tasha and the rest of the team will keep their original travel plans," Nyla continued.

Her assistant had made miracles happen, securing her and Nyla seats on a plane leaving London and meeting its owner in New York. From there, they'd hop another chartered flight to L.A. Tasha had even sent one of the dancers over to meet them with their passports and other essentials. Dani was willing to deal with the choppy travel if it meant getting home and coming up with a plan. She couldn't have spent all this time and done all this work to have Genesis back away at the last minute.

Yes, the deal with Genesis. That's the reason you're curled into the fetal position, your chest burning as if someone punched a hole through it. If you focus on the work, you won't have to focus on the pain you feel about Jameson and his dishonesty.

That pain cut so deep if she allowed herself to think of it, she could barely breathe.

This was her fault. She'd hastily opened herself up and allowed him access, not just into her body but into her heart, sharing pieces of herself she'd shown to only a select few. But it had been the quickness, and strength, of their connection that convinced her it was genuine. As her feelings had grown, she'd been thinking of all the obvious reasons they couldn't work—his being royalty, her being an entertainer, living on different continents—but in the end, it had come down to something that had nothing to do with the fantastical nature of their lives.

He'd betrayed her trust.

Annoyed for letting thoughts about Jameson penetrate her painstakingly reconstructed emotional fortress, she leaned forward and asked the approaching flight attendant, "Excuse me? Why are we still sitting here?"

The young man wrinkled his brow. "Let me check."

A few minutes later, the pilot came over the loudspeaker. "Sorry, Duchess. We were cleared for takeoff but then given orders to stand by. I'm waiting for further instructions."

Nyla bit her lip and shifted in her chair, but when Dani met her gaze, she shrugged.

Dani tightened the blanket over her shoulders and rearranged the voluminous layers of her skirt, cursing the impulsivity that had prevented her from stopping by her suite and changing out of her gown. She could always purchase an outfit when they got to New York, but that meant she'd be stewing in a puff of tulle for the next seven hours.

The phone in the galley rang. The flight attendant answered it, then pressed a button to lower the staircase.

Dani frowned. "What's going on? Is something wrong with the plane?"

Footfalls thundered up the steps and his massive frame filled the doorway.

Jay.

Still dressed in his formal white tie from the ball, albeit a little more disheveled. Still able to dwarf any space he was in, even the cabin of a luxury private jet, with his presence.

Damn him.

Nyla unbuckled her belt and stood. "I'll give you two a moment."

Dani narrowed her eyes at her friend's retreating back.

Traitor.

She exhaled audibly. "You need to leave."

Two long strides brought him to the seat Nyla had just vacated. "Dani, I'm sorry. I was going to tell you."

She turned away from him and stared out the small window. Looking at him increased the chances of her forgiving him. And she needed to remain strong.

"Dani, please. I made a mistake, but it wasn't malicious. I love you. I won't ever let you down again."

The pain in her chest howled at his declaration of love. Why did he have to say it now, when it was too late?

He reached out and grasped her hand. "I should've told you about the pictures and my grandmother's blackmail immediately. I felt like it was my problem because I should've known better. I should've been more careful. And when you confided in me why you'd agreed to do the concert and what was at stake for you . . . I didn't want you to worry."

Don't break, Dani.

She finally glanced at him. Damn, he was gorgeous. "It wasn't *your* problem, because it affected *me*."

"I know, but I wanted to protect you. Not because I don't think you're capable of taking care of yourself. You are. I—" He squeezed his eyes shut and bowed his head. "I watched the press hound my mother when I was younger. And there was nothing I could do about it. She was the person I loved most in this world and I . . . I could do nothing."

Tears scalded the backs of her eyes and burned her throat at the picture he painted of a young man helpless in the face of a seemingly overwhelming obstacle. A part of her understood that feeling, of wanting to do something but knowing the power to make it happen was out of your control.

"When my grandmother threatened you, I felt that same impotence. But my situation was different this time. I wasn't a young boy. I was a man. I thought I could protect the person I loved and the thing that was most important to her." He pushed from the chair and fell to his knees before her, dropping his head in her lap. "Dani, I'm sorry I wasn't better at it, but I won't let it happen again. I promise. Love . . . please . . ."

As she stared at his bent head, the vise tightening her chest eased. She loved him so much it colored what she felt, and how she acted. She believed him, trusted in his feelings for her and that his apology was heartfelt and genuine.

Plus, this man—this prince!—was on his knees! How could she believe anything else when faced with the intensity of his sorrow? It was like a Boyz II Men song come to life.

He had come for her, after all.

She ran her fingers through his hair. "Not the *most* important thing."

Jameson gaped up at her, his blue eyes overly bright. Questioning. Hopeful.

"You should've told me."

"I know. And I won't ever withhold information from you again."

"You'd better not," she warned.

"Thank God!" He stood and lifted her into his arms. "I love you, Dani. It killed me when I thought I'd lost you."

"Me too." She held on to him tightly, her heart thumping madly, brought back to life by his presence.

He brushed his lips tenderly against hers before exhaling in relief and setting her on her feet. "In light of the promise I just made, I need to tell you the Palace plans to issue a statement about us. Since you wouldn't go along with her plan, the queen is going to deny our relationship and declare they would never approve of our pairing."

She smiled bitterly. She wasn't surprised. The queen didn't seem like a woman with a weak follow-through.

"Okay. Then we'll deal with it. When I get home, I'll sit down with Bennie and my publicist and come up with a strategy."

"The problem with my grandmother's plan is me. You'll have me. She can't deny the existence of our relationship if I'm there with you. You don't have to handle this, or anything else, on your own. Ever again."

Her pulse soared, and it was suddenly important to her that he know what he meant to her, too.

"I didn't turn down the queen's offer because I don't love you. I do. And I want to be with you. But on our terms. They shouldn't get to dictate what we do or how we do it. Or have a say in my career."

She was still smarting over Marina's comment about her image not being good enough for their family.

"I agree. But, love"—he cupped her cheek—"they're not going anywhere. I will always be a member of the royal family. We'll need to work out how our two worlds can coexist."

Then they would. Because there was no way in hell she was giving up on this man. But she knew it wouldn't be easy. The queen was displeased with Dani. She'd be a force to be reckoned with.

"You do know our being together ensures you'll never live your life in obscurity again, right?"

"I know. But I'll deal with anything as long as you're by my side."

She was the rapper, but he was the one with a way with words. She glanced at him from beneath her lashes. "Can you handle things when I'm on top of you?"

He pulled her down onto his lap. "My favorite view."

"Excuse me, Duchess? Sorry to interrupt, but the pilot wanted to know if you're still planning to leave? We need to let the tower know."

"One sec," she told the attendant.

"Of course," he said, disappearing once again.

She laughed. "Your timing is impeccable."

Jameson pressed his forehead to hers. "I couldn't let you leave believing I didn't care."

"What are we going to do now? I have to get back to the States."

He clapped his hands together. "Let's go."

She scanned the plane, in case she'd missed it when he first arrived. Nope. "You don't have any stuff."

"I didn't have time. Nothing was more important than getting to you."

She pouted. "I wish you could come, but you can't. You need your passport."

He sighed. "That's probably for the best. Give me a couple of days to talk to my mother and Rhys and then I'll fly out to L.A."

"Are you sure?"

"I'm sure that I don't want to be without you."

"You are a sweet, sweet man," Dani said.

"Let's keep that our little secret. Come on. I'd better get out of here before anyone sees me."

They kissed, and this time his tongue slid into her mouth, claiming her with a wild, frantic urgency that dampened her panties. She clutched his shoulders, cursing the yards of fabric separating them, wanting one last chance to slide down his hard, thick length before they parted. While Dani had anticipated the despair she'd feel when the plane took off, at least now she knew their separation wouldn't be permanent.

Reluctantly breaking away, Dani informed the crew of their plans and Jameson motioned to the flight attendant, who once again opened the door. A roar sounded from the right and a million flashes went off.

"What the hell?" Dani peered out the window.

"So, about that idea of getting out of here unseen . . ."

"We should've expected this," Dani said ruefully. "There was no way you could ground my plane and think no one would find out about it. Especially after what happened at the ball."

He straightened his clothes and smoothed a hand over his hair. "Time to face the music."

"Together." At his startled look she stood and said, "You don't have to handle anything on your own ever again, either."

Jameson descended the five steps to stand on the tarmac. He held out a hand to assist her and slid his arm around her waist when she joined him. The throng of reporters, held a hundred feet away from them by the tall chain-link fence topped with barbed wire that bordered the airport, shouted a torrent of questions.

"Are the rumors true? Are you two dating?"

"Are you in love?"

"Prince Jameson, how is this different from your father?"

Dani stiffened but Jameson stood taller, that last question seeming to spark something within.

"I'm going to make an official statement. You're here because you've heard the rumors circulating about our possible involvement. I want to be clear: the rumors are true. I love Duchess. She and I are involved in a very serious relationship, of which the Palace has full knowledge, and members of the family have given us their blessing. Coming at the end of this week honoring the legacy of Prince John, I'd also like to state that my grandfather would've loved Duchess. I have no doubt they would've gotten along famously, and he would've been extremely happy for me. Since I know how these things work, let me further say that any 'sources' claiming anything to the contrary are simply the ravings of attention seekers who don't know anything about my family."

Dani's eyes widened as the import of what he said dawned. Not only had he acknowledged their relationship, he'd claimed it was approved by the Palace, placing doubt on anyone who came forward to say differently.

This would definitely help her with her business dealings, but more important, the world had been put on notice. She had her man.

As more flashes erupted, Dani hugged Jameson close. "Well done. That was an excellent statement. There might be hope for you yet."

He gazed down at her, and despite the blinding lights, she could see his eyes were warm and full of love. "Thank you. I took the statement the Palace intended to make and changed some of the details."

They kissed again as the inquisition continued.

"How long have you been dating?"

"Where are you going to live?"

"Duchess, what does this mean for your music career?"

"Will Her Majesty grant Mela-Skin a Royal Warrant?"

"That's all for now," a familiar voice called out. "His Royal Highness and Duchess have no further comment!"

Dani didn't think anything else could surprise her tonight, but seeing the Royal Household's senior events coordinator striding briskly across the tarmac to stand next to them proved her wrong.

"Girl, I hope you get overtime," she muttered to Louisa.

"I do not. Why? Can you do better?"

Dani smiled widely. "Yeah, I think I can."

It might help to have someone on her team who understood the ins and outs of the royal family, considering what Dani had just signed up for.

As they stood there at the base of the plane, in the glare of the airport and camera lights, the paparazzi ignored Louisa's decree and continued shouting.

All good questions.

All things she and Jay would need to figure out.

Later.

Epilogue

"Ask me for a feature?/ Who are you without me?"
                    —Duchess, untitled work in progress

On the nightstand, a phone covered in a glittery rainbow case vibrated against the hard surface. A second later it happened again. And again. And again.

What the fuck?

Samantha Banks raised her head from the goose down pillow and reached for the offending device. A list of notifications littered her locked screen.

People: "Is She the One? Prince Flips for Duchess!"

Us Weekly: "'Duchess for Real?' Will Duchess Give Up Her Career for the British Monarchy?"

TMZ: "Breaking News! Duchess Has Caught Herself a Prince!"

Bossip: "Palace 'Sky High' over Duchess and Real-Life Prince. #RoyalSwirlLove."

The phone buzzed again in her hand and a text from her manager appeared. Opening the app, Samantha saw what looked like an embedded video and clicked on it. Over an image of Prince Jameson and Duchess, still in their clothes from the event and standing at the bottom of steps that led up to a private plane, lights and cameras flashing, the announcer said:

"If you're just finding out about this, where have you been? The clip already has a million views on Instagram and YouTube. A royal love story between His Royal Highness Prince Jameson and American Royalty Duchess, rapper and entrepreneur. After the closing ball of the weeklong Royal Tribute in Honor of Prince John, the prince professed his feelings for his unlikely love."

"I love Duchess. She and I are involved in a very serious relationship, of which the Palace has full knowledge, and members of the family have given us their blessing."

"How long have they been dating? Where does the new couple go from here? How does the queen feel about them? Nothing has been announced yet, but we'll be following this story closely. They didn't take questions, but Duchess did have a message for her fans."

Duchess's face filled the screen, and Samantha hated to admit that she looked gorgeous as usual.

The bitch.

The rapper smiled. "You guys have been so supportive! Thank you! Meeting Prince Jameson and participating in this event has taught me a few things. One, it's important to stand in your truth. Two, if you put good into the world, it'll be returned tenfold. And three, own your shit. Do your own work. It's a rocky ride surfing the coattails of others."

She winked.

Anger filled Samantha as the taunt hit its target. Throwing back the duvet, she hopped out of bed and wrinkled her nose as she pulled on her dress from last night. She needed to get back to her hotel, shower, change, then call her manager. There had to be a way to capitalize on all of this. To use this new attention to shore up Samantha's own brand. Sliding on shoes and throwing on her coat, she went on social media to see what people were saying.

#PrinceLovesDuchess was trending.

"OMG, a real-life Duchess! Or Princess!!"

"What a role model!"

"Lissen, Samantha Banks needs to stop sweatin' Duchess. Periodt!"

Arghhh!!!!

Head in her phone, as she switched from Twitter to Instagram, she opened the front door, engaged the lock, and exited the townhouse.

"Oh my God! Is that Samantha Banks?"

Although she didn't look her best, the excited utterance lifted Samantha's spirits. She loved meeting people who recognized her and low-key coercing them into asking her to take a selfie. She lifted her head with a ready smile only to freeze when she saw the group of paparazzi blocking her path, cameras at the ready.

"Did Samantha Banks just walk out of Prince Julian's private flat wearing her ball gown from the evening before?"

Samantha winced and closed her eyes. Fuck! She'd been so focused on the news about Duchess she hadn't followed Julian's established protocols, which included calling the number he'd given her to alert his protection detail that she was ready to leave and exiting the home from the back entrance. On that brisk, cloudy London morning, the camera lights were bright and the shouted questions rang loud in the quiet neighborhood.

"Are you involved with Prince Julian?"

"Quite a walk of shame, Samantha! What would your Sparkle Sammies say?"

"You know he's married? How does it feel to be the other woman?"

"Did you hear about Duchess and Prince Jameson? Are you trying to get your own royal?"

"When can your fans expect new music?"

THAT AFTERNOON, BUCKINGHAM Palace issued a statement:

> *"It has come to our attention that rumors are circulating about His Royal Highness the Prince of Wales and his involvement with an American entertainer known as Samantha Banks. Prince Julian is a married man and denies the existence of such a relationship. Any claims to the contrary can only be seen as the machinations of someone desperate to haul herself into the ranks of British society. There will be no further comment."*

Acknowledgments

When I was chasing my dream to be an author, I could only see the end goal. I believed once I was published, the struggle would be over. I couldn't have been more wrong. Getting published is just the beginning; the path that follows is long (hopefully) but winding and sometimes rocky. I couldn't have done it alone, and this book is now in your hands because of a host of people I've depended on:

My agent, Nalini Akolekar, who's guided me through this journey with the perfect mix of "You're a great writer, your words are precious nuggets of gold" and "Girl, get it together and put it on the page!" It's a delicate balance, and somehow, she manages to bring the right dose to each occasion.

My editor, Tessa Woodward, who's always believed in my voice and the stories I wanted to tell. She continually pushes me to do better and never lets me get away with pulling my punches.

The talented Erick Davila, who drew this cover! I will never get over how gorgeous it is and how perfectly he captured Duchess. His artwork now has a permanent spot of honor on my office wall!!

Kristin Dwyer of LEO PR, whose excitement and expertise ensured readers everywhere learned about *American Royalty*. She is a professional port in a publicity storm!

The entire Avon team, including Alivia Lopez, Ronnie Kutys, Jes Lyons, DJ DeSmyter, Ashley Mitchell, and Ploy Siripant, who helped with the finishing touches and getting this book out into the world.

Mia Sosa, the brilliant, talented author I'm lucky to also call my friend. Easing on down Main St. of Romancelandia is so much better because of her wisdom, wit, and companionship.

Alleyne Dickens, who has been there from the beginning with her unconditional friendship and honest critiques. Best of all, when necessary, she shares my occasional jonesing for that delicious Peter Chang's.

Sarah MacLean, whose support and patience never wavered during hours and hours of phone calls where I questioned her about British royalty, protocol, and titles. *sigh* It's a lot, y'all.

My morning writing group, Alexis Daria, Adriana Herrera, and Nisha Sharma. Not only do they make starting my day fun, but I also couldn't have made it through this book without their consistent encouragement, and willing ear.

The other incredible women I've been so fortunate to know who continually show the best of this community and why it can be a fulfilling place to spend my time: Adriana Anders, Alexa Day, Tif Marcelo, Nina Crespo, Priscilla Oliveras, Michele Arris, LaQuette, Andie Christopher, Joanna Shupe, and Jen Prokop. There's many more I wish I could name, but you ladies know who you are. You get me through the day.

The gracious and supremely informative women of the OSRBC Facebook group who were kind enough to answer my questions about all things British: Talia Hibbert (who took time out of her own busy writing schedule), Ali Williams, Sarah Cheung Johnson, Shanti Mercer, Angela Terhark Milton, and Lucia Akard.

Dr. Toni Harris, one of my oldest friends, who educated me on the life of a professor. "What do professors get emails about?" was an actual text I sent her. And she answered.

My kids: Trey (my college man, who I miss dreadfully), Grayson (my emotional guru), and Will (my hype man, who sometimes seems prouder of me than I am of myself). I'm happy to say they now know the difference between Mom with a deadline way in the future, Mom whose deadline is in a week, and the crazy lady who wears a bathrobe and mainlines coffee when her deadline has been "extended." The knowledge has been a godsend for me, and whether they realize it or not, a lifesaver for them.

Last—but only because if I'd started with him, I wouldn't have gotten to anyone else—my husband, James. Twenty-six years later and he still has me sprung and in a constant state of heart-eye emoji. He's the reason why I chose and continue to write the stories I do, where heroes who look like him fall hard and deep for heroines who look like me. When we were first dating, it was slim pickings finding our story reflected on the pages of the books I loved. I write to change that . . . and to give my children, and other biracial children with black mothers and white fathers, positive love stories of their origins.

Until the next one,
TL

Dani & Jameson's story continues in 2023.

About the author

About the book

Insights,
Interviews
& More . . .

Meet Tracey Livesay

A former criminal defense attorney, TRACEY LIVESAY finds crafting believable happily ever afters slightly more challenging than protecting our constitutional rights, but she's never regretted following her heart instead of her law degree. She has been featured in *Entertainment Weekly*, the *Washington Post*, and on *CBS This Morning*. Tracey lives in Virginia with her husband—who she met on the very first day of law school—and their three children. ∾

Author's Note

To find the playlist I created that was inspired by *American Royalty*, go to my website: traceylivesay.com/books/american-royalty-series/american -royalty/.

Creating Duchess and writing this book reignited my love for female hip-hop artists. My affection was hard core when I was younger, but as I got older, I guess I let my disgust with the misogyny and, as Duchess said, the industry's insistence on the Highlander mentality pull me away. I admit I bought into the feuds, even "taking sides" several times. But don't believe the hype: there are many women in rap. For more information, check out two resources I found extremely helpful: *God Save the Queens: The Essential History of Women in Hip-Hop* by Kathy Iandoli and *The Motherlode: 100+ Women Who Made Hip-Hop* by Clover Hope.

Note: For those two books there were at least fifteen written by men that predominantly featured men. ∾

Reading Group Guide

1. Has reading *American Royalty* changed the way you think about consuming media, especially tabloid or gossip outlets?

2. Jameson is torn between his academic life/the woman he loves and the royal family. Do you think being born into the royal family means choosing duty over self? Even with regard to who you love?

3. How did Dani's background influence the decision she's making, to leave music for Mela-Skin?

4. Of the different "dates" Jameson planned for Dani, which was your favorite? If money were no object, what date would you like planned?

5. Do you think it was realistic for Jameson to believe he could live out of the spotlight?

6. If the next in line to the throne is not suitable/is awful, do you think they should be able to pick someone else?

7. Do you think it's necessary for a person to have grown up around the monarchy to be a great husband/wife to a member of the royal family?

8. Do you think Dani and Jameson underestimate how difficult it may be to have their happily ever after?

9. What do you think of female rappers using their sexuality as part of their persona? Does it affect how you view them? Why or why not?

10. The royal romance trope has ebbed and flowed in popularity throughout the years. With the increased awareness of real royals and recent revelations, do you think the trope has lost its luster?

11. Nyla is Dani's "oh honey, no" friend. Do you have one? What's the craziest thing they've stopped you from doing?

12. How would you handle Prince Julian and his comments to and about Dani? ∿